Praise for
Coast to Coast: Private Eyes from Sea to Shining Sea

"A tantalizing array of stories guaranteed to please fans of PI fiction. High fives all around!"
—MWA Grand Master Bill Pronzini

"Tough, taut and terrific. This cross-country collection of sleuthing stories—from the best writers in the private eye biz—is wonderfully written, always surprising, and completely entertaining."
—Hank Phillippi Ryan, Anthony, Agatha and Mary Higgins Clark award-winning author

"A bang-up read of PI fiction from a gallery of impressive authors. *Coast to Coast: Private Eyes from Sea to Shining Sea* is compelling, fun, and full of surprises. A treat."
—Shamus Award-winning author John Shepphird

Praise for
Coast to Coast: Murder from Sea to Shining Sea

"A sterling collection of coast-to-coast crime stories dripping with local color—all of it blood red."
—Chuck Hogan, author of
The Town and Devils In Exile

"Envelope-pushers! A truly WOW collection by the best mystery writers out there—full of surprises only they can pull off."
—Thomas B. Sawyer, best-selling author of
Cross Purposes and *No Place to Run*,
and head-writer of *Murder, She Wrote*

D0218713

COAST TO COAST

Private Eyes from Sea to Shining Sea

COAST TO COAST

Private Eyes from Sea to Shining Sea

EDITED BY
ANDREW MCALEER & PAUL D. MARKS

Down & Out Books
3959 Van Dyke Rd, Ste. 265
Lutz, FL 33558
www.DownAndOutBooks.com

Cover design by Eric Beetner

ISBN: 1-943402-35-3
ISBN-13: 978-1-943402-35-9

For Amy, wife, friend, editor, and who patiently
puts up with a writer's life
—Paul D. Marks

For my nephew Liam, a man wise
beyond his years
—Andrew McAleer

CONTENTS

CONTENTS

From the Editors

When we edited the first Coast to Coast anthology (*Coast to Coast: Murder from Sea to Shining Sea*) our plan was simple: gather stories from some of the best mystery writers in the country. But we noticed that the stories tended to crisscross the continent and thus the concept of "Coast to Coast" was born. And with the success of the first anthology (even garnering a Shamus nomination for Bob Levinson's story "The Dead Detective") we decided to embark on another coast-to-coast journey, this time with private eyes from sea to shining sea.

Crime isn't limited to one locale or one class. As you'll see here, crime is everywhere, from coast to coast and all points in between. This volume traverses the country from west to east, from the carnival of the Venice boardwalk to the gritty waterfront of Portland, Maine. From a wholesome small town in Connecticut to the flamboyant streets of New Orleans, and more.

Private eyes don't just work the mean streets of Los Angeles or New York, the city-that-never-sleeps, or other big cities. PIs are needed everywhere, even in the sleepy suburbs of D.C. (you might say "especially there...") or the quiet corn fields of Iowa City. PI work is hard to come by in some places, but as you'll discover in reading these stories, PIs always manage to get into the thick of things. Sometimes they're Chandler's heroes—"neither tarnished, nor afraid"— others are modern-day knights, even if their armor is somewhat rusty. Some are well-intentioned cowboys, others wisecracking jokesters, some are street-smart and world-weary

1

and sometimes they're naive bumblers. And some are hard-as-nails women or soft-spoken Southern gentlemen. Mostly they're underappreciated, maligned, used and abused. Underpaid and overworked.

This collection boasts many distinguished and award-winning authors. J.L. Abramo, winner of the St. Martin's Press/Private Eye Writers of America prize for Best First Private Eye Novel and a Shamus Award winner for his Jake Diamond mysteries; Eric Beetner, co-host of the Noir at the Bar reading series; Michael Bracken, two-time Derringer Award winner; Meredith Cole, St. Martin's/Malice Domestic winner and Agatha nominee; Matt Coyle, Anthony winner and Shamus nominee; Thomas Donahue, correctional officer turned writer; John Floyd, three-time Derringer Award winner and Edgar nominee; Gay Toltl Kinman, three-time Agatha nominee; Terrill Lee Lankford, novelist and writer/producer on the first two seasons of *Bosch*; Janice Law, Edgar nominee and Lambda Award winner; Andrew McAleer, Sherlock Holmes Revere Bowl Award winner; Paul D. Marks, Shamus Award winner and Anthony and Macavity nominee; O'Neil De Noux, Shamus and Derringer Award winner; Robert Randisi, Shamus nominee, winner of the Life Achievement Award from the Private Eye Writers of America and the John Seigenthaler Legends Award; and Art Taylor, Agatha, Macavity and Derringer winner.

Private eyes have come a long way since photostats, trenchcoats and gats. But that shouldn't stop you from sliding open your bottom desk drawer, reaching in past the stainless steel .45 for that bottle of bourbon, tipping your snap-brim fedora down low, putting your feet up on the desk (but be careful not to scuff it, your mom, wife, husband, maid won't like it), leaning back and reading this gutsy collection of PI stories.

—Paul and Andy

Windward
Paul D. Marks
Los Angeles: Venice Beach

Petrichor. That fresh smell of drying grass—or in my case wet pavement after the rain. You didn't know there was a word for it, did you? The rain had just cleared out. Everyone's been cooped inside, pent up energy building, seething. Bad guys couldn't do their thing. The rain stops, they come out to play. Shards of sun streak through a buttermilk sky. People in L.A. can't deal with rain anyway.

Petrichor. There's a word for everything. The word for my life at that moment was hell.

I was finishing up the job from hell, putting together the final bill on the Rence case. Identity theft. If you ever want your life to turn to shit get your identity stolen. Not only did it turn Rence's life to hell, but mine too. I'd spent three months on it, mostly barricaded inside, chasing leads on the dark web from the *hole*, my office. Three months of pure hell till I caught the bad actors—but Rence will spend five years trying to get her name back. I like what I do for a living, though lately, with computers and the Internet, it can get a little boring and tedious—they make it too easy to track people down. Not that it wasn't boring before, sitting on stakeouts or gumshoeing it, but at least then I was out in the world, among the living, even if it meant sweltering inside a parked car or hiding behind bushes, getting sunburned and having an excuse for all the crappy food.

A man opened the office door, the little bell on it rang. It's a concession to the old days that makes people feel comfortable, something they don't often feel when they have to hire a private investigator. It also makes a chime on my computer ring. I looked up, saw him enter on the video monitor. There wasn't an inch of my office, inside or out, that wasn't covered in a crossfire of cameras. I even had a camera on the restaurant across the street, shooting the front of my building. I'd done a little work for Lou Hernandez, the owner, and instead of taking money from her I asked if I could put a camera on her place. She agreed. I liked watching my little storefront PI shop on Windward Avenue in Venice. I particularly liked watching it from the hole.

I opened the door to the small front office, covered in pix of Venice from the old days. The piers and amusement parks, people in old-fashioned bathing suits on the beach. The canals and oil wells. And a young surfer dude standing next to his stick, stabbed in the sand. Originally a color photo, I'd printed it in sepia so it would match the others. It reminded me of who I used to be—I didn't get much surfing in these days. Actually, I hadn't surfed in years. I thought about it a lot though.

I'm talking about Venice, California. Los Angeles. Hey, the other one in Italy has canals and grand thoroughfares with colonnaded arches. We have grand canals and streets with grand colonnaded arches. Okay, so we don't have such grand canals these days, most of them have been filled in, including the Grand Canal. And Venice didn't quite cut it as the cultural paradise-by-the-sea that Abbott Kinney, its founder, had envisioned. Today it was an ever-changing kaleidoscope of people, dudes dancing on skates, musicians, artists. Maybe a few pickpockets here or there. But it was home. And I liked it here.

"Jack Lassen?" the familiar-looking man said from behind expensive shades, entering my place. Tan, very tan. Maybe the kind you pay for, maybe the kind you get from sitting by the pool, sipping mojitos, or whatever the in drink was these days. Loafers without socks—that told me a lot about him.

4

Pastel shirt, Rolex. Definitely not a walk-in off the beach looking for a handout.

I smiled. He didn't return it.

"You're a licensed private investigator in the state of California?"

"Want me to show you my photostat?" Of course we don't have photostats anymore but he was playing with me, I played back.

"Funny."

"What can I do for you, Mr...."

"Lambert, Patrick Lambert."

I knew the name. As in "A Patrick Lambert Production." Hey, this is L.A. Everyone aspires to a credit like that or "A Film By." Few get there. Lambert had been there for twenty years with no signs of coming down. Back in the day, he'd been a leading man of the George Clooney variety. Good looking, athletic. Heartthrob. And richer than God's Uncle Larry. He'd drifted from acting to producing and became an even bigger player, if that was possible.

"Have a seat," I started to say. But he was already making himself comfortable, leaning back in one of the guest chairs like he owned the place.

My office was neat as a pin, clean as a whistle—what other clichés can I come up with to describe it? I wanted customers to feel confident in me. On the other hand, sometimes I worried they'd think I had no business if there weren't a lot of papers strewn here and there, piles of manila folders and the like.

"My wife Emily is missing. The cops aren't moving fast enough."

"You want me to find her?"

"You're good." He stretched.

"Am I boring you?"

"You sure you've done this before?"

"Just making small talk."

5

"I don't need small talk. I need someone to find my wife."

"Did you lose her?" I knew I'd better stop.

He got up, turned for the door. Most people have trouble getting to the point, so I do a little friendly jousting with them. Not him, he was all business, or should I say *biz*? Unlike all those down and out PIs in the movies, my business was doing okay and I didn't need the money. But I didn't like the guy—wasn't sure why, sometimes you just don't. That didn't mean I wanted to let business just walk out the door—his money would buy me a meal or two at El Coyote as well as anybody's. Besides, I needed a break after the Rence case. You think it might have been that Hollywood swagger that put me off?

"Hey, Mr. Lambert, you come to a Venice PI you get a Venice vibe. Did you come to me specifically or was I just the closest one to you?"

"You're not the closest. You have a good rep, though I'm beginning to wonder why."

"Tell me what's going on?"

He seemed to collapse in on himself, lowered his voice. "My wife Emily's been missing for about a week now. I think she's been kidnapped."

"You're rich."

His face startled. Hollywood folks, the successful ones, are very wealthy and like to pretend they're "of the people," while sitting in their modest twenty-thousand-square-foot houses and their hundred and fifty thousand dollar Teslas.

"I'm just trying to figure out why someone would kidnap your wife. Motive and all that."

"We're comfortable. And to answer your next question, no, there's no ransom demand. Yet."

Comfortable, the old saw people said when they were way more than comfortable.

"I came home from work on Friday. Drawers dumped out. Whole house ransacked."

"Forcible entry?"

"The police said it looked like someone jimmied the sliding door open, but they think it was staged. They've lost interest. In fact, they think she ran off. That she faked the crime scene to make it look like she was kidnapped."

"Why would she do that?"

"She wouldn't." He sounded very sure of himself. Guys like that always sounded sure of themselves. They were, after all, God's gift to women and everyone else. Why would anyone ever want to ditch out on them?

"When I came home her car was gone. I think the kidnappers took her in it."

"Have the cops found the car?"

He shook his head. "Not yet."

"Alarm? Surveillance cameras."

"Neither was on. We don't always have them on when we're home, especially during the day."

"Help? Servants?"

"Off that day."

Naturally.

He handed me a stiff piece of semi-glossy paper with photos on it. Blonde hair, full lips. Overly made up. Pretty in that typical SoCal *IWannaBeAnActress* way—and if you did want to be an actress, why not marry Patrick Lambert, one of the hottest producers around? Yeah, she was an actress. Hell, what he'd given me was a six-by-nine composite card, the kind that actors hand out to casting directors. It had the standard studio head shot, plus action shots, bikini at the beach, climbing a tree. I'm not kidding. The best for last, steely-eyed holding a Goncz GA-9 pistol—cool looking high-tech gun, the kind Hollywood loves—dressed in a leather bustier and six-inch stilettos. I hoped that gun didn't have much recoil.

"Anything better? Normal, y'know snapshots."

He slid a wallet-sized photo across the desk. Without

makeup she really was pretty. "There's a ton of pictures of her on her Facebook page." He wrote down the password to her account. I wondered why he knew it.

I followed him to his *comfortable* Pacific Palisades house, er, mansion on an acre and a half overlooking the ocean. The house was small by Saudi prince standards, but was definitely comfortable. He showed me where the break-in occurred. Sliding door off a pool patio, a slight dent in the door frame.

"These are the official police photos." He showed me a dozen police pix from the crime scene. "I have some clout with the PD."

I bet you do.

The broken door. Ransacked dressers and closets. It was a little too perfect, everything just a little too perfectly out of place, strewn here, strewn there—like on a movie set maybe. But that didn't really mean anything. Bad guys don't always do everything according to Hoyle.

He said he'd wire me the money within the hour and gave me the names and numbers of Emily's besties and sister. He wanted her back, bad. I could see it in his eyes or maybe he was just afraid what they would say in the tabloids?

I called Laurence Lautrec, a Detective-II in the West L.A. station, from my cell. He was my department go-to. We'd worked together when I was on the force. Claimed he was related to Toulouse. The fact that Laurence was black and six feet tall and Toulouse white and barely five-foot didn't seem to bother him. And who knows, down the ancestral line anything might happen.

Every once in a while we'd get together to go shooting or just shoot the breeze, sometimes with guns.

"It's not my case," he said. "But from what I hear some-a the guys think she might-a pulled a 'Gone Girl' and—"

"What, faked her own kidnapping? Why? She's an actress

wanna-be, married to a player. Rich. Good-looking. Powerful. Nobody skips out on that."

He gave me a "who are you kidding" look, said he had to get back to work. He also said he'd send whatever he could regarding the case my way.

I hit Tito's Tacos on the way home. A little out of the way, but worth it and I sure as hell didn't want any of those too-hip hipster joints. With my taco fix satisfied, I parked behind my building, went in, slid down the ladder back into the hole—a 1950's bomb shelter built by some previous owner of this little building during the Cold War when trust was low and paranoia high. He was going to hide down here and be safe if the Big One came. Of course what he'd come up to when he opened the hatch might not have been much fun. The next owner had used this space for storage. The hatch door was solid steel, four inches thick. If I was down in the hole I could lock it so it couldn't be opened from the outside. I felt safe and snug down here, from bill collectors, home invaders and burglars, angry husbands and nukes. There was recirculating air and filters, electricity from batteries, generator and solar, and enough food and water for one person for a month. Well, it might not have been the best food but it would do—MREs. Plenty of books and DVDs. A link to the Internet. I could be happy here forever, if I didn't have to earn a living. And it was bigger than you might think, taking up the entire square footage of the building...and then some. The biggest problem was getting things down the hatch, but I managed. I also added running water, a shower and toilet and a great galley kitchen that HGTV would be proud of. Even had a chemical toilet in case the shit ever really did hit the fan topside and the regular one stopped working. All the comforts of home, including a million dollar view of the Venice boardwalk from the Venice Beach Live Cam, spread out on a sixty-inch flat screen. But it was quiet and that made up for a lot. And I didn't tell anyone except a handful of really good friends that it was here or where I lived.

By the time I got back to the hole, the material from Lautrec was already there. I downloaded it and perused the reports. Nothing jumped out at me.

I turned to Emily's Facebook page. A ton of pix. Nothing really out of the ordinary, no incriminating pictures. I printed a couple to show around along with the composite card should the need arise.

I made sure Lambert's payment cleared before I really dug into the job. Just because he's a big Hollywood muck doesn't mean he'll keep his word. I've been doing this gig for seven years on my own. Before that I had a partner for two. He preferred the safety of a steady paycheck—his wife's—and became a stay-at-home dad. Before that I was a cop for nine years, until I got shot in the hip, a nice euphemism for ass. I could have stayed on the department, but I like my ass. It gives me something to sit on.

I scanned the monitors to make sure everything was good. Nothing unusual happening on the Venice Beach Live Cam either, where the unusual is usual. I then looked at the outer office. The pictures on the walls. A clean, well-lighted place. My board. Even though I was just yards off the beach, I never seemed to get around to surfing anymore. I don't know why. I guess sometimes you just have to grow up, do grown-up things. Little games are for little boys, as the song says. On top of that, I just didn't have the time I had when I was younger. Every day it seems to evaporate like the fog snuffed out by the sun. So I kept that board, leaning on the wall, to remind me of younger days, better days. Glory days—like the high school football star who made the game-winning touchdown, then didn't do much with his life after that.

Turning back to the computer, I checked all the usual resources on Emily Lambert, Spokeo and Intellius. DMV and military records. She'd led a pretty ordinary life except for marrying Lambert. And was wife number three for him.

Lambert called, wanting to know what I'd done. It'd been about three hours since I left his house, and already he's bugging me. Hollywood Power Player thinking he owns me or Guilty Guy protesting too much?

I pulled up to Emily's sister's place in the Spaulding Square neighborhood of Hollywood at nine a.m. the next morning. Nice little Spanish-style houses built in the 1920s, around thirteen hundred square feet—on postage stamp lots of pure L.A. bliss going for a mil and a half—hell, my bomb shelter was bigger than that. Walking to the front door, I noticed she had torn out the front grass and put in an ugly xeriscape. Some xeriscapes are attractive. Not this one. It looked like the Iraqi desert after a brigade of American tanks had rolled over it two or three times. Erin Beckham, Emily's sister, answered the door. I intro'd myself, got the prelims out of the way.

She invited me in. The house was cozy. Offered me a cup of tea, which I declined. I took in everything about the room that I could, the décor, family photos, artwork. Several of the pix showed her with a man I assumed to be her husband. Buff and tough, like they're all trying to be today. Dirty-blond hair in a too-slick do. Another of him clowning, posing like the muscle men on Muscle Beach.

"Your brother-in-law, Patrick Lambert, is concerned that the police aren't doing enough to find your sister."

Her puckered lips, like she'd just tasted a sour lemon, gave away her feelings for her brother-in-law, even if she didn't say anything. "He's got a whole force of studio cops but he hires you."

"I'm not chopped liver you know. I have a pretty good rep if I say so myself."

"I didn't mean to put you down. Just that the LAPD sort of shills for the studios. But either way, I don't know anything."

"She have any run-ins with anyone?"

"No."

"How does she get along with her husband?"

This time a raised eyebrow. "As far as I know they get along fine. I mean, they fight like everyone does. He might be a little controlling, but nothing out of the ordinary."

"Maybe I can talk to your husband?"

She glanced over at the photos on the mantel. "He's too busy and he doesn't know any more than I do, probably less."

"What about other siblings, friends?"

"No siblings, just us. And she didn't have a lot of friends lately."

I asked if I could use the head. I didn't really have to; I wanted to see more of the house. I satisfied myself that Emily wasn't there. I stayed another ten minutes or so thrusting and parrying with her, getting nowhere. Maybe she didn't really know anything, but it's my nature—and my job—to be suspicious of everyone and everything.

"I'm sorry I can't help you," she said, eyeing the door. A not so subtle hint.

"Are you?"

I wanted to slam the car door—but didn't want to show emotion. And she sure as hell wasn't showing any, hardly seemed concerned about her missing sister. People do worry in different ways, but I knew she was full of shit. Problem was I didn't exactly know what she was full of shit about. Something didn't seem right.

"Strike one," I said driving off, heading back toward the beach. Made some stops on the way to talk with some of Emily's co-workers, then hit Pink's on La Brea, hot dogs to the stars. Pink's is nothing more than a ramshackle shack. But an L.A. institution. I'd rather eat at places like that or Tito's any day of the week than those new cooler-than-cool places that last a year or three, then spontaneously combust.

I parked behind my building in the secure private lot.

Made a pit stop at Lou Hernandez' restaurant for a beer and headed toward the boardwalk a few yards away instead of to the office. I popped the lid on a Lagunitas IPA and thought on it awhile.

Emily's co-workers, mostly actors and some below-the-line people, didn't have a lot to say. I figured they didn't want to get on Lambert's bad side and be blackballed. But they did turn me on to one of his exes—right in my own backyard. I looked her up on IMDB on my phone. She'd had a few small roles, but was mostly an appendage to Lambert.

Since the pea soup of winter laid a cold, heavy hand on the waterfront, I didn't know if she'd be on the boardwalk at all. I walked down there, passing a man in a Speedo playing a grand piano, just a little the worse for wear from the weather. I still haven't figured out what they do with that piano at night. Some detective, huh? I passed the Sidewalk Cafe and Small World Books, and, of course the ubiquitous tourists. Venice is the number one tourist destination in L.A., though for the life of me I can't figure out why. I guess they come to see the freaks. And since I lived here, I was one of them—my people.

After talking with several denizens—I like that word, don't you?—of the walk, Ja-ron, the fire eater, steered me to Haley Garrick Lambert. I'd seen her around, but never paid any attention. She was younger than I'd expected, early-thirties maybe. But still probably past her prime for Lambert. Short shorts and sandals—hey, it's an L.A. winter. Baubles and beads on bracelets and necklaces. A head scarf wrapped around long, golden brown hair that hung down below her shoulders. And two or three different colored tank tops layered one over the other. Yeah, she belonged in Venice. She worked selling handmade jewelry from a stand on the side of the walk.

I told her who I was, who I was working for. Asked the usual opening questions.

"I'd help you if I could," she said. That's more than Emily's sister had said. And why wasn't Erin worried? That worried me.

The sun cracked the clouds, glinting off Haley's dangly earrings that sported a distinctive dolphin design.

"You're looking at my earrings."

"They're unusual."

"Yeah and solid platinum. Patrick's very magnanimous. He gives all his exes earrings, 'cause he's sure stingy on the alimony," she squinted in the glaring sun. I could taste the sarcasm.

"How many does he have?"

"I'm the second. I guess Emily is the third now..."

"Can I ask you something?"

"That's what you're here for, isn't it?"

"What're you doing hawking this shit out here in Venice?"

"Oh, you think because I'm the great Patrick Lambert's ex that I should have my own alimony-mansion in Bev Hills, right? I'll tell you, I signed a prenup. I get a little and when I say a little—"

"You mean a little."

"Very little."

"So there's no love lost."

She hesitated. "I don't hate him if that's what you mean. I started out wanting to be a star like every other halfway decent looking girl in L.A. I thought Patrick was my ticket. We used each other. I didn't expect much on the back end. Just like in the movies, nobody gets their back end money. Almost nobody."

"He do that to you?" I pointed to a pink scar on her leg.

"Oh hell no. But it did happen on one of his locations in the Angeles National Forest. He finally gave me a bit in one his flicks, *The Atom Boys*."

"Don't know it."

"You're not missing anything, though it did make a lot of money. Anyway, I got hit by a falling light. You should have seen it right after. Searing red."

"I'll bet. So he didn't hit you, but maybe he was controlling?" I said, remembering Erin's comment and playing off my own hunch about Lambert.

"Everything from soup to nuts, as my grandmother would say. He's a control freakazoid." The venom gushed now. "I'd say that's why I left him, but he left me. Probably for Emily—probably had her waiting in the wings. But I don't care, I'm happy, I got the sun in the morning and the beach all day long. I'm not mad at him or her."

"You think he—"

"Well, yeah sure. He could have taken Emily out. Well, not Patrick. He pays people to do his dirty work."

"Like me."

"Yeah, like you."

I went away knowing a little more than I had when the sun woke up this morning. Erin was close-mouthed. Haley was friendlier. Maybe bitter about the breakup, about Emily taking her place. Motive to kill or kidnap her? Sure. She claimed not to hate Emily or her ex-husband. Nobody knew anything. Nothing they would cop to anyway. And I was suspicious of them all.

My phone buzzed. Lautrec wanted a meet. We hooked up at the Sidewalk Café, not too far from Haley's stand. I knew something was up as soon as he walked in. Tense, unsmiling. Shoulders tight.

"Hey."

We took a table, shot the breeze—how's your wife, how's the bunker, that kind of thing. But something was wrong. The conversation stiff, avoiding the subject at hand until…

He leaned in. "We're definitely liking Lambert for it now."

That came out of the blue. "You think he's the doer?"

"New thinking is he killed her and staged the break in to explain her disappearance." He downed a slug of Sam Adams. "This is under your hat."

I tipped an imaginary hat. "So why would he hire me if he killed her? You think he's trying to set me up?"

"Makes him look like he's doing something."

I toyed with my beer. "So what's wrong, that's not why you wanted a meet. I see it in your face."

"Every day it gets back-burnered a little more."

"That makes sense—much as anything I guess. You think he's the doer and somebody's warning you off it."

"And now I'm warning you off," he said. "Fair warning."

"I get it, the studios are comin' down on you. L.A.'s a factory town and Hollywood's the factory. Wanna make sure one of theirs is protected."

"Get outta here."

I walked home, looking at the colonnades along Windward, echoes from another time, and feeling uneasy about my meal with Lautrec as I entered the office. As soon as I did I saw something on one of the monitors that pissed me off. A green minivan blocking the gate to my little parking lot in back. I have to police that area because people will park there and go to the beach, even at night. Then I have to call a tow. It's a royal pain. I could see there were still people in the van; they didn't look like they were going anywhere. I went out back to tell them to move on. I walked by the van. Two men jumped out from behind a low wall, slapping something down over my head. Everything went black. They yanked the hood's drawstring tight, shoved me into the back of the van. I didn't think it was a random kidnapping. My first inclination was to laugh, crooks with a minivan. My second was, how the hell do I get out of here? Third, I left the damn door to my place unlocked. Shit.

Zip ties tore into my wrists as they lashed me to a cargo cleat in the back. I could smell the fear-sweat coming off them. The whole van was steamy and stunk up, like a gym on a humid night.

I tried to figure out where we were going, but it was hard to tell. My senses said we were heading north, up the coast somewhere. Nobody was talking. I tried to discern how many people there were from their movements. The two men who'd grabbed me were in back with me and a driver up front.

"You want to tell me what this is about?"

"Shut up."

The van bumped over rough gravel, probably a semi-paved beach parking lot somewhere up the coast. It had to be around six-thirty p.m., probably not anyone out at this hour. They cut the zip ties, yanked me out, threw me on the ground. Rip—the skin on my forearm shredding. Fuck them. I owe you now. I could hear the waves crashing a few yards away.

Damn! A kick in the ribs.

"Stay the fuck away from Emily Lambert. Hear me?"

"I hear ya." I felt him too. The kick wasn't hard, but it hit the right spot to give me a blast of pain.

"Or we'll be back."

"Did anyone tell you boys that kidnapping is against the law?" I loosened the drawstring on the hood. A drift of fresh air blew in through the gap.

Light from the open van door sliced across one of the men's faces as he bent over me. Familiar face—one I'd seen in a photo. Dirty blond hair and nicely cut gym rat muscles, the kind you'd find at Muscle Beach. Erin's husband, maybe, from what I could tell through the gap in the hood. Another kick. Wasn't very sharp. These weren't hard guys. They wanted to scare me off—why? They piled in the van. I threw a rock at the taillight, shattering it. They hit PCH heading south. I tried to figure out where I was. Maybe Will Rogers Beach. I had a good walk ahead of me.

I tucked the hood in my pocket, walked PCH back to Windward. Got home at seven bells on the dog watch. I didn't always think in those terms anymore, but I always liked "dog watch." And I was dog-tired. I slid down into the hole, sealed the hatch, salved my scraped arm. Put a couple of tortillas on the open-flame burner, spread butter on them and then hot sauce. And that was dinner. I set the alarm clock, lay down on my bed and drifted into some kind of dreamland where all the freaks on Venice Beach came out one at time and kicked me in the shins, like in some demented Fellini movie. The alarm went off at midnight sharp. I jumped in the shower, dressed and climbed up the ladder.

An eerie, cold, wet wind blew in off the ocean. I pointed the car east and drove, blasting Brigitte Handley and the Dark Shadows on fairly empty, fairly quiet weeknight streets. The part of Hollywood I was headed to wasn't quite as romantic as the one people imagine when they think of "Hollywood." It was the part where people lived and played, changed diapers and had sex, though maybe not in that order.

I parked a block away from my destination and walked that block like I owned it. A Nora Jones song filtered down the street from an open window somewhere. At oh-one-thirty not even a TV flickered through a window in the quiet house. I let my eyes adjust to the darkness, padded down the driveway toward the back of the house, looking for the out-croppings of a security system. Found it, disabled it.

Breaking in was easy peasy. I crept through the house on my steel-toed Doc Martins till I came to the master bedroom. I pushed the door open, quietly took a seat on the rocker by the foot of the bed and rocked slowly.

"W-what's going on?" Erin jumped up in bed. Her husband lurched up beside her. I shined the sun-bright LED flashlight at the end of my nine million volt stun gun in his eyes. He shielded them with a hand.

"Did you really think I couldn't figure out who you were?"

"What're you talking about?"

"Don't play fucking games." I hit the trigger on the

stunner. Zzzzzzzz, it crackled. "You want this upside your neck?"

"What do you want?"

I enjoyed watching them squirm. "I think you know more than you're telling. You want to keep me out of the loop—fine. But stay the fuck away from me. You're in a league you're not equipped for." I held up a piece of taillight from the van. "Fuck with me again, I'll turn you in. This piece of taillight belongs to your van, the one in your driveway. The one with the broken taillight I just snapped a picture of."

"Not legal," Erin said.

"Neither is kidnapping. Let's call it even and forget about it. When you decide to stop playing games you know where to find me."

The hole seemed particularly reassuring that night. Next morning, I wrote up a report for Lambert. Jammed by his house.

"You're not making much progress."

"I've only been working the case a couple of days." I didn't tell him about my being kidnapped or my field trip to Erin's house in the middle of the night. "You sure you don't know what might have happened to Emily?"

"Are you accusing me—"

"No, just that you might know about someone who could have been angry with her—or you."

"I wish I did. I really want to find her." He sounded sincere, but what did that mean? Like Shakespeare said, "All the world's a stage, And all the men and women merely players." Maybe he was a player in more ways than one—and maybe he was playing me. Driving back to the office, I tried to figure out my next step.

I looked through the photos again. A woman approached on one of the monitors. She glanced up and down the street, as if she was embarrassed going into a PI's office. I was up and out of the hole by the time the little bell over the door rang.

"Mr. Lassen."

"Erin. I'm surprised to see you here." I guess my late-night visit with the stun baton had worked.

"I'm sorry about what happened. We were just trying to protect Emily."

"Protect her?"

"She's been kidnapped." She sank into one of the chairs.

"Have you heard from someone? Has there been a ransom demand?"

"No, but I think someone wants to get to her husband."

"How does your kidnapping me help Emily?"

"Well, if she was kidnapped and you're nosing around they might hurt her." She squirmed. "I'm not sure how to say this so I'm just going to tell you everything. I'd been getting texts from Emily every day saying she's okay. But I haven't heard anything now in three days."

"Texts?"

"Yes, but not from her phone, from a number I don't know. I guess whoever kidnapped her is making her do it so we know she's okay."

"Anyone can send a text. No phone calls?"

She shook her head.

"How do you know it's really her?"

"She always signs off 'Lee-Lee,' what we called her as a kid. No one else would know that but these are signed that way."

She showed me the messages. Short, terse. *No cops or they kill me. Lee-Lee.*

"We can't go to the police. Don't you see? And that's why we did what we did last night. We wanted to scare you off."

"I get it." I thought I did but my suspicious nature made me wonder if she was telling me the whole truth and nothing but. "Does Lambert know about these?"

"No."

I understood her reluctance to share the info with Lambert at this stage. She showed me the last text message. It said something about curtains.

"Curtains?"

"It's our code. For where we used to go camping with our family in the Angeles National Forest. There was a wall of trees like a huge curtain."

"What do you think it means?"

"I think they might be holding her there."

She told me how to get to the place.

I hit Highway 2 in La Cañada-Flintridge, drove up into the forest, looking for the turn off that Erin had described. She couldn't remember exactly how to get there. The Angeles National Forest is known as L.A.'s body dump and I was looking for a body, hoping not to find one, at least not a dead one.

Driving in circles for an hour, waiting for the GPS to come back online, I wondered if Erin had sent me on a wild goose chase. Then I saw it. Rabbit Run Road. Not much to the little dirt road. It ended in a small campground. I parked, walked into the site. Deserted. A sliver of red flashed through the patchwork of leaves, glinting in the sun. Red Mercedes SL Roadster, behind a curtain of trees. Covered with dust and leaves, it looked abandoned. Hadn't been broken into...yet, but unlocked. Both of which surprised me. I guess it was so far off the beaten path, and especially in the cold of winter, nobody had found it.

I slipped on latex gloves, pulled out my little point and shoot—I liked it better than my phone for things like this. Snapped pictures of every inch of the car and surrounding area. The car was empty. No purse. No personal items. No dead body. Nothing. Looked like it had already been cleaned out. Maybe whoever took Emily Lambert had sanitized it to get rid of any incriminating fingerprints or DNA evidence they might have left behind.

I did a three-sixty around the car, then walked in successively larger concentric circles, trying hard not to disturb the land, hoping I wouldn't find Emily's body in a shallow grave. No footprints or breadcrumbs or anything. Someone had tossed her purse in a pile of leaves a few yards from the car. Emily's wallet remained, but her cash and credit cards were missing. Driver's license was where it should be.

Heading back to the car, something caught my eye. Two-inch wide dark tape wrapped around a tree branch, one end flapping in the breeze. Duct tape? Had they held her here? I walked over. No, gaffers tape, similar to duct tape, but used on movie sets and I'd been on enough of them to know the difference. Walked back to my car, found a spot where my phone would work, called the cops. And waited, and thought. Gaffers tape, movie sets. Lambert made movies. Was there a connection?

Something else caught my eye, shiny and sparkly, half covered by dirt. I picked up an earring. A familiar-looking earring.

I played Stratego on my phone till a black and white sheriff's SUV came trolling up the road.

"Jack Lassen?" Deputy Cantwell said. I knew his name from the badge on his shirt.

"Yes."

He made sure I wasn't armed. Luckily, I'd left my Beretta Nano in the car.

"Where's the car?"

I pointed.

"Stay here."

The deputy walked to Emily's car. Made sure there were no dead bodies in the passenger compartment. Popped the trunk. Clean. Scanned the immediate area around the car. Said something into his shoulder mic. Came back to me.

"You sure you didn't check out the car."

"Me?" Mr. Innocent.

"How did you come to find the car?"

"The owner's husband hired me to find her. She'd been missing."

"And how did you end up here?"

"Look, I don't want to tell the story eighty-six times. I'll just wait till the detectives get here."

He shot me a pissed off, don't-fuck-with-me look, but basically left me alone. He looked around, mostly just waiting for the detectives and criminalists to show. They took their sweet time. And when they did they gave me the third degree. I gave them most of what I had and they let me go down the mountain.

Halfway down, I pulled into a turnout. Figured I was far enough away from the scene of the crime that they wouldn't notice. Pulled out the earring. Familiar. I'd seen it before. On Haley at the beach. She'd had two. I wondered if now she only had one. Ex-wife, jealous of new, arm candy wife. Thrown to the wolves with a prenup that gave her virtually nothing. Maybe she'd hatched a kidnapping plan with a new boyfriend to make up for being shorted on alimony? It'd been done before.

Haley was holding down the fort at the little stand on the boardwalk. A chill wind slashed in off the ocean, biting my cheeks.

She saw me coming, had nowhere to go.

"Remember me?"

The scorn in her eyes said she did. She was wearing a pair of pearl stud earrings.

"How 'bout this, remember this? I think you lost it." I dangled the earring in front of her face.

She glared at me. "I didn't kidnap her. I had nothing to do with it."

"Then what was this doing where I found her car?"

"How would I know?"

"And that part of the forest is an interesting place. Not only did I find the earring. I also found gaffers tape. You know, like they use on movie sets. Like Patrick Lambert's movie *The Atom Boys* that was shot in the Angeles National Forest and that you were in according to IMDB and yourself."

"Get out of here. I don't have to talk to you."

"No, but you'll have to talk to the cops. You were there. Emily's car is there. I think there's a connection." I thought that was a good tagline, spun on my heel, walked off.

I could tell she was panicked. And she was definitely involved. She lost track of me in the crowd, crammed her phone to her ear. I ducked into an empty tattoo parlor, watching her from behind the window, like Bogart watched Geiger's bookstore from another shop across the street. Only I didn't have Dorothy Malone to keep me company. Haley closed up her little stand, double-timed up the boardwalk. I fell in behind her. She got into a Passat—I guess that was the ex-wife ride—and took off in a swirl of dust. I ran to my car. Beach traffic and red lights, the bane of L.A., slowed her down. I didn't have any trouble catching up to her. She drove PCH north, I drove PCH north, all the way to Santa Barbara. I could tell she was talking on the phone—I wished I knew to whom.

Santa Barbara. Nice place to be kidnapped, if there is such a thing.

She parked outside of a small real estate office—Josie Tremaine Realty—on State Street, the main drag. I went in the front door.

"Josie. Josie Tremaine." No sign of anyone. But I'd heard noises in the back when I first entered.

A woman came out. Pretty, not Hollywood-sexy, or should I say sexed-up? Dark hair, just a hint of makeup.

"I'm Josie."

I just looked at her, didn't have to say anything. She knew I wasn't here to buy a house. And I knew her name wasn't Josie. Her façade crumbled.

"You don't look any the worse for wear...Emily."

"Did my husband send you?" Emily said. "You're the PI, right?"

"I'm the PI. Your sister tell you about me?"

She sat, or maybe collapsed, in a chair. Game over. "I don't know why I thought I could get away with it."

"What're you trying to get away with? You wanna get some ransom money from your husband since you got screwed in the prenup like Haley?"

"Can't you just leave me alone? Pretend you never found me."

"I have a rep to protect." I was being flip. I don't think it worked. "Your husband's worried about you."

She stared past me. Through me. "I'm not going back. If you take me it'll be kidnapping."

"Like your sister and her husband did to me. I think we're at a Mexican standoff here."

"Why do you care if I go back to my husband?"

I didn't have a good answer to that. "I don't. But he hired me to do a job."

"And you always get your man—or woman."

"Something like that."

"I'll pay you twice what he's paying you."

"Why are you so desperate to get away from him?"

She sat closed-mouthed. "What kind of man are you?"

"Huh?" Nobody'd ever asked me that before, not so directly. I hadn't given it much thought. But I guess like most people I thought I was a pretty good guy—wasn't I?

25

"What kind of man are you? Honest? Trustworthy? Or a bum?"

"I'm as honest as the next guy, maybe more so. I like to think I'm a pretty decent person, try to do the right thing."

"Then do the right thing now."

"What's that?"

"Let me be."

I ignored her comment. "So why'd your sister turn me onto your car up there in the forest?" I said it loud enough for the people in back to hear. I'd seen Erin's van next to Haley's Passat. "You can come out now."

"We thought you'd find it, tell the police and they'd think that someone took her, murdered her. But that no one would ever find the body," Erin said, as she and Haley warily emerged from the back room.

"And she'd just *disappear*," Haley said.

"But you didn't plan to lose an earring, a very distinctive earring." I looked at Haley. "There was no kidnapping."

"No," Emily said.

I sat down, burned out. I'd been running on fumes since the Rence case. I was tired of all the assjacks I had to deal with every day. Assjacks I made my living off, but still..."You're all in it together? The ex-wives club."

"And ex-sister-in-law," Erin said, cracking the slightest smile.

"Have you told the cops yet?" Emily asked.

"Not yet."

"And maybe you won't."

"Tell me about it."

She pulled a manila envelope out of a locked desk drawer. Handed it to me. Several photos of her, black and blue and purple. Bruised up and down her body. "He did that to me."

"How do I know it's real? Not a Hollywood makeup job."

"That's why I wanted to leave. He gets off on beating me and he was getting more violent every time. He would've killed me eventually. I know he would have. I've been planning this over a year. Squirreling money away, a little here, a lot there. He never missed it. I'd tell him I was doing spa days with the girls. But come up here, work in another real estate office, till I founded this place. I got my real estate license, set up this office. Changed my name."

"And that's why you left your driver's license behind. Just to make sure everyone knew it was you, would figure you'd been kidnapped or worse."

She nodded.

I couldn't figure yet if she was being straight with me. "There's no reports of your being abused. And you were married to Mr. Wonderful, the dream guy for every woman in America. Mr. Perfect."

"Mr. Perfect has good PR and makes lots of money for the studios…" She fidgeted with the buttons on her blouse. "It's not makeup." She lifted the blouse, exposing a purple-going-to-yellow-bruise that spread like a Rorschach blot over her left kidney. "He thought he could buy me with money and promises of making me a star. I don't want the money—except what I took. And I don't want to be an actor anymore. He was never serious about that." She looked to Haley who nodded. "It was just something to keep me hanging in. And I don't want him. He'll kill me if I go back. I'm sure it's only a matter of time. He's narcissistic. He doesn't know love."

I turned to Haley, "You too?"

"Yes. He beat me too." She showed me the scar that she'd earlier told me was from a falling light. "Then, if I wanted anything at all, I had to sign a confidentiality agreement as part of the divorce settlement so I couldn't go to the press or tell anyone what a bastard he was. So Emily and I hooked up. I also got my real estate license. I'm planning to move up here too."

"And you?"

"I'm just the enabler," Erin said.

"You won't tell him, will you?" Emily reached for my hand.

"I don't know." But I did know. "You know, it's pretty easy to be found these days with the Internet and all. Even changing your name. If I could find you others will too. And Santa Barbara's pretty close to L.A., too close. One of his Hollywood friends'll see you around town or even come in here. If you really want to disappear, I'd move farther away, much farther and someplace more off the beaten path."

I turned for the door.

"Thanks. I'll take your advice."

"Get a new social security number if you haven't already. Both of you."

Emily nodded.

"If you don't know where to get one—"

"Down on Alameda."

"Yeah, but if you want a better one give me a call."

She smiled. The door closed behind me.

On the way home, I stopped at the Malibu pier. Walked to the end, listening to the waves crash, watching them roll in and out. The endless ocean. I reached in my pocket, pulled out Haley's dolphin earring, gave it one last look and tossed it as far off the pier as I could. It barely made a splash in the roiling water.

Dark clouds blew in off the Pacific. Storm warning. *Red sky at night, sailor's delight. Red sky at morning, sailor's warning.* How often did that hold true? Funny what you think of at times. A sting of salty ocean spray slapped me in the face, snapping me back to the moment.

Everyone's running from something. Emily was running from Lambert. More than that she was running from the Hollywood thing, the phoniness. What they used to call the rat race. She just wanted a normal life now.

What was I running from?

* * *

I hit Lambert's house. The housekeeper told me he was on location in Colorado. Really broken up about his missing wife. I drove home, clambered down into the hole and gave him a call on his cell. Filled him in, made the case sound colder than it was.

"What do you mean you can't find her? You found her car, the sheriff's office told me."

"She's in the wind—or dead. Trail's cold. Yeah, I found the car, but after that it's dead ends everywhere I turn."

"You're one fucking lousy PI. Give me my money back."

I enjoyed hearing the rage in his voice. "It's not like the movies, Mr. Lambert. Everything can't be solved in two hours. The money is for my time. Results are incidental. Read your contract."

"I'll destroy you. You'll—"

"What, I'll never work in this town again?" I laughed.

"Fuck you!" He clicked off. I'm sure he missed the days when you could slam a phone down and really show the person on the other end how pissed you were. He didn't seem to miss his wife much—maybe he suspected what really happened. He probably already had a new starlet on the hook, and I didn't feel guilty about letting his wife get away or taking his money. He might be able to hurt my rep a little, but what would it be without integrity anyway? On the other hand maybe it would help once I got the truth out. Besides, my purpose in life isn't to prop up the Patrick Lamberts of the world.

I scanned the monitors, nothing exciting. Then I saw it, leaning against the wall in the outer office. My stick. The one I hadn't used in what seemed like a lifetime. I climbed out of the hole, walked down Windward, toward the beach, board under my arm, the wind pounding in from the ocean. I guess like all those people cooped up inside, with their nervous energy building, I didn't want to be cooped up anymore either.

Went surfing.

The Fedora
Terrill Lee Lankford
Los Angeles

I didn't get into this job for romantic reasons. I never watched the old detective movies. I didn't even really know who Humphrey Bogart and Alan Ladd were. I never liked old movies. Especially ones that were in black and white. I became a private investigator because my uncle had a business and he said I could make some dough running down insurance scams and tracking down debtors on the dodge. He didn't usually handle divorce cases because no one cared why anyone got divorced any more. And he knew if someone wanted a romantic partner followed it was because they wanted to find out if that partner was cheating on them. And if they did find out and the offended party went bonkers and killed the cheater or cheaters then my uncle could get sued and his insurance would go through the roof. So he specialized in insurance fraud and debt collection. There was more than enough of that to go around.

All that changed when my uncle's pal Milo asked us to keep an eye on his wife, Deloris. Milo was going out of the country for six months to work on an oil rig in Dubai and he couldn't take his wife with him. He wanted to make sure he was the only one in the family who would be working the drills during that time, if you know what I mean (and I think you do). So my uncle made him a sweet deal and told him that I would keep an eye on Deloris while he was away. I'd do it in my spare time, checking in whenever I could, so it wouldn't break Milo's bank while I was at it. Milo said it would be easy to keep track of Deloris when she went out at night because she always wore a fedora. I didn't even know what a fedora was. I had to look it up on Wikipedia. It's a hat. A guy's hat at that. But guys don't wear hats anymore, so I didn't understand why a woman would.

But then I saw her in it.

It was the very first night I was watching her house after Milo had left for his rig. She came out at precisely nine-fourteen p.m., wearing her fedora and a raincoat. It wasn't raining out. It wasn't going to rain. As a matter of fact it wasn't even cold. Even though it was December, it was warm out. We were in L.A. for Christ's sake. Why would anyone wear a raincoat when it's not raining? Despite the fact that she was wearing a raincoat and a hat, she looked sexy as hell as she walked to her car in the driveway. I could tell she had a figure and she was using it, swaying with every step. I knew this lady was up to no good. Something about being so covered up made her look extra naughty. What was she hiding?

I followed her out of Santa Monica all the way up into the Valley to a little jazz club on Ventura Boulevard. Along with black and white movies, I never acquired a taste for jazz. Rock and roll was more my style. Bob Seger. Tom Petty. Skynrd! But I liked the music that was playing in the joint. A sexy Asian girl named Grace Kelly was playing with a four-piece band. She played the sax and sang too. She was really good.

Deloris took a seat at a table off to the side in the club and watched the band through both sets. I thought she was waiting for someone, but if she was they never showed. A couple of guys approached her at different times and asked if they could buy her drinks. She refused politely and they left her alone. She was being a good girl.

But I still didn't trust her.

She never took off the hat and the place was pretty dark, but I saw her face a few times by the light of the little candle on her table and I could tell she was beautiful. I just couldn't tell exactly how beautiful. Milo was nuts to have a job where he had to leave her for six months at a time. Any time you don't spend with your woman, someone else will.

She had only the required two drinks while she was there. No more. And no food. She seemed to just be there for the music. During the break between sets she read a paperback book. Not one of those electric devices everyone reads on nowadays, but an old fashioned paperback book. Like my dad used to read. I couldn't see what the title was, but it must have been good, because she never looked up once from it until the band returned to the stage.

When the show was over she got up and left. I followed her home. As far as I could tell, she never noticed me. Not in the club and not on the road. She didn't seem interested in anything except listening to music and reading her book.

So this is how it started. We'd repeat this same exact experience every night for the next few weeks. Sure, she'd go to a different little jazz club in the city and she'd see a different little jazz group. But nothing else would change. She would always just watch them quietly. Always just have her two drinks. Always read her paperback book during inter-mission. (Although it seemed to change every other day or so. Once in a while I could spot a title: *The Deadly Yellow Rain*, *The Smiling Dog*, *The Long Goodbye*. I wrote down any title I could read from a distance, but I didn't know crap about books.) And she always left without anyone in tow and drove back to her house in Santa Monica. I had found a great spot to watch her place from a block away. A large oak tree gave me cover and I could lean forward and check on the place from time to time, then lean back without her ever being able to see me from her house or her yard. I had a clear view of the street so if anyone showed up to visit, I'd know it. Her backyard butted up to a neighbor's backyard. Unless she was having an affair with a seventy-two-year-old woman named

Gloria Carthem who was good at scaling fences, that was not an angle I needed to cover. If she was having an affair with anyone, the guy must have been using a tunnel to get into the place. I checked up on her during the day whenever I could. But she never seemed to go out in daylight. I think she was sleeping most of the time, because when she would come home at night I could always see the light from her TV flickering in her bedroom until daybreak. She either watched TV all night or she went to sleep with it on. Occasionally her drapes would be open a little and I could see a piece of the TV. It was always one of those black and white movies I had no interest in. This lady was a freak. But not the kind I thought I'd be following. I don't know why Milo was worried about her. She seemed to have no interest in any man who approached her in the clubs and she certainly wasn't entertaining anyone at the house—at least not on my watch. But every now and then I would see her shadow moving on the other side of those drapes and I got why Milo was worried. A body like hers needed guarding. No matter what her head was up to.

I found myself being distracted by thoughts of her during my day work. I was becoming less and less interested in the various insurance cheats I was following and photographing and more and more interested in keeping Deloris distant company at night. She was mysterious and despite the fact that I said I didn't get into this business for romantic reasons, every man likes a mystery. Especially a hot mystery.

I had been on her tail for almost a month before the trouble began. She was in a joint called The Baked Potato in Studio City watching a group called The Open Hands when the tall guy approached her table. He bent over and said something to her. She shook her head no, but he sat down anyway. He leaned into her ear and said something else. It went on for more than a minute. She just sat there, listening. The brim of her hat created a shadow under the stage lights so I couldn't get a read on her expression. She was just sitting rock still. After he was done she spoke into his ear for about thirty seconds. He smiled. Shook his head, got up and walked out of the club. She went back to watching the group. I have to admit they were good. I was starting to like this jazz stuff. You listen to anything long enough and you are bound to find something about it to like, right?

She seemed fidgety for the next ten minutes. Like she wanted to leave. I had a feeling she was going to split, maybe to rendezvous with the tall guy. It looked like her hubby was right. But who could blame her? She'd been without a man for a month. Some women can't handle that. She took one last sip of her drink, left the rest and a tip on the table, gathered her stuff and walked out. I gave her a thirty second head start, then followed after her.

When I came around the corner and looked into the parking lot I assumed my suspicions had been correct. She was standing at her car, lighting a cigarette. The tall man was walking towards her, a big smile on his face. I couldn't tell if this was an old relationship or a new one starting to blossom, but in a moment I realized my entire theory was wrong. The tall man put his hand on Deloris' shoulder and leaned down to say something. What neither he nor I had noticed was that Deloris had her right hand in her purse. He didn't see it happen, but I did—she brought her hand out of the purse and deftly shot him in the face with pepper spray.

He stumbled backwards and started yelling, "What the fuck! You bitch! You fucking bitch!" and variations on that theme. She'd been a cool character when she sprayed him, but now she looked a little nervous. He charged forward, but he was blind, so she sidestepped him easily and he crashed into her car. She jumped away as he swung toward her, but he caught the shoulder of her rain coat in his hand. I crossed the distance between us in the parking lot without thinking. He was yanking her towards him and had raised his free hand in the air to slap her. But I went low and head-butted him in the stomach, slamming him back against her car again. He was shocked by the unexpected attack, but brought his knee up in reflex, catching me in the jaw. I saw some stars, then went to work on his lower body with some quick jabs, then an upper-cut to his nuts that ended the squabble. He flew into the air and landed on the hood of her car, trying to grab his nuts with one hand and his eyes with the other. He slowly rolled off the car onto the asphalt, moaning. There was a big ass dent where he had landed in the center of the hood.

I stood up fully and looked at Deloris. My head was still swimming from the knee shot, but I could see that she had lost her hat in the ruckus and she was standing in the light of the club's large marquee. It was the first time I really got a good look at her and, boy, was she gorgeous. She had long dark hair that had fallen loose during the struggle, full pouty lips, and sparkling green eyes (or were they blue? I couldn't be sure in that mixed light). She had high cheekbones and a soft round chin that kept her out of supermodel status but made her look human enough to approach.

She looked at me and said, "Thanks."

I wasn't sure how to react. I had blown my cover, but maybe I could salvage things and save my job.

"No problem," I said. "Is he your boyfriend?"

"Don't be ridiculous. I've never seen that guy in my life." She had a low, husky voice. I couldn't tell if it was an act of if she was born that way.

"What happened?"

"He approached me in the club. Made some inappropriate comments. I told him to scram. I thought he had, but he had messed up my vibe so I decided to go home. I didn't know he was out here waiting for me. But when I saw him coming toward me I decided I'd had enough of his nonsense."

"What did he say to you in the club?"

"I'd rather not repeat it."

"It was dirty stuff?"

"Filthy."

I walked to the front of the car where the guy was still laying and moaning. I put a knee on his chest and slapped his face a couple of times to get his attention.

"You're a dirty little scumbag, aren't you? You like to attack women? She's half your size!"

"I didn't attack her! She attacked me!" He screamed it like a three-year-old would.

I looked up at her. She was watching us, a small grin on her face.

"You want to call the cops and have this guy arrested?" I asked.

"No. I just want to go home. I've had enough excitement for the night."

I stood up and looked at her car. "He dented the hell out of your hood. He's should pay for it."

"He already did. In humiliation. Besides, I have insurance."

"What about your deductible?"

"You have a point."

I kneeled down beside the guy's face. He was rubbing his eyes with both hands now, trying to clear them. His head was resting in a puddle of tears.

"The lady said she is willing to not have you arrested. But you need to cover the deductible on the insurance."

"Fuck you. Fuck you both!"

I grabbed his hair and slapped him on the side of the face again—twice—to help him clear his eyes. "I'd take her up on the offer. Otherwise I'll stay here with you and file my own report with the cops. I've got nothing better to do. You'll definitely end up in a cell tonight."

He started to reach under his jacket. I put a hand on his arm and controlled it as he brought out his wallet, just in case he had something else waiting under there. He dropped the wallet on the ground. I picked it up and opened it. The guy was loaded. He had twelve hundreds and a bunch of smaller bills.

"What's your deductible?"

"I think it's five hundred."

"You sure? It's usually more like a grand."

"Might be. I'd have to look."

"Forget about it. It's a grand."

I reached into the wallet, pulled out the bills, counted out ten of the hundreds, then dropped the wallet and the rest of the money on the guy's face.

"You're covered. Jerk. But I see you around this place anymore and I'm going to take it personal."

I got up and the guy turned over onto his belly. He was still hurting all over.

Deloris was standing by her car door now. She had picked her hat up off the ground and was putting it back on. I handed her the grand.

"I should give you at least half for your services."

"This was no heist. I'm just trying to make things right."

"You've done a fine job of it. Thank you."

"Are you okay to drive?"

"What?"

"Aren't you rattled? You were just attacked."

"No. I'm fine. But you can follow me home if you want— to make sure I drive properly."

"Why would I do that? I'm not a cop."

"Well, you've been following me ever since my husband left town. Why would you stop now?"

My face turned red. I couldn't help it. I was so busted. I was worried I had blown my cover, but there had been no cover to blow. She had been on to me from the start. Some private investigator I was.

"Okay. I'll follow you. Just to make sure you get home safely."

"Right."

We got in our cars and drove out of the parking lot, leaving the tall guy to consider the error of his ways underneath a BMW, where he had decided to rest. As I followed her my mind went to places that it shouldn't have. She knew she had been followed from the start. And she didn't mind. If anything, she seemed to like it. She had a real twinkle in her eye when she exposed me. I was definitely feeling some chemistry there. And now she wanted me to follow her home. That sounded like an invitation. But what was her game? Had she been playing the good girl all along because she knew I was following her? Or had her husband told her I would be on the job from the start so she would behave? I was beginning to feel played. I just wasn't sure which one of them was playing me.

By the time I pulled up in front of her house her car was already parked in the driveway and she was opening her front door. She went in without even looking back at me. Any fantasies I might have had of being asked in for a drink immediately faded away. I watched the house for the next hour. Same routine as always. Dark windows as she got ready for bed, then blueish and gray shadows in her bedroom as she watched TV. Annoyed with the situation, I went home early. But I didn't sleep well.

I decided not to show up at her house for the next few days. I didn't know whether to discuss what had happened with my uncle or not, so I put that conversation on hold until I could get a read on what the scam might be. If there was one.

But I kept thinking about her. She had gotten into my head.

Finally I couldn't take it anymore. I went down to her house but her car was not in the driveway. I parked right across the street this time, not even trying to be subtle. It started to rain and I fell asleep. When I woke up her car was in the driveway. I checked my phone. It was after three a.m.

I'd been out for hours. The TV was on in her bedroom but I could see no movement behind the drapes. The rain was still coming down. We were having a rare series of storms, the Pineapple Express is what they called it, but no matter how much rain came down, a few days later they would still be telling us we were in a drought. You could flood this place and it would never drink enough to be well. It was a desert! Why did they think they could plant twelve million thirsty people on it?

The rain made me drowsy again and soon I drifted off to sleep. I was awakened by rapping on my window. I jumped like a bunny, thinking the cops were rousting me. But it was her. She was standing in the rain, an umbrella keeping her from getting soaked. I started my car and considered speeding away, but instead I lowered my window.

"Why are you being stupid?" she said to me.

"Huh?"

"Why are you sitting out here in the rain?"

"It's my job."

"Why don't you come in? I'll make you some tea. Or coffee. Whatever."

"I don't think that's a good idea."

"Sure it is. And don't tell me you haven't been wanting to come inside for a long time now. I saw how you looked at me in that parking lot."

Damn. She had me figured. She was ahead of me every step of the way. I gave up. Turned the car off and followed her inside.

"Take off your shoes," she said after we were on the other side of the door.

We both took off our wet shoes. She was wearing that raincoat of hers. It had finally rained! She kept it on and led me into the kitchen.

"Coffee or tea?"

"Coffee."

"Mind if it's reheated? I still have half a pot from this afternoon."

"No problem."

She nuked us both cups of coffee and we sat in the kitchen, drinking them black.

"Don't you want to take off your raincoat?"

"It's not just a raincoat. It's a trench coat. Feel it."

She stuck out her arm and I felt the grey material. It was soft.

"Raincoats are made out of waterproof material. This was made for warmth and comfort. It's a trench coat. There's a difference."

"Okay. Don't you want to take off your trench coat?"

"Can't. Got nothing on under it."

"Oh." I took a sip of coffee. Tried not to spill it.

"I like your voice," she said. "It sounds like you've been up all night drinking whisky and smoking cigarettes."

"I don't smoke. That's for suckers."

She smiled. "I smoke."

"I know."

"So you're a private eye? A real private eye?"

"I'm a private investigator."

"That's what the 'eye' stands for."

"Oh. But we don't call ourselves that. That's for old movies."

"I like old movies."

"I know."

"Have you been peeping into my window at night?"

"No. But I can see the light from your TV. It's almost never in color."

"You have no idea how much this whole thing excites me. A private eye following me at night. It's like a girl's dream come true."

"That would make you a pretty strange girl."

"I'm old fashioned. I like the old things. I'm not much interested in the way things are today. All this technology. There's no more romance anymore."

"I follow your thinking there."

"I wish I was born in the twenties. I would have loved to be young in the forties."

"You'd be pretty old now. Or you'd be dead."

"But I would have lived. Really lived. How great would it have been to live through the forties and the fifties and the sixties? Those were exciting times. Face it. We were born in lame times."

"I don't know. I think life is what you make of it."

"That's because you're an animal. You'd be fine no matter when you were born. You'd have been fine as a gladiator."

I smiled. "Yeah. That would have been fun."

She finished her cup of coffee, then took mine while I was in mid-sip, put them both in the sink, then took me by the hand and said, "Let's go."

She led me into the bedroom. It was dark in there except for the TV, which was on mute. One of those old gangster movies was playing. Bunch of guys in suits shooting it out.

She turned to me and opened the trench coat. She was right. She wasn't wearing anything underneath. Hell, she was right about everything. I'd never seen anything so right in my life.

She dropped the coat on the floor and stood there, waiting for me to make the next move. The blue light of the TV played over the curves of her body. She wasn't one of those skinny girls I'd been dating lately who looked like they only ate one meal a day. But nobody would mistake her for an aerobics instructor either. She was full bodied. Firm, but not lean. Not muscular. She had a body as old fashioned as her taste in movies, music and books. Big breasts, big hips. A natural beauty, not a calculated one.

I took her in my arms and kissed her. She gasped and I felt

a jolt go through her body, like she was being attacked. I stopped and looked at her.

"I thought..."

"It's okay. I just haven't been touched by anyone in a long time. Not even by my husband. I forgot what it felt like."

"You and Milo?"

"Not for over a year."

"His mistake."

I kissed her again. This time she met me halfway. Soon we were off our feet and into the sky. We did everything we could think of and then a little bit more. She was the hungriest woman I had ever met. And that made me hungry too. I know there are chemicals that run our bodies and brains and they make us feel things like "love" and "passion," so a person should always take that kind of thing with a grain of salt. That stuff wears off after a while and if you take it too serious it just makes things complicated. I was fully aware of the tricks that were running the show, but it didn't make a difference. Whatever those chemicals were in both of us they combined and turned into dynamite that first night. We were just one long explosion for the next few hours, wrapped so tightly around and inside each other we had no idea where I ended and she began. It was intense.

By the time we came up for air, the sun was on the rise. We lay still on the bed for a long time before she spoke.

"Do you like what you do?" she asked.

"Sometimes. It's fun to catch cheaters in the act."

"What about us? We're cheaters now, too."

"I look at this as a moral failure. I blame my parents. They didn't raise me right."

She laughed.

"I knew you were a bad pony the moment I set eyes on you."

She stopped laughing and looked serious.

"I'm not bad. Not usually. I've never done this before."

"Really?"

"Really."

"Then why did Milo want you followed?"

"I have no idea. I don't think he ever did that before. If so, I never knew about it."

"I must be pretty bad at my job if you spotted me right away."

"You stand out in a jazz club."

"How's that?"

"You spent more time watching me than watching the players."

I looked at her beautiful body glistening with sweat in the dawning light. "You're a lot more interesting to look at."

And then it began again. It was noon by the time we stopped. I was tired. But it was the *gooood* kind of tired.

We began a bit of a routine, if you can call it that. We kept playing our parts, in public. It excited her. I would follow her to a club at night. We would never talk to each other there. I would follow her home. I would wait in my car for an undetermined period of time, then I would slip into the house and we would make love like horny teenagers. We would never know exactly when it would happen. The suspense drove us both wild. She loved being followed. She said it made her feel like she was in one of those old movies she watched all the time. I started watching them too, when we would rest. They were pretty good. Those people definitely had style back then. And it was usually pretty easy to tell the good guys from the bad guys. It was as simple as, well, black and white. I could see what she liked about them.

We only talked about her husband once more. She said he was a very jealous man. His work took him to far off places for long periods of time so his paranoia had been growing as the years went on. And his paranoia had begun to manifest in a hostility towards her. One that extended into the bedroom. He wasn't sure if he was mad at her or bored with her, but he no longer made sexual advances. He didn't want her, but he didn't want anyone else to have her either. She had considered leaving him, but never had the guts. And she couldn't imagine starting over again. Even with me. She said she'd rather play out the string. Live out her days in a world of fantasy, because nothing, even what we had going, could live up to the world she had built for herself in her mind. I wasn't sure I understood everything she said, but I knew she lived in a lonely place. Even when I was with her.

I usually tried to leave before daybreak so the neighbors wouldn't notice. One morning around five a.m. I went out to my car, only to find my uncle leaning against it.

"Kind of following a little close, don't you think?" he said, shaking his head.

"What the hell are you doing here?"

"Your reports started sounding like bullshit, so I thought I should check up on you."

"That's fucked up."

"Really? You're going to play the injured party? You know we take money from her husband, who happens to be a friend of mine, while you are in there banging her, right? That's what's fucked up."

"Okay. I admit it. It's a bad situation."

"Yeah? Well, it's about to get worse. Milo is coming back to town."

I stared at him as he walked toward his car. He turned and looked at me as he opened his door. "End this shit. Now. Or don't come back to the office. Ever."

I didn't sleep the rest of the day. I was between insurance investigations. I had not been given a case in two weeks and now I knew why. My uncle knew I had compromised the company and he was deciding my fate. He didn't want to get me tied up on anything if he was going to fire me. How long had he known? But I had the feeling the visit was more about warning me that Milo was going to return than scolding me for my indiscretion. After all, we were family. Milo was just his friend.

I was sitting on my deck, watching the sun set over L.A. when she called me.

"He's home."

"I heard."

"Even worse. He says they've offered him a permanent position in Dubai. We're moving there."

"When?"

"Immediately."

"What?"

"We're leaving in two days. He just came back here to get some of his things and tell me to pack a couple bags. The movers will be shipping the rest. He's selling the house!"

"Where are you?"

"I'm at home."

"Where is he?"

"In the shower. Wait...He just finished. I've got to go."

"Hold on..." But she had hung up.

Later that night I drove by the house. The lights were all off, but her car was in the driveway. He had two vintage rides in the garage, a '67 Mustang and a '70 Challenger, so she could never park in there. I wondered if he was going to ship those cars to Dubai along with my lover. I returned later that night and sat across the street for a while, hoping to get some hint of what was going on inside. But there was nothing. Not even light from the TV.

I spent the next two days freaking out. I had never let a woman get to me like this one had. Not since I was a kid at least. I didn't want to lose her now. But she wasn't mine, was she? I was the interloper. The intruder. I thought she would call but she didn't. Either she couldn't or she didn't want to. I had no way of knowing.

I tried to think of a course of action that would bring us happiness without creating chaos. I couldn't come up with a thing. So I decided to charge forward and let the chaos begin. I would find her. I would tell her to leave him. I would take her from him and she would be mine. And if Milo tried to stop us I would break him in half.

I went to her house. Her car was not in the driveway. I stayed in front of the place all day and through the night into the next morning, but the car never returned. I tried her number, but it was disconnected. She was gone.

As the months rolled on the intense feelings I had for her slowly faded and things returned to normal. Our time together began to seem like some kind of mysterious dream. My uncle forgave me—or at least he said he did. But I knew our trust had been broken. I worked, but not as often as I used to. He gave me only the simplest of jobs. And they never involved beautiful women. Even ones who had "slipped and fallen" in the grocery store.

I found I had developed a taste for jazz and old movies though. I started watching Turner Classics late at night and downloaded a bunch of jazz to listen to while on observation. I even dropped into the clubs to see one of the acts. And maybe hope to find her there one night as well, sitting in the dark in her trench coat and fedora, sipping a cocktail, tapping her foot to the beat.

One day, about six months after she left, I found a package next to my front door. A medium sized box covered with international stickers. It took me a moment to realize that it was from Dubai. I opened it without even going into the house. In it I found a fedora, just like hers. I smiled. She hadn't forgotten me. She had sent me a gift. I took it into the house, dropped the box on the floor and put on the hat. I looked at myself in the living room mirror and realized it was too small for me. I looked ridiculous in it. But then I thought about it and began to get nervous.

I picked the box up and looked inside. There was a note there that I had missed. It read: *Thought you might want this hat as a trophy. Deloris won't be needing it anymore.*

I took off the fedora and looked at it more closely. It wasn't a gift she had bought for me. It was her fedora. And Milo had sent it to me. He knew. I saw a dried, crusty substance on the back of the fedora. I wet my fingers and drew some of it from the lining of the hat. As I rubbed it between my fingers they turned dark red.

I looked at myself in the mirror again, standing there, holding the fedora. And a fool looked back.

The #2 Pencil
Matt Coyle
San Diego

San Diego.

L.A. lite. Less traffic, bluer skies and a place where people say hello to strangers. A city of nearly one point four million that still thinks it's a small town. People come to San Diego from all over to reinvent themselves. North, east, west. And sometimes south of the border.

When the reinventing gets interrupted and the police can't help, they come to me. Or, more often, people like me. I'm near the bottom of the private investigator food chain. A lone coyote in a city of wolf packs, fighting for scraps left by big agencies that'll cater to whatever the police don't handle or let go cold.

The woman had the face of the children who tug at your shirt peddling Chiclets on the streets of Tijuana. Ripe cheekbones, flat forehead, coal eyes. But grown up, beaten down and scared.

She wore jeans and a white T-shirt. The unofficial uniform of under the table, and probably under the border, domestic help for affluent San Diegans. She clutched a straw handbag against her chest when she entered my office.

"Mister Duncan?" Her voice was high and brittle.

"It's Durgan. You can call me Chet." I stood up from behind my desk and pointed to one of the two secondhand office chairs across from me. "Please, sit down."

She sat and mashed her purse tighter to her chest. Her eyes

were black drops surrounded by O's of white that darted around my office. I couldn't tell if she was afraid of everything or just me.

I waited for her to complete her inventory. It didn't take long. I rented a ten-by-twelve-foot cubbyhole between an accounting office and a tanning salon in a strip mall. It had been a utility closet until the mall owner cut a window in it and found me to fill the space.

"So, what can I do for you miss...?"

"Maria." She flashed a quick smile and then the fear dropped back into her eyes. "Me husband no es...Me husband es missing."

"How long has he been gone?" I pulled a legal pad, a pen and a standard contract out of a desk drawer and readied for notes on the chance I had a paying case.

"He no come home for two days."

"Has he done this before?"

"No. *Nunca.*"

"Did you call the police?"

"No." She shook her head and long tendrils of black hair whipsawed across her face.

Fine by me. If everyone called the police every time they needed help, I'd be waiting tables or selling insurance. And making more money. But then I wouldn't have a ten-by-twelve-foot office all to myself.

Missing person cases were hard to solve. Especially if the person missing wanted to stay that way. Or, if someone else wanted him to. The outcome was rarely good. Sometimes tragic. However it worked out, I had to get paid. Especially since I hadn't had work in a couple of weeks. My daily fee was three hundred, plus expenses. That money adds up quickly when you're sitting on the wrong end of it.

"Maria, please read this, fill in your name and address and sign it." I slid the contract and pen across the table to her. "Then I can get started on finding your husband."

She stared at the contract and kept her hands glued to her purse. "I have money. I no sign. I give cash."

"Cash is fine. But, I still need a signed contract. That's the way I do business."

"No sign. Cash." She pulled an envelope out of her purse and set it on the table. "Me husband tell me never sign paper."

I looked at Maria and then the envelope. She opened it and pulled out ten crisp one hundred dollar bills that looked like they'd come straight from a bank. Well, cash *was* king.

"It's three hundred a day, plus expenses." I put the blank contract back in the desk drawer. "This might take a while, Maria."

"It's okay. You take. I bring more if you no find Manollo in three days. Please, find him."

Manollo Fuentes was a day laborer. One of the work-booted, straw-cowboy-hatted, sun-hardened men who dot Home Depot parking lots waiting for building subcontractors in pickups or homeowners in SUVs looking for cheap help.

From the photograph Maria gave me, Manollo looked to be in his early-thirties. The picture could have been a mug shot for all the emotion Manollo showed in it. Flat stare, black eyes, faint mustache over a thin mouth. The sun had etched lines into the brown skin around his humorless eyes.

I showed the picture around the Home Depot parking lot in the strip mall across the road from my office. According to Maria, it was Manollo's job hunting ground of choice. I got there early Tuesday as the store opened at six a.m. The January morning hung low and cool under a thick gauze of fog.

The chattering hit mute whenever I approached one of the cliques that stood sentry at the entrance of the parking lot. I got a lot of head-shakes when I showed the picture. The men weren't impressed with my broken Spanish and none offered any broken English in return.

Maybe if I tried a more universal language.

I pulled a twenty out of my wallet, waved it in the air and tried my Spanish in a loud enough voice so that everyone could hear. "First man who can prove he's a friend of Manollo Fuentes gets this."

Nobody moved for a couple of seconds, but I kept waving the double sawbuck. Then a kid, maybe eighteen, in a holey sweater and threadbare jeans shuffled over in front of me. He avoided my eyes and mumbled something I didn't understand.

Before I could respond, the kid shot a wide-eyed glance over my shoulder and walked away. I turned and saw a Baja Cowboy. He wore a white Stetson, clean and crisp. Shiny black cowboy boots, stiff blue jeans, bomber jacket. I made him for sixty, but he could have been younger. The sun had creased and tightened his skin over the years. I guessed he'd worked outside most of his life. Before he'd started running things.

"Help you, amigo?" He fixed black eyes on me that could've cut diamond. There wasn't malice in them. Just certainty.

"I don't know. But the kid you just sent away was about to."

"He's a foolish boy. His head's full of mota and the Kardashians. He knows nothing."

"Well." I locked onto his eyes which hadn't blinked since we started talking. "What do you know?"

"I know you're not police." He smiled without warmth. "Or a rich La Jollan looking for Mexicans to pave your driveway.

"Manollo Fuentes." I flashed him the picture, but his eyes never left mine. "His wife is worried about him. Hasn't been home for a couple of nights. She asked me to find him."

"You didn't talk to his wife." His voice was flat and even.

No accusation in it. Just a statement of fact. Had Maria lied about being married to Fuentes?

"Wife. Girlfriend. I don't care. She's paying me to find him. I'll give you fifty dollars today for good information. If it helps me find him, I'll come back and give you fifty more."

His eyes stayed on me, but the bill of his cowboy hat dropped a half inch and then leveled again. I pulled another thirty from my wallet, added it to the twenty and handed the cash to him.

"I haven't seen Manollo for two days." He slid the money into his jeans pocket and left his thumb in there with it. "He's not a reliable *jornalero*. Sometimes he doesn't come for a week."

I asked him where Manollo liked to hang out when he wasn't working and he gave me the same names of two bars that Maria had, plus one more. I thanked him and turned to leave, but he took hold of my arm.

"Sometimes a man doesn't want to be found when a woman looks for him."

I couldn't argue with that. I headed across the intersection back to my office.

I'd been in dive bars before, but this one owned the deep end. Chipped mirror behind the bar. Rickety tables sans cocktail waitresses. Spilled beer and sweat stink. Wooden plank floor covered with sawdust that hadn't been changed since San Diego was a quiet Navy town. In some spots the nails had come loose and inched up to form a pronged mine-field. Every third step was a stumble. I sat in a torn vinyl diner chair at a bar that looked like it had been made out of wood leftover from the floor.

I'd spent the last two nights sitting in bars listening to Tejano music and drinking Negra Modelo. I hadn't learned anything about Manollo Fuentes but I'd earned a couple of nice beer buzzes. The other two bars had been in Linda Vista, a community east of Mission Bay where fresh Hispanic and Indochinese immigrants and Navy folk shouldered up against each other to form a diversity cocktail. The bars there had been a shade more upscale; no sawdust, real barstools and cocktail waitresses.

This one was in Barrio Logan, a town wedged between the Port of San Diego and Interstate 5, known for Chicano Park, graffiti murals, and junkyards. I was the only Anglo in the bar. War's "Low Rider" blared over the sound system. Challenging stares from hard men drinking Budweiser bounced off my face.

The bartender, a rusty, squat man in his sixties, scanned the bar when I showed him Manollo's picture. I couldn't tell if he was looking for Manollo or checking how many eyes were on him. He shook his head and moved down the bar, wiping it with a stained dish towel.

"The Rail" looked less like a hangout for day laborers and more like one for ex hard-timers. Not a single cowboy hat, but plenty of bandanas smothering bald heads. Dark blue prison ink ran down mens' arms and around their necks. A hand and the number "13" were the common images. La Eme. Members of the Mexican Mafia. The toughest prison gang in California. A couple of Chicanos had tattooed tears dripping from the corner of their eyes. Killers.

I feared for Manollo's life.

A hand clamped down on my shoulder. I feared for my own.

"You lost, homey?"

I turned and followed the hand up a bulging arm to sofa-sized shoulders and a round, bald head. No neck. Just a goateed bowling ball of a head. I didn't think flashing Manollo's picture would soften his features.

"Bitch, I'm talking to you!" No Neck grabbed my jacket and yanked me off the diner chair.

I once spent a long night in the downtown jail. Negotiation showed weakness. Violence demanded respect.

I surprised No Neck with a left hook to the ribs and followed with a straight right to the bowling ball. His nose or my hand, or both, cracked and pain bolted through my knuckle up my forearm. Blood trickled from his nose and reddened his lips. He lunged at me and I sidestepped him and smashed a short right to his temple. He hit the ground like a dropped sledgehammer.

I swung around and readied for a charge from No Neck's homies. My hand throbbed but I fought the urge to shake it and, instead, balled it into a fist. A thin, gray-haired Chicano in Harley leather pulled back from the opposite end of the bar and ambled over to me. No one else moved, but all eyes were on me.

The man's arms were sleeved but dark blue tats crawled up his neck. Three tears trailed down from his left eye. A white scar ran down below his right. His hands were in his jeans pockets and a thin smile straightened his mouth. He stopped in front of me and we traded stares. Then he looked down at the mass of muscles laid out below me.

"Burro, you takin' a nap?" He nudged No Neck in the shoulder with a motorcycle boot. The man struggled up to his hands and knees and shook his head. Rivulets of blood splashed down onto the sawdust.

White Scar nodded to the far end of the bar and two smaller versions of No Neck rose and walked over to their fallen comrade and escorted him over to a table.

"Mr. Fast Hands, my friend asked you a question before he fell and bumped his head." White Scar continued with the smile but his eyes didn't share the mirth.

"I'm looking for a man named Manollo Fuentes."

White Scar nodded to the front door and another leather clad man went over and closed it. Then locked it. The two men who'd tended to No Neck came over and straddled me at the bar.

A thousand bucks hardly seemed worth it now.

White Scar's minions shot their hands around my arms and shouldered me to the bar. He punched me in the stomach a fraction after I tensed my ab muscles. It still forced the breath out of my diaphragm and left a knot sucking for air like a clogged vacuum. I gasped and finally inhaled enough air to live. White Scar punched me in the gut again. The two toughs holding me let go and I collapsed onto the floor.

"You some kinda friend of his, White Boy?"

My face was buried in saw dust that my teeth were trying to filter as I gasped for oxygen. A kick blasted my ribs. I groaned and covered up waiting for the next one. When it didn't come I pulled myself upright along the bar and faced White Scar.

"I'm a private investigator." I spit some sawdust from between my teeth back down onto the floor. "Someone hired my partner and me to find Fuentes. We'll pay for good information. If you don't wanna tell me where he is, fine. I'm outta here."

I threw the partner story out so they'd think someone knew where I was. Someone who could contact the police if things went bad. Or worse.

The two thugs still bracketed me. The front door was still locked. White Scar still pointed his unfriendly smile at me. I took a step toward the door and my sentries grabbed me and slammed me back against the bar.

"You'll leave when I say so, *Pendejo*." White Scar pistoned his finger into my chest. "Who's looking for Fuentes?"

My clients' names and intentions are their business and mine. But since I'd already told the Baja Cowboy who my client was, coupled with the fact that Maria hadn't signed a contract or sworn me to secrecy, I felt free to answer the question. And, even if neither of those things had been true, I valued my life over a client's trust.

"A woman. Claims to be his wife. Might be a girlfriend. I don't give a crap, either way."

This time the punch landed on my nose. White sparks shot across my vision and pain exploded in my face. Then the blood started. It dripped out of my nose, off my lip and into my mouth. Warm. Metallic. Mine.

"That was for Burro." White Scar riffled my pockets until he came out with one of my business cards. He looked at it and then waved it in my face. "Maybe we'll meet again, Chet Durgan. Someday when you don't expect it and we won't be so friendly. In the meantime, forget about Manollo Fuentes."

He shoved me toward the door and I stumbled over some nails jutting up from the floor and reunited with the sawdust. I wobbled my way up and the bartender appeared from behind the bar. He draped my arm over his shoulder and slid his arm around my waist and shuffled me toward the door.

Once we were outside, he asked where my car was and guided me to it. Fog grayed the black of the night and smudged the street lights. The car door handle was cool and slick.

"Listen." The squat man looked back at the bar and saw that no one else had come out. "Give me two hundred dollars and I tell you where Manollo is."

I guess he hadn't listened to what the man with the tattoo teardrops told me.

Maybe I hadn't either.

"So, you lied to me in the bar." I wiped fresh blood from my nose. "Why should I believe you now?"

"I couldn't tell you in there. Manollo is a thief. He steal things and gives La Eme a cut."

The man's eyes bounced between me and the bar. His fear was real. He gave me an address and I gave him a hundred with the promise of another if it panned out.

* * *

The address was a well-kept California Craftsman bunga-low in North Park, a slightly less polished version of Hillcrest, its gentrified neighbor to the west. The house had a garage and there was no car in the driveway. It was a bit after nine. I parked a house down across the street and checked myself in the rearview mirror. My nose was twice its normal size. Caked blood hung above my lip like a bad mustache. Even in the dark, I could see the blue beginnings of two black eyes. I'd looked worse. But that was when I was young and stupid.

Now, I was just stupid.

The Mexican Mafia. As soon as I saw the prison tats and ink tears I should have slunk out of the bar. Would have saved me a busted nose and a few less enemies. There were garden variety street toughs and then there were the gangs that grew out of the toughest prisons in America. Life was cheap inside and not worth much more outside. These men feared nothing. Not prison. Not death. Not me.

Maybe one of the big detective agencies in town was hiring. Maybe I could land a worker's comp fraud case where the only person who gets hurt is just pretending.

A late-model sedan pulled into the Craftsman's driveway interrupting my job contemplation. A woman got out of the driver's side. She looked to be blonde and nicely proportioned in the hazy street light. A man exited the passenger door and I had my one chance. I started the car, flicked on the headlights and pulled away from the curve at a sharp angle. The lights caught the man's face as he walked along the driveway toward the house.

Manollo.

Case closed. Retainer earned. Now, I just had to deliver the bad news.

* * *

I was working on a crossword puzzle with a #2 pencil and a good eraser when Maria showed up at my office at nine a.m. the next morning. If she had signed a contract or given me a credit card, I would have given her the news over the phone. But, since this was a cash deal and I was owed for expenses, I gave it to her in person.

She asked me about my broken face and I told her I ran into a door. I had enough bad news to tell her. I didn't want guilt to mix in with the grief that was to come. She sat in the same chair as before and set her purse down on the floor below the desk. She wore a rainbow blouse and her black hair was in a tight pony tail. It made her look more urbane, like she'd shaken off her village upbringing in just three days. Her eyes weren't quite so big this time. There was more anticipation than fear in them.

I gave her the address, then told her about the blonde woman. Anger squinted down her eyes, then she buried her head in her hands. A couple of sobs seeped through, but when her head came up her eyes looked dry. A grimace pained her face.

"Why?" A sniffle. "Why he do this?"

There were plenty of "whys" whenever there was a man and a woman involved. I didn't know which one to choose. And if I had, I would have kept it to myself.

"Maybe there's an innocent explanation." Not a chance.

"*Ay, Dios mio!*" Tighter grimace and a hint of liquid in the corners of her eyes.

I went around the desk and patted her shoulder. She turned her face into my chest.

"Mister Durgan, can I have water, please?"

I went over to the mini fridge I kept in the back of my office and grabbed a bottled water. When I returned to the desk Maria was wiping her nose with a tissue. She thanked me for the water and took a sip, then stood and gave me the expense money.

"Thank you, Mister Durgan." She dabbed her nose again with the tissue. "Can I have your card if I need talk to you again?"

"Sure." I grabbed a card off my desk and handed it to her. She took it with her tissued hand and dropped it into her purse. I opened the door for her and she trudged off, head down, through the parking lot toward the bus stop.

I went back to my desk, grabbed the expense money Maria had given me and left the office. I headed for the Home Depot parking lot across the street to pay the Baja Cowboy the fifty I owed him for information. While I waited for traffic to clear, Maria buzzed past me behind the wheel of a late-model convertible Mustang.

Maybe I had her all wrong. Didn't matter. I'd done my job. Gotten paid. Life moved on.

I paid off the Cowboy and went back to the office to finish my crossword puzzle, but couldn't find my pencil.

The next morning, I read the paper in bed and flicked on the local morning news.

Then bolted off the bed for a closer view of the TV.

A reporter stood outside the California Craftsman where I'd tracked Manollo Fuentes. She didn't give any names but said that inside a man and a woman had been murdered.

Manollo and the blonde? Maria and Manollo? Murder? Murder, suicide? The Mexican Mafia? I grabbed my cell phone out of my pants and punched Maria's number.

"Hello?" The voice was less accented and lower than when I'd talked to her in person.

"Maria? Thank God you're alive."

"No Maria here. Sorry."

"Maria, I know that's you."

"My name's not Maria." A chuckle. "It never was."

The puzzle pieces finally snapped into place.

"Why did you have to kill them? He cheated on you, but life goes on. You could have just walked away."

"Cheated on me, no. Cheated me, yes. Ours was mostly a business relationship. Bye, bye, Mister Duncan." She gave my name an exaggerated accent. "Look me up the next time you're in Mexico."

Click.

I redialed. It rang, then stopped. No voicemail. Probably a burner.

I dialed the San Diego Police Department and got dressed while I waited on hold.

Then a fist pounded on my door. I opened it and two plain clothed detectives were backed by two Uni's.

I hung up the phone.

"Chet Durgan?" The lead detective was old school. Desk belly, Basset Hound eyes, porn mustache. "We have a warrant to search the premises."

He handed me the warrant and I gave it a quick look and invited them in. I didn't have anything to hide.

I volunteered the whole story before the cops ever asked me a question.

"So, you never actually met Manollo Fuentes? Never had any dealings with him?" The detective asked.

"No."

"And you don't know this Maria's real name, don't have an address, and don't have a signed contract?" His Basset Hound eyes drooped.

I shook my head and gave him her phone number. He dialed it, got no answer and hung up. Then his phone rang. He answered it, listened, said "thanks," hung up and turned his attention back on me. "Is there anything else you want to tell us or are you going to blame everything on the mysterious woman?"

"There's nothing more to tell. She used me to find Fuentes and then she killed him."

"So, this supposed peasant woman duped you?"

"Yes."

"And that explains why you've been asking about Fuentes all over town and your car was seen parked outside of the house where he was later found murdered?"

"Yes!" This was heading in the wrong direction. Right at me. "I left there once he arrived at the house. I never went inside."

"Really? Then I wonder why your business card was found at the murder scene. And why the fingerprints on the pencil sticking out of Mr. Fuentes' eye match yours on file with the Bureau of Investigative Services."

"It wasn't me!" The walls of my living room closed in on me to form a perfect frame.

"Cuff him. We're going downtown."

Vengeance is Mine
Gay Toltl Kinman
San Bernardino/Lake Arrowhead

The backstory, one year ago.

"How's your hand?" Lara Chisolm asked.

"Hurts like hell. How can two fingers that are missing still hurt this much?" said Angie Shay. "Never mind, that's a rhetorical question." Her blonde hair swung around her ears as she shook her head.

"You said you had some wine chilling?" Lara opened the refrigerator.

"White Zinfandel," Angie said as Lara pulled the wine out. "Opener's in that drawer." Angie pointed with her left hand, her bandaged right still rested on her kitchen table. "Get the good glasses. They're in the dining room cabinet. The pink ones. To match the wine. They were my grandmother's."

Lara set the opened bottle on the table, and then returned with two long-stemmed, antique crystal glasses. "These are beauts," she said, holding one up to the light, turning it and looking through the rosebud pink glass. Then she set them on the table. She held one by the base and gently flicked a finger on it. It rang musically. "Real crystal," she said as she poured the wine.

They clinked glasses.

"Good thing I'm a lefty," Angie said looking at the wine glass she held with her good hand. "Now what did you want to talk to me about?"

"I've got an idea," Lara said. "I want us to open a private investigator agency and call it 'Vengeance Is Mine.'"

"As in, 'sayeth the Lord'?"

Lara touched her glass again to Angie's. "You got it, partner."

"We have to have some rules, otherwise this could go over the edge."

"Just happen to have paper here." Lara reached down into her briefcase, past her gun and her badge, and pulled out a yellow pad. She brushed dark brown curly bangs away that made her forehead itch in the July heat. She felt them instantly spring back.

"You're serious," Angie said, leaning back in her chair.

"Dead serious."

"What happened today? You were testifying in court, weren't you? Don't tell me that slimeball got off."

"You got it in one." Lara drained her glass and poured another. "The scuzzy walked. I won't even tell you the details. I'm thinking of walking, too."

"Why, Lara? You've got ten years on."

"So do you."

Angie waved her bandaged hand, then flinched and set it gently back on the table. "I can't be a cop if I'm missing two fingers. I mean, not a real cop. Doesn't matter that I got shot in the line of duty."

"And because you're a lefty one scuzzy is off the streets—permanently."

"Amen to that."

"I didn't hear that they were making you pull the pin," Lara said.

"Might just as well. The chief said I could have any desk job in the department that I wanted. Even in his office."

"Ah, I get it. The operative words are 'desk job.'"

"Lara, I don't want to sit behind a desk. It would break my heart. Reading reports of what everyone out in the field is doing. I'm not going to catch any bad guys sitting at a desk. I'm ready, willing and able to hop back into our plain Jane car this very minute. I'm an investigator, not a desk jockey."

"Okay, okay, I get it."

"But you're still an investigator. No one's making you take a desk job, so why do you want to leave?"

"Think I lost something when you lost your two fingers, and especially now that I've lost you as my partner," Lara said.

Angie finished her wine. "You'll get another partner. A good one."

"Maybe," Lara filled Angie's glass.

"Let's do this," Angie said, "Work our first case or two, then you can decide if you still want to quit."

Lara played with the pen on the yellow pad. "I'll make a deal with you. If you stay, so will I. You can be a desk jock for the department—or an investigator for V.I.M."

Angie laughed. Lara felt a weight off her chest that her friend and partner found a moment of merriment in her pain-filled month.

"Clue me in about the business you've got in mind. I can tell you've been thinking about this a lot."

Lara nodded. "Basically what we're doing on the job, only we work one case at a time not a file drawer full. I want us to be the resort for lost cases. I want us to balance the scales of justice when the police and courts aren't able to."

"Can't say a few people wouldn't welcome it," said Angie.

"Clem, Don and Racine said they'd work for us on their days off. They don't want to give up their day job."

"Whoa. You've already talked to them about this?"

"Been talking to them ever since you got hit. How to get the scuzzies off the street. They started telling me about all the cases where the victims' families wanted justice. And had no place to go. That's what gave me the idea."

"I see," said Angie. She poured the wine this time, empty-ing the bottle. "We've got to think this out, make strict rules, otherwise you're talking vigilantism."

"I want us to offer a thorough investigation, so we're sure

we've got the right culprit. One hundred percent sure. If we're not, we walk away, give the money back to the client. But we've got to charge a high fee. I'm talking really high. Our investigations will be more thorough than any police agency could even do with the workload and budget restrictions."

"I'm listening, partner," Angie said.

"Our contract will have the clause that if V.I.M. does not solve the case we will deduct a reasonable portion for expenses and return the money."

"That's pretty generous. Other PI agencies charge whether they get results or not," said Angie.

"Another type of justice we offer."

"I like it," said Angie. "You're making me feel better already. Let's start writing up the rules."

Lara nodded. She looked at the empty wine bottle, picked it up and dumped it in the trash. "Thought I saw another one in there," she said as she opened the refrigerator again. "Ah, there you are, you can't escape!"

"We'd better make those rules fast before we finish the second bottle."

So they did.

Toward midnight, Vengeance Is Mine was born.

THE CLEMENT CASE
The present.
Location: Redlands, California.

Lara's appointment was a referral from the lawyer in whose lot V.I.M.'s mobile office/motorhome was now parked. Mrs. Clement had gone to the lawyer with her problem. His solution had been to give her a V.I.M. business card. To help Mrs. Clement further, he had offered parking space for V.I.M.'s mobile office.

The Clement Case were the first words Lara wrote on her

notebook page. Mrs. Clement, the mother of the deceased, said that her son, Bobby, had left their home at nine p.m. one year ago. He had told his mother he was going to walk to the local mini-store a few blocks away to buy milk. An hour later, not far from their home on Clark Street, he was found dead on the sidewalk by a neighbor about to walk his dog. Bobby Clement had been shot.

The door-to-door canvas of the street by the police found no witnesses. A drive-by shooting was the consensus of the detectives, but out of character for the neighborhood. Their investigation failed to turn up any information, not even a gangbanger willing to trade secrets for a lesser charge. That didn't lessen the fact that the shooting had all the earmarks of a drive-by. A shot in the back of the head, execution-style, but not up close, so the police ruled that theory out. Perhaps a lucky shot. The location of the bullet in the body was not revealed, as the police always held something back.

"We live in a nice neighborhood here in Redlands," Mrs. Clement told Lara. "Not a place where people go shooting other people. I've lived in our house for over forty years, bought it when we were first married. My husband's gone now." After a pause, she said, "And now my only child is gone."

Lara studied Mrs. Clement. The woman was about five feet, over sixty years old, topped with light reddish hair, her face marked with grief.

Redlands had many nice neighborhoods with a population of close to seventy thousand. It was an old community, and had a university founded in 1907—old for southern California. The first white men on the scene included Father Francisco Dumetz in 1810 from the San Gabriel Mission come to convert the Indians. Since they had arrived on the feast day of Saint Bernardino of Siena, he named the region

San Bernardino Valley. The land had been claimed for Spain, but in 1822 it all became Mexican territory after the War for Independence. The town was first populated in 1890 with a little over nineteen hundred souls, probably not counting the members of the Morongo and Aguas Calientes tribes Father Dumetz had come to covert.

With the arrival of the railroad in the 1880s for transportation, the citrus industry took off. The hot, dry climate and ready water was perfect for fruit trees, particularly oranges. Redlands was named after the color of the adobe soil, and became the last stop on the Big Red Car line that connected cities in Los Angeles county, a boon for bringing people to the area, even just for the weekend. The proliferation of the automobile served as the death of this unique transporttation system and spawned a tangle of freeways.

In their new, although temporary surroundings, Lara had researched all this to get a feel for the area. She liked to know the history of where she was. It might, but not always, help them solve the crime.

Lara thought about the drive-by theory and considered it could be the proving ground for a gang member to get initiated. Wouldn't want to do it in his neighborhood where someone might recognize him, the driver or the car. On the other hand, it could have been a drive-by shooting by someone who did have a motive. That's the theory they would work.

Bobby Clement had no milk with him. Had he even walked as far as the small Rockview stand, which had, in fact, been closed?

"I never thought about it being closed when he left," Mrs. Clement told Lara. "Just before he went out he took a phone call and became upset during the conversation. I heard one sentence because he shouted it. 'I want to marry her.' After he hung up, he told me he was going out to get milk. He seemed quite agitated, so I didn't ask him then but I was so surprised about him saying he wanted to marry someone. He'd only been home for two weeks after living in Alabama for five years. He hadn't mentioned anything about marrying. I was so happy to hear that. I thought it might be a woman from there. I wanted him to get married but I was hoping he wouldn't be moving back to Alabama. I wanted him here. I wanted to be able to spend time with my grandchildren when he had them. I was going to ask him about it when he came back—but I never had the opportunity."

Lara could see Mrs. Clement was stoically trying not to cry, but she did dig a tissue out of her purse.

Because of their high fees, Lara told her V.I.M. had the time and resources to spend on an investigation. Lara noted that the police department had done as good an investigation as they could under the circumstances with no leads or witnesses. Because they had nothing, they had labeled the case Open and Unsolved. Lara was sure, like all other police departments, they had new murder cases coming. Ones where the trail was fresh with leads, witnesses and evidence—and with a higher possibility of being solved, the murderer caught and brought to justice. Cases that could be worked. Not like the Clement case, which was a dead end.

But not to V.I.M.

Mrs. Clement had brought in the requested documents—and a check as this was what she wanted to spend her money on. Fittingly, the money was from her son's life insurance policy.

Lara asked her for her thoughts, any suspects she might have in mind, gossip, rumors, anything. It was hard asking a mother if she thought anyone wanted to kill her son. The only other information that she offered was that she had bundled up the papers on her son's desk and brought them with the items Lara has asked for. Other than that Mrs. Clement had no further information.

The V.I.M. team was Lara, business partner Angie, and part-time investigators Racine, Don and Clem. They would review everything and develop a plan. The plan was really a big to-do list. Even though they had other prospective cases, they worked only on one case at a time. Not something any law enforcement agency could do.

And because their cases took them all over, Southern California in particular, they had outfitted a motorhome as a mobile office with small living quarters so they didn't waste time traveling to and from the site. In the living part, they each had a small bedroom, more like a murphy bed room they joked.

Home for Lara was an apartment in the building where their permanent office was located, and Angie had a house about a half-hour away from there. The mobile office turned out to be more of a boon than they had anticipated, especially with the Redlands case, an hour's drive away from their permanent office.

So they set up business at the scene of the crime. The lawyer's parking lot was fenced so the gate could be locked at night, giving them privacy. They had driven the mobile office with Lara's car hitched on.

That evening, the five members of the team conferred. Lara had gone through the bundle of papers from Bobby Clement's desk and found names of people living in Alabama with whom Bobby Clement had a connection. The police department, because of budget restrictions, couldn't send two investigators to Alabama to interview the contacts.

But V.I.M. could.

Plus, V.I.M. could hire a PI agency there and get the insider information.

Clem and Racine were happy to go. They spoke the language, they said. Racine was a New Orleans-bred black man, and Clem described himself as a redneck farm boy from Alabama. Both of them were highly experienced, savvy and motivated investigators. Plus they could get the time off from the police department.

Two days later they reported in on a conference call with Lara, Angie and Don.

"These people here Bobby Clement met with are meaner than a nest of scorpions," Clem said.

"Don't take any chances. Come on back, we can return the money," Lara said, realizing she sounded like somebody's mom. With one person already dead—maybe from the Alabama connection—she didn't want to take any unnecessary risks. She oversaw the office, coordinated the reports, and felt responsible for their welfare. Angie was the lead in the investigation.

Clem went on as though Lara hadn't said anything. "Bobby Clement was working with a local group to get gambling legalized in this state. That was the job he came here to do."

Lara wanted to say "Be careful" again, but she bit her lip. Those two were pit bulls, so once they got their teeth into something they wouldn't let go. Not that she would have either.

"How is that PI agency working out?" Angie asked.

"They've got more stuff in their head than they have in their files—a real font of information about politics and the people here," Clem said.

He brought them up to date on what they had done so far, and the leads they were going to follow up on.

From his last local job in Redlands, they knew Bobby was "let go" because he had "expanded" his expense accounts.

Not much money and it seemed a stupid thing to do. Why jeopardize a good job for just a few dollars? The answer to that one was that Bobby Clement had said he was framed and the paperwork forged. He had a lawyer who started a wrongful termination suit. The W.T. suit had been filed, but no one had been served so no further legal action, such as getting a court date, had happened.

Angie's assignment was to find out if any other legal paperwork had gone out, like interrogatories, Notice of Deposition, etc., but the lawyer of record was no longer in the law biz. No listing for him in Redlands. And he hadn't paid his bar dues. At first glance, he'd disappeared off the face of the earth. Lara followed up on that with a few key strokes into a specialized database and located him at Lake Arrowhead. She downloaded the information and put it into a report.

Lara emailed that and the info about the expense account debacle on the W.T. suit to the two investigators in Alabama. Had Bobby Clement been accused of trying to cheat his new employers? If he had, was that the motive for his murder?

Another lead for Racine and Clem to follow up on in sunny Alabama.

Next, Angie worked the streets of Redlands while Don tracked down and interviewed former co-workers. Angie knocked on doors in the Clements' neighborhood. True, the police had already canvassed the area. She made sure, as the police had, to interview the dog walker who had found the body. He and the dog hadn't gone far as the body was on the street, one arm flung out on the walkway to the house. The dog owner pointed out a small stain on the cement, which he said was left by the fatal wound. The only other information Angie gleaned from him was that he knew Mrs. Clement, as he lived on the same street, a block away. He didn't know

Bobby, but he'd heard a lot about him since the murder.

I'll bet, thought Angie. He could add nothing more to their investigation. She hadn't expected to learn anything new about the shooting, but she was after gossip, what the neighbors thought about the Clements, particularly those who'd lived here for a long time. She hoped they'd tell her more than they would a police officer.

She believed there should be an adage, proverb, or old saying about being nice to your neighbors as they would tell all when given the opportunity. Because it was true.

Mrs. Clement got high marks for being a good person. Bobby, not so. A charmer, yes, but he used it to get what he wanted when he was a kid—an extra cookie, money for a movie, a tip after being paid for mowing the lawn. Seems he didn't change much as an adult—except to get worse. The word "charmer" was used more than once.

Don found out much the same from former co-workers. Two were still on the job that Bobby Clement had been fired from. Two former ones he was able to interview at other jobs.

A picture of Bobby Clement emerged—and it wasn't good. Mrs. Clement had no idea how many people would line up for a license to kill her son.

All the reports from Clem and Racine in Alabama, and Angie and Don from Redlands, were e-mailed to Lara who combined everything into their own version of a murder book—available electronically to the team.

When Racine and Clem came back after their week in Alabama, the five members of the team sat around the conference table in V.I.M.'s mobile office to discuss the case.

Lara opened the meeting by saying. "We're recapping what we've done. It's a two-pronged approach to this case— Alabama, and locally here, in Redlands, which is the scene of the crime. I'd like Clem and Racine to start with their reports."

"Pardon my French, but this boy was fuckin' everybody's wife. I mean everybody." Clem shook his head in amazement. "The get-out-of-town clincher was when he put the make on his high school buddy's wife. The very guy who invited him there with a lucrative job offer."

"Nothing else to do in that town for some folk," added Racine. "He was real close to being tarred and feathered. That's why he skedaddled back home to momma."

"That bad?" said Angie. "Tell us more about the job he had there, and why the heck he went to Alabama when he was living here in the land of milk and honey."

"Now that you mention it, honey was probably the reason he left here and left there. Too many honeys, if you get my meanin'."

"You've got your Alabama accent back," said Lara, laughing.

Clem laughed, too. "You shoulda heard Racine here talkin' to all his supposed kinfolk. He had them convinced he was some sort of distant cousin. They were tellin' him about every crime in the county for the last hundred years and who was guilty and never went to jail."

Racine shrugged. "Everybody's related. And we're talkin' black folk, so they aren't passin' on a lot of information to white folk pole-ece officers. Yep, they told me lotsa stuff. I could have solved a bunch of cold cases, but that'd mean the sheriff would have to lock himself up because he was one of the bad guys. But Clem's right, this Bobby Clement guy was sweet talkin' every married lady who'd give him the time of day."

"Willing? No forcible stuff?" Lara asked.

"As willing as it gets," Clem answered. "But back to basics. He went there as a political advisor to help lobby the legislature to set up gambling in the state. Lotta greedy people. They all just needed the right advisor. And Bobby was it. Invited there by his old high school buddy—Duff Parker."

"Besides a bunch of husbands with buckets of tar, was he in hot water for doing anything else? Cheating on an expense account, like he'd been accused of here?" Lara asked.

"Nothing like that," Clem answered. "Dirty tricks. Typical campaign stuff only with a harder edge. Circulating rumors that weren't true."

"He put out a piece that the candidate opposing the gambling measure had a black ancestor. Bad as having a Jewish ancestor in Nazi Germany," Racine said.

"So a few of them are suspects?" Lara asked.

Clem gave her a list. "We narrowed it down. The high school buddy who hired him—Duff Parker—is at the top of the list. The only motive we came up with for any of the others was the adultery angle. We couldn't find any motive coming out of the job he did. Even from the other side of the political fence."

"You think one of them came here and shot him?" Lara held up the list of five names.

Clem and Racine nodded. "We checked out their where-abouts as best we could for the time period when Clement was shot. The only one we couldn't verify one hundred percent where he said he was was Duff Parker," Clem said.

Racine continued, "Supposedly he was on a hunting trip, out in the wilderness, alone. No witnesses."

"Any leads to follow up on as to whether he was actually out there?" Lara asked.

Clem shook his head. "Here's the description and make of his car."

"You think he drove here?" Angie asked.

"No paper trail that way." Racine said.

"He could have had someone else rent a car for him," Lara said.

"What's your gut feeling?" Angie asked.

"It could go either way," Clem answered. Racine nodded.

"Okay. I like the Alabama angle. Seems strange the guy didn't kill him there," Angie said.

"Maybe he didn't have the opportunity. Clement left in a big hurry," Clem said.

"So the buddy waits two weeks, then goes on a hunting trip?" Angie asked.

"Have to tell you, the trip was planned, had the time scheduled off work and he did come back with a big buck," Racine added.

"He could have used the opportunity, waited until trip time, pretended to go hunting, and came here to hunt a different kind of game," Angie mused. "It would be smart of someone from Alabama to murder him here, rather than there. That would be a red herring—we're all looking for someone here. Throw us off the track. Make it look like a drive-by shooting. Clever, really. We need to look at this guy Duff Parker more closely."

"Or," Lara said, "somebody waiting until he came back here to shoot him. Maybe they didn't want to expend the effort to go to Alabama."

"Or couldn't," Angie added.

"Like I said, the only motive we came across there was the adultery one," Clem said.

"Gotta say he wasn't the only guy in the pack cattin' around, he was just better than the others at seducing. And he was fresh blood," Racine added.

"Any other husbands besides Duff Parker in a murderous state?" Angie asked.

Clem pointed to the list. "They all had the same motives. They all had the means. No lack of guns there. When we get down to opportunity, meaning someone who wasn't accounted for, wasn't in town for that time period when Clement was shot—here's what we have. Two have alibis on the iffy side—meaning they were supposedly out working their marijuana farm. And the other two were gone off on a gambling junket. Rumors in both instances."

"But rumors from people in the know," Racine said.

Clem nodded. "Duff Parker's the only one we can't verify."

"I'd say he had the biggest motive—betrayal by a friend, not to mention his wife," Angie said.

"Why she slipped under the covers with Clement is another story. None of these characters are so sterling they can throw stones at someone else," Racine said.

"Which of the wives was Clement talking about marrying?" Angie asked.

Clem and Racine looked at each other, both puzzled. "That's the first I've heard of marrying," Racine said. Clem nodded.

"His mother heard him talking to someone, saying he wanted to marry someone. She thought it might be someone from Alabama."

"Don't know anything about that," Clem said.

"And I doubt it," Racine added.

"Any gut feeling, either of you?" Angie asked.

"Nobody has 'I did it' tattooed on their forehead," Clem answered.

"Nada," said Racine.

"Okay, I'll get that PI agency in Alabama to check out these alibis. And whatever they come back with, you two may have to go back and check it out for sure," Lara said. "And I can see why you said they were a nest of vipers."

Then she turned to Don. "Okay, you and Angie are up next."

Don reported on the disappearing lawyer who had been handling Bobbie Clement's wrongful termination case. "The manager of his old law office building told me a few things. The lawyer, Sam Moorehouse, left. Didn't come back or leave a forwarding address, so the manager cleaned out his office and put everything in storage. Then after a year, he dumped it."

"And we learned," Angie added, "that Clement selected that particular lawyer because they went to high school together."

"Same as the Alabama connection," Racine noted.

The three men went back to work at the police department while Lara and Angie continued the Clement investigation. The men would come back, as needed, on their days off.

Angie went to visit Mrs. Clement. "Of course, I knew him. Sam and Bobby and Duff. They were like the Three Musketeers in high school. Always together. Hung around until Duff moved to Alabama, but he kept in touch."

Angie didn't talk about the wrongful termination suit, or why Mrs. Clement's son left Alabama hurriedly. She just said they were checking out every connection. Had she talked with Sam or Duff lately?

Mrs. Clement shook her head. "Neither of them came to the funeral. Sort of surprised me. Think they both knew about it as I made sure it was in the high school alumni newsletter. I've got Duff's address. Don't know where Sam is now."

But Lara and Angie did. Samuel L. Moorehouse lived in the Lake Arrowhead mountain area, about forty minutes away. Been there almost five years. Why he had abandoned his files and his profession wasn't in any specialized database.

Back in the office, Angie told Lara what she had learned.

"Bobby hires Sam to file the W.T. case," Lara said.

"Then Bobby leaves for the job in Alabama and nothing is done with the case," added Angie.

"Let's go up and interview Mr. Moorehouse," Lara said. "See if he can clear up some of our questions."

The next morning, Lara took the 18 through Wildwood to Lake Arrowhead while Angie, in the passenger seat, tapped away on her laptop. Missing two fingers on her right hand didn't slow Angie down much. As Lara drove, Angie reviewed all the reports on her laptop. She asked Lara a few questions and added her own notes to the reports, sometimes in the form of questions, sometimes as a to-do item, and sometimes as a humorous comment.

It was about twenty-five miles to Lake Arrowhead Village, all up hill, the double-lane curving highway narrowing to two lanes, one each way, and even more curvy after the sign saying they were entering the San Bernardino National Forest. Signs along the way announced the altitude, three thousand, four thousand, five thousand, then fifty-four hundred feet just before approaching the Village where there were roads off to Lake Gregory, Crestline, Rimforest, then Cedar Glen.

"I'm adding about the temperature," said Angie, still tapping away.

"February twenty-second, and it's going to be seventy-nine degrees at noon in Redlands. Here it's fifty-four," Angie said peering at the temperature gauge on the dashboard. "Isn't it amazing that we go up five thousand feet and down so many degrees. Good thing we didn't come up here a month ago. That's when there was a big snow storm." Angie was looking at a website, commenting on the information.

"You sure wouldn't know that now," Lara said. "Only a few clumps of snow and they're so gray they look like rocks."

"Would you believe they have a homeless problem here?"

"Homeless is bad enough but to be up here in the winter. They can't survive." Lara heard a few more clicks of the keyboard.

"Been a few dumpster deaths."

"Eww, don't tell me. I had to investigate one of those. The

most gruesome body I've ever seen. You were off on vacation in Bermuda or someplace."

"That's why I went." Angie turned her face so Lara could see her grin.

"Ha, ha," said Lara. "I don't want to have to do one of those again, so change the subject." She was now heading her car through the archway that read *Lake Arrowhead Village*.

"Look, seagulls!" Angie yelled.

Then Lara saw them, flying circles over the parking lot that was surrounded by stores and restaurants, and beyond that, the lake. "I didn't know they hung out at lakes."

"I wonder why?" Angie said.

"We can find out, but let's get some lunch before we head over to Moorehouse's office."

A few visitors wandered around taking pictures, going into the shops, while the locals walked purposefully to their destinations, some with dogs on leashes.

One restaurant caught Lara's eye as it was on the upper level and facing the parking lot. Papagayo's. There they indulged in Nachos Supremas, a huge plate they shared but weren't able to finish.

As they ate, Lara looked out of the window admiring the beautiful view of the lake at its best on this sunny day. The gulls still swooped around.

They knew a little of Moorehouse's background, specifically that he was in the real estate business. They expected he would be able to answer all their questions on Bobby Clement's lawsuit. Was the evidence forged as Clement claimed? Had he wanted his job back? Why did they drop the suit? And why did they both leave town for different jobs at the same time?

When they found his address, it was a house. As they walked to it, Lara looked up to see the blue sky through the tall, green trees that gave off a piney smell into the oxygen-rich air. She took a deep breath while Angie knocked on the door. From his front step was a wide view of the lake.

Sam Moorehouse opened the door.

Lara and Angie introduced themselves. Angie said they wanted some information about the lawsuit he was going to file on behalf of Bobby Clement.

He looked at them for what seemed a long time. Then he nodded, and stood aside, gesturing to the sofa and chairs. The area was part office and part living room. Nice way to make customers feel at home, thought Lara.

Lara sat in the center of the sofa, Angie chose a stuffed chair on one side, while Moorehouse took the matching chair on the other side.

Angie started off. "We'd like to know why Bobby Clement dropped the W.T. case."

Moorehouse leaned back in the chair, folded his hands over his tummy, and looked at the ceiling. "There are several ways to answer that question, but I'll tell you this—it was a bullshit case. The evidence of him falsifying the records had been so blatantly forged that I could have got him reinstated like that." He snapped his fingers. Then sighed.

"I talked with his boss, and explained about the ramifications of him, the boss that is, breaking the law with the forged documents. He more or less admitted that it was not a clear-cut case. I had to guffaw at that. But then he told me why he wanted to get rid of Bobby. I won't go into that right now. What you want to know is—I dropped the case, not him."

It was obvious to Lara and Angie that Moorehouse was reliving whatever had happened. He was getting red in the face and his voice changed. From mild to wary to anger.

At that very moment, the front door opened and in came a beautiful, blonde-haired young lady pushing a stroller with a boy of about four in it. She had a baby in a sling across her chest. Moorehouse sprang up, went to her and hugged her. "This is my daughter, Samantha," he said then introduced

Lara and Angie, saying, "These are friends from Redlands."

"Did we used to live there?" she asked, her words coming out slowly, her face with a confused expression.

"A long time ago," he answered. Still with his arm around his daughter, he looked at Lara and Angie, and nodded toward the sleeping boy, "These are the angels of my life."

Samantha bent to check her child. He was definitely as angelic looking as his mother. As she bent, Lara could see that the baby was asleep also.

"Can I make coffee?" Her expression changed to hopeful.

"Would you, love? We would all like some coffee especially if you make it for us." Moorehouse smiled, his face the opposite of what it had been a few minutes ago.

"I'll be right back." She pushed the stroller out of the room.

A heavy blanket of silence fell on them. They looked at each other.

"You see," Moorehouse said, "my daughter is a little simple. Brain damage at birth. My wife died during the complications, but they saved my daughter." He stood up and began to pace. "She may not be fully *compos mentis*, but she's loving, beautiful, always happy. And she's a wonderful mother. Christopher and Timothy are like her dolls." He turned away from them.

Lara knew he was trying to stifle a sob. He pulled a handkerchief out and put it to his face.

She looked at Angie who gave a slight lift to her eyebrows. They gave him a few moments to recover.

"The reason I dropped the case was because I found out that night while we were working on it that Bobby had been with my daughter. He said he wanted to marry her. I almost killed him right then and there. I knew what a tomcat he was and he was my age, old enough to be her father. He was the last guy in the world I'd let marry Samantha. The last!" He dabbed at his eyes, his face becoming florid again.

"I left Redlands the next day, brought Samantha up here. I already owned this home. I realized I didn't want to have to deal with scumbags like him again. So I took up a new profession. Liked using my hands building houses, got my contractor's license and then my real estate license. A lot of people want to come up here for vacations—winter and summer. It's a beautiful place." He took a breath, stood and then paced a bit.

"Bobby left town that night. A high school friend of ours, Duff, had offered him a job in Alabama. That's where Duff had moved to years ago. He knew Bobby was brilliant when it came to politics. No holds barred for him, which is what the Alabama guys needed to get the gambling law through. If anyone could do it, Bobby could. I'll say that much for him."

At that moment, Samantha came in with a cart as though she had exchanged the stroller for a rolling trolley. She was pushing it the same way, eyeing the cups and saucers and pot as if they were her children.

Moorehouse let her serve everyone. Lara and Angie took their coffee black. Samantha fixed two cups with cream and sugar, gave one to Moorehouse and held the other cup, all the time smiling beatifically.

Lara felt her heart break.

"Samantha, why don't you have your coffee with Christopher and Timothy?"

"Okay. Let me know when the pot is empty." She left, balancing her cup on the saucer.

After she closed the door, Moorehouse sat down. "Then it became obvious that she was going to have a baby. I can't tell you how mad I was. Good thing Bobby was a lotta miles away. But that's not the end of the story. When he got back from Alabama, he came up here, still wanted to marry her. I told him that wasn't going to happen and to stay away from her—or else. I didn't tell him about Christopher. But what I didn't know was that he'd come back up here the day before just to see Samantha. Well—more than see. When I discovered that he'd been here, I called him up and—well..."

Moorehouse drew a few more deep breaths, downed his coffee in one gulp. "That's basically what happened to Clement's boss. His daughter became pregnant, thanks to Bobby. That's when her father falsified his expense sheets to incriminate Bobby and have a reason to fire him. He arranged for his daughter to have an abortion. I didn't give it a lot of consideration to his predicament. I was too busy working on the wrongful termination case. Until it happened to me." He fumbled with his handkerchief.

Lara got up and poured them more coffee, adding cream and sugar to Moorehouse's cup.

"But I have to tell you, my grandsons are a complete joy to me. They look like Samantha, not like that scumbag. I used to loathe every time I thought of him as the father, but I've come to consider him as just a sperm donor. Gotta thank him for that." He looked at his watch. "The boys are going to be waking up soon from their naps. I usually play with them..."

The hint for them to leave was in neon. Lara and Angie said nothing.

"Can I answer any more questions for you?"

"Do you think he really wanted to marry your daughter?" Angie asked.

It took him a minute to answer. "Yeah, I do. I knew what he was like, randy, but he'd never talked about marrying before. Thought about that a lot. Yeah, I think he did. It's the only good thought I have about him."

In answer to Angie's next question, yes, he knew that Bobby Clement was dead—he'd read about it in their high school alumni newsletter.

"Did you go to see him in Redlands?" Angie asked.

When they were investigators together on LAPD, Angie had asked the questions while Lara had observed. That's what they were doing now, with Lara studying his body language, looking for "tells" to see if he was lying, or leaving out part of the truth.

He stared at Angie. "You mean, did I go down to Redlands and shoot him? Only in my imagination. That's too quick a death, a shot to the head. I'd rather have strangled him slowly. Or beaten him to a pulp with a baseball bat. But like I said, I got over that. He was just a sperm donor."

"Would you introduce your grandsons to their grandmother?" Angie asked.

"But my wife is dead," Moorehouse said.

"Their other grandmother. Mrs. Clement."

"Oh, God," Moorehouse moaned.

"She's lost a son. Two grandchildren won't make up for that, but they would certainly help her in her grieving and give her some happiness. Give her some of the joy that they have brought you."

Moorehouse nodded. He seemed to be the one grieving now.

"Soon," Angie said. It was a statement. She stood.

Lara twisted on the sofa to watch Angie as she walked behind the sofa where there was an alcove. A black screen decorated with an egret in mother of pearl. Behind the screen hid most of what was in the alcove, but partially visible was a gun cabinet. Lara realized Angie had seen it from where she sat, but Lara hadn't since it was behind her.

Angie looked at the guns and said, "How did you know it was a bullet to the head?"

Lara turned quickly to see Moorehouse's reaction. He had none. He was frozen, like an ice sculpture.

"Uh...uh...it was in all the newspapers...I get the *Los Angeles Times*. The Redlands paper..."

"The *San Francisco Chronicle*?"

Lara almost laughed at Angie's question. Under other circumstances it would be sarcastic, but Lara heard a note of sadness in her voice.

"Uh...I might have read it."

"I don't think so."

Lara could see out of the corner of her eye that Angie had turned and was facing Moorehouse. "There are only two ways you could have known about that. Reading the internal investigation report on the shooting, which you don't have access to—or having shot him yourself. A shot to the head."

Silence in the room. Lara heard the traffic on the road below, the cry of the seagulls, and a child's voice somewhere in the house.

"No..." Whatever he was saying no to, he stopped. "They'll be waking up from their nap soon, coming in here..." His shoulders sagged, as though at the thought of the confrontation.

Angie took a few steps closer to Lara and put her hand on her shoulder. "We're former police officers. Our whole working life has been to bring murderers to justice, meaning having them convicted and in prison. That's what we're about. That's why we formed our PI agency and that's why we called it Vengeance Is Mine."

A sob came from Moorehouse. He stared at her, horror in his eyes, his mouth open.

Lara held her breath. She wasn't going to go against Angie's decision, but—

"We're about justice, justice for everyone. Your daughter and her sons need justice, too. You going to prison would not accomplish that. Your daughter and her sons have to have your support and physical presence. As you pointed out, your daughter wouldn't make it on her own."

Moorehouse gripped the arms of the chair.

"The Redlands Police had labeled the case Unsolved and Open—"

Christopher, the four-year-old burst into the room. Samantha followed with the wide-awake baby in her arms. The boy ran to Moorehouse who pulled him onto his lap. He buried his face in the boy's blond hair. After a moment he looked up at Angie.

"We are going to let that decision stand," Angie said.

Lara let out her breath and nodded when Angie looked at her for confirmation.

They took a few moments to thank Samantha for her hospitality, great coffee and whatever they could say to flatter the young mother before they took their leave.

At the door, Angie said, "We're stopping by Mrs. Clement's to give her the good news."

Moorehouse nodded, holding the chattering, wiggling child.

On the way down the hill, Lara said, "Yeah, his daughter and those two boys need him."

"What about the money?" Angie asked. "Return it after we deduct our expenses?"

"What about suggesting to Mrs. Clement that she set up a trust fund for the boys." Lara said.

"Great idea! And all of it their father's money." After a few moments, Angie asked. "What's our next case?"

"The Chu Case," answered Lara. "Their daughter was beaten to death by the son-in-law who got off on the criminal trial, but had to pay big time in a civil judgment."

"And Mom knows where she wants to spend that money," said Angie. "Where are we moving to?"

"Home."

"You mean, I get to have a real shower in my house where I don't bang my arms on the walls and my head on the shower?"

"Or sleep in our murphy bed rooms," Lara laughed. "I've got bruises on my arms, too."

"Are you truly satisfied with my decision?"

"As satisfied as you are, partner. It was the right decision."

Lara took a hand off the steering wheel to reach over and squeeze Angie arm. "Next stop, Mrs. Clement's to give her the news about her grandsons. And then we're heading home for a non-combatant shower."

"Amen to that," said Angie, holding up her left hand for a high five.

Kill My Wife, Please
A Danny Bardini Story
Robert J. Randisi
Las Vegas

"Take my Wife, please."
—Henny Youngman

1.
Las Vegas, 1960s

When my office door opens without my phone ringing first it's either Penny or my buddy, Eddie G.

"Danny," Penny said, "there's somebody here to see you." She closed the door behind her.

"Oh? Who's that?"

"Larry Tequila."

"Tequila?" I asked. "The comedian?"

"Yup," she said, "one half of Tequila and Martini."

Tequila and Martini were a poor man's Allen and Rossi, who in turn were a very poor man's version of Martin and Lewis. Their whole bit seemed to be Martini singing, and Tequila whining, sticking his jaw out and asking "Whatay-mean by dat?"

"What's he want?" I asked.

"He says he has a case for you," she said. "I thought I'd come in and tell you, rather than buzz you on the phone. Besides, I didn't want to stay out there with him. He thinks he's funny, but he's gross."

I didn't know what Larry Tequila was doing in my office.

It was pretty well known to show biz people that when you had a problem in Vegas, you went to Eddie G., over at the Sands.

"Well, okay, doll, show him in."

She nodded, went back out to the reception area, then showed the gross Mr. Tequila in.

Part of the shtick between Tequila and Martini was Tequila's wild shock of hair, which made him look like he'd just stuck his finger into a light socket. Other than that he was fortyish and overweight. Maybe he and his partner were more Abbott and Costello than Martin and Lewis. If so, he was the Lou Costello, only not as talented.

"Mr. Tequila," I said, standing up but staying behind my desk, "what can I do for you?"

"I'll tell you what you can do for me, gumshoe," he said, making no effort to shake hands, "keep my *fakakta* partner from killin' me."

"Why don't you have a seat and tell me more?" I suggested, sitting down.

Tequila sat down heavily in my visitor's chair, but immediately his right leg started to bounce up and down.

"You got somethin' to drink around here?"

"I'll have Penny bring you some coffee."

"No," Tequila said, "I mean a drink, damnit!"

"Sorry," I said, "all I've got is coffee."

"Ah, forget it, then," the comedian said.

"Mr. Tequila, where's your partner now?"

"We're playin' the Flamingo," he said. "We have suites there. That's where he is, I guess. Probably with some showgirl. The bastard cheats on his wife every chance he gets."

"Why do you think he wants to kill you?"

"We're not real fond of each other," Tequila said. "I mean...you know how it gets with partners? Like Martin and Lewis?"

"Martin and Lewis broke up," I said. "They never tried to kill each other."

"Yeah, well, we dislike each other a little more than they did," Tequila said. "We ain't so civilized, ya know?"

"Why is that?"

"He's the pretty one, he sings, he gets all the babes," Tequila said. "Me, I'm just the funny one, the one with all the talent."

And the ego, I thought.

"What exactly do you want me to do?" I asked.

"I want you to go to Sam and tell him you know what he's up to," Tequila said.

"I thought your partner's name was Johnny Martini."

"Yeah, right," Tequila said. "He was born Sam Epstein and he's always been Sam to me."

Yeah, I thought, like your name is really Tequila.

"So you want me to tell him you know he's going to try to kill you?"

"Hire somebody," Tequila said. "He's gonna hire somebody to kill me."

"And how do you know that?"

"Easy," Tequila said. "he's gonna hire the same guy I tried to hire to kill him."

2.
"Who's on first?"
—Abbott and Costello

The Flamingo was a few steps from the Sands, so I stopped in to pick the brain of my buddy, Eddie G. We had both grown up in Brooklyn, and I was actually friends with his older brother. After Eddie's brother was killed we lost touch until he surfaced in Las Vegas. Looking for a change of scenery myself, I relocated to Vegas and we became close friends who also worked together. Eddie was a longtime pit boss at the mob-owned Sands Hotel & Casino, where the Rat Pack hung out. And when Frank, Dino and the guys needed help, they went to Eddie, who had the whole town wired.

I found Eddie at the bar in the Silver Queen Lounge, working the phone. He'd been moved out of the pits by the Sands boss, Jack Entratter, and turned into a "casino host," so he could work his magic without any interference from other casino business.

He saw me, waved me over, and had hung up the phone by the time I reached the bar. Someone outside the lounge hit a jackpot on a slot machine and the sound of the coins being caught in the tray rattled my eardrums. I hated slot machines! My fervent hope was that, sometime in the future, they'd go away.

"Beer, Danny?"

"Why not?" I replied, claiming the stool next to him. "I haven't had lunch, yet."

He waved to the bartender and held up two fingers. In moments we each had a beer. At the other end of the bar glum-looking Red Skelton was working on a drink of his own.

"What's his beef?" I asked.

"We won't increase his credit line."

"Why doesn't he go someplace else?"

"He likes it here. What brings you here?" He looked at me.

"I was on my way to the Flamingo to see Sam Epstein."

"Johnny Martini?" he asked. "Why?"

"Jesus," I asked, "do you know everybody's real name?"

"What can I say? I'm clued in."

"His partner came to see me this mornin'," I said. "Claims his partner is gonna hire a hit man to kill him."

"I knew they weren't getting along, but come on," Eddie said. "How does he know?"

"Because the guy he hired to kill Martini says that Martini is also tryin' to hire him to kill Tequila."

"Wait," Eddie said, staring into his mug, "I thought this was my first beer of the day, but—"

"Yeah, I know," I said, "it sounds crazy. Both of these guys are hirin' the same hitman to kill each other."

"Jesus," Eddie said, "As crazy as I think the showbiz crowd is, every once in a while somebody just goes totally batshit. What are you going to do?"

"Well, I'm gonna talk to Martini, but the fact is I know the guy Tequila says they hired."

"The hitman?"

I made a rude noise with my mouth.

"Hitman, my ass," I said. "Frankie DelBoccio is a con man. He's got both of these jokers believing he's a hired killer. He's takin' them both for a couple of grand each."

"Are you going to tell them?"

"Why? If I do, they might each go out and find a real hitman."

"So what are you going to do?"

"Well first, I wanted to know if you knew anything about the two of them."

"Only that they're not A-listers," Eddie said. "As far as I know, they have no bookings after the Flamingo. This might be it for them."

"So if one of them gets killed, that'd be good publicity for the other one, right?"

"Right."

"Wow," I said, "murder for publicity."

"Or the whole thing is being done for publicity," he said. "Hire a well-known private eye, leak it to the press..." Eddie shrugged.

"Well-known?"

"Reasonably," he added, with a grin.

3.
"I was talking to the duck..."
—Anonymous bar joke

I stopped at the Flamingo's front desk and asked for Johnny Martini's suite number.

"Uh," the girl said, "Mr. Martini doesn't want to be disturbed."

I could've asked Eddie to make a call and clear the way for me, but I decided to do it on my own.

"Would you call him and tell him my name is Danny Bardini and that I'm here to talk to him about Frankie DelBoccio."

"Del..."

"Boccio."

"Yes, sir."

She called the suite on the phone at the end of the desk, spoke from there so I couldn't hear her, then hung up and came back.

"Mr. Martini asks that you come right up." She gave me the room number.

"Thanks."

I rode the elevator to the fifteenth floor and knocked on the door of Martini's room. It was answered by a girl wearing a towel. Well, partially wearing a towel. I could see the tops of her big breasts, and her thighs very clearly. If she was a showgirl, I bet she went topless in a show in one of the second-rate casinos. She didn't have the build to play the Flamingo, or the Riviera, or any of the other top shows. She was too busty, her thighs were too heavy, and she wasn't tall enough. But she was probably perfect for what Johnny Martini was using her for.

"Johnny's gettin' dressed," she said. "He says to come in."

She backed away and I entered, closing the door behind me.

Martini came walking into the room from the back bedroom, buttoning a powder blue shirt, wearing grey slacks and a pair of brown loafers.

"Better get dressed, babe," he said. "You got a show."

She turned and as she walked past him, I could see the towel did not quite cover her generous butt. He slapped her on the ass and she gave a little scream and hurried from the room.

"Hey, sorry about that," he said to me. "I wasn't dressed to answer the door."

"Yeah, well, neither was she."

"What, did that bother you?" Martini asked. "I thought hardboiled gumshoes liked naked babes."

"We do," I said, "at the right time."

"You want a drink while we wait for her to leave?" he asked, moving behind the bar.

"No, I don't need one. And we don't need to wait for her to leave."

"Yeah, we do," he said, pouring himself a generous helping of scotch. He lowered his voice a couple of decibels. "If DelBoccio sent you, I don't want her to hear—"

"DelBoccio didn't send me."

A frown clouded his handsome face. He looked to be in his early-forties, with a great head of curly black hair and just the beginning of a double chin.

"Whataya mean?" he asked, ironically using part of his partner's catch phrase. "The girl on the phone said—"

"She said what I wanted her to say so you'd let me come up here," I said.

"What the fuck—" he said. "She told me you were a private eye workin' for DelBoccio."

"My name's Danny Bardini," I said. "I'm a private eye working for your partner, Tequila."

Now he looked surprised.

"What the hell is Larry doin' hirin' a private eye?"

"Apparently," I said, "you guys have each hired somebody to kill the other."

"What?" Martini seemed shocked. "That *schmendrick* hired somebody to kill me?"

"Actually," I said, "he hired the same guy to kill you that you hired to kill him."

Martini took a mental step back for a moment, then said, "I never said I hired anybody."

"But when I mentioned DelBoccio's name, you let me come up here."

"Del...what? Is that supposed to be the hitman?"

"He told you and Tequila he's a hitman," I said. "He's actually a con man."

"What?"

"He took you both for...what? Two grand a piece?"

"That sonofa—" Martini stopped himself. "Look, I ain't admittin' I hired a hitman, but if Tequila did then don't you have to turn him over to the cops?"

"If I did that," I said, "I'd have to turn you both over, wouldn't I?"

"Hey, I didn't admit nothin'."

"No, but DelBoccio would," I said. "I'd have to hand all three of you over."

"Shit." He drained his glass, poured himself some more.

"What's going on, Johnny?" I asked. "Or should I call you Sam?"

At that point the girl came out, wearing a short halter dress that showed off all her best parts, like the towel had.

"I'll see you later, Johnny."

"Sure, Candy."

She came over to the bar, kissed him shortly, then smiled at me and said, "'Bye."

"Good-bye."

"Look," Johnny Martini said, "whataya doin' here, gumshoe? Whataya want?"

"I want both you and your partner to know that you got took," I said. "And I want you to know that if either of you manages to go out and hire a real hitman, and one of you gets killed, I'll be goin' right to the cops. So find a different ways of ironing out your differences."

"You know," he said, "Larry's just a jealous shmuck. He brings his wife along to our shows, keeps her in his room, then bitches when I have girls in mine."

"And how does your wife feel about that?" I asked, remembering that he was also married.

"She's home with the kids, where she belongs."

"Just remember what I said, Martini," I told him. "No more murder for hire. You guys are way out of your league."

As I got to the door and opened it he shouted, "Hey, how about gettin' my two grand back?"

4.
"To get to the other side."
—Anonymous chicken joke

Tequila had a suite one floor down—they hated each other so much they didn't even want to be on the same floor. He told me to come down when I was finished with Martini.

He answered his door and pulled me in, shushing me at the same time.

"My wife's about to go out shoppin'," he said. "Don't say nothin' til she leaves, huh?"

"Sure."

When she came out of the back bedroom I was stunned. Now this woman looked like a showgirl. Late-twenties, tall, slender with good breasts and great blonde hair. She was wearing high heels, a short skirt and a scoop-necked top.

"Okay, sweetie," she said, kissing him shortly on the cheek. She had to lean down to do it, as she was a good six inches taller than he was. "I'll see you later."

"Spend money," he told her.

"You know I will." She stopped to look at me. "Who's the handsome man?"

"Jackie, baby, this is a friend of mine, Danny."

"Hi, Danny." She smiled broadly. "'Bye, Danny."

"'Bye," I said.

She went out the door and I couldn't help myself. I pointed at the door and said, "That's your wife?"

"Gorgeous, right?"

"And how!"

"How do I rate that?" he asked. "Easy, I got talent, and I got money. Dames flock to me."

"Lucky you."

"Only I don't cheat," he went on. "Not like my partner. You talk to him?"

"I did," I said. "I told him what I told you, no more hitmen. I'm serious, Larry. I'll go right to the cops if one of you turns up dead."

"Yeah, yeah, I know," he said, "I wasn't really serious. Only he was. You wanna drink?"

"No thanks."

His suite was pretty much the same set up as Martini's. He was wearing a loud Hawaiian shirt with lots of orange, and a pair of shorts that showed off knobby knees. He was barefoot. He went behind the bar and poured himself a drink from a bottle of rum.

"I hear the Flamingo's your last gig," I said. "Is that true?"

"Pretty much," he said. "We're washed up."

"So what are you guys gonna do?"

"Split up, go our own ways," he said.

"You got plans?"

"I do," he said. "I've got a three-picture deal with Zanuck."

"Really?" I couldn't hide my surprise.

"Shockin', ain't it?"? he asked. "I told you, Sam's jealous, he always has been. I got the talent, I got a beautiful wife—you know he tried to lay her? When she told me I almost killed him with my bare hands. We been done a while. After this gig, it's official."

"So what's he gonna do?"

"He'll go back to doin' what he was doin' when I found him seven years ago," Tequila said. "Singin' in two-bit lounges and cheatin' on his wife."

"Well," I said, "I'm done. I'm assumin' your check will clear?"

"Don't worry, it'll clear. I got an advance on my picture deal. I'm rollin' in it!"

I stared at him. He was no Lou Costello or Jerry Lewis, that was for sure. I wondered how his films would do.

"Well," I said, "I wish you luck."

"Thanks for takin' care of this, Danny," he said. "If I had to see Sam off stage I think I'd kill him myself."

"So you guys only see each other on stage?"

"If we can help it."

"Where did it all go wrong?" I asked.

"Seven years is a long time for two guys who never really liked each other," Tequila said. He raised his glass. "Here's hopin' we both walk away healthy."

"I'll be seein' ya, Larry."

"Hey," he called, as I reached the door, "you want tickets?"

I waved the offer away and went out into the hall.

5.

"That's what she said."
—Wayne Campbell, *Wayne's World*

A week later, Penny buzzed and told me there was a cop to see me.

"Anybody we know?"

"Detective Hargrove," she said.

I made a face and said, "Send him in."

As Hargrove opened my door and entered, followed by another new, nondescript partner, he said, "That's a nice tidy piece of ass you got out there, gumshoe."

"I'm sure she'll be thrilled to hear your opinion," I said. "Who's the new guy?"

"Mills," he said, and that was it. Mills looked bored.

Hargrove was so unlikeable he had a hard time holding onto partners. He had only two goals in his job, to make my and Eddie G.'s lives miserable.

"What can I do for you, Detective?"

"I'm workin' a homicide, Bardini," Hargrove said. "Seems you know the people involved."

"Oh? And who are they?"

"A coupla fellas named Tequila and Martini. I hear they're supposed to be a comedy team."

"That's true."

"Well, I wouldn't know," Hargrove said. "I'm a Marx Brothers guy. Nobody else is funny to me."

I sat back in my chair and shook my head. So they did it anyway, even after I warned them.

"Which one is dead?" I asked.

"Neither one," Hargrove answered.

"You said it was a homicide."

"It's the wife," he said. "She's dead."

"The wife? Which one?"

"The only one that's in town," he said. "The little funny lookin' one's wife. Jesus, how did he get a piece like that? Well, it doesn't matter. She's gone, now."

"What happened?"

"The maid went into their suite to clean it, found her dead in the bedroom."

"How?"

"We're waitin' for the autopsy," he said. "I saw the body. Could've been blunt force, could've been strangulation. We'll need the doc to tell us that."

"You make an arrest?"

"We're holdin' the husband," Hargrove said. "He gave us your name."

"Why?"

Hargrove shrugged. "Instead of askin' for a lawyer, he asked for you. He claims his partner killed her."

"Have you talked to him?"

"We can't find him."

"He's on the run?"

The detective shrugged again. "He's not in his suite and nobody's seen him since yesterday."

"Have you called his wife?"

"In L.A.," Hargrove said, with a nod. "She hasn't seen or heard from him in days."

"So what do you want me to do?" I asked.

"Well, the funnyman wants you to come to the station and see him," Hargrove said. "That's up to you. I just want you to tell me what you know about these two."

I stood up and asked, "Your car or mine."

"Take yours," he said, "so nobody has to drive you back."

When we got to the station, Hargrove made me talk to him at his desk before he'd let me see Tequila. I wasn't quite sure why I did it, but I didn't give them away. Instead, I just told Hargrove that Tequila had hired me to find out who was threatening him. I also told him it turned out to be nothing.

"Maybe not so much nothin'," Hargrove said. "You didn't come up with anybody?"

"I worked two days on it, and then he stopped payin' me."

"Well," he said, reluctantly, "I guess it's not your fault, then. Come on, I'll take you to him."

He walked me down the hall to the interrogation rooms and let me into number two.

6.
"I don't get no respect."
—Rodney Dangerfield

"Jesus Christ, it's about time!" Tequila said, as I walked in.

"You've gotta have a better attitude than that, Larry, or I'm out of here," I said.

"Oh, hey, no, no, no," he said, waving his hands, "I just meant it's about time the cops let you in here to see me."

He was wearing another loud Hawaiian shirt—more yellows than oranges—shorts, and a pair of sandals.

"Where did they pick you up?" I asked, sitting across from him.

"At the hotel pool. Grabbed me, told me my wife had been killed, and brought me here."

"Have they questioned you?"

"Some, but I said I wanted you here,"

"Why didn't you just ask for a lawyer?"

"Wouldn't that make me look guilty?" he asked. "I mean—geez, I didn't kill my own wife." He covered his face with his hands. Amazingly, his hair was still standing straight up.

"Larry, I gotta ask," I said. "You and Johnny, you still tryin' to kill each other?"

"Naw, naw," Tequila said, "we agreed we was bein' stupid. We gave that up." He looked as if something just occurred to him. "At least I did. Geez, you don't think—"

"Why would Martini have somebody kill your wife?"

"I dunno! Maybe they made a mistake."

"They killed your wife thinkin' it was you? Come on, nobody's that blind."

"So you're sayin' somebody killed her on purpose?"

"Maybe somebody broke into your room and she surprised them," I said. "Could've just been a burglar."

"Then why are they holdin' me?"

"That's just murder one-oh-one. The husband is always the first suspect. If they have no evidence, they'll have to release you."

"There ain't no evidence because I didn't do it," he wailed. "I loved Jackie."

"Then sit tight and you're right. Don't ask for a lawyer—not unless they charge you."

"And you don't think they will?"

"Not if you're tellin' me the truth."

"I am!"

"Then like I said, sit tight. Do you know where your partner is?"

"He ain't at the hotel?"

"Nobody's seen him. His wife hasn't heard from him in a couple of days."

"That ain't unusual."

"When did you see him last?"

"At last night's show."

"So nobody saw him yesterday during the day, but he made the show?"

"I guess."

"And now nobody's seen him today."

"Ah, he's holed up with a showgirl somewhere."

"The same one?"

"He never sees the same one," Tequila said.

"I saw him with a girl named Candy last week," I said. "You know what show she's in?"

"Candy?" he repeated. "The only Candy he was with was one he picked up in a strip club somewhere on the strip."

A stripper. I didn't know why that had never occurred to me. When he'd told her that she had a show to do I just thought she was a showgirl.

"Look, gumshoe," Tequila said, "you gotta find out who killed my Jackie."

"This is an open police case, Larry," I said. "I'd be riskin' my license—"

"I told you I got a big advance from the studio," he said, cutting me off. "It's yours if you find out who did it."

I thought about it. "Okay, but if anybody asks, you hired me to find your partner, got it?"

"I got it."

"I'm gonna talk to the detective and see if I can get you out of here," I said. "If not, I'll get you a lawyer."

"I appreciate it."

He was holding his head in his hands when I left the room. Hargrove was waiting for me right outside the door.

"What have you got on him?" I asked.

"Nothin'," he said, "unless he confessed to you."

"He says he didn't do it," I said, "and I believe him."

"Sure you do. He's your client, right?"

"He was, last week."

"And now?" he asked. "You tellin' me he didn't hire you to find his wife's killer? I mean, if he didn't do it?"

"Detective, you know I wouldn't risk my license workin' on a case of yours."

"Uh-huh."

"However, he did hire me to find his partner."

"Good!" Hargrove said. "I wanna find that guy, too. He tell you where he might be?"

"Just that he's probably shacked up with a babe somewhere."

"What babe?"

"He doesn't know," I said. "A showgirl, maybe a stripper."

He poked me in the chest with his forefinger. "You find him, I better be the first to know."

"Of course."

"Look," he went on, "these are supposed to be funny guys, but I don't find nothin' funny about murder. Got it?"

"I got it, Detective," I said. "For once I agree with you. There's nothin' funny about murder. Are you cuttin' him loose?"

"Yeah," Hargrove said, sourly. "You can wait up front."

7.

"How hot was it?"
—Johnny Carson

I needed to do three things: look at the crime scene, find Johnny Martini, find a stripper named Candy.

I loaded Larry Tequila into my car in front of the police station and drove us to the Flamingo.

"Can't I go to my suite and take a shower?" he asked.

"We're goin' to your suite, but not so you can take a shower," I said. "I wanna see where your wife was found."

"Oh Christ!" he said, as if he just remembered that his wife had been killed there.

"It's a crime scene," I said. "We may not even be able to get in. We can get you another room from the management, since you're playin' there."

"Where the fuck is Sam?" he said, harshly. "If he had anythin' to do with this—"

"Take it easy," I said. "Let's not jump to any conclusions. You told me you guys talked and you weren't gonna do anythin' crazy, anymore."

"I told you we agreed," he said. "That don't mean he stuck to the deal."

"Look, let's go slow," I said, "see if we can get in, get you another room, and then I've gotta make some calls. Try to sit back and relax."

When we got to the Flamingo I let Larry Tequila take me to the very nervous, middle-aged hotel manager, who was happy to give him another suite.

"This is terrible," the man said, "just terrible, Mr. Tequila. We can't tell you how sorry we are—"

"Relax, pal," Tequila told him, "I'm not gonna sue your hotel."

The man seemed relieved.

"Have you seen Mr. Tequila's partner, Mr. Martini, today?" I asked.

"Uh, no, sir, not at all."

"Okay, thanks."

"Uh, sir, do you know what we should do with your, uh, other suite?"

Tequila looked at me.

"Are the police done with it?"

"Apparently," the manager said.

"Let me take a look and I'll let you know," I said.

"And you are...?"

"Workin' for me," Tequila said. "You really don't wanna get sued, do ya?"

"Oh, no, sir!"

"Then relax," Tequila said. "We'll tell you when we're done with the suite."

"Very well, sir," the manager said. "As you say."

We left the manager's office and took the elevator to the floor Tequila's first suite was on. There were no cops on the door.

"It's locked."

I looked at him in his loud shirt and shorts and asked, "Do you have your key?"

"Oh, yeah," he said, digging into the right pocket of his shorts. "Stuck it in here when I went to the pool—here it is!"

He used the key to unlock the door and we went inside.

"Where'd they find her?" I asked.

"The bedroom," he said. "I don't have to go in there, do I?"

"Only if you want some clothes."

"Uh, can you...?"

"Yeah, sure. Just relax."

I went into the bedroom and looked around. Apparently, the cops had done their thing in record time and released the room.

There was blood on the rug, a splotch about the size of a head. If she was strangled, she had probably been struck over the head first. I looked around. The chest of drawers was partially open, left that way during a police search. The same was true for the closest. The bed was unmade, the covers looking as though someone had either tossed and turned, or struggled on them.

Other than that there didn't seem to be evidence of a struggle.

I found a suitcase in the closet, threw some clothes into it. At the last minute I also grabbed a suit from the rack in the closet, and carried them all out to Tequila.

When I got back out to the other half of the suite, he was behind the bar, nursing a drink. I put the suitcase on the floor, the suit on the sofa.

"Larry, do you know what your wife was wearin' when they found her?"

"I think she was still dressed for bed," Tequila said. "A nightie. She tended to sleep late."

"Not you?"

"I like to go to the pool early."

"Did you and your wife have sex? I mean, in general?"

"You saw her," he said. "Whatayou think?"

"What about last night?"

He hesitated, then said, "I was drunk last night. No, we didn't have sex."

"The bed looks a mess," I said.

"She tosses and turns."

"You said your partner tried to sleep with your wife."

"Yeah."

"It never happened?"

"No."

"What about somebody else?"

"You're askin' if my wife cheated on me?"

"That's what I'm askin'," I said. "The bed looks used. Maybe she had a lover come in after you left, they had sex, had a fight, and he killed her."

He bit his lip, poured himself another drink.

"I know how it looks, funny lookin' guy in his forties with a young, sexy wife. Why wouldn't she cheat? But she didn't."

"And you?"

He laughed. "Married to her? Who would I cheat with? Why?"

"Showgirls? Strippers?"

"I wouldn't lower myself," he said. "That was Sam's world, not mine."

"Is that why you disliked him?"

"Partly."

"What's the other part?"

"He just isn't a nice person."

"And why did he dislike you?"

"Because he knew I knew," Tequila said.

"Knew what?"

"The real Sam Epstein."

I picked up the suitcase. "Come on, let's get you to your

other room. You can take a shower, change your clothes."

He came around the bar and picked up the suit from the sofa.

"Thanks, Danny."

That was the first time he'd called me anything but "gumshoe."

"Sure, Larry."

8.
"Mom always liked you best."
—The Smothers Brothers

While Tequila used the shower in his new room I made some phone calls. First I called Eddie G.

"Jesus, Danny," he said, "do you know how many strippers there are in this town named Candy?"

"No, I don't," I said. "That's what I was hopin' you'd be able to tell me."

"Do you know anything else about her?"

I told him what she looked like, how she was built, and that she was spending time with Johnny Martini.

"At the Flamingo?"

"That's right."

"Okay," Eddie said, "that might narrow it down a bit."

"How?"

"I'll check with my Flamingo contacts."

Eddie knew all the valets in town. I had my own Vegas contacts, but Eddie had all the casinos wired.

"Okay, Eddie, I appreciate it."

"You gonna be out and about?"

"Yeah, but Penny'll be at the office. Give her a call if you find out anything."

"Maybe," he said, before hanging up, "I'll give her a call even if I don't."

* * *

"Man, that's better!" Tequila said, drying his hair as he came back into the room. He was wearing another loud shirt and pair of shorts I had tossed into his suitcase. He headed right for the bar. "Drink?"

"Not now," I said. "I'm waitin' for some word on where I might find Candy."

"Martini's stripper? What for?"

"I want to find him," I said.

He stopped rubbing his head and put the towel down on the bar. As he poured himself a drink, I stared at him. It was first time I'd seen him without the electric frizzy hair. It was odd.

"You think Sam had somethin' to do with killin' Jackie?"

"I don't know," I said, "but I don't like that we can't find him."

The phone rang and he picked up the one on the bar.

"Hello? Oh, yeah, sure." He held it out to me. "It's for you."

I walked to the bar and grabbed the receiver from him.

"Yeah?"

"I got what you want," Eddie said.

"Already?"

"One of the valets at the Flamingo saw them the other day, recognized the girl," Eddie said. "You'll find her at a low-brow, off-the-strip dive called Cheaters."

"Really?"

"That's what I got."

"Thanks a lot, Eddie."

"Watch your ass," he said, "although that's not why guys go there—I mean, to watch your ass, they go to watch—"

I hung up on him.

"I've got to go out," I said. "Stay in this room, don't go anywhere."

"What if I get hungry?"

"That's what room service is for."

I left the suite, thinking if my wife had just been killed, would I be thinking about food?

Cheaters was low-brow, all right. The parking lot wasn't even paved, and the "ER" lights were out on the sign, so that it said CHEAT__S." Although why they had the sign turned on when there was still a couple of hours of daylight I didn't know.

When I stepped through the front door, I was immediately confronted by a big goon in a tight T-shirt. His biceps strained the short sleeves, but his gut was doing some straining of its own. Although he worked in a place with naked women, he was reading a girlie magazine.

"Ten bucks," he said.

"I'm not goin' in to look, I just wanna—"

"If you go in," he said, "you're gonna look. Ten bucks."

He was right. There were naked girls in there and I was gonna look.

I gave him ten dollars.

"Is Candy here now?" I asked. I figured as many strippers as there were in Vegas named Candy, they wouldn't be at the same strip joint.

"Yeah," the guy said, "don't worry, you'll get to see Candy. But the one you really wanna see is Stella."

"Stella?"

"That's right," he said, leering, "Stella Starlight. Best stripper we got."

"Is she here now?" I asked, despite myself.

"Naw, she comes on at night."

"Right. Thanks."

He went back to his magazine and said, "Enjoy."

I went through a curtained doorway and was immediately in the dark. But it was only by comparison. I waited a few seconds and my eyes started to adjust. There were three stages—two long ones, and one center, round one—that were outlined by footlights. On each stage was a girl, doing her job.

I sat down at an empty table in front of the center stage. Looking around, I saw there were only three or four other guys in the place. A waitress with big tits and wide hips came over, holding an empty tray.

"Two drink minimum," she said.

"Bring me two drinks."

"Of what?"

"Beer," I said, "two beers."

"Sure."

"Hey, can you tell me when Candy'll be out?"

"In ten minutes."

"Okay, thanks."

I considered trying to get backstage to see her, but that would have been more trouble than it was worth. There was another burly goon standing by the backstage door with his arms crossed. By the time I convinced him to let me go back, she'd be on stage.

The waitress brought the two beers. They were in small glasses, but she charged me as if they were pints. I eyed the glasses suspiciously, and decided not to try them.

I watched the girl on the center stage, a skinny black girl with a body like a boy and big nipples as dark as tootsie rolls. I didn't know what she had ever done to deserve the center stage. To me she didn't seem to be expending any more energy, or showing more talent, than the two girls on the outer stages. Or maybe which stage they were on didn't make a different, they simply rotated.

When Candy came out she was on the left stage. I got up, left my beers on the table, and moved. There was one other guy, sitting across from me, on the other side of the stage, making it rain singles for her.

I waited until she looked at me and then showed her a twenty.

She got on her hands and knees, crawled over to me and asked, "What do I have to do for that, honey?"

"Just talk," I said.

She frowned. She really did have the perfect body for a stripper. Large boobs with heavy undersides and pink nipples, chunky thighs and butt and, from the looks of what was sticking out from the G-string, a lot of pubic hair. But as far as dancing, she had no talent at all that I could see.

"When you're done," I said, "just sit with me and talk."

"You got it, handsome."

She got back on her feet and returned to the other guy, who seemed to have no shortage of one-dollar bills.

When her music stopped, she collected her singles from the floor of the stage. She grabbed her top, but didn't bother to put it back on while she stepped down and came over to me.

"Twenty first," she said, sticking her hand out before sitting down.

I gave it to her, and she sat.

"Whataya wanna talk about, lover?"

"Johnny Martini."

She frowned, then brightened.

"Wait," she said, "I knew I saw you before. You were in Johnny's room!"

"That's right."

"You a friend of his?"

"Not exactly."

She looked around.

"He ain't here?"

"He's not anywhere, as far as I can find out," I said. "Nobody's seen him since yesterday. What about you?"

"I saw him...two days ago," she said. "In his suite. I

thought he was gonna be here yesterday, but he never showed."

"What about today?"

"I didn't really expect him today," she said. "He usually comes when I work nights, not days."

"When do you work nights again?"

"Tomorrow."

I didn't have until then. I needed to find Martini before that.

"I need you to find him, Candy," I said. "It's very important."

"What's goin' on?" she asked. "It's not that crazy partner of his, is it?"

"What do you know about his crazy partner?"

"Just that Johnny complains about him all the time. He's gonna dump him after this Flamingo date and go out on his own as a singer. He's as good as Dean Martin, you know."

"Did he tell you that?"

"He didn't have to," she said, proudly. "I've heard him sing."

I wondered what promises Martini had made to this girl?

"You know he's married, right?"

"Of course I know that," she said. "I'm a stripper, but I ain't stupid!"

"Do you know where he hangs out?"

"I don't know if I should say—"

"Candy," I said, "his partner's wife has been murdered. The cops are lookin' for him."

"What?" She looked panicky. "He wouldn't do that. Why would they think he'd do that?"

"I don't know," I said, "but it might be better for him if I find him before they do."

"Oh, God," she said. "Okay, there's a small club, out on the edge of the desert, he goes there some nights…"

"To drink?"

"No," she said, "he goes there when he needs to get away from that crazy partner of his." She hesitated, then added, "He goes there to sing."

9.
"When I'm bad, I'm better."
—Mae West

I followed Candy's directions to the edge of the desert and found myself parked in front of The Desert Palm. There was a marquee out front, but I didn't recognize any of the names on it. If Martini was there to sing, maybe he just sat in with the band. He certainly wasn't on the marquee as Martini, or Sam Epstein.

I parked and went inside. There wasn't much surrounding it, since it was literally on the edge of the desert, but inside it didn't look bad. It was just small, and simple, not dirty or rundown.

There were maybe a dozen tables, most of them occupied, and a small stage with a trio playing on it. Waitresses worked the floor, dressed modestly, but still managing to show some shoulder and leg. Somebody with money probably could have done something with the place.

"I can't say I'm surprised," a voice said from behind me.

I turned, saw a man with thinning hair and a small pot belly, wearing a white suit and black tie. The only thing I recognized about him was the drink he was holding.

"Martini?"

"No," he said, "not without the hairpiece and girdle. Here I'm just Sam Epstein."

"I didn't see your name on the marquee."

"Why would I put my name on the marquee?" he asked. "I own the joint."

"You own...oh. Candy didn't tell me that."

"She doesn't know. She just thinks I sing here, sometimes. Come with me."

I followed him along the bar, where several men and women were sitting, enjoying the soft music and what I assumed was un-watered down drinks.

We went down a narrow hallway to an office door. He opened it and went in and I followed, closing it behind me. He sat behind a small but neat desk and waved me to a chair.

"Why'd you come here?" he asked.

"Why'd you say you're not surprised?"

"You're a detective, aren't you?" he asked. "And I haven't been to the Flamingo in a couple of days."

"Haven't you?"

He was in the act of sipping from his drink, stopped with the glass halfway to his mouth.

"No," he said. "Larry and I had a fight. I left."

"What about your act?"

"Let him do it alone," he said. "He thinks he has all the talent, anyway."

I still couldn't believe I was talking to the same man. Without the hairpiece he looked ten years older.

"This is where I belong," Sam Epstein said. "Right here."

"Are you tellin' me you don't know what happened this mornin'?" I asked.

"What are you talking about?"

"Jackie Tequila," I said, "if that's the last name she uses. Somebody murdered her."

He put his glass down with a bang, spilling part of it.

"Jackie? Dead?"

"The police questioned Larry, and now they're lookin' for you."

"So that's why you're here?" he asked. "You think I did it?"

"Did you?"

"No, why would I?" he asked. "I had no reason to kill

116

Jackie. Larry, yeah, but not Jackie."

"What about your wife?"

He frowned. "What about her?"

"Well, your partner told me you tried to sleep with Jackie. Was your wife jealous?"

"My wife knows what I do on the road," Epstein said. "We have an agreement. But no, I never tried to sleep with Jackie. Larry told you that?"

"He did. Is there any reason why he'd think that if it wasn't true?"

"Just if he was lookin' for an excuse to have me killed," he said. "Not that he needed one. We both pretty much hate each other. But then Larry hates everybody—including himself."

"And his wife?"

He hesitated, then said, "They fight...a lot! He's a hard man to be around. But I guess he loves her."

"Why would a woman like that marry him?"

"Jackie was a very honest woman," Sam Epstein said. "She married him for his money."

"Does he have a lot of money?"

"Not up to now," he said. "Maybe after we break up he'll make some. After all, he always says he has the talent."

"He told me he's signed a picture deal with a studio."

"I'd take that with a grain of salt, if I was you."

"So he lies?"

"Constantly."

"What about your wife and his?"

"Our wives like each other," he said. "I like Jackie and Larry doesn't hate Barbara, oddly enough. There's no trouble with our wives, only with each other. If I was dead, you'd suspect Larry. If Larry was dead, you'd suspect me. But the wives? I don't get it. Who would want to kill Larry's wife?"

"Well," I said, "there's always a number one suspect when a wife is killed."

10.
"To the moon, Alice!"
—Ralph Kramden

One of the first things I'd noticed about Larry Tequila was that he wasn't funny. I had never really seen the Tequila and Martini act, except maybe for a few seconds on TV, once. As far as I knew he popped his eyes a lot and depended on his funny hair. Martini sang okay—or Epstein. Whatever.

When I got back to the Flamingo it was fully dark, but the strip was lit up—the casino names, the marquees were all flashing, and the Flamingo marquee shouted TEQUILA & MARTINI, albeit beneath the name Nat King Cole. They were never going to headline a big Vegas showroom. Not unless something made them more famous.

Like murder.

And if not the murder of a partner, why not the murder of a wife? However, it was just a theory, and I needed to back it up with some facts.

I took the elevator to the floor I knew I'd find the security office on. If this was just a hotel and not a casino, I'd be looking for the house dick, but here I needed the head of security, who I knew slightly from a previous case.

The other offices on the floor were closed for the day, but the hotel and casino were open twenty-four hours.

I entered and two men looked at me, one from behind a desk, the other from in front. Both were wearing suits. The man behind the desk was the one I wanted. He was in his fifties, obviously the man in charge. The other man, in his late-twenties, stared at me curiously.

"Well, well," he said to the younger man, "Look what we have here, Harry. This is a real live private eye, Danny Bardini."

"Hello, George," I said.

"All right, Harry," George said, "hit the floor."

"Yes, Mr. Rawlings."

He went past me out the door, giving me one last look.

George Rawlings had been a lawman in Las Vegas for over twenty years, first with the Sheriff's Office, and then with the Las Vegas Police Department. For the past five years he had been in charge of security for the Flamingo Hotel and Casino.

"Have a seat, Danny, and tell me what's on your mind," George said.

"This is about the killing this mornin'."

"Ah, the comedian's wife, Mrs. Tequila. The cops let him go, didn't they? They're lookin' for his partner?"

"I found him."

"Of course you did," George said. "You're the best private eye in Vegas. Did you turn him over?"

"No," I said, "I don't think he did it."

"Hmm, then who do you think did?"

"I have an idea, but I need to clear up a couple of things first."

"Like what?"

"I need to talk to the maid who worked on their room."

"Tonight?"

"In the morning will do," I said. "First thing?"

"I'm at your service," George said. "I'll have her here at...eight?"

"Make it nine-thirty," I said. "I've got some calls to make, too."

"Nine-thirty it is," George said. "What about the police?"

"I'll call Hargrove when I have something substantial to give him."

I stood up.

"That's it. Why don't we go down to the bar and have a drink?"

"I'll drink with you after I'm done, George," I said. "And I'll buy, in return for this favor."

George put his hand out and said, "I'll see to it you keep that promise."

We shook hands and I left.

I was back at nine-twenty the next morning, after making a couple of phone calls.

"This is Lily," George said. "She cleans the Tequila's suite."

"Thanks, George."

"I'll be downstairs." He poked me in the chest on his way out. "You owe me that drink."

"Lily," I said, "my name is Danny Bardini. I'm a detective. Please, sit."

She sat down, and I sat behind George's desk.

"I haven't done anything wrong." She was young, and a little scared. "Are you gonna arrest me?"

"I'm not a police detective," I said, "I'm a private detective. I just have some questions for you, and then you can go to work."

"Oh," she said, "well, all right."

"Tell me about Mr. and Mrs. Tequila."

"What do you want to know?"

"What only the maid knows," I said. "Something you heard, or saw while doin' your job?"

"Well...they fought a lot," she said, dropping her voice.

"About what?"

"He always thought she was cheating on him," Lily said. "He accused her all the time."

"Did you ever see another man with her?"

"No, sir, never."

"Not even Mr. Tequila's partner?"

"Mr. Martini? No, he was never in their suite." She lowered her voice even more. "Mr. Tequila and Mr. Martini hate each other."

"I see," I said. "What about the morning she was killed. Are you the one who found her?"

"Y-yes," she said, "I went in to clean the room, make the bed, and there...there she was."

"Did you see anyone near the room?"

She hesitated.

"Lily?"

"Mr. Tequila, he would...spy on her."

"Spy?"

"In the mornings he'd put on one of those terrible shirts, his shorts and sandals and go down to the pool. But he would sneak back, listen at the door, try to catch her with somebody."

"But he never did?"

"No."

"And yet, he was convinced she was cheatin'."

"Yes, always," she said. "He was always accusing her. He's a horrible, horrible man."

"Anythin' else?"

"L-like what?"

"Did you ever hear him threaten her?"

Her eyes went wide. "Do you think he killed his own wife?"

"It's a thought."

"He threatened her all the time," she said, her voice hoarse. She looked around before continuing. "He once told her if he caught her with another man, he'd kill them both."

"Men say that all the time, don't they?" I asked.

"That's true," she said. "I've heard many husbands say it to their wives in this hotel. But in those cases—well, this is Las Vegas. Many of those wives and husbands were cheating. But this lady..."

"Never?"

She shook her head, her eyes filing with tears. "Never!"

"All right, Lily," I said. "Thank you."

11.
"Kill my wife, please"
—Larry Tequila

Larry Tequila was at the pool.

I could see the purple shirt and shorts from across the way. As I approached, I saw that he was stretched out on a chaise lounge, his sandals underneath, a pink drink in his hand, seeming to all the world unconcerned that his wife had been killed twenty-four hours ago.

He saw me coming, removed his sunglasses and waved to me.

"Danny," he yelled, "pull up a lounge. There's a pretty waitress around here someplace. Let's get you a drink."

"A little early for me, Larry."

"I thought you gumshoe types had bourbon for breakfast?"

"You've spent too much time in Hollywood."

"Well, you should have one of these," he said, holding up the pink drink. "Cranberry juice and champagne."

"Champagne?" I said. "Are you celebratin' somethin'?"

"Huh? Hell, no, what would I be celebratin'?" He put the drink down on the table next to him and put his sunglasses back on. "What the hell kinda question was that?"

"Well," I said, "you're out here by the pool drinkin' champagne, Larry. What else am I supposed to think?"

"Fer Christ's sake!" he said. "I'm just...I'm just tryin' to, ya know, get by...get on with it." He squirmed uncomfortably, then went on the offense. "You find that bastard Sam?"

"I found him."

"That's great!" he said. "You give him to the cops?"

"Nope."

"Why not?"

"Because he didn't do it."

"Whataya mean he didn't do it?"

"Just what I said. He didn't kill your wife."

"That sonofabitch!" he swore. "How did he convince you of that?"

"It's my bullshit detector, Larry," I said. "I get near Martini and it's quiet as a mouse. But I get near you and it goes bong-bong-bong like crazy! Why do you think that is?"

"I don't know what the hell yer talkin' about!" Tequila snapped.

I sat down on the lounge next to him. Which seemed to make him more uncomfortable.

"I'm gonna be real honest with you, Larry," I said. "I think you killed your wife."

"Wha-a-at?" he said. "Are you nuts? Why would I kill Jackie?"

"Two reasons," I said. "One, you think she was cheatin' on you, and two, for the publicity."

"Publicity?" he asked. "What the hell I need publicity for? I'm dumping that dead weight partner of mine and going to Hollywood. I told you, I got a three-picture deal—"

"You've got nothin'," I said, cutting him off. "I called a buddy of mine in Hollywood, and he did some checkin'. You don't have a deal with Zanuck or anybody else. You've got nothin', so some publicity—like maybe a dead partner, or wife—would be real helpful to you."

"You know," Tequila said, swinging his feet to the ground and feeling around for his sandals, "I don't hafta listen to this."

"Yeah," I said, kicking his sandals into the pool, "you do. I think you had one of your fights yesterday mornin', it escalated, you killed her, and then went down to the pool like always and left her for the poor maid to find."

He could have continued to deny but instead gave in to ego and said, "You can't prove a thing, gumshoe!"

"Maybe not," I said, "but I will, funnyman. I will. You can count on it."

He stood up quickly, and I did too, blocking his escape. Instead of trying to get past me, he took a clumsy swing at me. He wasn't any better a fighter than he was a funny man. I sidestepped the swing. He stumbled off balance, and I had two choices—catch him, or let him stagger past me into the pool. I decided to help him...into the pool.

He went flying, hit the water with a huge splash and a sound like a belly flop. I sat in his chaise lounge and watched him flounder at the deep end, wondering if he could swim, and knew I didn't have enough to call Hargrove with, yet. But suddenly I was very sure I had more than a theory.

Larry Tequila had killed his wife, and I was going to prove it.

Gun Work
John M. Floyd
Dodge City

Will Parker sat alone on the wooden platform beside the pulpit in the empty church. He was watching, through one of the side windows, the bay horse he'd tied to the hitching rail half an hour ago and the rippling rust-colored leaves of the trees in the distance. It was a sunny October morning, bright enough to light up every corner of the little sanctuary, and the breeze through the open windows was cool but not cold.

Parker crossed his legs, took off his hat, and balanced it on one knee. The pews facing him were as empty as the church, but he had chosen this seat—which wasn't really a seat—because it offered a clear view of the front door. Whenever possible, he sat this way, facing a room with his back to a wall. He remembered what had happened to Bill Hickok.

For the tenth time, Parker checked his pocket watch. He'd been intentionally early, but it was now twenty minutes past the time his client had set for this meeting.

His client. That still sounded strange to him, even after several years as a private investigator. But Parker liked the job, and the agency he and his brother had founded in San Francisco had been surprisingly successful. Granted, most of his recent work was dull—checking backgrounds, locating beneficiaries of a will, uncovering shady deals and/or relationships, etc. (unlike the tough assignments he'd had during his short time with the Pinkerton Agency years ago)—but occasionally he was given something interesting and challenging. He had a feeling this case might be both. After all, he wasn't often instructed to meet a client at a church in the middle of the week, in the middle of nowhere.

"Mr. Parker?" a voice said.

He looked up to see a tall man in a brown hat and vest standing in the front doorway. Parker had heard no hoof-beats, no footsteps. A quick glance confirmed that his own horse, rented from the livery stable in Dodge early this morning, was still alone at the hitchrail. So much for being watchful.

"Who else would I be?" he said. "We're probably the only two people within miles."

"Sorry I'm late," the tall man said.

Parker stayed seated, watching him. "How'd you get here?"

"Quietly. My horse is tied some distance away." A smile touched the man's lips, but only for a moment, there and gone. "The cautious, I have found, live longer."

"Cautious of what?"

"Of everything."

With that, the man strode casually down the aisle and extended his hand. "Cole Bennett."

They shook hands and Bennett took a seat in the front pew, facing Parker from a distance of eight feet or so. Cole Bennett appeared to be in his late-fifties, maybe ten years older than Parker. But he looked strong and fit, and had what Parker's wife Bitsy would call a world-weary face. Bennett took off his hat and set it down beside him. "Thanks for coming," he said.

"You paid for my transportation," Parker reminded him. "I arrived on last night's stage."

"But not from San Francisco. Your brother wired me that you were already fairly close to here, at the moment. Redemption, he said?"

"Yes—my wife lived there when I met her. We're visiting her parents."

"That was convenient for me."

"Convenient for me, actually. Less expensive for you." Parker hooked his thumbs in his gunbelt. "How can I help you, Mr. Bennett?"

Bennett blew out a long sigh. "First I need to tell you a story."

"I'm listening."

"Do you remember the Ford brothers? Jesse and Dalton?"

"Barely."

Again Bennett hesitated, obviously choosing his words. "Some time ago," he began, "a U.S. marshal, Sam Ewing, shot Dalton Ford during what was said to be the robbery of a bank up in Hays City. The marshal lived here in Dodge but was in Hays the day this happened. Anyhow, Marshal Ewing shot Ford and killed him. Afterward one of the witnesses said Ford was in the bank, sure enough, but wasn't robbing it—he said Ford was chatting with one of the tellers. Whichever way it happened, the marshal got word he was there, entered the bank, and Dalton Ford—a man wanted for multiple crimes— wound up dead as a pine knot. Dalton's brother Jesse, who was in prison at the time, heard about the killing, and when he was released a year later he showed up at Ewing's house just outside Dodge with two of his buddies."

"Looking for revenge."

"Yes," Bennett said. He paused and studied his folded hands.

Will Parker waited, saying nothing.

"According to the official report," Bennett continued, "Jesse Ford—I'll just call him Jesse from now on—and his friends arrived one day in July to find Ewing and his twelve- year-old son Andrew home in their farmhouse north of town. Not far from here, actually. Mrs. Ewing had died three months earlier, some kind of fever, and Ewing had retired as marshal and took to raising crops and some cattle. Apparently Jesse and his men surprised them. They struck Ewing in the head in the kitchen, held him and the boy at gunpoint, and

Jesse ordered his two men to go outside and wait. Five minutes later, Ewing got the jump on Jesse and shot him dead, then went out and killed one of Jesse's friends as well. The other one got away."

Parker thought that over. "The official report, you said?"

"Yes. It's what Ewing told the sheriff, afterward."

"Go on."

"No more to tell. That's the background," Bennett said. "The current situation is, I received word recently that things didn't happen the way everyone thought they did that day at Ewing's house. I've been told that Jesse Ford was shot in the back. One of his two companions was killed with an entry wound in the chest, just like Ewing reported, but—again— Jesse's wound showed that he was shot from behind."

"And how did you find all this out?"

"From an old friend of mine. He'd been a sheriff's deputy in Dodge, back when the incident took place, and saw the two bodies the sheriff brought in. He told me this a few weeks ago, on his deathbed. A week or so after that, I noticed an ad in the newspaper about your agency, and sent the wire requesting your services."

Parker waited for more. When it didn't come, he asked, "So what is it that you need?"

Bennett turned to look out the window at the small stand of oaks Parker had been watching earlier. The wind had died; the leaves were still. Like Bennett's expression.

"I need to know what happened that day," Bennett said. "What really happened."

"Why don't you just ask the sheriff?"

"Because the sheriff is dead. So is former marshal Sam Ewing, and even his son Andrew. The son died young, from an accident on a cattle drive, south of here. They're all gone now."

Parker studied Cole Bennett for a moment. "What haven't you told me, Mr. Bennett?"

"I haven't told you when all this happened."

"When did it happen?"

Bennett let out a lungful of air. "Sam Ewing shot Jesse Ford twenty-two years ago."

"What?"

"My friend—the deputy—said he kept the secret all those years because the sheriff asked him to. Said everybody in town loved Sam Ewing, all the Ewings. Said the sheriff figured what good would it do to tell the whole story? Jesse Ford was dead, along with one of his cutthroat friends, and the world was better off for it. Why complicate things? The deputy said he and the sheriff, and of course Ewing and his son, were the only people who knew Jesse was back-shot. And that only the two Ewings knew how it happened."

Bennett went quiet then, staring down at his boots as if in deep thought.

Parker let the silence drag out, then said, "I think we have a problem here, Mr. Bennett. If this took place more than twenty years ago and everyone involved is deceased, why do you think I could find out any more than what you just told me?"

Bennett raised his head. "Because I don't think they're all deceased."

"You just said—"

"I said the deputy told me Sam Ewing and his son were the only people who saw exactly what happened. But I think there's someone else." He leaned forward in his seat, his eyes locked on Parker's. "I heard Sam Ewing's son Andrew had a childhood friend his own age, and I heard that in the summers they were inseparable, those two boys, especially in the months after Sam's wife passed. Way I heard it, this kid was at little Andrew Ewing's house most every day." Bennett paused, drew a breath, and said, "I'd be willing to bet—in fact, I guess I am betting by hiring you—that whoever this boy was, he was probably there with Andrew the day Jesse

Ford and his men came to call. I'm betting he never got mentioned because everyone involved was trying to protect him. Again, why make a simple matter complicated?"

Parker gave this some thought. "Do you have a name?"

"No. But I have confidence you'll come up with one. And when you do..." Bennett paused again, his face solemn. "When you find him, maybe he has what I need to know."

Another question was nagging at Parker. An important question.

"Why do you need to know?"

Cole Bennett settled back into the pew. "My wife," he said, "was a Ford. Jesse and Dalton, as worthless as they were, were her nephews. Her brother's sons. I told her what my deputy friend, before he died, told me about Jesse's death, and it's driving her crazy. She says she has to know what really happened in that kitchen that day."

Parker mulled that over. "All due respect," he said, "why do you need me? Why couldn't you ask the same kinds of questions you want me to ask?"

"Because you're the expert. I checked out the references your brother gave me." Bennett picked up his hat and stood. "I'm trusting you to solve this for me, Mr. Parker."

Parker, who had spent a lot of time doing this kind of work, knew a lie when he heard it. He knew Cole Bennett didn't want to ask around about this matter for the same reason Bennett had picked a remote spot for their meeting today: he couldn't afford to be connected to all this. What are you hiding, Mr. Bennett?

Parker rose to his feet also, and the two men stood facing each other.

"Your brother told me your name's Will," Bennett said.

"That's right."

"It occurred to me that you bear some resemblance to another Parker, well known in this part of the country years ago. By reputation, at least."

"What kind of reputation?"

"He was a gunman. A killer, I'm told."

"Is that so."

Bennett tilted his head, narrowed his eyes. "This man's name was Charlie Parker."

Parker felt himself shrug. "Sorry. No relation."

Bennett studied him a moment more, nodded, and left. Parker remained standing where he was. This time he did hear hoofbeats, moments later, receding into the distance.

Parker sighed. All God's chillun got secrets, he thought.

After another minute or so, Charles William Parker walked outside to the hitching rail, mounted the bay, and headed back to town.

It took Parker less than six hours to narrow things down a bit. Unlike the procedures he'd followed to gather information the last time he'd visited these parts—a missing-person case in the small town of Redemption—he didn't bother with the saloons and the stables and the blacksmith and the stock-yards. This time he concentrated on places where he could find and talk with the womenfolk. After several hours of visiting the general store, a dress shop, the schoolhouse, and a church—this one with more pews and more windows than the one this morning—he'd discovered that young Andrew Ewing was well remembered by some of the older teachers and ladies. One, a widow with the unfortunate name of Ophelia Reardon, recalled that Andrew had indeed made one especially close friend during his long-ago school years.

"Truitt," Mrs. Reardon said, smiling at the memory. "Can't recall his first name, but little Andrew Ewing played a lot with Daisy Truitt's boy. Never saw one of them without the other."

"When exactly was that?" Parker asked. "When they were teenagers?"

"Earlier. When they were eleven or twelve, probably." A thought seemed to come to her, and Mrs. Reardon's smile faded a bit. "Around the time Andrew's mama died, and that outlaw Ford came and tried to kill Marshal Ewing," she said.

Which was exactly what Parker wanted to hear.

"Is Mrs. Truitt still here in Dodge?" he asked, holding his breath.

"Sure is. Husband died five years ago. She and her son live on the other end of town." Ophelia Reardon pointed toward the reddening sunset. "You turn left there at the stage office, their place is about a mile south, on the right side of the road. White house with a tall barn."

Parker thanked her and set out in that direction. Five minutes later he climbed the front steps of a white-painted home and rapped on the front door. The small woman who answered the knock looked about as old as Cole Bennett was, which made sense. Twenty-two years ago she would've been about the right age to have a twelve-year-old child. She was holding what looked like a damp washcloth.

Mentally crossing his fingers, Parker identified himself and, without giving a reason, asked if he might meet her son and ask him a few questions.

She stared at Parker a long time before answering. "You can certainly meet him," she said at last. "But I'm afraid questions won't do any good."

"Excuse me?"

She heaved a sigh and motioned him inside. The house was old but neatly kept. Parker followed her down a dark hallway and through a door to a room containing nothing but a bed and two small tables on each side. Propped up on pillows in the bed was a pale, thin-faced man in his thirties, with sandy hair. His eyes were closed, his breathing slow and peaceful. His forehead and cheeks looked wet. Parker now understood the washcloth.

When Parker turned to look at her, Daisy Truitt gave him

a sad smile. "My poor boy Wilson. He's been that way six months now," she said. "Got kicked by a mare while he was trying to shoe her. Doc says it caught him square in the left temple, at just the wrong place. When his brother got here he went out and shot the horse dead, not that that did anybody any good." She studied her visitor again and added, "He can't speak, Mr. Parker—he can't even hear us. Could I be of some help instead, with your questions?"

Parker, stunned, shook his head. "I doubt it, ma'am. Unless he might possibly have told you something—anything—about the day Jesse Ford was killed, up at the Ewing place."

She looked shocked. "Wilson? No, I'm afraid not. I doubt he knew anything about that."

"Well, then, I'm sorry to have bothered you."

"No bother at all."

They retraced their steps to the front door, but Parker was barely aware of it. His legs felt heavy, like chunks of firewood. What a disappointing way to end his search. And his assignment.

Parker thanked Ms. Truitt again at the door and was turning to leave when it hit him. He stopped and looked at her in the gathering twilight. "You said his brother shot the horse?"

"That's right. My second son."

"You have another son?"

"Two years younger," she said. "His name's Tommy."

Parker swallowed. "Could he have known Andrew Ewing? The marshal's boy?"

"Oh my, yes. Those two were best friends."

Tommy Truitt, it turned out, lived in the town of Hopeful, about half a day's ride from Dodge. Will Parker, hopeful now also, sent a wire that night to his wife and another to his brother Robert at the agency's home office. He assured Bitsy he'd try to be back by the end of the week and informed his brother that he had met with Cole Bennett and was making progress. He rewarded himself with a thick steak at a café called Delmonico's and a beer at the Long Branch, and after that retired to his hotel to sleep the sleep of the weary and guiltless.

Or at least the weary.

It was hard, Parker had decided, to escape the past. Years ago, young and reckless, he had chosen all the wrong friends and all the wrong endeavors, and his steely nerves and uncanny skill with firearms soon found him steady employment and built him a reputation from Fort Smith to Deadwood. Inevitably, many who heard about Charlie Parker wanted to challenge him, and those who did, died. When maturity and self-preservation finally convinced him to give up gun work, he went east, started using his middle name instead, and landed a job with the Pinkertons in Washington, one that required brains over bravado. Since then he'd done some security work, even a stint as a deputy, before joining his brother at Parker Investigations in San Francisco.

Even now, though, after all this time, a lot of people remembered the name Charlie Parker. When that happened he usually pled ignorance, which occasionally worked. He doubted that it had worked with Cole Bennett.

What a career change, Parker thought. He'd gone from being a hired gun to being a liar.

He fell asleep wondering which was worse.

Will Parker got up early, had a leisurely breakfast, and rode into Hopeful just past noon. The town was appropriately named, he decided; there seemed to be nowhere for it to go but up. He counted a dozen dreary houses and a half-dozen dreary stores, all clustered around the intersection of a sluggish creek and a muddy road. He hoped Tommy Truitt lived on this side of the creek. The wooden bridge looked too rickety to support a man, much less a man on a horse.

At one of the buildings—a sort of combination saloon and dry-goods store—he was told that Truitt owned a small ranch west of town. There was no real road out that way, but the directions Parker received seemed simple enough. An hour later he found the spread.

He also found Tommy Truitt, on his knees in the doorway of a barn, shoeing a gray horse. Given the family history, Parker figured it to be a scary task. The horseshoer looked up as Parker rode in, and eased the gray's foreleg to the ground. Something about the man's eyes verified that he was the son of the woman Parker had spoken to the night before.

Parker stopped ten feet away and propped both arms on his saddle horn. "I've come a ways to find you, Mr. Truitt. Can I interrupt your work for a while?"

Truitt put down his tools, stood, and sleeved sweat from his brow. "Don't know. I'm having an awful good time, here."

Both of them smiled.

"Help yourself to water for you and your horse," Truitt said, pointing to a well and bucket. "I'll be right with you."

Fifteen minutes later introductions were made and Parker's task was explained. The two of them sat in rockers on the front porch of the house. Truitt's wife and daughter, he said, were visiting his wife's mother, in town. Chickens pecked and strutted in the dusty yard, and small white clouds cast moving pools of shade across the flatlands. The wind was chilly.

Tommy Truitt exhaled a deep sigh. "Yes, I was there that day," he answered. "And no, I've never spoken of it to anybody, not even my ma and pa."

"You didn't tell your brother?"

"So you know about Wilson? A sad thing, that horse kicking him. I go over as often as I can, help Ma with chores…"

Truitt paused, adrift in his thoughts. Then he blinked and said, "No, I never told him. Wilson was a bit older, and for some reason we never got along. Guess that's why I played so much with Andrew."

Parker, wondering how to proceed, decided to be direct. "Do you remember what happened, that day?"

"I'll never forget it," Tommy Truitt murmured.

A silence fell, during which Parker had the good sense to keep quiet. After a full minute or more, Truitt took a long breath and said, "We'd been playing in a patch of woods behind his house, with a bow and arrow we'd made out of sticks and a springy branch. We were trying to shoot a rabbit, and Andrew kept saying we needed that old eight-gauge shotgun his pa had, not a homemade bow and a little stick with an arrowhead tied to the end. He said his pa had put away all his weapons when he retired, but Andrew knew where the shotgun was stored. He said we ought to sneak it out and shoot that rabbit. Said there wouldn't be nothing left but a cotton tail."

He stopped for a beat, and Parker saw him smiling a little, at the memory. The smile didn't last long.

"That was when we heard hoofbeats coming down the road from town," Truitt said. "By the time we got back to the house—"

—three horses were tied to the porch rail. Tommy Truitt didn't recognize any of them.

He and Andrew climbed the steps, crept inside, and found three men in the kitchen with guns drawn, and Andrew's father sprawled on the floor with blood on his forehead. Greenish-white peas were scattered on the floor, some still in their hulls, along with a broken bowl and an overturned chair. Tommy figured the intruders must've caught the marshal shelling peas and hit him with a gunbarrel. "Pa?" Andrew cried.

When Marshal Ewing saw them—Andrew's pa would always be Marshal Ewing, to Tommy—he propped himself up on one elbow and groaned, "Run, boys. Get outta here."

One of the three men told him, in a bored voice, to shut up. This was the ringleader, Tommy could see that. He was the oldest and the meanest-looking, too. He had dragged one of the kitchen chairs over to the wall beside the spot where Andrew's father was lying and was sitting in it, leaning back against the wall. The glare he gave the two boys sent chills up Tommy's spine. The man said, to one of his friends, 'Get rid of 'em, Dixon."

For just a second Tommy wondered what he meant, and then understood. The man the leader had spoken to seemed to understand, too. "No," he said.

The leader turned to face Dixon. "What did you say?"

"I said no. I'm not shootin' any kids, Jesse."

It was then that Tommy knew who the leader was. Jesse Ford. He'd heard the name mentioned, in town. Tommy had thought Ford was in jail.

But he wasn't. He was here, in Andrew's house, sitting in a chair against the wall and pointing a gun at Andrew's pa, lying at his feet. It felt like a dream, a scary one. But it was real.

"Then I guess I'll have to," Jesse Ford said.

"No." Dixon shook his head. "Nobody's shootin' a kid."

The two men stared at each other for what seemed a long time. Sam Ewing was still propped on one elbow, opening and closing his eyes and breathing hard. Finally Ford said, "What do you suggest, then? We can't let 'em go—they done seen us, and can tell the Law."

"So can that woman we saw in the field, a few miles back. She got a good look at us."

"We shoulda killed her too," Ford muttered.

"Jesse's right, Dixon," the other man said, a short guy with a face like a weasel. "I'll do it if you won't."

Ignoring him, Dixon said, "We don't have to kill 'em. We could tie 'em up. Or lock 'em up someplace. All we need is time to get this done and get far enough away."

"You could lock us in the pantry," young Andrew said, speaking for the first time. Tommy turned in surprise to look at him, and so did everyone else. Even Marshal Ewing's eyes were open now, and watching.

"It's right there," Andrew added, his voice shaky, and pointed to the wall against which Jesse Ford's chair was leaning. "The only door's just around the corner, and it locks."

"Who in the hell would put a lock on a pantry?" Ford growled.

"My ma, years ago. She kept stuff in there, kerosene and poison and such, that I wasn't supposed to get into."

Dixon walked to the corner, then came back. "It has a latch, with an open padlock on it."

Jesse Ford sighed and nodded. "Get 'em in there, then."

Within seconds the two boys found themselves inside the long, dim pantry. Dixon had steered them through the door, and afterward Tommy heard the lock snap shut. Narrow bars of light seeped in under the door and through the spaces between the wall boards.

The first thing Tommy heard, from the other side of the shared wall, was Jesse Ford's voice: "You men go outside, you and Dixon both. Bring the horses round to the back door here and wait for me. I won't be long."

"You gonna kill him?" Weasel Face said.

"That's what I came here for. Now get out, both of you."

Tommy, who had been listening and peering into the kitchen through the tiny slits between the boards, heard Andrew moving around in the back of the pantry. "What are you doing?" he whispered. Andrew didn't answer.

On the other side of the wall—Tommy could see the dark outline of Jesse Ford's back as he sat in the chair only inches away—Ford said, "Well, well, Marshal. Here we are, just you and me. You beginning to be sorry you killed my brother?"

Weakly, Sam Ewing said, "Wish I'd had a chance to kill you too."

Ford cackled a laugh. "I got news for you, Marshal. Them two boys of yours are gonna die too, soon as I finish with you. I'll just shoot the lock off the door and take care of 'em both. Might have to shoot Dixon too, afterwards. Looks like he ain't got the grit I thought he had."

All of a sudden Tommy felt Andrew pushing him aside. Andrew had something in his hands, but Tommy couldn't make it out. He was about to whisper a question when Andrew placed one end of whatever he was holding—a long stick?—against the wall Ford was leaning back on and squatted down behind it.

"Ain't no use wastin' time," Ford's voice said. Tommy heard the click of a pistol being cocked. "This is for Dalt—"

Jesse Ford never finished the sentence. Tommy heard an explosion—it sounded like a blast of dynamite only inches from his right ear—and suddenly there was a fist-sized hole in the pantry wall. Light poured in from the kitchen, smoky gray light, and then he saw Andrew standing beside him. Andrew was saying something to him, shouting it, his lips moving, but Tommy could hear nothing. Finally he saw Andrew motion to him to get down. Tommy ducked and heard yet another explosion, above his head. He looked up to see that the pantry door was open, the wood splintered in a huge circle around the spot where the lock had been. Andrew stormed past him and out the door, holding his pa's double-barreled eight-gauge, and Tommy stumbled after him, ears ringing. Andrew was reloading as he ran, stuffing in fresh shells.

There was no need. They rounded the corner to find the kitchen empty. Jesse Ford's body was lying in the middle of the floor, lying where Andrew had blown him out of the chair and forward six or seven feet. Marshal Ewing was nowhere to be seen. Blood was everywhere.

Before Tommy could get his mind around all this, he heard—through his left ear—a pistol shot, and followed Andrew out the back door. Standing there in the yard were two men: Dixon and Marshal Ewing. Dixon had his hands raised, and Ewing was leaning against a tree, his smoking revolver pointed and rock-steady. At first Tommy wondered where Ewing had found a pistol, then realized it must've been Jesse Ford's, picked up off the kitchen floor after Andrew had shot him. A short distance away, lying at the feet of one of the three horses, was the motionless body of Weasel Face. His shirt was bloody and a gun lay in the dust beside him.

For a long moment no one said a word. The boys gawked at the two men and the two men stared at each other. Somewhere nearby, a crow cawed.

With the back of his hand Andrew's father wiped blood from his eyes. He was covered with it, from head to toe, and Tommy realized most of it was Jesse Ford's.

"Give me a reason I shouldn't kill you," Marshal Ewing said.

Dixon shook his head. He looked sad, and strangely unafraid. "I can't."

Ewing cast a quick glance at his son and Tommy, then said to Dixon, "You don't seem the same kind of man as those other two were. What are you doing in this bunch?"

"I'm more like them than not," Dixon said. "But there's some things I won't do."

"Like murder a child."

"Yes."

Another long silence passed.

"Get out of here, Mr. Dixon. And don't come back."

Without a word, Dixon lowered his hands, walked to his horse, mounted up, and rode away. Tommy and the two

Ewings watched until he disappeared around the curve of the trail.

Then Andrew put the shotgun down and ran to his father. Tommy did too. Marshal Ewing scooped both of them into his arms, then stopped when his son cried out in pain. As it turned out, Andrew's right shoulder was badly sprained, from the kick of the eight-gauge. And he had even fired it a second time, Tommy remembered, to blow away the door lock.

All three of them, as if at a signal, turned to look at the shotgun, lying in the dirt.

"Guess I won't bother hiding it anymore," Ewing said.

"And that's what happened." Tommy Truitt looked at Parker and shrugged. "They're all gone now. Marshal Ewing, Andrew, everybody. Except me."

Parker nodded. He had started out taking notes, but had soon quit and just listened. "You all agreed, I guess, never to talk about it."

"That's right. To anybody. And the marshal insisted on hiding the fact that Andrew was the one who killed Jesse Ford, and that I was even there at all. If anyone else ever showed up looking for revenge, he said, simpler was better. Three men came, two died, one got away."

Parker wondered what it would feel like, to live through that and never tell anyone about it. Maybe telling it, at long last, had helped a little.

"Andrew was a tough kid," Truitt said. "And smart. He talked a bunch of killers into locking us in a room that had a gun hidden in it."

Parker nodded. "Smart and lucky. Lucky two of the three men were outside, lucky that Jesse Ford sat where he did, lucky that Sam Ewing was on the floor, underneath the line of fire."

Truitt didn't reply. He just sat, slowly rocking, looking out at the flat plains, and his memories. After a while he blinked and studied Parker's face. "You said you came a long way, for this. Did you get what you needed?"

"I got what my client needed. You cleared up a lot of things."

"Now I plan to forget about it," Truitt said.

He rose to his feet, and Parker followed.

"You're welcome to stay for supper," Truitt said. "My family'll be home soon."

"Much obliged, but I need to go." Parker turned to leave, then paused. "One question. You said you'd heard the name Jesse Ford, before all this happened."

"That's right."

"Well, he wasn't the only one did gun work, back then. Ever hear of Pete Lawson, or Merrill Smith, or Charlie Parker?"

Truitt thought a moment, then shook his head. "Don't think so."

"Good," Parker said.

The temperature dropped like a stone that night, and the following afternoon was windy and cold and overcast. The orange, yellow, and red leaves of the trees outside the small country church seemed to be struggling to stay on the branches, and many of them failed. Parker arrived just before three o'clock. This time Bennett was early; Parker found him standing at the head of the center aisle. They shook hands and settled again into the same seats they'd taken earlier.

"Let's hear it," Bennett said.

Twenty minutes later the story had been told. Parker left nothing out. Using many of Tommy Truitt's own words, he told Bennett about the intrusion, the spoken threat to the two boys, Dixon's challenge to Jesse Ford's order, the locking of the boys in the pantry, the shotgun blast through the wall, the shootout in the back yard, the departure of the third attacker.

"I believe every word he said," Parker concluded. "That's the way it happened."

For a long time Bennett sat there in silence, fingering the buttons of his overcoat. At last he said, "It makes sense. I couldn't see Sam Ewing as a backshooter. But I had to know." He stood up. "You've done good work, Mr. Parker. I'll be sending full payment to your office tomorrow morning." He turned and moved away toward the front of the church.

"Give my best wishes to Mrs. Dixon," Parker said.

Bennett stopped in his tracks. For several seconds he stood motionless, then turned again and locked eyes with Parker. Parker hadn't moved. He was still sitting there, on the platform beside the pulpit.

Very slowly Bennett walked back to the first pew. It was so quiet in the church Parker could hear the wood creak as Bennett sagged into the seat. His face was blank.

"Are you even married?" Parker asked him. "Or was that a lie, too?"

"I'm married. But my wife wasn't a Ford. And she has no nephews." Bennett paused for a beat, then said, "How did you know?"

"That you were the third man?" Parker sighed. "I'm not sure. Maybe it takes somebody with a guilty conscience to recognize it in someone else. Besides, you were so certain that Andrew had a playmate who would've been there at the time. Why were you so sure? And something else that bothered me from the start was that you felt you couldn't pursue this on your own. I finally realized that if you had, if you'd discovered the identity of Andrew's friend, and approached him yourself to ask him questions—"

"He might've recognized me. From that day."

"Right," Parker said. "And I assumed you had a reason why you'd rather not call attention to your past."

"My reason is, I'm an elected official now. A mayor. Back east a ways."

"I know. And I know where. My brother checked, and contacted me this morning."

Bennett stayed quiet a minute, gazing out the window.

"You think anyone'll find out?" he asked.

"About your former life? That you rode with Jesse Ford? No. Even if they do, so what? You're a changed man."

"What about Tommy Truitt?"

"The two of you live far apart. I doubt you'll ever meet."

Bennett rubbed his face wearily. "Maybe we should." He looked Parker in the eye and said, "I went there that day to help murder an innocent man. What I did got two people killed."

"What you did saved three people, too."

Bennett gave that some thought, and nodded. This time both of them stood. "Thank you, Mr. Parker."

"What should I call you?"

"My name's Morris Dixon."

They shook hands. "Have a safe journey home, Mr. Mayor."

"You too."

Parker watched through the window as Dixon rode away, then he pulled up the collar of his coat and stomped outside to his own horse. He had already swung into the saddle when he saw a grizzled old man in a fur hat and a bearskin trudging up the road toward him. Parker loped over to the man and reined in.

The old-timer looked up and patted the shotgun he held in the crook of his arm. "Good day for squirrel huntin'," he said.

Parker burrowed deeper into his coat. "If you say so."

The old man chuckled, then frowned. He leaned forward and squinted. Parker knew what was coming.

"I know you, from someplace," the hunter said. "Ain't you Charlie Parker?"

Parker raised his head a moment, gazed up at the trees and the falling leaves and then at the woods and the straight, flat road that led to his wife and his brother and the rest of his life. He thought about past deeds and past decisions, and about Cole Bennett, also known as Morris Dixon. Then he looked back down at the old-timer.

"I used to be," Parker said.

Mr. Private Eye Behind the Motel with a .38
Michael Bracken
Waco

Waco is a city of hypocrisy, a city where Baptist ministers condemn homosexuality yet laud the high-scoring exploits of the local university's lesbian basketball star; a city where the wealthy attend high-dollar charity events, but won't drop a quarter in a homeless man's hand; a city where a banker spends thousands of dollars on hookers and his wife pays me only a few hundred to follow him around and take photographs.

"This is a good one." Joan Wilkes-Tower flipped my iPad around so that I could see the buxom redhead astride her balding, corpulent husband.

I earn most of my income helping small companies combat workman's compensation claims, taking photographs of back-injury claimants doing things like hoisting deer carcasses into the beds of pickup trucks, and I'd become quite comfortable with my digital camera. The photograph of Charles Tower and the redhead was a particularly good example of the photographs I had taken through a fleabag motel room window the previous night. I said, "She actually looks like she's enjoying herself."

"For what Charles paid her, she probably did."

The redhead had been provided by an escort service operating out of Austin. The service charged extra for the two-hour drive north, and Charles paid the surcharge to avoid hiring local talent for his sexual assignations.

My client wore a black silk robe with a sash fastened loosely around her waist. I said, "A shame he finds it necessary to rent affection when he has a beautiful woman waiting for him at home."

Aghast, Joan said, "You couldn't pay me enough to have sex with that man."

"He's your husband."

"Second husband," Joan said, "and we have a marriage of *inconvenience.*"

When she leaned across the table and took my left hand in hers, her robe gaped open and I caught a glimpse of her black lace bra and the swell of one breast.

"Are you married, Mr. Blake?"

I wore no jewelry on my fingers, but that wasn't answer enough. I said, "No."

"Seeing anyone?" my client asked as she stroked the back of my hand.

My body reacted to her touch and I shifted slightly in my seat. "Not in quite a while."

"That's a shame," she said, "a handsome man like you having to do without."

I'm not handsome, not by the stretch of anyone's imagination, but neither does my reflection break mirrors. My client was flirting with me and I expected a proposition to follow. She surprised me by drawing her hand back and tapping her manicured fingernail on the iPad screen. "Send me this one."

I already knew her email address because I had sent her photos from several of her husband's previous assignations at the same motel. As I emailed her the photo from my iPad, she rose from the table and returned with her wallet.

She withdrew a trio of Benjamin Franklins, pressed them into my hand, and said, "I'll call again the next time I think he's going to that place."

My client always paid cash and she refused to sign a confidentiality agreement. Though I preferred having a paper trail, not everyone wants it known that they've hired a private detective, and I didn't put up a fuss because I needed the cash.

After I pocketed the Franklins, I grabbed my iPad and stood. I followed her from the dining room, through the foyer, and to the front door. After she opened it, I stepped past her and turned back.

I can't remember what I intended to say because the words caught in my throat when the sash slipped off and my client's robe fell open. As she closed the door, she said, "I'll call you if I need you."

I needed a cigarette. I tucked my iPad under my arm, pulled a crumpled pack of Camels from my jacket pocket, shook one free, and stuck it between my lips. I lit it and then headed down the steps toward my car.

Known for years as a rest stop on the trip between Austin and Dallas-Fort Worth, Waco gained national attention when law enforcement burned to death David Koresh and his followers; when one college basketball player murdered another and coaches covered it up to prevent NCAA sanctions; and again when a firefight between rival motorcycle gangs and law enforcement left nine dead and nearly two dozen injured.

The good never quite outweighed the bad—the creation of the Waco Mammoth National Monument , the media attention that came from the local university's increasingly successful sports program and construction of the new football stadium, the television couple renovating Waco one home at a time—and so residents had to take their joy where they could find it. For me, a bachelor who prepared meals in a microwave, joy came from dining in the local restaurants, and I was sitting in a plastic lawn chair eating lunch at Schmaltz's Sandwich Shoppe when Lieutenant Bobby Spencer stepped through the door.

He nodded in my direction and then joined me after he'd ordered. Spencer—my sergeant when I was a uniform patrol officer—was a man whose ambitions were superior to his investigation skills. He had been promoted into plainclothes and then into homicide by failing to offend anyone within the department, but his sights were set even higher. Our paths didn't cross often, but with the courthouse only a block from my office we couldn't avoid one another, either.

When I was in uniform, I made the mistake of detaining the wrong teenager for speeding and I found him holding enough cocaine to put a black man in prison for decades.

Spencer had pulled me aside as soon as I brought the boy into the station. Under his breath he asked, "Don't you know whose son that is?"

I had come to Waco from Midland via Texas A&M, following in my father's academic footsteps but not his career path. As an Aggie in Bear country I had to tread lightly, so I glanced at the boy. "Does it matter?"

"You're damned right it matters," he said. "If you don't kick the kid before he phones his father, you'll be lucky to find a job as a security guard."

"I'll take that chance," I said, and before the month ended I was drawing unemployment. Instead of applying for a security guard position or asking for my father's help, I turned private. I almost starved to death before a bottom-feeding lawyer on the east side hired me to tail a client he actually thought was innocent.

As he settled onto the chair opposite mine, Spencer asked, "Still a dick?"

"The best kind," I said. "Private."

"Too bad you threw your career away trying to prove a point," the lieutenant said. He had spent his law enforcement career ensuring that justice didn't touch Waco's wealthy and socially connected, and, by sucking up to them, hoped to someday join their ranks.

Someone behind the counter yelled "Forty-nine, number forty-nine." The lieutenant raised his hand and a young waitress delivered his sandwich. When Spencer returned his attention to our conversation, he told me he was waiting for his turn to testify in a murder trial, and that the trial was on lunch break.

"We have the guy dead to rights," the lieutenant said. "He killed his girlfriend's husband for the insurance money, but he wasn't too bright. Any thirteen-year-old who's ever played Clue would have known it was Mr. Boyfriend in the garage with a monkey wrench. If he had money, his lawyer could convince the jury the murderer was Mr. Transient in the potting shed with a meat cleaver."

After lunch, I sat at the desk in my one-room office and divided Joan Wilkes-Tower's three hundred dollars into two uneven stacks. The income was off the books, unlikely to be discovered by the IRS unless I deposited it into a bank account. I slipped two bills into the false bottom of one of the desk drawers, where they joined several dozen others already hiding in the dark. The balance went into my wallet to pay for my assorted vices.

I had just slipped my wallet into my pocket when my cellphone rang. I didn't recognize the number, but answered anyway. After identifying myself, I listened as a prospective client spilled a world of misery into my ear.

"My son's baby mama is not taking care of my grandbabies," said Luby Watkins. "My son's over there in Afghanistan and she's back here. The little girl ain't going to school regular and she don't change the baby's diaper and he's got a rash and—"

"And what can I do for you?" I asked.

Mrs. Watkins said Mark Cain, the bottom-feeding lawyer who had hired me a few times, had suggested she call. "He said you could follow her, take pictures of her doing those things she's doing so we can show Darrell what his baby mama is doing and he'll believe us and help us take them away so we can raise them right."

I told her my day rate. "Plus expenses."

"Don't you worry about your money. I got money saved up."

I explained that I would require a signed contract and an advance before I began work.

"You come now," Mrs. Watkins said. "I'll sign your paper and give you the money."

I had nothing on my calendar for the rest of the week, but I said, "I have an appointment at two, but I could come after."

That afternoon I collected my signed contract and advance, and that evening I began work. The woman Mrs. Watkins hired me to tail was every bit as bad as she described, giving five-dollar hand jobs while her children were locked in the family beater. I killed a few cigarettes in the privacy of my own vehicle while snapping photos and, after two days, decided to speed the process along. I used a burner phone to make an anonymous call to the police about two children locked in a car and the parents nowhere in sight.

That evening I downloaded all the photos I had taken to a memory stick, printed a few of the more incriminating on photo paper, and took everything to show Mrs. Watkins. She paid my bill without complaint, even the expense charge for the burner phone.

Waco is a city divided by more than the Brazos River, with old money families funding the arts, supporting the charities, and plastering their names on the buildings, while the long term residents on the other side of the divide struggle to keep the utilities turned on and the rent paid. New money injected into the city's social structure following explosive expansion of the academic and the medical communities brought new ideas, new attitudes, and new growth, including the revitalization of a downtown long thought dead.

Old warehouses have been converted into loft apartments, long-shuttered businesses replaced by new, and several food trucks line University Parks Drive near the intersection with Franklin Avenue. The weather was unseasonably warm, so I walked from my office in the ALICO Building on Austin Avenue to the food trucks a few blocks away and purchased a beef-and-lamb gyro with a side of feta fries.

The fair weather had brought out young and old, and all the tables were occupied, though not all of them at capacity. I settled onto one end of a picnic bench in front of Xristo's Cafe and ate while I watched the pretty young women ignore me as they walked past.

A blonde in a Mustang convertible caught my eye, and I watched as the Mustang parked at the opposite end of the row of food trucks. The blonde climbed out and meandered from one to the next, stopping to examine menus, and then moving on without ordering. Wearing a sleeveless white silk top, dark form-fitting jeans, and red strappy pumps that added two inches to her height, she walked as if she knew the roll of her hips caught the attention of every man dining outside that afternoon and she didn't care. As she drew closer I realized she wasn't as young as I'd first thought—early-thirties, maybe mid-thirties—and she carried a few extra pounds. Before long she reached Xristo's Cafe, where I was sitting near a blackboard with the day's menu chalked on it. After examining it for a moment, she turned to me. "What do you recommend?"

I recommended the beef-and-lamb gyro and the spanakopita.

"This seat taken?" she asked, indicating the bench on the opposite side of the picnic table.

When I told her it wasn't, she sat.

Pale blue eyes examined me as I examined her. She looked

familiar, but Waco is still small enough that almost everyone looks familiar. I asked, "Have we met?"

"No. I think I'd remember you if we had." She wet her red-painted lips with the tip of her tongue and held out her hand. "Ashley Robinson."

Her name meant nothing, and I clasped her hand long enough to tell her my name. I liked the way her hand felt, but I didn't let my hold linger.

"You come here often, Joe?" she asked. Before she drew back her hand, she took a fry from my basket, and she ate it while I answered her question.

"Once, maybe twice a week. My office is over there—" I gestured vaguely in the direction of the ALICO Building. "—and the walk is good for me."

"I've never been," she said. "I don't get downtown much."

I told her about the food trucks and the menu items I preferred at each of them.

"You a food truck connoisseur?"

"Bachelor," I said, "and I can't cook."

"That's too bad," she said. She took another fry from my basket without asking, and I watched as she drew it between her lips. "Neither can I."

I don't remember our entire conversation, but I do remember that the rest of the world ceased to exist for several minutes. By the time we rejoined reality, I had finished my gyro and she had finished my fries.

While we talked, her fine, shoulder-length hair blew into her face and stuck to her lipstick. I reached across the table and pushed a strand behind her ear. She smiled.

"I like the way you did that."

"Yes?"

"I'd like you to do it again sometime," she said. "Maybe over dinner."

I named the time. She named the place.

Then she left without ever having ordered lunch, walked

directly to her Mustang, and, with a wave of her fingers, drove away. I made no attempt to move until the Mustang was long out of sight.

Dinner wasn't on Ashley's mind when I arrived at her home in one of the sparsely developed subdivisions springing up along Highway 84, nor was it on mine. We left a trail of clothing from the foyer, up the stairs, and into the bedroom. For the next hour all of our communication was physical, punctuated by gasps and sighs.

As we lay in bed afterward, moonlight streaming through the open window and no neighbors in the surrounding unfinished houses who could see in, she rose up on one elbow, looked down at me, and asked what I did. I told her I was a private investigator.

She used the tip of one finger to twirl my chest hair as she stared into my eyes." Are you going to investigate me?"

"Should I?"

Ashley smiled coyly. "You never know."

I needed a smoke. An ashtray on the nightstand let me know Ashley was not opposed, but I had no desire to go stumbling about in the dark looking for my jacket. Not during that visit. During subsequent visits, I lay in her bed smoking and telling her about some of my cases—the cheating spouses, the insurance fraud, and the stolen property I'd recovered.

"That all sounds so exciting," she said.

Though it was more exciting than joining the family oil business in Midland, I said, "Most of the time it isn't. Usually I just sit in my car and wait for stupid people to do stupid things so I can take their pictures."

"Take me with you sometime."

I gave a non-committal response and changed the subject by pulling her to me and repeating what we'd done earlier.

Later, after we'd satiated ourselves, she opened the drawer of her nightstand and showed me a .38 and a box of shells.

"What's that for?"

"Protection," she said. "I live out here all alone and I worry about things happening. But now that I have it, I don't know what to do. I don't even know how to load it."

I took the revolver from the drawer, ensured that it wasn't loaded, and showed her how to point and shoot, telling her to squeeze the trigger and not pull it. Then offered the gun to her. "You want to try?"

After she shook her head, I loaded the .38, pushing each shell into place with my thumb before returning it to the nightstand drawer.

Old money occupied Castle Heights, a neighborhood centered on and adjacent to Austin Avenue that consisted of massive two-story homes built in the early 1900s. I lived not far away in Brookview, a neighborhood of small ranch homes built in the 1950s. Once home to up-and-coming middle-class families, slumlords had been turning their homes into rental property as the residents died off. About three weeks after my last stop in Castle Heights, and the morning following a late-night vigil outside her husband's favorite fleabag motel, I returned to Joan Wilkes-Tower's dining room with more photographs.

My client wore a different silk robe, but one no less revealing than before, and I caught glimpses of the tan lines on the swell of her breasts each time she flipped a photo on my iPad, making me suspect she was braless beneath the silk. Her husband's bleached blonde the previous evening had ridden him much the same way all of his previous assignations had, making me wonder if the escorts feared being crushed to death.

"Does looking at these photos excite you?" Joan asked.

"I don't think so." I remembered sitting in the cold waiting for the right moment to stick my camera lens through a window with a broken latch, and I did not find the resulting photographs the least bit stimulating.

"That's a shame." She captured my left hand and toyed with my fingers as she wet her lips with the tip of her tongue. "There are so many ways I could use you."

"Here's where you tell me you love me and you want to run away with me," I said, "but first we have to kill your husband."

She tilted her head back and laughed so hard her breasts threatened escape from the confines of her robe. When she caught her breath, she said, "You're awfully full of yourself, aren't you, Mr. Blake?"

"Maybe I've watched too many movies that end badly for the schmuck who falls for the beautiful dame."

Joan released her hold on my hand and stood. After crossing the room to retrieve her purse, she handed me a trio of Franklins and said, "Email me that last photo."

I stuffed the Franklins in my shirt pocket, emailed my client the photo of the bleached blonde riding her husband, and then stood to leave.

"There are easier ways to earn a living," Joan said. She unfastened the sash of her robe and confirmed that she wore no bra.

I didn't pretend to look away. Instead, I appreciated the view for what I thought it was—an attractive middle-aged woman whose husband no longer valued her sexually trying to seduce a younger man. If I hadn't been heavily involved with Ashley by then, I might have been tempted.

Instead, I let myself out of the house, lit a cigarette while standing on the porch, and then returned to my office. I disbursed my cash earnings in a long-familiar pattern, letting two of the Franklins join those already crowded into the false bottom of one of my desk drawers.

* * *

Several small towns clung to Waco's borders as the city expanded, and the communities pressed hard against one another. Some—Hewitt and Woodway—are home to new money and middle-class families escaping the Waco Independent School District. Other communities are not as fortunate, and it was to these less fortunate communities that I was often drawn by my work.

I spent two days trailing a man who lived in Bellmead until I finally caught him engaged in an activity that his supposed back injury should have precluded—carrying a large, brand-new flat-screen television into his mobile home. My photos helped the man's employer contest his workman's compensation claim, and the employer's insurance company had cause to pursue a criminal charge of insurance fraud.

I told Ashley about my most recent cases during post-coital cigarette breaks, and she asked questions about each as if she were truly interested in how and why I did what I did. I told her about my brief time as a member of the Waco Police Department and my decision to go private. And I mentioned—though I never used his name—Charles Tower's string of semi-regular assignations at a fleabag motel along the highway on the other side of the Brazos River. I even told her how I'd slipped into the room one day after I realized he always rented the same end unit, and how I'd broken the window's lock and greased the slides so I could open it from the outside without making undue noise.

"So the women," Ashley said one night as she shifted position on the bed and straddled me. "How do they do it? Like this?"

"Yes," I told her as she lowered herself onto me. "Exactly like that."

* * *

Though Waco is growing, it is still small enough and inbred enough that those of a certain social status carry similar names. Some female descendants of the founding families hyphenate their names upon marriage, while others give their family name to their children as middle names. This ensures that everyone knows from which well-to-do families their children are descended.

Charles Tower's forbearers had founded one of the banks when cotton was king, and Charles was the latest in a string of Towers to serve as president of the financial institution. Status came with his family name. So did money. Joan Wilkes-Tower's family name wasn't as prominent and her first husband, now deceased, had squandered the money they'd had. She'd settled into her role as her second husband's slightly soiled trophy wife, her own heritage just prominent enough that no one thought he'd married down. She appeared with him at various social functions, always hanging on his arm and smiling as if she knew which side of the bed her bank account was buttered on, but they slept in separate bedrooms and she seemed to get pleasure from examining photos of the women her husband hired to satisfy his carnal desires.

Several weeks had passed since my last assignment from her, so I wasn't surprised when my cellphone rang and her name appeared on the caller ID.

"My husband phoned and said he's working late," she said. "That means he's going out again tonight."

"Tonight?"

She must have sensed hesitation in my voice. "That a problem?"

"No," I told her. I had plans with Ashley I would have to cancel. "Not at all."

"If you get anything good," she said, "email it to me."

Every previous time she had hired me to tail her husband, she had also invited me to her home the following morning to share my photographs. Beyond thinking that I had resisted her advances once too often, I didn't take time to wonder why she had not extended another invitation. After my conversation with Joan ended, I phoned Ashley to break our date.

When I told her why, she asked to join me. There was nothing dangerous about sitting in a car and taking a few pictures, so I told her she could.

"You'll have to pick me up," Ashley said. "My car's in the shop."

Twenty minutes later, Ashley met me at her front door. She wore black running shoes, dark jeans, and a dark blue work shirt that failed to conceal her feminine figure. Thin leather gloves and an oversized black jacket completed her outfit. "How do I look?"

"Good enough to take upstairs and forget about tonight's job."

Ashley laughed. "Maybe later."

Not bothering with a purse, she pulled the front door closed and followed me to my car. Soon, we were parked where we could watch the bank's parking lot, and two hours after the bank closed for the evening, well past the time most of the other employees had vacated the building, a balding fat man waddled out of a side door and looked around.

"That's him."

I started my car and, as expected, followed Charles Tower to a fleabag motel on an Interstate 35 frontage road north of Waco, just shy of the border with Bellmead. He parked his Mercedes in the darkness behind the motel and made his way around the building to the end unit farthest from the dimly lit office, a room he rented on a weekly basis so it was available whenever he needed it. The highway noise would have kept me from falling asleep if I'd rented a room, but it didn't seem to bother the truckers who were the motel's primary occupants, and Charles Tower wasn't there to sleep.

I parked nearby, and we watched as he slipped into the room. A few minutes later a buxom blonde climbed out of a

Corolla and tapped on the door. The door opened and she stepped inside.

As soon as I felt certain they had begun their business transaction, I grabbed my camera. I had disabled my interior light, so my car remained dark as I stepped out. I crossed the parking lot and approached the window I'd doctored a few months earlier. After looking around and seeing no one watching me but Ashley, I eased the window open, slid the lens of my camera through a gap in the curtains, and snapped several photographs of the blonde riding my client's husband.

When I finished, I let the curtain fall back into place and eased the window closed. Then I returned to my car, slipped behind the steering wheel, and continued watching.

Sometime later, Ashley slid one hand into my lap and leaned against me. "How long do we have to sit here?"

My attention wavered. "Until he leaves."

"Well, I have to pee."

I glanced around. There was nowhere she could go and I didn't think suggesting the bottle I sometimes used for long stakeouts would be appropriate. "We can't leave yet," I said, "and there's no place—"

"I've held it as long as I can." She opened the car door.

I grabbed her arm. "Where are you going?"

"Back there." She pointed vaguely behind the motel. "I'll hurry."

I released her arm and she disappeared into the darkness.

She had been gone several minutes when Charles Tower exited the room and walked around the end of the building. I sat up straight and was about to open my door when Ashley came hurrying back. She had her jacket wadded into a ball, but she was still wearing her gloves when she climbed into the passenger seat.

I asked, "Did he see you?"

"No, I was careful," she said. "Did you get what you needed tonight?"

"I got what I could," I said.

Ashley slid her hand into my lap again and lowered her voice seductively. "Then take me home."

I usually waited until Charles Tower drove out of the motel's parking lot before I vacated my post, but Ashley's hand provided ample incentive to leave first, so I did.

Her hand remained in my lap for most of the trip, but once we reached her home, Ashley insisted we review the photographs I'd taken. As we sat naked in her bed, she pressed against me and I flipped through them.

She helped me select the best photograph, one that left no doubt that Charles Tower was the man beneath the blonde, and I emailed it to my client.

Then I devoted my full attention to Ashley, and she to me until I could pleasure her no more and I fell asleep.

I never stayed the night, and a few hours later she sent me home.

I woke late the next morning, made coffee, and turned on my iPad. I surfed the Internet for several minutes before checking the local newspaper's website and discovering that morning's breaking news.

Prominent banker Charles Tower had been found dead behind a local motel.

I read the story, learning that the banker had been shot to death, that a motel employee had found his body, and that the police were pursuing all possible leads.

I phoned my client, but she didn't answer. Then I phoned Ashley, but she didn't answer, either.

I showered, dressed, and drove downtown to my office. I was chain-smoking Camels and digesting the news about my client's husband when Lieutenant Spencer rapped on my office door and let himself in. I tamped a half-smoked cigarette out in the coffee mug I was using as an ashtray as I greeted him.

Without preamble, he asked, "Where were you last night?"

"On a stakeout job," I said.

"Anyone see you?"

"Would I be any good if they had?"

"Apparently, you're not that good," Spencer said. "We received an anonymous tip after the news broke about Charles Tower. The tipster rattled off your license plate number, said you were sitting in the car watching Tower's motel room, and that you drove off shortly after he left the room."

Spencer couldn't find his ass with both hands, even with a Google map providing directions, so I was surprised that he knew as much as he did. What I didn't know was how much information the anonymous tipster had provided, though I knew better than to dispute what we both apparently knew to be true.

"You took some dirty pictures and tried to peddle them to his wife," Spencer said. "I don't know how you tumbled to Tower's extra-marital activities, but you've been snapping pics for a while, and you targeted his wife because you knew she had more to lose than he did. She said she's been paying you to keep quiet."

I said nothing.

"You didn't learn your lesson the last time I gave you good advice," Spencer said. "You don't mess with old money."

"I wasn't working alone that night," I told the lieutenant. "My girlfriend was in the car with me."

"Think she'll confirm that?"

Even though Ashley had not returned my calls, I said, "I don't see why not."

"What's her name?"

"Ashley Robinson."

"You're using Tower's stepdaughter as your alibi?"

"Stepdaughter?"

"Ashley Wilkes Robinson."

Ashley had never told me her middle name, and I'd never thought to ask.

"I've already spoken to Ms. Robinson, and she's her mother's alibi. According to them, they were together all evening," Spencer said. "What's more, a neighbor saw Ms. Robinson arrive around four that afternoon and her car was in the driveway all night as far as anyone knows. That Mustang convertible of hers is hard to miss. Another neighbor saw her leave her mother's house this morning."

I leaned back in my chair, the events of that evening rearranging in my mind.

After the lieutenant vacated my office, I did some Internet sleuthing and learned more about the two women who had dominated my life for the previous few months. I confirmed Ashley's relationship to Joan Wilkes-Tower and Charles Tower, learned that her biological father—Joan's first husband, John Barnes Robinson—had let his inheritance run like water through his fingers, and learned that Robinson had died an untimely death that left Joan so deep in debt that she and Ashley became social pariahs. Joan's debt and social status had returned with her marriage to Charles Tower several years later, and his standing had improved as well with the merging of his family with that of another founding family.

I stopped trying to contact Ashley, certain that her value as my alibi disappeared the moment she and her mother vouched for one another, and I wondered which one needed the other more. Ashley had been with me that night, and she had been out of my sight long enough to have popped her stepfather, but anyone could have been waiting in the darkness behind the motel.

Anyone.

I crushed out my last cigarette, drove to the 7-Eleven for a fresh pack, and stopped at the row of food trucks to pick up a lunch I barely touched.

Lieutenant Spencer was sitting behind my desk and another detective stood beside him when I returned. My office had been ransacked, my desk drawers had been pulled free and overturned, and papers from my file drawers littered the floor. I took it all in with a glance but concentrated my attention on the lieutenant as he unfolded a search warrant and placed it atop my desk.

"We found a few things we're taking with us," he said. He fanned a stack of Franklins and stuck them in an evidence bag. He also had the other detective search me, and then placed my iPad and cellphone in other evidence bags along with my digital camera.

I said nothing.

"We'll be talking with you again real soon."

After the two men left, I looked over the search warrant and saw that it encompassed my home, my office, my car and my person. They had already trashed my office and emptied my pockets, so I went downstairs to see what they'd done to my car. I arrived in time to see it disappear around the corner attached to a tow truck.

The next time he visited my office, Lieutenant Spencer had bad news. "You're under arrest for the murder of Charles Tower. You have the right to an attorney...but you know all that, don't you?"

I didn't resist, though I certainly considered the option, and soon I sat in an interrogation room at police headquarters watching our reflections in the one-way mirror and listening to the lieutenant spell out his theory of the events leading up to the murder of Charles Tower.

"Mrs. Wilkes-Tower thought you would leave her alone after she paid you the first time, but you wouldn't. You kept approaching her with new photos of her husband—she showed them to us—so she started marking the hundred-dollar bills she used to pay you. We found several of them in the false bottom of your desk drawer. We also found hundreds of photos in your camera and on your iPad that prove you've been stalking Charles Tower for quite some time."

He paused for a moment, as if waiting for me to express admiration for the story he was spinning. When I said nothing, he continued.

"The last time Mrs. Wilkes-Tower met with you, you demanded more. You wanted her, and you suggested killing her husband so that you could have her." Spencer shook his head, possibly for the benefit of the people watching from the observation room on the other side of the one-way mirror. "You never were very bright. We found the murder weapon under the front passenger seat of your car with your thumb-prints on the shells. We also found two Camel cigarette butts near Tower's Mercedes with your saliva on them.

"So here's what we think happened: You waited behind the motel long enough to smoke two cigarettes. When Tower finally came out, you killed him. Two shots to the back of the head, so close there are powder burns inside the wound. He likely never saw it coming."

After a moment of silence, he pushed a notepad and a pencil across the desk. "You want to make a statement?"

"I want a lawyer."

The Waco legal community is a good-old-boys club awash with Baylor Law School graduates that closed ranks against outsiders rather than let any sauce drip from the gravy train. Finding a high-powered criminal defense attorney willing to represent me when the victim came from Waco's socially prominent old money and the preponderance of evidence seemed insurmountable was a mug's game I didn't bother playing. I phoned Mark Cain from jail, he fronted for my father's attorneys in Midland, and I was out on cash bail within twenty-four hours. My guilt or innocence was none of Mark's concern, but as we walked down the courthouse steps, he asked, "What the hell have you gotten yourself into?"

Without my car, camera, cell phone, or iPad, I felt powerless, but I said, "I'm about to find out."

We parted company at the bottom of the stairs. Mark returned to his office across the river and I walked to mine. The place was still in disarray, but I sat at my desk and began to put things in order.

I rented a car and drove to the east side, where I purchased an unregistered .38 and a box of shells from the trunk of a low-rider Impala. On my way back through town, I bought a sack of tacos, supplies to clean the .38, a cellphone, and a new digital camera with a telephoto lens.

I didn't know if I should start with Joan or her daughter, because they were obviously working together to deprive me of my life. Ultimately, I chose to drive to the new subdivision where Ashley lived because it would be easier to watch her without attracting unwanted attention and because I had her pegged as the shooter. She had used a feigned urge to urinate as the excuse to slip out of my car, had popped her stepfather in the darkness behind the motel, and had returned with her revolver wrapped in her jacket to slip under my car seat. Then we'd gone to her home for a night of spirited sex that had distracted my attention from earlier events.

I tucked the rental car in the rear-entrance garage of an unfinished two-story house across the street from Ashley's home and took up residence in the front room. I ate my tacos while I unpacked my new camera and read the instruction booklet. Then I cleaned and loaded the .38.

I don't know what I expected to happen, and several days passed before anything did. In the meantime, I kept one eye on the local news. No one ever questioned what Charles Tower was doing behind a fleabag motel, but Joan played the suitably grieving widow, Ashley the devastated stepdaughter, and Lieutenant Spencer the appropriately heroic detective, who in a matter of days, had cracked a particularly heinous crime.

That's why I was surprised a few evenings later when Spencer parked an unmarked patrol car in Ashley's driveway, walked to the door, and was greeted by my former bed partner. She wore nothing but a diaphanous white babydoll and a grin that matched his.

I barely had time to grab my camera before the lieutenant scooped Ashley into his arms, carried her into the house, and kicked the door closed. I snapped off a few quick shots and then ran up the unfinished stairs to the second floor, into the bedroom facing across the street toward Ashley's bedroom.

As always, her curtains were open, and I took several photographs of Ashley doing things with the lieutenant she'd never done with me.

I waited several hours until he left, she extinguished the light in her bedroom, and I felt confident I could drive away without waking her.

Twenty minutes later I parked my rental car in the alley behind Joan Wilkes-Tower's home, popped the lock on the kitchen door, and let myself in. I had only ever been in the foyer and the dining room, so I had to find her bedroom by trial and error. When I sat on the side of her bed and switched on the bedside lamp, she woke with a start.

Joan didn't scream, but her eyes went wide with surprise. She recovered quickly and said, "I wondered when I would see you again."

"We're going to have a nice quiet chat," I told her. Joan sat up and leaned against the headboard as I asked, "Why did your daughter kill your husband?"

"She didn't."

"You knew she was going to kill him that night," I said. "You helped her fabricate an alibi."

"That wasn't me," she said. "I only played along for their sake."

"Their sake?"

"My daughter and Bobby. They're planning to be married," Joan said, "but he isn't from money. He needs some other form of status and what could be better for my daughter than to marry the man who caught her stepfather's killer?"

"You knew they were going to kill your husband and you did nothing to stop them?"

"Why bother? I didn't love Charles and never had. That fat bastard didn't rescue me from the situation my first husband left me in out of the goodness of his heart. He needed to find an appropriate wife before he became a social pariah, and I needed the right husband to stop being one."

I pushed myself off the bed and backed away, afraid that close proximity to her cold heart would give me freezer burn.

"Bobby's the one who suggested I hire you in the first place," she said. "He said you were too stupid to stumble onto any of this. I guess he was wrong."

I let myself out the way I came in, considering what I'd just learned. I knew I had been set up, but I hadn't figured Spencer for the mastermind. He had never been one to rub two thoughts together and spark an idea, but he'd been quick to finger me for the murder. Too quick.

From Joan's home, I drove to the Mountainview neighborhood where Lieutenant Spencer lived. When I saw the lights go on in his house, I knew he was getting ready for work, so I found a place in the shadow of his garage where I could wait.

Getting the drop on the lieutenant proved easy enough. I waited until he exited the house and crossed the lawn to the unmarked police car parked in the driveway before stepping from the shadows. I pressed the muzzle of the .38 against the base of his skull, just as he had pressed one against the base of Charles Tower's skull.

"I'm surprised to see you," Spencer said. "No one thought you'd make bail, and I figured you'd blow town after you did."

He had only ever seen me as a starry-eyed police officer and a private investigator eking out a living on the fringes of the local legal system, never once questioning where I'd come from or how I'd been raised. That was his first mistake.

"What do you want?"

I hadn't yet spoken to Ashley, so I lied. "The ladies have ratted you out," I told him. "They say this whole thing was your idea and that you pulled the trigger on Charles Tower."

"Just you," he said. "The only thing I gave them was you."

"You gave them more than that," I said. "Who marked the bills for Mrs. Wilkes-Tower? Who found the .38 for Ms. Robinson? Who—?"

"I did it all for Ashley," the lieutenant said. "The set-up was her idea, a way for us to get married without causing a ripple in society, and her mother was glad to be rid of her husband."

"And you got to step up in class."

"Everybody got what they wanted."

"Everybody except me," I said, "me and Charles Tower. You figured everybody would buy the story you told: Mr. Private Eye behind the motel with a .38?"

"I knew you couldn't afford an attorney who could sell a different story."

He was right. I couldn't, but my father could.

Better still, I could put the pieces together myself. When they decided to kill Charles Tower, they needed a fall guy, and Lieutenant Spencer provided my name. He knew I didn't travel in Waco's prime social circles. So, Joan hired me to tail her husband, a man whose expensive infidelities provided reason enough, and she paid me with bills marked by Spencer.

Then Ashley seduced me, knowing they could call their plan off if I stumbled onto her relationship with my client. When I didn't, Spencer provided the .38 I loaded for Ashley, and she collected my cigarette butts from the ashtray in her bedroom.

The night Ashley joined me, she drove to her mother's house, left her car in the driveway, and slipped out the back where Spencer was waiting to drive her home.

Later, I picked Ashley up and drove her to the motel, where we watched her stepfather. Just before he left the room, Ashley slipped out of my car. She was waiting in the dark behind the motel to surprise her stepfather, distracting him for the brief moment it took Spencer to shoot him. I'd not heard the shots because of all the highway noise. Ashley wrapped her jacket around the revolver and hurried back to my car as the lieutenant dropped my cigarette butts onto the ground near Tower's car. While I was concentrating on the drive to Ashley's home, she slipped the revolver under my passenger seat.

Later that night, after Ashley kicked me out of bed, Lieutenant Spencer arrived and drove her to her mother's house. Neighbors noted her departure later that morning— just as they had noted her arrival the evening before. The two women alibied one another, and no one thought to look at Lieutenant Spencer.

My story was as plausible as the one he had spun in the interrogation room, but I knew that he wasn't the mastermind. Someone else had put everything together, and I had yet to confront her.

The sun was rising as I returned to Ashley's home, and she sat in her living room listening as I laid it all out for her. "I figure this entire scheme was your idea. Bobby hasn't the brains to think up something like this and he's so eager to move in better circles that he'd do most anything you asked of him."

Ashley smiled but said nothing.

I asked, "But why me?"

"Because you're just a dick," she said, "and a dick was all I needed."

After I left Ashley, I phoned Mark Cain and had him set up a meeting with the assistant district attorney, who listened that afternoon as I laid everything out for him. He didn't believe a word of it, but the lieutenant crumbled when it was put to him. As soon as Spencer crumbled, mother and daughter turned on him, insisting that he had masterminded the entire thing and had forced them to participate.

They turned state's evidence, were far more convincing than Lieutenant Spencer, and he finally learned the lesson he had tried to teach me all those years ago: In Waco, you don't mess with the old money. When it was all over, Joan and Ashley were sitting pretty, but Bobby Spencer got the chair.

I gave up smoking, closed my office, sold my house, and headed west. With Waco in my rearview mirror, I thought I might give Midland another chance. After all, I'd been raised with the boom and bust of oil money, and I owed my father a few years in the family business.

Out of Business
Eric Beetner
Iowa City

I hefted the box in one hand, turned back to face my office and clicked off the light. Staring at it in the dark gave me my first real pang of sadness. I'd known it was the last day I'd be in business, but it hadn't sunk in until right then. It'd been a normal day for me—sit around and play solitaire. Look up a few things on the Internet, go down a deep hole on YouTube watching old Hawkeyes' highlights from Rose Bowls past. A long lunch out at the Airliner and then back to the office to check messages, of which there were none.

So this was it. My last day as a PI. I pulled the door closed and looked at my own name stenciled on the frosted glass. "Cleve Kershaw" in a rainbow arc across the top. "Confidential Investigations" under it. Whoever moved in after me would have it scraped away and probably not give a second thought to the man who spent six years here trying to make a go of the private dick business.

Iowa City, as it turned out, was not the hotbed of secrets and lies I thought it was. Or maybe, I'd come to believe, it was too damn good at keeping those secrets. And everyone was so damn full of their own lies, everyone feared exposing someone else's in case it started a flood of realizations that would overrun the town.

We were a small town, and small towns stick together. They don't like to rat out their neighbor, even when he's cheating on his wife.

I'd just turned my back on the door forever when I heard a muffled phone ring. The second floor of my building was mostly storage for the university, so I was often the only living soul up there. And I think I owned the only telephone on the floor. I'd kept the land line because so many people trusted it more than reaching a guy by his cell phone to hire him for PI work. Something psychological, I guess.

I almost kept going for the elevator. My phone rang so infrequently I figured it had to be a wrong number. Happened often enough.

For old times' sake I set the box down, went back through the door with my name on it and picked up the phone.

"Kershaw Investigations."

"Mr. Kershaw?"

It was a woman, perhaps expecting a secretary to answer.

"That's me."

"I need your help."

Music to a private eye's ears. But I wasn't one anymore. I was thirty seconds retired. But what the hell, I was the boss, right? And when I looked at my watch, it was still five minutes to five. Office hours still open.

"How can I help?"

"It's my neighbor," she said with some concern, as if he might be listening in on the line. "He's...well, I don't like the way he watches my daughter. I want you to check up on him."

"You want me to run a background check?"

"Yes. Well, whatever you call it. I want you to make sure he's safe. Safe to live next door to."

"Do you not feel safe, Mrs....?"

"Kellen. Stacy Kellen. And no, not lately."

I ran through the usual questions before I took on any case, and I wasn't too keen on taking this one. I'd already mentally checked out. I could use any extra cash however...

"Have you reported this man's behavior to the police?"

"Yes, I have. They said there wasn't anything I could do about someone just looking. He stays in his yard, he never says anything to her so they said it wasn't harassment. They told me to build a fence."

"Yeah, Iowa City's finest." Sympathizing with the client helps build trust. "Have you talked to him about it?"

"No. I don't dare. He gives me the creeps."

I sighed. "Okay, well, I can do a routine check. Give me your address and I'll come meet you and we can discuss the details."

What the hell, right? I had no other job lined up. No prospects. I didn't want to end up back at the rail yard. I'd gotten free of the Burlington Northern Railroad for a reason. I figured to hit up the HR department at the university, but that wasn't until Monday. Might as well take the weekend and work up a few bucks in my pocket.

She gave me an address on Raven Street and I drove out there, my box of possessions in the trunk of my car. I'd be working remotely on this one. The practice I'd shut down of my own accord, the office I was being evicted from for lack of payment.

Suburban street. Used to be close enough to the edge of town you could still smell the fertilizer, but now just one twist in the maze of single family homes pushing the farmland farther out. Her house was a split level, built in the seventies, probably. The one next to it was a two story, overgrown lawn, peeling paint. Definitely looked like a creep's house.

She met me at the door and invited me in. She pointed to her daughter playing in a room as we passed.

"That's Olive."

The kid was maybe six or seven. Not the age you want your daughter to get unwanted attention from a weird neighbor. But that's any age, really, isn't it? Just because I'm not married and don't have kids, I still know that much.

She played quietly, her tiny voice acting out parts to her

dolls. She had big eyes, filled with innocence like maybe we all did at one point.

We sat at a small table in the kitchen and Stacy set out coffee.

"Thanks." I took out my small notepad, a ball point pen. "Do you know his name?"

"Mr. Douglas. He moved in about four months ago. Never goes out. Well, rarely. I don't know if he has a job or not."

She laid out the strange behavior. She'd catch him watching Olive in the backyard, just staring. She said he rarely wears a shirt when he stands in his window or when he's out back watering the grass, which she said he did so much she was surprised it wasn't a swamp.

He was watching at her birthday party a few weeks back. Every time Stacy looked up, there he was, watching. Even hearing her describe it made me a little uneasy. I felt good about answering the phone. I wanted to help her and her daughter. It would be a good last case, make the ending less bitter, more sweet.

"I'll see what I can dig up," I told her.

"You don't think I'm being paranoid?"

"No such thing when it comes to our kids." I smiled, felt like a kindly grandpa, even though I'm only forty-four. "Do you mind my asking," I said with a little caution. "Does Mr. Kellen have any opinion on this? Has he noticed the same behavior from Mr. Douglas?"

"My husband is in prison, Mr. Kershaw. I should have told you."

I felt awkward, tried to backpedal. "I shouldn't have assumed—"

"He's in there because he hit me and Olive. He went away for ten years. I put off calling the police about Mr. Douglas. I put off calling you. But I know what it means to be scared, Mr. Kershaw. And I vowed not to live my life in fear ever again."

Her strength seemed to be built around a shaky middle, but I admired her for it. She was doing right by her child and stood up for herself when she needed to.

I closed my notebook, gave her a soft look that I hoped eased her mind. "Nor should you."

She managed a weak smile.

The next day was research day. Amazing how few people start there themselves. So much of PI work is just doing what average citizens can do on their own but never bother to. First things first—check the sex offender registry.

My first attempt yielded results. Seems our Mr. Douglas was a registered sex offender, and worse, a pedophile. Charles Douglas, Chuck to his friends—which he had none of—arrived four months earlier after eight years in a Michigan prison for exposing himself to a playground and then masturbating in full view of the kids until the police showed up to stop him. He'd been out over a year, hard to track his whereabouts during that time without more resources, but he landed in Iowa City and had so far been clean.

It made his obsession with Olive all the more scary, though. Mrs. Kellen was not going to like this.

But this is America. Innocent until proven guilty, right?

Well, Douglas had been proven guilty on two other minor charges over the years. The playground incident was not an isolated one. I decided to meet the man face to face.

I was never a wigs-and-funny-hats kind of detective. My role playing was limited, but I could pull out those two years of high school drama club when I needed to. When I showed up at Douglas' house I had my ruse all worked out. All I needed was a few minutes of the guy's time. Just to get my own take on him and whether I thought he was as dangerous as his rap sheet made him out to be.

I knocked and a few moments later the door eased open. The man kept inside, away from the light. He looked up at me from under his brow, suspicious and nervous looking. His face was thin, like I expected it might after eight years behind bars. Clean shaven, but that didn't help make him look like an upstanding citizen or anything.

"Yeah?"

"Mr. Douglas? I'm here to ask you, sir, if you've considered the benefits of solar panels on your home?"

"Solar panels?"

"Yes, sir." I took a small step forward, wedged my foot in the open door. Classic tactics never go out of style. "The economic benefits are profound, not to mention the environmental impact." Around most of this solid red state they couldn't give two shits about the environmental impacts, but in a college town, you never knew.

"I ain't interested." He gave the door a shove but my foot was there and he backed off. I leaned in a little more, peeked around the door. The house was dour and dim. Things were still piled in boxes. No art on the walls.

"Mr. Douglas, did I mention that the initial cash outlay for you, sir, is zero. You heard right. Absolutely zero dollars for us to install and maintain your new solar panels." I peeked around the other side of the door as I talked. "Be honest, haven't you ever wanted to live off the grid?"

I felt like that one got to him a bit. It gave me a second to register what I was seeing in the living room. Video equipment. Monitors, cameras, stacks of tapes. Not good. Made me wonder how many of those had shots of young Olive on them.

I didn't know if this was enough to obtain a warrant for the police, but it should help Mrs. Kellen's case.

"I said I ain't interested." He pushed harder on the door now. He'd seen me notice his little hobby room and was eager to get me out. I'd gotten what I came there for.

"Well, sir, if you change your mind." I thought of something on my way out. "Say, Mr. Douglas, can you tell me if you think the neighbors will be home? I hate to waste my time, you know."

I pointed to Stacy's house, saw him glance that way, but not linger. Like there was something there he didn't want to see.

"I wouldn't know."

I acted like I was trying to recall some information. "It's a Mrs. Keller, isn't it? Kellogg? Woman and her son?"

"Daughter," he said. His eyes darted away. "I think."

He shut the door on me. I went home to write my report.

"Oh my God, oh my God, oh my God."

I knew she wasn't going to like what I had to say to her. I'd typed it all up, made it official looking. I told her to bring this to the police and ask for a warrant. If Olive was on even one of those videos, they'd have him back in jail for violating parole.

"Do you think they'll arrest him?"

"I honestly don't know, Mrs. Kellen." I tried to hide my skepticism. In truth, I thought she'd hit a dead end with the cops. She'd be better off moving.

She looked out her kitchen window up to his house on the rise, his windows staring down on her house ominously.

"I just want him gone."

As I packed my notebook and file folder, I chuckled. "That will cost you extra."

Bad joke, maybe. I felt some levity was needed right then. She felt something else entirely, I learned.

"How much?"

I paused, a pen half in and half out of my breast pocket. I looked at her. "I was joking, Mrs. Kellen."

"Mr. Kershaw, did you think what you told me was going to make me feel better about the man living next door? Do you think I'll sleep soundly tonight?"

I shook my head.

"The man who's been staring at my child is a convicted pedophile. And the police told me last time they were here that unless something happens, I have no grounds to stop him from doing whatever it is he's doing in his own house. Well, what something do you think needs to happen before they'll act? We both know what. The only question is—does he rape and kill my daughter, or just rape her? And which is worse?"

Stacy was beyond crying. Her anger had hardened her tears into stones. Her pupils bore through me. Anger at the system, love for her daughter, knowledge of what men could do all built a wall inside her.

"Do you own a gun, Mrs. Kellen?"

"No. Not yet."

"I hope it doesn't come to that."

"It doesn't have to."

I left her in the kitchen with my report and a bill for three hundred dollars.

When I got home I had money on my mind. I got out my accounts sheet, ran the numbers. I still owed two months on the office. I was behind on my house payment, my car was due the following week. Gas, electric, cable all due or past due.

When I had a business I could more easily convince myself things would work out. Now I had nothing. No job, no prospects. If I got lucky, the university would be hiring security guards. Maybe I could get a job guarding the Jackson Pollock or something, flirt with a few college girls.

The other prospects looming were to head back to the rail yard, if they'd have me. Or I could go way back in my employment history, work in a chicken rendering plant again. Send a thousand chickens a day to their deaths. Or maybe go the full Iowa and find work in a cornfield.

My phone rang. Stacy Kellen.

"He's watching, Mr. Kershaw. Just sitting up in his window and staring down at us. It's like he doesn't even care we can see him."

"Invest in some curtains."

"I thought you told me to buy a gun."

"Curtains are cheaper."

"Money is no object. I made quite a lot in a settlement against my ex-husband. I have a lot. I just need the right person to give it to."

"That someone would have to earn it."

"Earn it doing a good thing."

"That depends on which side of the doing you're on."

"You know what side is the right side."

I did. I looked at the bills spread before me on the table. The last job wasn't turning out to be such a sweet send-off as I originally thought. Here she was, offering me the chance to write my own check. All I had to do was to get rid of an awful human being.

But I'd never gotten rid of anyone before.

I'd never been evicted before, either.

I thought of Olive. Her big, innocent eyes. If something happened to her, I'd feel it the rest of my life. I knew, now, what Douglas was capable of. He may not have taken that extra step before—or maybe he had but never got caught—but I knew the pattern. Chuck had an illness. But it was Olive who would suffer from it.

Maybe it was time for me to take the extra step.

I had a few drinks to think it over. For a lot of men, courage came in a bottle. For Stacy's husband, I bet. What would it do to a woman who'd already been through what she had, to endure a predator at her doorstep drooling over her daughter?

Probably before I should have, I took a drive. I made loops around the U of I campus, past the football stadium, the basketball stadium. I went past the gold dome of the old Capitol. Everywhere I looked Herkey the hawk, the school mascot who was equal parts cheerful and fierce, stared out at me from banners, billboards, bumper stickers and flags hung on frat house porches. If I'd have been smart, I'd have named my detective agency Herkey Investigations. Appeal to the alumni crowd.

But I hadn't been smart. I'd lost it all. And I started to come to the realization that I was about to be not smart again.

I parked in front of Stacy Kellen's house. The drinks had left my system and I was stone sober now. My decision was made with a clear head.

"I'll do it," I said when she answered the door.

She didn't ask how and I didn't know then anyway. We talked terms, never once saying the words kill or murder, just go away and disappear.

I drove away with a check for twenty grand in my pocket.

The next night I parked on Raven Street and waited. I didn't worry too much about how to do it and not get caught, I figured the best way to avoid all that was for there to never be a body. That was my plan. I'd lined my trunk with garbage bags, ready for a corpse.

I'd gotten from Stacy that Tuesday was garbage night. The cans would go out to the curb and get picked up bright and early Wednesday morning. She confirmed that Douglas' cans were always out the night before.

Around nine o'clock, under a welcome cover of darkness,

he stepped out his side gate pulling two garbage cans to the curb. The whole night I'd been running over worst case scenarios in my head. Olive as a victim of the most horrific crimes I could imagine. I'd turned Douglas into the worst possible monster. I'd convinced myself he'd done it before and gotten away with it. I'd convinced myself he needed to die.

I wouldn't let myself think anything else or I might chicken out. Part of it was the risk to Olive, part of it was having to tear up that check.

I got out of my car with a thin rope in my hands, heavy work gloves on. I didn't want any blood. I wanted Mr. Douglas to just vanish. People would assume he jumped bail, ran off to go live his sick fantasies.

Douglas kept his head down as if he didn't want to be noticed by the world. It made getting close to him easy. By the time he looked up I was already reaching for him, rope taut between my hands. I saw the wheels spin—he recognized me from somewhere, but could not place where and why the hell did I have that rope?

I slid to the side of him, looped the rope over his head, then moved behind and pulled. The loop made a noose and cut off any screams. I looked up and down the street for any dog walkers or nosy neighbors. Nothing. Then I looked down at Stacy's house where Olive sat playing in the living room. She hadn't taken my advice on curtains.

As I kept up the tension on the rope, I dragged him back down the walk and behind the gate. My mind was a blur of all the horrible crimes this man had committed. Even if he hadn't yet, I was saving the next little kid, and the one after that. I was doing good. The right thing. Justice.

And getting paid for it.

I don't know how much time passed before I snapped out of my own head. My arms burned, my fingers cramped. Sweat rolled down my back and off my forehead. Cicadas sounded their sirens in the trees and I finally let go of the rope. Douglas was dead.

In the trunk with Chuck were four cinder blocks, two lengths of chain, and rubber boots. I was behind the wheel and still sweating like crazy. I'd thought about the Iowa River. It's right there, running through town. But it's too close, and not deep enough.

I had to make the drive to the big boy—the Mississippi. I headed south and then cut east over to Burlington, a river town a bit down on its luck and probably no stranger to things going into the river that people want to get lost. Maybe an old car, empty beer bottles, a broken washing machine, the occasional ex-wife.

I'd called ahead and arranged for a boat. Just a little flat bottom with an Evinrude on the back. I'm not much of a boat guy so I wanted something I could handle.

I couldn't get it until the next day so I parked myself in a motel that had seen its best days last century and tried not to think about the body in my trunk, and my role in how it got there. How I slept that night is beyond me. It became like any other part of a job—you just did what needed doing. Part of me wished I felt worse about killing a man, then I thought about what kind of man I'd killed and it all felt like steps on an assembly line.

Next morning I made my way down to the river. I signed out my boat and then puttered away and around a bend where I'd stashed my car up the bank a ways. I slid on the boots and slogged through the mud to bring the body, which I'd wrapped in the plastic lining the trunk.

I managed to get Chuck loaded without capsizing, chained him up with the cinder blocks and away I went. I dumped him closer to the Illinois side just because I didn't want a man like that at rest on Iowa ground.

And like that it was done. Well, there was one unfortunate part. I knew the cinder blocks would hold him down, but to make extra sure, I had to avoid the intestinal gasses that cause a body to bloat and rise to the surface. So I got him all set to dump, slid one block into the water which made me lean perilously to one side. I thought sure as anything I'd start taking on water and sink, which would be hard to explain to the rescue boat or the rental place. But once I got him all set for the final push, I drew a knife I'd brought along and I used the momentum from his slide over the edge to hold the knife against his belly and let it slide a wide gash through his middle. By doing this, the gasses wouldn't have any place to get trapped and he wouldn't bloat up like a rubber ball. Plus, the fish would get at him sooner and start feeding, which was a bonus.

I took on a fair amount of water in my little boat, but I bailed out pretty easily after that and I stayed out for three hours just riding up and down so it wouldn't seem weird to the rental place that I took a boat out for a fifteen minute ride.

The Mississippi is actually really beautiful around there if it weren't for the damn bugs everywhere.

When I got back to my car I kicked off my muddy boots and sat on the bumper, thinking how my money problem had gotten a reprieve and also how I could very well have just started a lucrative new business.

My phone rang. It was Stacy.

"I got him." Her words were flat, like she was calling me from her sleep.

"What? Who?"

"He grabbed Olive. He...he took her into his house. So I..."

Impossible. "Stacy, slow down. What happened?"

"I took your advice. I got a gun. He came for her so I...I killed him."

I didn't understand. Douglas was at the bottom of the river.

"You killed who?"

"Him. Douglas."

"Stay where you are. I'll be there soon. Is Olive okay?"

"Yes. I got him before he could..." I could hear tears, but I knew her well enough now to know they were falling down stoic cheeks.

"Hang tight. I'll be there."

My mind reeled, spinning more out of control than when I had a rope around his neck. I'd taken care of Chuck Douglas already. I started thinking maybe Stacy was the crazy one. Maybe she'd made it all up.

When I got to Raven Street I had my answer.

Stacy had Olive down for a nap. She answered the door looking shell-shocked. I'm sure I looked the same to her.

"Is he here?"

She shook her head. "His place."

"Stay here."

I went next door. A man lay on his back in the middle of the room filled with video equipment. He was naked to the waist and three bright red spots clustered around his heart, weeping blood. The skin around them was swollen and the blood pooled beneath him had started to harden.

The man looked familiar. Same basic face, but with a scraggly beard. Tattoos spotted his chest and arms, all in basic blue ink, mostly smeared and blurry on the edges. So she'd shot someone, but who? I put my detective skills to the test like they'd never been in my six years of anemic practice.

Back at Stacy's I got online and did some more research. What I learned I took back to his house and did a little more recon than I was able to do from his front doorstep during my solar panel ruse.

In less than a half hour I had it figured. I also figured that I was a shit detective, or I'd have known it from the start.

Chuck Douglas had a brother. He'd been released to big bro Thomas' recognizance after he left prison. Thomas was there to babysit, to make sure Chuck didn't get into any more trouble. It was a deal struck during his parole hearing. That explained why he answered to Mr. Douglas when I showed up at his front door. I hadn't thought to ask which Mr. Douglas.

Thomas was the one I'd met. And the one I'd killed.

I got sick in the bathroom off the hall, wiped it down as best I could, and went back to Stacy's to explain. When I saw her, I decided she didn't need to know. All she needed was the assurance that I'd take care of it.

I'd be making another trip to the river.

She offered to pay me more for disposing of the real Chuck's body, but I turned her down. It didn't matter. This was my last job. And any brief fantasies of starting a murder-for-hire business were gone now.

Maybe I'd invest in a little cinder block and boat rental business. Business seemed to be booming.

Featuring Martin and Lewis
O'Neil De Noux
New Orleans, Louisiana

Eastern Airlines Flight 55, nonstop from New York to New Orleans, finally arrived, the silver DC-4 landing smoothly on the wet airfield, its wheels spraying water in the air. It was a pretty plane, much prettier than the Dakotas—military version of the twin-engine DC-3 that ferried my Ranger battalion to North Africa, Sicily and Italy during the war. The new DC-4 was longer, wider, a dark blue stripe on its silver fuselage just beneath the name of the airline and Eastern's logo—red eagle on a two-tone blue background.

The plane was two hours late arriving and the people waiting with me put out their annoying cigarettes, smiled now, let out audible sighs of relief. About fifty people lined the low fence between the terminal and runway. Most were moving back into the terminal now that the plane had landed.

A prim man in a light blue suit and wearing old-fashioned pince-nez glasses atop his long nose, bumped into me, said, "I wonder what delayed them?"

"Ducks most likely."

"Ducks?"

I handed the man my early edition of the afternoon *New Orleans Item* he'd been eyeing as I read it. Not much happening on Tuesday, March 8, 1949. Biggest news, beyond the communist Chinese spreading out from Peking to conquer the rest of China, was France signing an accord with the emperor of Vietnam in an attempt to hold on to what they once called French Indochina. I was just a private eye, but it didn't take a rocket scientist to realize a corrupt emperor had little chance against the dedicated communists of Ho Chi Minh who had simultaneously fought the Japanese and French during World War II and the Chinese after. It seemed that communists were everywhere nowadays.

A line of passengers came single file off the DC-4, heading for the terminal. I figured I could pick out Miss Jacqueline Balsley, a woman traveling alone from New York. I envisioned a long, cool Manhattan socialite in a slimming skirt-suit and high heels. Most likely black, due to the circumstance. What I got was more like a bobby-soxer. Well, almost. Her pink skirt wasn't exactly a poodle, and no socks, although she wore flat shoes and a light-weight short-sleeved sweater, a tad too tight.

She also didn't look to be about thirty as described by the Empire Insurance Company investigator who called yesterday. She did have brown hair and eyes and a pretty face, which she turned to me as she arrived at the fence gate and said, "Are you Mr. Cain?"

"Lucien Caye. Miss Balsley?"

She switched her purse to her left arm and stuck out her hand to shake as a loud family of short people babbling in a foreign language nudged past her, shoving her into me. I grabbed her elbows and pulled her aside.

"They jabbered all the way in the plane," snapped Jacqueline Balsley. "Spanish."

"Portuguese." I let go of the lady's elbows. She was tall, only a few inches shorter than my six feet, my hair a darker shade of brown. An old girlfriend once described my eyes as Mediterranean brown. Jacqueline's were lighter and her complexion much fairer. Her curly hair was cut in the new short style which outlined her round face. Jacqueline had a small mouth and pouty lips that made her look even younger.

"I'm sorry for your loss, Miss Balsley."

She took in a deep breath, said, "I haven't seen my father in eleven years. Let's get this over with."

We went into the terminal for her baggage and I carried her suitcases out to my pre-war, gray DeSoto. I'd washed it that morning and dripped a few drops of Purleen on the rear floorboard so the scent of the pine forest permeated the old upholstery.

"What's the smell?" Jacqueline said immediately and looked into the back seat.

"Ran over a pine tree on the way over."

She gave me the look I usually got from women who didn't think I was funny. She put on a pair of dark sunglasses, rolled down her window as I put on my own sunglasses and pulled away from Moisant Field. It was easy cruising down Airline Highway with little traffic, through Jefferson Parish toward the city. We flew past an occasional café and I wished I'd eaten lunch. Lots of open flatland here, marshy land with few trees. As we neared the city limits, we passed a series of small motor hotels with creative names: Come Inn, Shangri La-La Motel and the brazen No Tell Motel.

"You'd think they'd have a better line of places for people coming in from the airport," Jacqueline said, looking out at a filthy Gulf Oil station.

"First time in New Orleans?"

"First time below the Mason-Dixon Line. And you don't sound Southern."

"This isn't Atlanta. I sound like I'm from Brooklyn, right?"

Jacqueline tapped her glasses down, gleeked me over the top and nodded slowly. A spotted dog tried to follow the DeSoto, barking madly as it realized the car was already past.

"Any more articles in the paper about my father?" She crossed her legs, turned her knees toward me, and leaned against the door.

I shook my head, eased on the brake. Hell, I hadn't seen the original article, if there was one. We were at the parish line now. Black families on porches of unpainted shotgun houses watched us as we waited for the light to change.

"The insurance investigator showed me one from your *New Orleans Eagle* that called my father a mad scientist. He wasn't a scientist, more a chemist, although he was a little off his rocker."

The motor hotels in the city along Tulane Avenue were a little nicer, less trash in the parking lots, cats instead of dogs. The Orleans Parish Coroner's Office, along the White Street side of the hulking brown-gray concrete Criminal Courts Building at Tulane and Broad, was familiar to me. Too familiar. The morgue was in the street-level entrance of the building, almost a basement but there were no basements in a city below sea level.

Jack Concannon, who'd worked the Third Precinct with me before the war, was now the chief investigator for the coroner and was expecting me. He checked out Miss Jacqueline Balsley's sweater as she slipped her sunglasses back in her purse. He nodded approval to me as she moved past and he took us through the unpleasant formaldehyde scent to the refrigerators.

The body wasn't as mangled as I expected from a man who died in a lab explosion, at least his head and shoulders weren't torn up. Clyde Balsley was a pasty-faced white male, about sixty, thin with a receding hairline. Jacqueline let out a mousey squeak, then moved around the drawer and took a good, long look at the dead man. She nodded and there were papers to fill out in a small air-conditioned office upstairs.

We had to wait a few extra minutes for the ancient secretary to fill in the name on the death certificate. I bought two copies, one for the daughter, one for the insurance company. Concannon slipped me a copy of the autopsy report and when I shook his hand on the way out, I passed my old buddy a sawbuck for the quick work.

Jacqueline stopped outside the building, turned her face to

the sun falling in the western sky and let the orange light warm her face.

"He came down here on a business trip when I was in college. An eighteen-year-old freshman at NYU. He met a woman and never came back. My mother never recovered although she pretended. She was always looking over her shoulder, hoping he'd be there, that he'd come to his senses."

Jacqueline walked down to the DeSoto and I unlocked the door for her. Eleven years ago she was eighteen, which made her twenty-nine. A young looking twenty-nine. I still had a couple of years on her.

"On her deathbed, she thought he was in the room."

When I climbed behind the wheel, I asked if she was hungry.

"No. Just take me to the hotel."

I parked on Baronne Street, a half block up from the Roosevelt Hotel, carried her suitcases to the door where a bellhop with gray hair and dark brown skin with a name plate that read "Alfred" took it from me. One of the city's best, the Roosevelt stood twelve stories and had about four hundred rooms and luxury suites, the cozy Sazerac Bar and the Blue Room night club where I'd seen Lena Horn, Louis Armstrong and Frank Sinatra.

Jacqueline had a reservation and I tipped the bellhop and started to leave. Don't trust everyone to tip like I do and Alfred thanked me.

"Mr. Caye," she called out before I made a clean getaway. "Were you serious about dinner?"

"The city's got some great restaurants."

Looked like she was about to say yes, at least her eyes were saying yes, but she said no.

"I'll just get room service." She turned to follow Alfred, looked over her shoulder and said, "See you in the morning."

"Nine o'clock. Right here." I pointed to the floor.

Which was exactly where I stood the following morning in

my black suit, gray tie, two-tone black-and-white Florsheims when she came into the lobby. If it wasn't for her hair, still curly and short, I would not have recognized her.

Holy moly. Who taught her how to apply makeup overnight? Those crimson lips stood out all the way from the elevator as she came my way. She wore a sleek black dress that caressed her body, showing she had a figure, long and lithe. When she arrived she was eye-level with me now in those high heels. Did I mention the way she walked? It was more of a glide with those hips rolling but not shaking.

"Right on time," she said and moved around me and I followed her into the morning sunshine. Didn't catch her perfume until we were in the confines of the car, light but not familiar. Enough to catch my attention and not make me sneeze. She sat with her legs crossed and looked out the side window occasionally. She put her sunglasses on first. I followed.

I found a spot on Esplanade a half block up from the cemetery and led the way through the black, wrought-iron gates of Saint Louis No. 3, and watched Jacqueline's head move from side to side until she had to take off the sunglasses to get a clearer view of the above ground cemetery—the marble crypts and cement sepulchres, the brick mausoleums, the most elaborate marble and concrete angels adorning many of the tombs here.

"Are all the cemeteries this elaborate?"

"This is the newest of the Saint Louis Cemeteries, dating from the mid-nineteenth century and all are pretty elaborate. The Metairie Cemetery is the biggest, used to be a race track." I led her down the central grassy lane. A squirrel raced past us for one of the oaks on the other side of the cemetery. "This one was the burial site for yellow fever victims. Mostly Irish. That Storyville photographer Bellocq is buried here."

I saw she had no clue, so I told her about the man who took hundreds of pictures of the brothels of Storyville at the turn of the century. Mostly half-naked or nude daughters of joy. Not a bad gig.

"Daughters of joy?"

"Victorians thought prostitutes were nymphomaniacs."

I spied the hearse and a group of people in black to the right. Clyde Balsley's tomb—bottom left slot in a wall of oven tombs sandwiched between a group of crypt of Sisters of the Sacred Heart and another of Franciscan priests. Empire Insurance Company even provided the tombstone that would seal the tomb after the casket was slid inside.

Eleven people were there before we stepped up, including a minister who said a few prayers. I have no idea which denomination he was because I was raised Catholic and all Protestants were the same—purgatory bound. When the minister, a small, balding man, mentioned the kind people of Boreas Chemicals, I realized that's where these people came from. Six men and four women, all looking a little bored, except for the two hawking out Jacqueline. One in a light gray suit looked familiar.

The eldest man, a tall dead-ringer for John Carradine, waited until the service was over to come and talk with Jacqueline. I gave them room, stepping to another crypt. Their conversation wasn't secretive as the manager of the chemical company spoke so loudly all around could hear him praise Clyde Balsley as a dedicated chemist who worked long hours. The long hours got him killed when he managed to blow himself up at three a.m.

The familiar looking guy moved around to get a better view of Jacqueline and spotted me watching and looked away quickly. Where have I seen him before? He turned away and stepped around a brick sepulchre only to find me on the other side.

He was maybe an inch shorter than me, thinner, which was hard to be. His deep-set eyes blinked at me and he tried to smile, only his tiny mouth seemed lost in the wrinkles. His black hair made him look younger than he was up close.

"Hello," he said. "You must be a detective by now."

If I learned one thing as a PI, it was to keep my mouth shut when someone else was volunteering information.

"You remember me," he said. Is this a question or a statement?

I just stared into his shifty eyes.

"Elvin Cini," he volunteered. "You busted me back in forty-one, Officer Caye. Just before the Japs bombed Pearl Harbor. I was the one you caught with the gold watches from Bergeron's Jewelers."

It came back to me in flashes—a dark night, prowl cars zooming to Canal Street while my partner George Crane figured we'd stay in our beat and watch and sure enough we spied this moron cutting across Decatur Street in front of a bus that almost flattened him. He had a bag in his hand and ducked away from us behind the French Market. Crane dropped me off at one end and took our prowl car to the other and we walked the backside of the market until Elvin Cini spotted Crane and turned to run past me and ran into my redwood nightstick instead. The bag had twenty-something gold watches and bracelets.

"I still have a knot on my knee." Cini rubbed his right knee. He leaned closer, looking to make sure we weren't overheard. "Spent five years in Angola, but I'm good now. I hope you won't tip the stiffs about me. I've been working there a year. I'm good now."

I've said it before. New Orleans was nothing but a big, small town. There were few strangers here. Well, the man paid his debt to society. Who was I to ruin his new life?

I passed him my card. "I'm a private detective now."

He let out a low whistle. "Just like Sam Spade. Philip Marlowe."

I nodded. "Just like them." Some people watched too many movies.

His eyes lit up as Jacqueline came around the tomb behind me and put her sunglasses back on. We went to get her suitcases at the Roosevelt on our way to Moisant. I waited in the lobby, watched two men assemble a marquee for a coming attraction at the Blue Room. The picture on the marquee featured two guys, one with black curly hair, the other with a crew cut and a goofy smile on his face.

"The Blue Room Proudly Welcomes the Toast of New York—Martin and Lewis."

Dean Martin and Jerry Lewis. I'd heard of them, think I caught a snippet of them on the radio. Comedy team.

Jacqueline came out of the elevator followed by Alfred the bellhop. Her sunglasses still on, she breezed up, put a hand on my shoulder, leaned over and fidgeted with one of her high heels. Her perfume was nicer up close. She stood up, tapped down her glasses and gleeked the marquee poster for a moment, let go of my shoulder, and then led the way out.

She gave Alfred a nice tip and he doffed his sky cap, said, "Y'all come back soon."

Jacqueline said nothing all the way to the airport and I let her sit there in her own world. She seemed sadder and I just thought about the report I had to write and send to the insurance company to get my pay for escorting her to provide a positive identification of the body. I'd read the autopsy report overnight.

Cause of death—blunt trauma to chest and abdomen.

Manner of death—accidental.

One interesting note—cirrhosis of the liver. Heavy drinker.

Tomorrow I'd get a copy of the police report. It would tell me more about how the body was found. I liked getting extra for my clients.

She said nothing until we were at the gate, just before she boarded the plane. She took off her sunglasses, tucked them into her purse and turned those light brown eyes to me. Her lipstick looked just as bright, just as glistening, just as red.

The boarding started.

"My father's going to miss their movie."

"Movie?"

"Martin and Lewis. Their first movie, *My Friend Irma*, is playing in New York. Daddy really liked those two." She leaned forward, her eyes looking at my lips now as she licked hers then she kissed me and I kissed her back. When I felt her tongue, I French kissed her and felt electricity surging through my body. She pulled away, licked her lips again and gave my lips a peck. Jacqueline turned and walked out to board the plane and didn't look back.

It hit me when I was half-way home—"Daddy really liked those two." If her father ran off eleven years ago, how'd she know that? Martin and Lewis started up after the war. Mysteries like that bother me.

Maybe they'd spoken over the phone, I told myself. Maybe he visited New York because this was the first time she'd been south of the Mason-Dixon line. It bugged me. By the time I pulled my DeSoto in front of my building and the rain had started, I realized it didn't matter about Daddy liking Martin and Lewis. If the death was accidental nothing else mattered.

But it still bugged me.

The next afternoon I had insurance investigator Lucius Trebblehorn on the phone, explained to him the police and fire department arson investigators agreed. The explosion was not suspicious. Fumes from two experiments mixed and boom.

"The report does not actually say 'boom,' does it?" Trebblehorn had a Midwest accent.

"It says 'bang' actually."

"If you could be so kind as to include a copy of everything with your report, especially the death certificate, then I will send you a check right away."

"Who is the beneficiary?" I asked, as if I didn't know.

"Jacqueline Ellen Balsley of Brooklyn." He sounded as if

196

he was shuffling papers. "She gets fifty thousand dollars. Her father took out the policy twenty years ago, twenty-five thousand dollar double indemnity if he dies accidentally. Usually means car wreck. Not industrial accidents, but that counts. I told you she was a pretty girl."

"That you did."

I told him it was nice doing business with him, hung up and turned back to my typewriter to get this over with.

By May first the Yankees were 10-2 and in first place in the American League again. Far from the aberration of 1948's third place finish. The newspaper headline told me a scientist discovered a second moon around Neptune. Same guy discovered one of the moons of Uranus as well. Interesting work, I supposed.

Later that day—at noon, just as the church bell of Immaculate Conception Church on Baronne Street chimed, I started to cross Canal Street when Jacqueline Ellen Balsley stepped off the Cemeteries Streetcar. She spotted me immediately and her face became cartoonish—eyes bulged, mouth circling into a big O, before she turned and slipped into the crowd and hurried off. Going to church? It is Sunday.

Wherever she was headed in a red satin dress and high heels on a Sunday she was in a hurry. I thought about shadowing her, but didn't want to stand up my lunch date with Bethany Adams, my contact at the DA's office. A PI's gotta keep up his contacts. I kept my lunch date with Bethany, bought her a nice meal, listened to her for an hour, my mind wandering back to Jacqueline stepping off the streetcar, seeing me and scampering. My mind continued to wander and woke me early the next morning. Why? I wasn't sure. It's a free country and she can go anywhere she wanted. But why was she here? Early in my career I learned there's no such thing as the perfect case. Not that this was much of a case. Since I was pretty much between gigs with a nice bottom line on my bank account I figured—first thing—locate Jacqueline. She had to be staying somewhere.

The following morning paper had a story about Israel preparing to celebrate its first anniversary tomorrow—a lot of people didn't think they'd make it. I wasn't one of them. Two of my Ranger buddies were over there, helping with the Israeli army. One wrote to me these were tough, determined bastards, like we were when we trained with British Commandos at Carrikfergus, Northern Ireland, then Scotland. Of the five hundred who volunteered for the 1st Ranger Battalion, only eighty-seven of us survived the war. Goddamn Nazis.

My building door closed and a shadow moved outside the smoky glass door of my office here on the first floor of 909 Barracks Street, in the lower French Quarter where the rents were low and people yelled at each other a lot. Ever see *A Streetcar Named Desire*? Stanley Kowalski screaming, "Stella!" That was a few blocks from here. My friend Tennessee Williams told me that.

My door opened and I pulled my feet off my oversized desk, folded the paper. Elvin Cini stepped in wearing the same gray suit he'd worn at the funeral back in March, looked around the room, decided it was safe and closed the door behind him. He held a fedora in his hands, his beady eyes locking on to mine as he crossed the big room. My office once housed an entire upholstery shop before my landlord tore the walls down.

He arrived at my desk, looked at the two chairs in front and chose the one on the right, which most people tend to do. Haven't figured out why yet. I leaned back in my captain's chair as he cautiously put his hat on his knee.

"I need your help, Detective Caye." He had the business card I gave him back in the cemetery in hand. He looked freshly shaved, his hair cut in a fresh crew cut.

"Go ahead."

He turned to the row of windows along the Barracks Street side of my office.

"I need you to tell the police something for me."

I tried not to laugh.

"Go on."

He leaned forward, placed a bill and my card on the edge of the desk. "Tell them I didn't take any of the money."

I waited.

"It was all Clyde Balsley's idea. All I did was find a lookalike." Cini looked around again, as if someone was about to pop out of the kitchen on the side of my office, or maybe one of the closets.

"Wasn't hard. Found a skid row bum who looked like Clyde. Pumped him with booze, delivered him to Clyde and got out before the evil deed."

I nodded, took the Parker T-ball Jotter from my pocket, clicked it, opened my note pad, asked, "How much money he promised you?"

"A grand. He keeps putting me off. I'm leaving town. Forever. I was gonna send you a letter, but I want you to take this." Cini stood up, lifted the bill, showed me it was a fifty. He laid it on the desk and started backing away. When he was close enough to the door to figure I couldn't come around and catch him in time, he smiled. It wasn't pleasant.

"I can't get in trouble if I didn't get any of the insurance money, can I?"

"Why don't I pick up the phone and ask the police?"

He pointed to the bill on the desk. "You can't. Client's confidentiality. I just hired you." He opened the door.

"You watch too many Perry Mason movies." I reached for the phone and he bolted. I went to the windows to see what he drove off in, but he must have run down Barracks or around the corner. I was in no mood to chase him. Hell, I didn't have to prove Clyde Balsley blew up a bum. I just had to prove the son-of-a-bitch was still alive. Why else would

Jacqueline Ellen Balsley be in town?

I went back to my phone and called Lucius Trebblehorn of Empire Insurance Agency, who dropped his receiver when I told him what just happened. He snapped up the receiver and said, "You shittin' me?"

"No, sir."

"Damn. Too late to stop the check to the beneficiary." I heard papers shuffling.

"You want me to see if I can locate Clyde Balsley?"

"You think he's still in New Orleans?"

"His daughter is."

"Son-of-a-bitch! You're damn right I want you to find Balsley. I'll wire another retainer to your bank right away."

I slipped the fifty into an envelope and slipped it into a paperback located on the large bookshelf behind my desk. Not just any paperback, but Mickey Spillane's *I, the Jury*. Hey, why don't people think I'm like Mike Hammer? I've shot people.

Clyde Balsley's last known address was listed on the autopsy report. Concannon must have got the signed driver's license he'd returned to Jacqueline, along with other personal effects of her father. Clyde lived on the left side of a pale yellow shotgun double at the corner of Annunciation and Philip Street. His landlady lived on the right side of the double.

"I'm Malva Huddleston," she said, looking at my business card she held in her left hand as she lifted her glasses out of the way. She could have been five feet tall if she wore heels, which she did not. Her dark dress nearly reached to the floor, so did the white apron. She pulled up those cat-eye glasses and touched her steel gray hair as if primping, although her face remained unsmiling.

"I'm working for the insurance company," I began. "How long did Mr. Balsley live here?"

"You got a warrant?"

I glanced over my shoulder in case a prowl car had slipped up and a host of cops were there.

"No, ma'am. I'm not here to search anything or arrest anyone. I'm a private detective."

She closed and latched the screen door.

"Did you know Mr. Balsley well?"

"I don't like cops." She looked at my card again. "You're a PI. Like Philip Marlowe?"

"Do you like Philip Marlowe?"

"No. I don't like Humphrey Bogart."

First person I'd ever met who didn't like Bogie.

"Well, I'm not like Philip Marlowe." I tried my best smile. "I'm better. What did you do with Mr. Balsley's belongings?"

That lit a fire in her dark eyes. "I didn't take a damn thing. His daughter came and took it all."

"Daughter?"

She started to close the door. "Go away or I'll call the cops."

"I thought you didn't like cops."

She shut the door on me. I tried the neighbors. Only one remembered Balsley, an even older lady across the street.

"He's been living there since before the war," she said. "Didn't have a car. Took the streetcar."

"Did he have any friends?"

"No, Officer. I don't associate with Protestants." She closed the door on me as well.

I found a couple of boys tossing a football in the street and they told me Balsley was an okay guy, never yelled at them for anything like the grouchy old ladies, not even when they unscrewed the fuses on the back of the yellow double on last New Year's just as the fireworks stared up down the street. The old lady threw a tantrum, but Balsley figured them out and just laughed.

"Did he have any friends, companions, women?"

"Pretty lady came by for his stuff," one of the boys said. "She was in a K&B purple car."

No other friends they saw ever came by. I gave them each a quarter. Big money for nine year olds.

Next stop—red beans and rice and a beaded pork chop at Laiche's. I made a mental list as I got into the DeSoto, call my contacts at the power company, telephone company, gas company. I wanted to find the bastard before I had to call my buddy Lieutenant Capdeville. I preferred handing him a case *fait-accompli* before he started telling me I wasn't a real detective after all.

A week after Jacqueline Balsley stepped off that streetcar I had nothing. I had one more long shot to play. Stake out the streetcar at the same time today, in case it was a routine. She may have something to do every Sunday around noon. Who the hell knew?

According to the morning *New Orleans Eagle*, Sunday, May eighth, the Soviets agreed to lift the Berlin blockade while sixty-two thousand workers at Ford were still on strike in Detroit. My Yankees were playing the Tigers in Detroit today after beating the White Sox 8-1 yesterday. Casey Stengel had the Yanks 14-4 and cruising along.

I spotted something more interesting in the entertainment section. Martin and Lewis in a one-night show at eight p.m. tonight at the Blue Room. How had Jacqueline put it? "Daddy really liked those two." Okay, if she didn't get off the streetcar today, I had one more long shot. A real long shot.

At eleven-thirty a.m., I positioned myself at the corner of Baronne and Canal Street to watch for the Canal-Cemeteries streetcar. She'd gotten off it at noon a week ago and it could have been a routine. It wasn't. I waited until almost one-thirty and thought as I walked away, if Clyde Balsley didn't come to see Martin and Lewis, I had no choice but to go to the police.

There was no way I could wait in the lobby of the Roosevelt and watch everyone go in without being spotted and I didn't want to get a table because the place was too big, about fifty tables. Then I remembered Alfred, the bellhop. I found him easily and he took me to the lighting director's booth above the stage where I could look out the one-way mirrors at the audience below as they arrived. I brought my small binoculars, opera glasses, and watched the people come in. I slipped Alfred a ten as well as Mr. Jefferson, the lighting director. Insurance company expense money, which paid off immediately as I spotted Jacqueline Balsley come in with an older couple—a tall, thin, man with a receding hairline and a moustache and wearing a blue suit and glasses, along with a tall woman in a black evening gown with sequins. Her light brown hair, streaked with gray, was worn up on her head, along with a thin tiara with plenty gemstones. Is that a black pearl necklace? She wore bracelets on each wrist, one could have been diamonds, the green stones on the other could have been emeralds. Whoever she was, she wasn't at the funeral.

Jacqueline wore a fitted-blue dress and looked pretty damn good up close. She had a wandering eye tonight, watching the men looking at her. The man pulled the chair out for the older woman and she pecked him on the cheek. So now I knew why Clyde Balsley hadn't blown town. Did he really think a moustache and glasses were a good enough disguise? Maybe in a big berg like New York City.

The lights drew down as the orchestra played soft music and the talking subsided. I watched my prey as they settled in their seats. Below me, Dean Martin came on stage with no introduction, moved to the lone microphone as people started clapping. Tall, dark and handsome, this Italian crooner's hair was jet black and curly and he waited for the applause to wane. He looked backstage and shrugged.

Dean announced, "A great writer, O. Henry, who lived here in New Orleans for a while once said there are only two

romantic cities in America. San Francisco and New Orleans."
He looked backstage again.

"This song is for New Orleans." Dean started *That's Amore*. Finished the first stanza when a loud shout from the back of the room stopped him and a spotlight hit a man in a waiter's white jacket. I recognized the crew cut immediately. Jerry Lewis ran into the room, bumping into people and tables, going "Uuuaaaauaaaa!"

The band stopped and laughter echoed as Jerry Lewis plodded his way toward the stage, knocking people's drinks over, pulling a woman out of her chair to dance with her, twirling her around and letting her go before he continued bumbling along. I headed out. Played another hunch, going outside to find the K&B purple car. Didn't want to get caught up with the show. Heard they were a riot and I didn't need the distraction. Found the car parked down Baronne Street. Katz and Besthoff Drug Stores, K&B, used a distinctive shade of purple, a sort of lavender, in their logo and on the cartons of their ice cream. It looked odd on a 1949 Packard, Super-8 four-door sedan. I copied down the license plate before moving my DeSoto around to Common Street to cover the Packard if it went down Baronne or turned up Common. Both were one-way streets.

Most of the time, following someone along the streets of New Orleans was like trying to follow an ant after you step on its anthill. Don't go when the light turns green because some smart ass is about to run the red light since it was yellow a second ago, and stop signs were just a suggestion. Yield? Who the hell yields in New Orleans?

A private eye following a car who lets a car get between them so his car isn't in the rearview mirror all the time, invariably gets behind a plow-jockey from Georgia or a Kansas mule-skinner who "ain't never seen one of dem iron balconies" before and sure enough—"Slow down, Jethro, that gal over on Bourbon Street is 'bout to show her titties."

The Packard was incredibly easy to follow because the older woman drove it carefully, like a good driver should. She ran no red lights or stop signs and didn't go over thirty all the way to a three-story white house on City Park Avenue between Saint Ann and Dumaine Street. She parked in the driveway and all three went inside. The lights went out at eleven-thirty-five.

The next morning at ten-thirty-five, I picked up my phone to call Lieutenant Frenchy Capdeville after I discovered the electricity at the house on City Park Avenue was listed to Dorothy Katz, as was the '49 Packard. Before I was half-way through dialing the number my office door opened and Jacqueline Balsley glided in.

She wore a tight, white blouse, her skirt blood-red with a slit that went half way up her right thigh, all the way to the top of her stocking and white, garter-belt fastener. Black high heels gave her legs that sleek look and a black beret topped off the outfit. Her lips glistened crimson. She stood just inside the doorway, small purse dangling from her left shoulder, hand on her right hip as she stared at me.

"They're filming a French movie down the street?" I asked.

"Has my father been here?"

"Isn't he in Saint Louis Cemetery?"

She started across the room, moving slowly, purposefully, eyes still locked on mine.

"We spotted you following us last night," she said.

Damn.

"He has binoculars and watched you from the house." She arrived at my desk and sat in the chair on the right.

"He has a gun," she added as she sat and crossed her legs, the skirt opening to show nearly all of her right leg.

"I have a gun, too. And shooting me won't solve your problem. Why are y'all still here?"

"The widow Katz. She keeps telling Daddy no one born in New Orleans ever leaves—willingly."

"When did he find her? That's not the woman he left your mother for, is it?"

"No, they just met."

"So he grows a moustache and starts wearing glasses?"

Are those tears in her eyes?

"The widow is filthy rich. Daddy wants to make a deal. Give the money back to the insurance company."

I shrugged. "Empire might go for that but murder usually isn't for sale."

"Murder?"

"Yeah. Remember the dead guy we slid into the tomb?"

I reached for the phone and she let out a mousey squeak.

"You're going to turn us in?"

"Why wouldn't I?"

Her lower lip quivered. "I thought we had something special."

It was my time to look around, in case someone I didn't know had come into the room.

"Jacqueline, you're not making sense."

"But. But. We kissed." Her eyes didn't look a bit crazy. She should meet my friend Tennessee. He loves a good actress.

"I kiss a lot of women. Even some thieves, like you."

"But. But. Our tongues touched."

Lord, help me. I picked up the receiver and started dialing.

She stood and I didn't miss her uncrossing those legs. That's when I spied the gun in her hand. Looked like a .32 caliber, maybe a .25. Little nickel-plated semi-automatic. She started backing out of the room. I sat very still.

"If you follow me, I swear I'll shoot you."

"Okay. I won't follow you." I hung up the receiver and eased my chair back in case I had to duck. I didn't have to. She hustled out the door and I sat there for a moment. This was almost like *The Maltese Falcon*, except Jacqueline Balsley wasn't actually a femme fatale and I wouldn't be able to turn her over to the cops personally. I picked up the phone.

Frenchy Capdeville always answered his phone with one word, "Talk."

"Dorothy Katz," I said. "She related to the Katz and Besthoff Drug Store people?"

"How the hell do I know, Pretty Baby?" I heard him take a drag of his ever-present cigarette. If Frenchy liked you—he called you Pretty Baby. If he didn't—you were a Sack-a-Roaches. Since I was his protégé, more or less, he gave me a break.

"I think I solved another murder for you."

I held the receiver away from my ear as he went through his usual litany of curse words before he caught his breath, then said, "All right. Who the hell got murdered?"

"I don't know exactly, but I know where he's buried and who killed him."

"Okay. Talk."

A Necessary Ingredient
Art Taylor
North Carolina

I am not a detective—not a real one, as you'll see—and I didn't set out to write a detective story here.

But sometimes you end up in a place you didn't intend to go. Sometimes what you discover is different from what you expected to find.

For the past few years, I've rented a second-floor office in a downtown desperately committed to revitalizing itself. My office is upstairs from an ice cream parlor that's been around for decades. Next door stands an old movie theater rehabbed for party rental but rarely rented. Down the block are a pair of consignment shops trying to look like antique stores, a barber shop with an old-school rotating pole, and a tea shoppe that opened two years ago—the latter with two p's on the sign but never much business inside. Re-gentrification even at a loss is the case with a lot of small eastern North Carolina towns, I imagine.

From my vantage point, the glass on my door reads:

Ambrose Thornton
Private Detective

Outside that door, a wood box holds business cards—and brochures listing the kinds of cases I won't accept. No matrimonial work, for example, and nothing involving child custody. No skip tracing or bail bonds work. No insurance fraud. No corporate espionage. Nothing involving labor relations. Nothing that requires me to spend my days at the mall searching for shoplifters.

In fact, with so many things ruled out, not much is left I will handle, and that's by design. Maybe if a murder investigation comes along...but the chances there are slim, and the correspondence course I took to get my license hardly equipped me to investigate crimes like that.

The bad news is that I make no money. The good news: it doesn't matter. I rent the office solely to get my father off my back.

"It's important for a man to have a job, a purpose," he told me more than once in the years after I graduated college. "A reason to get up in the morning and put in an honest day's work and then bring home a paycheck to show for it."

By that point, my father himself had transcended the business of business and simply reaped the profits, his own desk cleared of everything but the morning paper and an afternoon cocktail, and the money flowing his way while other people's desks grew cluttered and burdened.

He liked to see other people busy—and other people specifically included me.

But my father's success had become my lifestyle. Trust fund baby, thanks to his industriousness and my mother's finagling—my late mother. Gentleman's Cs through high school and college—undoubtedly helped along by donations to school coffers. Too many of those bright college years still a haze of bourbon and pot and afternoons spent reading piles of pulp fiction while the business and economic textbooks slid further and further to the side—while the nagging and indignation grew and then grew exponentially the older I got.

"Son," he'd said one day, snapping his suspenders like the punctuation to a pronouncement, "you need to find something you love to do and do it."

The thing I could've asked: What if my passion might not bring home a paycheck?

Today, even with the rent on my workspace, there's still enough stipend left to keep filling the bookshelves lining two walls of that office—classic detective stories, pulp crime novels, some of them collector's editions. I spend my days reading and rereading them, watching the sunlight travel from one side of the office to the other, watching a door that stays mostly closed. But it's a door at least, an office, a business, and isn't that what my father wanted?

My first case arrived late summer a year or so after I'd opened shop. Despite the windows shut tight against the mounting heat, the sounds outside still seeped through: children playing in the greenway that runs through the center of downtown (in off-sync stereo with the squeals from the ice cream parlor downstairs), the occasional toot of a horn at the intersection, lately an occasional helicopter passing overhead. Military maneuvers, the paper had said. The sunlight had travelled halfway across the floor and then begun to fade. The radio droned softly, election updates again—the governorship teetering over business interests and concerns about the economy, the incumbent embattled, the challenger an up-and-comer with rising poll numbers. My father talked heatedly about withholding his own endorsement until he saw which way the wind blew, but I'd tuned him out and tuned out the newscast then—focused instead on my eighth or ninth reading of *Trouble Is My Business.*

That's when my own trouble walked in.

That line sounds like your traditional hard-boiled story, I know, but she wasn't tall and leggy with flowing blonde locks and an overabundance of cleavage nicely framed for my viewing pleasure. She was short and trim with a boyish haircut. She wore an off-white oxford and scuffed jeans. And instead of some swirl of perfume, she smelled like garlic.

"I'm Esmé," she said, offering me her hand. She had a firm grip, confident instead of dainty, but her nails were bitten to the quick. In addition to garlic, there was cumin too, and maybe cinnamon, and I don't know what else.

"Esmé," I repeated. "Like the new restaurant down the street?"

"We're one and the same."

Esmé's Bistro had opened up two months before, and I'd caught whiffs of those same scents in the air walking back and forth to my car.

"Have you been in?" she asked, taking her seat as I moved to my side of the desk.

"Not yet."

"And there's part of my problem."

"Business troubles?"

"Sort of." She nibbled lightly at her lower lip. It wasn't unattractive.

I was already placing bets about it. Someone on the wait-staff mishandling the tips or culling credit cards numbers. Something to do with immigration and visas, undocumented workers huddling back in the kitchen. Or maybe there was a customer who'd gotten too friendly. Stalking—another crime I steered clear of, some flipside of matrimonial work. I was already angling for an exit.

"What do you know about...tonkas?" she asked.

There in the pause before the word, she'd looked at me—green eyes intently focused my way, like she was waiting for my reaction, not just watching but watching for something, and she'd needed the pause to prepare for it. Her eyes didn't leave mine, even after I'd shrugged and answered.

"I played with them as a kid. A dump truck, a front-loader, something like that." I took a deep breath. "But I need to tell you upfront: I don't handle child custody cases"—a reminder to myself to revise the brochure outside.

Another pause, more watching, before she shook her head. Her disappointment was palpable.

"I'm not talking about toys," she said. "I'm talking about the tonka bean. It's a spice, a very powerful one." Another glance, another bit of watchfulness.

Again, I could offer nothing but bewilderment.

"I'm not a grocery store either," I said.

"It wouldn't matter if you were." Her eyes finally turned away from me. "The FDA outlawed tonkas back in the fifties. They're considered toxic. The coumarin in them, it can cause liver damage."

"So you're not looking for them," I said. "You're trying to steer clear of them. Poisoning? Someone's slipping these beans into your kitchen?"

"No, no, not at all." She rolled her eyes—the stupidity of it all, that was the message, maybe my own stupidity. "The ban is ridiculous, given how much you'd need to consume to risk any effect. And you only need a little of it to...to open up a dish." She moved forward in the chair, holding her hands out as if she had a bean in her palm. "When you shave the tonka, it releases these...powerful aromas. Vanilla and cherry and a whiff of cinnamon maybe, with a complexity to it all, and the taste carries those same layers and more. Caramel and honey flavors too, and...I don't think I'm doing it justice." She moved her hands to her face. Her cheeks had flushed. "Magic, that's the better word. It's like a drug almost, that smell, that taste. Standing above it as you shave the bean can be intoxi-cating, overpowering. Empowering really."

Vanilla, cinnamon, honey...most of the flavors she men-tioned seemed fairly ordinary. But the way she was saying them and the expression on her face were anything but. She seemed transported herself simply talking about it.

"I'm still not sure what you need me for," I told her.

"My restaurant is new, and I want it to be a success, and more than a success, a..."

When she leaned in, I caught a glimpse of her breasts. I couldn't help it. And thinking about that now, maybe this moment marked another turn toward this becoming a real detective story. "Someone here in the county is growing them," she went on, barely a whisper. "I've heard it—from a reliable source—and I want some for myself. I want in."

From Esmé's description and from some quick work on Google, powering up my laptop while she sat there, I gathered a few quick facts about the tonka. It's grown mostly in Central and South America—Venezuela, Columbia, and Brazil primarily. It looks less like a bean than a long raisin or a thin prune—dried, wrinkly—and the inside has the look and texture of chocolate. Even a shallow cut into the bean would release those aromas she described as intoxicating.

"French chefs have a name for it," Esmé told me. "*La fièvre tonka*. Tonka fever." It sounded like a disease she'd be glad to catch—the breathless way she said the words—and the way she navigated that French accent suddenly left me a little breathless too.

"You're French yourself?" I asked.

She smiled, shrugged. "Somewhere up the family tree maybe."

"And your restaurant. French too?"

Another shrug, but the smile had faded. "Eclectic, let's say. If it's not barbecue in a town like this, does the marketing matter?"

"You're not from here, then?"

"I was a sous chef in Raleigh"—she named a restaurant everyone knows—"then got lured down here to open a place of my own. Inexpensive taxes, the promise of a supportive community. Opportunities—that's what I was told."

Seemed like none of that had panned out.

The FDA had indeed outlawed the bean in 1954, like she

said, and there had been cases where the government had stepped in to enforce the ban—"significant fines, negative attention," Esmé explained. "The kinds of risks any beginning restaurateur would be loath to take."

Despite that ban, I found some for sale online as we sat there.

"Some of those are meant for luck, as talismans," she explained. "Dried and shellacked. You can't cook with them."

I squinted at the screen. "The description here says 'can be used in desserts and stews,'" I said. It also mentioned "used in spells" beneath it, but she didn't let me get that far.

"Most suppliers will refuse to ship to the United States anyway. And if they did ship, chances are it would be tracked."

I clicked the button to place the order anyway.

"Cancel it, please," she said, suddenly jittery.

"Why? Couldn't hurt to see what happens."

"I've talked with you. I can't risk the association here, not officially, not where it can be documented."

"You make it sound like the FDA is watching now."

"You can't know that they're not!" She leaned forward again, her hands clasped like she was begging—her fear as palpable as her desperation before. "You've read how the government tracks our emails. What if the FDA raided me? My business means everything—it's all I've got!"

"Okay, okay," I said, clicking to cancel—but the screen froze. I'd need to handle it later. "You mentioned a reliable source. Someone here in town? So you already have a connection with the grower..."

"That's a dead end for me. The supplier in the case"—she put a stress on the word supplier—"showed me a few beans, but the price for more was too high. I need"—she seemed flustered—"I need someone closer to the source."

If some of her descriptions of the tonka had made it sound like a drug, this last part surely did. I conjured images of dealers on the playground, handing out samples, hooking clientele, driving hard bargains afterwards. Her desperation wasn't quite like an addict's, but it was driven by the same need. I could see it in her eyes—that deep green there, soulful and needy.

"I'll do what I can," I said with more assurance than I felt. Whatever nerves she wrangled with, I caught them too, for my own reasons—the first client I'd ever accepted. "I'll need to get you to, uh, pay a retainer. Then there might be daily expenses. And…" I pretended that it was all routine, but I had no paperwork on hand. I promised to get it to her soon. "The retainer can serve as a contract for now."

She pulled a checkbook from her purse, glanced at the register with hesitation, then wrote out the amount. I'd caught a glimpse of her balance—barely a couple of hundred more than I'd requested. I decided I wouldn't cash the check immediately, maybe not at all.

At the door, she turned again to face me—a similar pose to when she'd walked into the room. I was struck by how my image of her had changed in our short time together. The same off-white oxford, the same jeans, the same boyish hair-cut and sharply bitten nails. But now she seemed cosmopolitan somehow, mysterious, seductive even.

She pointed to my name on the glass. "Thornton," she said. "You're related to Ben Thornton?"

"My father," I said. "You know him?"

"My landlord," she said. "At the restaurant—or rather he's connected somehow to the company I rent from. I didn't know it myself until he became a customer too."

Other people's desks cluttered and burdened, like I said, and the money simply flowing my father's way.

I'm not sure if I can stress enough the point I've made about not actually being a private investigator.

The private detective is a myth—at least how many people picture the job. These days it's mostly background checks of one kind or another or maybe insurance fraud—usually handled in-house by the businesses themselves. On the domestic front, anyone trying to prove a partner's infidelity hardly needs a detective, what with cheap hidden cameras and recording devices or a quick search of a smartphone or a computer's browser history.

I had regularly steered potential clients in those directions, toward online resources or the webpage for Radio Shack or sometimes to local law enforcement. A friend of mine from high school, Randall Norton, was a police officer now, and I often passed along his card. Randy told me I'd have made a killing on commissions if any money had ever changed hands.

But here law enforcement couldn't help, since the tonka was illegal. Passing Esmé along wasn't an option. And I couldn't admit that I'd never taken a case before—couldn't turn her away, could I?

Maybe I simply didn't want to.

After some more research online, I visited several produce stands the next morning. More than one mystery had the solution hidden in plain sight, right?

About a block and a half from my office, a white tent was usually popped up in front of an abandoned gas station. I'd stopped by before.

Weeds broke through the concrete, and table legs leaned into holes, barely balancing baskets of apples and peaches, small containers of figs, several piles of muscadine grapes. Another table was bunched with greens—signs for "Collard" and "Mustard" and "Kale." The nearest things to the tonka's shape were some gray butterbeans.

April, the woman who ran the stand, was cutting peaches into a paper plate labeled "Samples, Take One." I did.

"I've got a recipe that calls for this specific bean, the tonka bean," I told her. "I've tried the grocery store, but you know how that is…"

Play to a source's importance, that was key.

April wiped the knife on her apron.

"You got a new girlfriend?"

"How's that?"

"All you ever buy is salad and fruit." A smirk teased one corner of her mouth. "Who's the lucky girl? Or are you the lucky one?"

"We'll wait and see how the recipe turns out."

"Never heard of tonkas, but we've got plenty of beans." Before I could interrupt her, she was working through the list: those butter beans, limas, green beans, pole beans. "Maybe you could substitute. That's what I always do, but a lot's out of season already."

"No, I really need this one." I pulled out a picture I'd printed from the Internet.

"Looks like a coffee bean almost," she said.

"It's more of a seed really, from what I understand."

She handed me the printout. "I don't do much with seeds, but that big market out on 70 does."

By the time I'd reached that one, the sun had risen high and the heat with it. This structure was elaborate—a wood frame and big plywood signs handwritten in green, orange, and red paint. "Boiled Peanuts" and "Home Made Pies" and "Cantaloupe" and "Watermelon." I'd stopped there before.

"Bean seeds," the farmer running it said with a curt nod, and he walked me toward a carousel of small manila packets, hand-labeled in purple ink: "Blue Lake," "Kentucky Wonder," "State Half Runner," "Yard Long Giant." I peeked into a couple on the off chance that one might hold what I needed.

"It's a specialty seed," I said. "Grown mostly in tropical climates."

217

A helicopter passed overhead, low enough and loud enough that I started to repeat myself, but he'd heard.

"Tropical?" he said. "You think this heat wave is gonna last long enough to grow a tropical plant?" He must have been sweltering in all that denim, but he didn't seem to have broken a sweat.

"Well," I said. "I wasn't really thinking about how to grow it."

"Sunlight," he said. "Heat and lots of it, months of it. And moisture probably, depending."

I stared at several piles of tomatoes on the table beside us. One pile sat under a sign that said "Heirloom." The other said "Hothouse."

"Would a greenhouse do it?"

He sent me to my next stop, a more professional operation with an aluminum sales area fronting a network of long greenhouses. The man who helped me there wore a thin red tie and jeans that looked like they'd been pressed with an iron.

"Tropicals?" he said. "Sure, right this way." A side door led into one of the greenhouses—hotter and muggier than outside. But when we got to our destination, the tables were all flowers: ferns and philodendrons, African violets, bromeliads, orchids, something called a bird of paradise.

"It would be more of a tree than a plant," I told him, looking at my notes. "A cumaru tree, it's called."

"Not one I've heard of," he said. "But if it's a big enough tree, you'd need more height than we have here"—pointing at the glass roof only a few feet above our heads.

All in all, a waste of time—proof maybe that I was better off not taking cases.

I could've picked up the telephone and called Esmé to update her on my progress—lack of progress—but I decided to stop by the restaurant that night instead. I hadn't been in, after all. It might help to get the lay of the land. That's what I told myself.

Business was indeed slow. I bypassed the hostess—a disinterested teen I vaguely recognized, daughter of some somebody in town—and took a stool at the bar that dominated half the restaurant: mirrors and sleek mahogany, the counter itself curved into a loose L-shape, only one couple there, hovering over a half-bottle of wine. The dining area was crisp white tablecloths and tall candles, high-backed chairs, dark plank floors. Three tables had diners, and their voices echoed hollow in the space. A couple of them I recognized, and we exchanged brief waves. Friends of the family, friends of my father—the country club set, their days as idle as mine but dodging the judgment.

An open kitchen stretched two-thirds of the back of the restaurant, Esmé on the other side of a stainless steel counter, busy chopping something. I glanced at the cocktail menu— leather bound, labeled "Speakeasy Classics"—ordered an Old Fashioned with Booker's, and then watched Esmé for a while, hoping she would notice me and come out to speak, but she was intent on her work. Focused, I thought. Driven. It helped drive my own goals. I was going to find her those beans.

I took out my notebook and revisited what I'd learned back in the office about the growing season for the cumaru tree, why they would struggle to survive, much less thrive, in North Carolina's climate. It would indeed take a greenhouse—and given the trees' height, one several stories tall. How would you hide that? Was it worth building a greenhouse like that—and then hiding it—for a handful of seeds?

None of it made any sense.

Then I started thinking of what else might need a lot of light and heat to grow. And what someone might want to keep hidden—and from bigger guns than the FDA.

Slowly, it began to make more sense.

The door opened as I finished my notes, and my father's voice preceded him into the room. "Evening, Melissa," he said to the girl at the hostess stand and, "My usual spot"— which turned out to be the bar.

He didn't greet me at first but called out hearty hellos to those same folks in the dining area who'd waved my way before, stepping over to glad-hand one of the men. As he perched himself on the barstool beside me, he called out "Manhattan" to the bartender, but then stopped him as he reached for the Maker's. "On second thought, let your boss lady make it when she's free"—gesturing toward that open kitchen and Esmé within. "She knows what I'd like."

His voice boomed and carried, and I thought I saw Esmé glance out at us, then quickly glance away.

I caught myself, same as some other times, wanting to ask my father what self-respecting Southerner would drink a Manhattan. But instead I gave him a curt "Dad" as he adjusted himself on the stool.

"Son," he said. An awkward moment passed. Between his teeth, he clenched an unlit cigar, which he took out and propped between two fingers. Then he returned it to his mouth. "Buy you a drink?" Before I could gesture toward my Old Fashioned, he saw it himself. "But guess I've already bought you that one. Almost forgot that your tab's still my tab these days."

"I'm working," I said.

"One of us tosses that word around without knowing what it means."

"I am working," I said. "Actually doing work. I have a case."

"Let me guess. Someone at the library misshelved a book and they need help locating it. Or maybe the neighbor lost her cat. You always liked cats, didn't you?" He leaned over toward me, whispered, "Or maybe it's another kind of pussy you're tailing? Some cheating woman, and the husband hiring you to dig the dirt?"

"I don't take matrimonial cases."

He leaned back on his stool, stared at me as if I were a stranger he was trying to recognize. "Son, do you have any idea how real people speak?" He tapped his finger against the counter. "I'd be glad to know you were getting even a look at the fairer sex. Always thought you needed too much encouragement in that direction."

Esmé walked up to the counter, wiping her hand on the apron she was wearing.

"Evening, little lady," my father said. "Have you met the sire of my loins here? Heir to the fortune?"

He was overloud again. Esmé blushed, maybe both of us did. My father didn't seem to notice and didn't wait for either of us to answer before ordering his Manhattan again.

Despite asking for "the boss lady" in particular, he critiqued each step of her drink-making: moving her up a higher shelf in her choice of bourbon, questioning if those were the best bitters she had, cautioning her not to bruise the vermouth.

Fine liquor was his only vice, my father used to say, and then fine women too, after my mother died and he found himself on the hunt again. She'd been the buffer between us for years. Both of us missed her.

I didn't like to think of my father dating, but if his treatment of Esmé offered any indication of how he treated women, it didn't seem like an issue.

Esmé set the cocktail on the counter before him. "Compliments of the house."

"No, ma'am," he said, pulling out his money clip and sliding a twenty from it. "It's good business to pay for what you get."

For some reason, that made Esmé blush too. She seemed prone to it.

* * *

My father is not a fat man, though I realize I may have implied that somehow: the cigars, those suspenders, his booming voice. He's not a fat man, no, but he's a big man, and he fills whatever room he's in.

Sometimes there's not much space left for anyone else.

My father gave the Manhattan a curt taste then told Esmé she'd only slightly missed the mark. He asked about the business, asked about the night's specials, protested that he'd already eaten when she offered a menu, suggested she add more pork dishes—"think about what people want to eat, not what you want them to eat." He complained about a small placard on one of the bar shelves, advertising for the challenger in the governor's race—"wear your affiliations on your sleeve, you'll alienate half your clientele." He talked about me too, that phrase "heir to the fortune" again and then some blunt comments about bigger questions of inheritance, about the traits that are passed down or should be passed down and then something about recessive genes—"or is it regressive? I can never remember."

I'm not sure exactly what I said or how I fumbled through the conversation, what Esmé may have said or done or looked like through it all, except that she appeared truly beautiful to me now in a haunted, melancholy way and I suddenly felt like I should stand up for her or for myself—and then felt equally foolish for thinking that.

"Spends his days reading," my father was saying. "Walls of bookshelves, packed tight, up in his office."

"They're reference books," I said. "Think of lawyers, their libraries."

"Want to practice law, you should've gone to law school." My father swigged the rest of his cocktail. "Want to play at law or whatever you're doing..." He waved the empty glass toward Esmé, gesturing for another.

"Reading isn't a bad thing, knowledge," said Esmé, but she was watching me like she had the first day, with suspicion beneath it now. Any authority I had with her was quickly slipping away.

That was the way the conversation went. Before long, I left—putting off my update to Esmé. After all, I didn't have much to report anyway.

I called my friend Randy the next morning and asked to meet—away from the police station.

"Another referral?" he asked.

"A consultation," I said. "I need some insider perspective."

He was free after lunch. We planned to meet downstairs early afternoon.

As I hung up, my office door opened, and Esmé stepped in. She wore a skirt this morning—her legs tan and taut, I couldn't help but notice. She had a basket under her arm.

"Croissants," she said. "Fresh out of the oven. Have you had breakfast?"

I pointed to the coffee cup on my desk—still half full. "I have more in the pot and another mug."

Another blush. "I brought a French press," she said. She pulled that out of the basket along with a couple of jars of jelly, knives, napkins—cloth ones. The cups she poured were dainty but the scent was robust.

"What's the occasion?" I asked.

"We didn't get the chance to talk last night." She cut open a croissant. "Grape or strawberry?"

"Surprise me," I said, then: "I've got a lead, just need to see where it takes me."

She'd chosen strawberry, and the knife paused briefly against the croissant—enough so I caught it. "I thought when you came by last night—"

"I'm working on it," I said. "But no, no tonkas yet." I held my hands out, palms up. She examined them, like there might actually have been a bean sitting there. Her shoulders sunk. Her whole body seemed to deflate.

"Maybe I should pay the price," she said, almost to herself.

"Is there a rush? It's been a day, hardly that. Have some faith"—trying not to think about how my father had undermined me the night before. Reminding myself to have faith too.

She nodded—unconvincingly—then handed me the croissant.

"So tell me," I asked her, "have you always wanted to be a chef?"

"Since I was a girl," she said, carefully opening a croissant for herself. Something about her words and the movement and her smile gave me a glimpse of that child she was talking about: simple and unguarded, pure excitement, a contrast to those hard-bitten nails. "I used to burrow into the cabinets of my mother's kitchen, pulling out pots and pans, banging them around, pretending I was making something. When I was old enough, five or so, my mother gave me a chance to cook for real—or that's the way I remember it. I'm sure she helped more than I knew. She was a great cook herself, taught me everything I know. Cooking school was...perfecting some of what she'd taught me. Trying to perfect it. Understanding it in a different way."

"Sounds like you were born for it," I said. I held up the croissant. "Delicious."

She took a bite of her own. A dab of jelly clung to the corner of her mouth before she licked it away. "My mother said I had a special talent—a gift for it. And I wanted to be special, to feel like I was destined for something, you know? But destiny...you have to work at it. You make your own destiny, that's what I've learned."

"You and my father would get along well," I said.

It was a casual comment really. I didn't expect Esmé to bristle at the comparison. That unrestrained smile closed up quickly, her lips tightening.

"Did I say something wrong?" I asked.

"Your father," she said. "He didn't seem very...kind...to you. Last night."

I waved my hand. "I'm used to it."

"You shouldn't get used to things like that."

"Not much choice where family is concerned."

That same watchfulness from the first day. "I hope that's not the case." And then the smile again, but forced now—a purposeful attempt to lighten the mood. "Your turn," she said. "Something about yourself. What's been your most interesting case as a detective?"

I took a bite of my croissant to cover up the pause, buy myself time, then gave her a slimmed-down version of the plot of *Red Wind*—a set of pearls connecting a woman to her one true love, a blackmailer who stole the pearls and demanded payment or else he'd tell the woman's husband about the other man, and then the detective in the middle (me, as I was telling it) trying to get those pearls back.

"But when the pearls turned up," I said. "You know, she was probably going to protect them better, get them insured, whatever. But here's the kicker—they weren't real. That one true love of hers had given her cheap fakes. So I couldn't deliver them back, couldn't deliver that news, could I? So I pretended that the blackmailer had sold the real ones, had planned to sell fakes back to her—and I got a fake pair myself, clearly fake so she wouldn't recognize them as her own, and said that I'd done my best. She didn't get the pearls back, but she got to keep the memories. You see?"

It was a favorite case, even if not my own.

I'd earned back a real smile from Esmé, some genuine warmth behind it. "Who would've imagined there was so much intrigue in a town this size?"

"Who would've imagined there was a South American tree growing here," I said, "with an outlawed bean, a magic bean?"

She held up the last bite of her croissant, angling it like she wanted to toast, though it took me a few seconds to catch on. I tipped the corner of my own croissant toward hers, felt some real connection as the edges touched.

It was a day of eating indulgently. I met Randy that afternoon at the ice cream parlor downstairs. He bought Rocky Road, I had vanilla. Ms. Florence, who's run the place since both of us were kids, offered Randy his cone on the house, but I insisted on paying for both.

"If buying me a cone is a good exchange," Randy said on our way out, dodging a family hurrying in, "then it must not be very valuable, this information you're looking for."

"You saying you're open to bribery?"

"If I was, it might take more than ice cream."

"Would you have rather met for a bourbon?"

"Still on duty," he said.

I don't think he would've minded, but I did. More privacy out in the open than side-by-side with whoever might have shown up at a bar, even that early in the day. Plus, given the heat, the ice cream wasn't unwelcome.

"So what're you buying here with your single scoop?"

"What you know—off-the-record—about some criminal activity that might intersect with a case I'm working."

"Criminal activity?" he said. "Intersect?"

"Intersect at best," I said. "Unrelated ultimately—directly I mean."

He waited a second, took another lick of the cone, nodded toward a park bench set off from the few small crowds on the green. Three kids took turns chasing one another with water guns. Two women sat with a stroller at another bench.

Further down the green stood a table covered with political signs—these promoting the governor and a second term.

Where we sat was far enough away from all of them. No one could hear us.

"Who's growing marijuana in the county these days?" I asked once we were settled.

Randy laughed. "You looking for a buy? Missing those high school days of ours?"

"Not for me," I said. "And not small stuff, not some set-up in a closet. I meant a big plot." Big enough for a tree? The tropical plants covering for the growth underneath? I was still feeling my way.

He whistled, held up the cone. "You should've made it a double scoop." I waited. "If I knew about someone with a large-scale marijuana operation here, wouldn't I have already arrested them? Kind of my job these days."

"Could be something you know about," I said, "but you're not acting on it yet. Could be you're waiting for the right time to deal with it."

"A lot of could be's. What's leading you that way?"

"I don't think the helicopters that have been passing by are on military maneuvers."

The kids with the water guns rushed past us, squealing and shooting. Randy called after them to watch their aim, shifted his elbow.

"Caught in the crossfire?" I asked him.

He looked at me out of the corner of his eye. "By them or by you?"

"I don't know what you mean."

"The helicopters," he said. "Not ours—not that we could afford helicopters, not with our budget—and not military either, you're right there. But government somehow."

"So what are they doing?"

"Above my pay grade," he said quickly, some bitterness laced under the words, then took a bite of his cone. After a moment, he tossed the cone to the ground in front of us.

"What's the fine for littering, Officer?" I asked.

"Birds will eat it," he said. "Or ants. Tastes like cardboard anyway."

Already his ice cream was puddling. I took a bite of my own cone. It tasted fine.

"The helicopters," I said again. "They're looking for marijuana, right? Hidden greenhouses? Something like that?" But he wasn't having any of it.

"Back early this summer, end of the school year, prom night," he said, "the chief stationed several cruisers on the roads leading away from the high school. He wanted to be all zero tolerance, hard as nails, catch the kids drinking and driving, pull 'em over, run 'em in." He let out a long, low breath.

"Happy senior year, yeah?" I said.

"Exactly. And I didn't want to do it, not ruin some kid's graduation. I thought about letting them ride, whoever I saw. But then that wasn't good either—some drunk kid getting into an accident, killing somebody, himself, a whole carload of kids. You know where I'm coming from?"

I did, but I didn't. I knew what it meant, couldn't see how it connected. "So you pulled them in."

"And drove them home," he said. "Got hell for it the day after from the chief. And you know what I told him?"

I shook my head.

"I told him, when's the last time you had us stake out the roads up and down from the country club on a Saturday night?"

What he was telling me, it made sense and it didn't. The helicopters were like the police staking out prom when they should've been staking out someone else? I told him as much.

"They're not looking for anything," he said. "Not as far as I can tell. That's the funny thing. I asked and was told I shouldn't ask, and then I asked again anyway."

He stood up, gave me a sad smile.

"Me, my hands are tied." He squinted, like seeing something in me he hadn't seen before. "But maybe you can get further with it, given your position and all."

It wasn't lost on me here, a classic detective fiction set-up—the detective able to work outside the law, able to find what the authorities couldn't find.

"You want a lead," he said, "maybe talk to Harley."

Which proved part of my point: that Randy knowing something didn't mean he would act on it.

Detecting, no doubt about it, was a complicated business. Randy wouldn't give me any more information—didn't have any, he said—nothing specific about the helicopters, nothing about marijuana, nothing that might lead me closer to the heat at the core of the case, the literal heat, the kind that might grow not only marijuana but the tonka. That was all I cared about, even if that bean and Esmé herself were quickly getting lost under other troubles.

Harley went to high school with Randy and me, and he'd been the go-to source for weed. It had been years since I smoked pot—I'd grown up some, no matter what my father might think—and years since I'd seen Harley. But out of sight and out of mind didn't mean out of business.

Dust swirled as I pulled up the dirt road toward Harley's trailer. When I knocked on the front door, I heard shuffling inside. He looked like I'd woken him up. Maybe I had.

"Well, well," he said. "Here come old times rolling up to the door."

We shook hands, exchanged hellos. Harley sank down into a La-Z-Boy and motioned me toward a plaid couch, frayed at the arms—a cat, I felt sure. I hadn't seen one, but I caught a whiff of litter box mixed against the pot smell that had seeped into the couch and the walls and into Harley himself.

I mentioned that Randy had sent me his way, explained what had brought me out.

Harley nodded like he knew something. "Old times rolling up, and now looking to roll something himself." Then his loose smile morphed into puzzlement. "But you don't need me to roll a joint for you, do you?"

"Looking for some information," I said. "I wanted to ask about your supply channels."

He stiffened at that, pulled himself onto the front edge of the recliner.

"You cutting in on my business?"

"I'm not interested in your business," I said. "I mean, I am, but—"

"I'm not going to be strong-armed. I've been doing this too long to be treated like that. You push me, I'll go over your head. Don't think I won't."

He was all but bouncing in his chair, spittle clotting at the corners of his mouth. A cat did appear then, skittering out from under the couch, darting through the kitchen and deeper into the trailer.

"Harley," I said, trying to bring him back to reality. "Listen to me. I'm not buying, and I don't want to sell either. That's not why I'm—"

"You? Selling?" he said. "Hell, no, I know you better than that. Keep up appearances, that's you in a nutshell, even back in high school. And like you'd ever need the money. But then behind the scenes, when there wasn't nobody looking—different story, yeah? And now you want to slide right into the middle here and…"

Already he was pulling me up, pushing me out of the house—more threats, his anger deepening. Classic paranoia, I thought, and I tried to tell him that, but he wasn't listening. He slammed the door behind me, curses still pushing through the trailer's thin walls.

Back in the car, I felt stunned. Why had Randy sent me out

this way? Had he known how Harley would react? Surely he couldn't have anticipated what happened.

Harley peeked out from around the curtains, yanked them closed.

One of the helicopters passed, not directly overhead but not far away, and Harley peered out again, then gave me the finger.

I sat for a while, thinking.

Maybe it wasn't paranoia, I decided. Maybe Harley had reason to be spooked. None of it was clear yet, where I was headed, but as I watched the chopper, I began to wonder where it went.

I was stuck to two-lane roads winding awkwardly through the farms outside of town, while the helicopter went where it wanted to. But over a couple of hours, watching the horizons, watching the skies, I got sense of its flight paths, its area of surveillance.

I drove back into town and got to the courthouse a good forty-five minutes before it closed. The office for the registrar of deeds was in the basement, a large windowless room with linoleum floors. The clerk was a girl I'd known from school, as it turned out, a few years older—Sheri was her name. I'd had a crush on her years before. She was married with two kids now, had a plumpness about her.

She helped me find the names I needed—people and corporations both. Then I went back to my office, picked up the mail—a Ross Macdonald I'd ordered—and started up the laptop.

A couple of hours later, my research revealed no connections between the names I'd written down and what I thought was going on here—what I felt I knew, based on Randy's comments about the country club and Harley's accusations about me putting myself in the middle.

No connection at all.

But I did find a connection between the farmland the helicopters were monitoring and some real estate closer at hand.

All of which—I admit this with some pride—was exactly what I'd anticipated.

That night, I returned to Esmé's.

I arrived later than I had before, giving the dinner crowd, such as it was, longer to finish up—a single table still eating, a foursome in the back corner. My father was already at the bar, Manhattan in hand—likely not his first. Esmé stood back in that open kitchen.

I eased onto the barstool beside my father, ordered another Booker's Old Fashioned. The bartender rapped the counter with his knuckle, turned to make the drink.

"You're becoming a regular here," my father said, not looking my way but at the row of liquor bottles along the wall.

"Came for you, actually," I said.

"That's unexpected."

"I had a few questions about business."

He did glance my way then. "Very unexpected."

"I've always had an interest, sometimes more than others." The bartender set down my Old Fashioned. "Hear you're moving into agriculture these days."

My father sipped his Manhattan. While I waited for him to talk, I took a sip of my own. It was sweeter than I expected. Or maybe that was the moment seeping over.

"I've always kept a diverse portfolio of interests," he said. "Good business all around."

"Investments in that direction going well?"

"Better than some." He gave me a pointed glance. I wasn't an investment that was going well.

I let it slide—both the remark and the look. "So no worries about those helicopters?"

The mirror behind the bar was obscured behind the rows of liquor bottles and the placard for that gubernatorial challenger, but from what I glimpsed, my father may have actually smiled.

"Is this the case you've been working on?" He crossed his arms. "You're wasting your time. Here's the thing about business, son. By the time you reach my age, my position, you not only know how to make a deal, but you know how to be discreet about it."

"Hide it?" I asked.

"Semantics," he said. "And then there are the deals that aren't recorded at all. Those are sometimes the strongest. Power isn't always on paper."

"I wouldn't think you'd risk dirtying your hands—man of your integrity."

"Who said I was dirtying my hands?"

"Marijuana?" I whispered it. The bartender was drying some glasses at the other end of the bar—still close enough to hear. I glanced over my shoulder. The foursome in the back corner had broken up and was heading out. The waitress cleared their table. "Remember the way you used to talk about it when I was a teenager?"

My father didn't tone down his own voice. "As much money as I've been funneling to you over the years, I figured I could at least make some of it back from your kind at the other end."

"The helicopters," I said again. "Those can't be good business, can they?"

"A political dispute, that's all."

I thought of the governor's campaign heating up—the embattled incumbent, the ambitious challenger, the business vote, the power that wasn't on paper.

"The governor is extorting your endorsement."

"The words you choose, son." He tsk-tsked me like I was a toddler. "We businessmen are key to his support. We're in negotiations, that's all."

"Everything's negotiable, huh?"

"Always."

Esmé was wiping her hands on a towel, looking our way—heading our way, it seemed clear.

"Okay then," I said. "Let's you and me negotiate."

This time it was definitely a smile. I couldn't see it in the mirror, but I could feel it. Or maybe it wasn't meant for me at all, but for Esmé who was indeed rounding the bar.

Fine liquor and fine women—those were the things that drove this.

"The tonkas," I said as she came up. Her eyes widened, a cautious smile there too. "That's the case I've been working on, the case I've solved."

"Solved?" my father said. "This little lady has known where to find them all along."

"But she couldn't get them," I said. "That's why she needed me."

"A moment please," Esmé said, shifted from one foot to another. That hint of a smile had faded. "Why don't you take off the rest of the night?" she told the bartender.

"You sure?" he asked, but he was already laying down his bar rag.

"And tell Maria she can go too." The waitress I'd seen, I assumed.

While he gathered his things, Esmé looked at me in silence—from me to my father and back—with that same watchfulness she'd brought to my office the first day. That was her whole point, I think—watching us and waiting.

When the help had left, I pointed to the leather-bound cocktail menu: *Speakeasy Classics*. "This is the connection, right? And that?" Pointing to the Manhattan.

"It wasn't the drink," Esmé said. "That was only the start."

My father sighed.

"You reach a point in your life when it's all about enjoying the day," he said. He picked up his drink, stared into it. "This is the perfect cocktail—or nearest to perfection. I've got time on my hands. I wanted to see if I could indeed perfect it."

"Abbott's bitters," I said. "Made with the tonka."

Outlawed in the U.S. in the fifties along with the bean itself, I'd found. I remembered my father chiding Esmé about the bitters she used the first night I stopped in, if those were the best she had—rubbing it in, playing his hand.

"A necessary ingredient,'" he said. "The original Manhattan, way it should be, until some neb in Washington mucked it up. I found a recipe for them, figured how hard would it be to make a batch of those bitters myself? Hell, I probably could've found an antique bottle easier, paid a pretty penny for it maybe, but the money didn't matter. It's a point of pride to make something for yourself." He looked at Esmé. "Turns out I can't cook. But then someone came to town who could—or at least I thought she could."

I turned toward Esmé. "You open your business, advertising speakeasy cocktails, and he comes in with a proposal."

"He brought in a quarter pound of the tonkas." Her voice cracked. "A plastic bag, as if it was nothing. He laid it on the counter here, and the recipe beside it. He said that it should be enough, if I'd be willing to make it. And I could have, I would have." She was knitting her fingers together, clasping and unclasping them. "But infusion, the aging—it takes time."

"Six months," my father said. "That's what she told me, and in the meantime, she wanted more beans for herself. And I told her sure I had them, told her they were growing like wildflowers, how many did she want?"

"He never let me touch even the first batch," she said. "As

soon as I asked about additional ones, he pulled the bag away from me."

"Simple supply and demand," he said.

I turned toward Esmé. "You told me in the office that the price was too high. What was the price?" I knew the answer already. Another of those blushes confirmed it.

"I wanted conversation," my father said. "Friendly companionship, that's all."

"It wasn't companionship that you wanted," Esmé said, barely a whisper.

"A fine drink goes better with a fine woman."

"He threatened to pull the lease," she told me.

"I merely reminded her that whether her restaurant succeeded or not, the rent was due on the first of the month," he said. "Every month. For two years."

"A lease that's not in your name," I said, "though it is in the same name as the land those helicopters have been keeping under surveillance. So what? You claim it when it's convenient, don't when it's not? And meanwhile, use it for whatever leverage you can? There's a difference between a date and a deal, Dad."

My father leaned back and smiled, reached up and gave his suspenders a satisfied pluck.

"Don't you forget, son," he said. "The little lady here used you for leverage too. Shake you up, shake me down—isn't that right, honey? And then shake some seeds out of it all for herself."

"I wasn't using him," Esmé said. "But I thought if anyone could reason with you, could influence you to—"

"Influence is the definition of leverage," my father said.

"Stop it, both of you," I said. "However we got here, here's where we're at." I faced my father head on. "The marijuana isn't the case I was hired for, and what's going on between you and the governor, that's between you—for now. But I'll go to the local police with it and to the press—I'll bring it all down on you, the FDA too—if you don't give Esmé access to your other agricultural interests—those cumaru trees you're growing."

"A coo-ma-what?" he asked. This time it was genuine perplexity—on his part and Esmé's too, but different in each case, a difference maybe neither of us had expected.

"It's the tree that grows the tonka bean," I said. "Tropical trees, in your greenhouses."

"Growing like wildflowers," Esmé added. "That's what you told me."

My father snorted—the perplexity shifting toward something else: comprehension, confidence, pleasure.

"You ever heard of a figure of speech," he said. "Grow a tree? Why the hell would I do that? Nah, I ordered the seeds online, get as many as I want. And whatever this one kept telling me"—a thumb toward Esmé—"there's nobody from the FDA been breaking down my door to get them either. And what the hell would I care if they did?"

He drank down the rest of his Manhattan, used two fingers to slide the glass to the other edge of the bar.

"Deal's off between us, missy," he said, "and that leverage you two are working on, it doesn't mean a...a hill of beans." He laughed, sharply, then stepped down off the barstool. At the door, he turned back briefly toward us. "You two are made for each other, you know that? She lives in as much of a fantasy world as you do. Waiting for magic beans to save this business, same as you sitting and reading while the world passes you by. Rent's still due same as usual, first of the month."

After he'd left, Esmé and I were alone. I thought about the things I could say to her. That I was sorry for the way my father acted. Sorry I couldn't get the beans she wanted. Sorry there weren't any beans at all—not like she'd thought.

I wanted to tell her I was there for her still. But she spoke first.

"If you do it right, it all comes together in the end," she said. "That's what my mother told me. She was talking about cooking. The ingredients, the steps—the magic there at the end. And it wasn't simply the meal itself that you created but something else for yourself. Pride maybe, or peace, or...But you have to do it right, and this business..." She waved a hand at the empty restaurant. "I don't have enough money to pay the rent next month."

"You think getting the beans would have made the difference? Would've saved you?"

"Everything could've been different," she said, talking almost to herself now. "I didn't have to know that he ordered them online. I could've denied it if the FDA did come in. And maybe they'd have been what I'd needed, if I'd handled all this better."

"Would you have slept with him to get them?" I asked.

I didn't need the answer there, either. She'd already mentioned in my office her temptation to pay the price. And then there was the crisp elegance of the bar where I sat and the dining room behind me, the bottom line on that check register I'd glimpsed when she hired me, the look on her face now—that same blush, deeper than ever.

You build your future, I could've said. You build your destiny. But even then sometimes you end up somewhere you never intended to go.

I pulled from my pocket the check she'd written, unfolded it and left it on the bar beside what was left of my Old Fashioned. She didn't stop me as I headed out the door, didn't say a word.

For better or worse, I'd closed the case.

The next morning, Randy called to ask what I'd found out. I don't think he ever knew it was my father at the end of that search—only country club types in general, class and power and something he couldn't reach and thought I could, not because of my position as a detective but because of who I was, the class I was born in.

My turn to play coy with him. No, I hadn't found what I was looking for. And that was true. The marijuana hadn't been my case at all.

That afternoon, the tonka seeds arrived—the ones I'd ordered myself. I'd forgotten to cancel them.

Esmé said they would likely be shellacked—good luck charms of some kind instead of usable ingredients—but when I cut into one of the beans, the fragrance filled my office. Vanilla and honey and caramel and cinnamon and something joyous about it, exactly like she'd described it.

I bought a can of clear varnish and sprayed the rest of the beans, packaged them up with the invoice and added a note that she'd been right after all, probably the same kinds of beans my father had dangled before her—letting her know they wouldn't have worked, wouldn't have been worth it.

I'd mail the package, since I didn't plan on stopping by again.

And then I got back to business myself—the Ross Macdonald collection that had arrived the day before. *Strangers in Town.* I'd been waiting for it, and it for me.

Life Goes to the Dogs
Meredith Cole
Washington, D.C.

Matt's new client was a walking, talking country song in action. He had lost his wife, his house, his truck and his dog. But it was apparently only the loss of the dog that had really stung, since he was hiring a PI to recover him.

"What happened to your dog, exactly?" Matt said, clearing his throat. Divorces were often contentious, but this one seemed unusually bitter.

"I think my ex sold him," Joshua Henley said as his head jerked towards his shoulder. He was, Matt quickly discovered, physically unable to sit still. His body was one big twitch.

"Sold it?" Matt tried to imagine how he would feel if his girlfriend ever did something so low as to sell his dog. The trouble was, although he loved his mutt, he couldn't imagine anyone wanting to pay money for him. He'd destroyed several carpets and chairs as it was.

"She always hated Rocco. And she knew how much I loved him." Joshua's left eye twitched several times before he could speak again. "My therapist prescribed him for my anxiety disorder. And he really helped me."

Now the dog rescue was sounding like a medical emergency. "What kind of dog was Rocco?"

"A Samoyed."

Matt leaned over and did a quick search on his laptop for the breed. He could see why the guy missed Rocco. The dog looked like a miniature polar bear, all fuzzy white with a goofy grin. The site also claimed that the dogs could go for up to seven thousand dollars. Seemed like a lot to pay for a dog. "They're expensive."

"It's a valuable breed, and he was a perfect specimen. He had papers from the kennel club and everything."

Matt had never understood why people paid a lot of money for fancy dog breeds. But he wasn't going to talk himself out of a job. Sorting his bills and invoices this morning, he couldn't help but notice that the bill pile was higher. Much higher. His private investigator business was still getting off the ground. If the guy wanted his dog back and was willing to pay, Matt was willing to look for it.

"When did the dog disappear?"

"I'm not sure. Last week, I went to pick him up at my old house. I'd finally moved into a place that accepted dogs. And my ex said he was gone." Joshua looked completely miserable and he twitched again. Wearing a tweed jacket and khakis, Joshua looked like a college professor but Matt knew he was a programmer for some kind of tech firm. The kind of guy who could afford a fancy breed of dog.

"Could he have run away?"

"I don't think so."

"And she won't say what happened?"

"No."

"When was the last time you saw him?"

"About a month ago." Joshua explained that every time he'd tried to see the dog, his ex had fobbed him off. And the dog was never there when he went to sneak a peek. Joshua hyperventilated at one point while telling his story and had to put his head down between his legs until he calmed back down.

After Matt got Joshua a glass of water, they spent a few minutes haggling. They established a price (Matt's hourly rate) plus a deadline (one week to reconvene). Matt also got Joshua's ex-wife's phone number and address so he could do his own sniffing around.

Within an hour of Joshua's leaving, Matt decided that he would likely regret taking this case. He was in way over his head. If this case had been about D.C. politics or the CIA, he would know where to start and who to talk to. But fancy dogs were another matter altogether.

A quick call to the SPCA and the local shelters came up empty. He called shelters up to two hundred miles from D.C. and still got nothing. But he left his name and number everywhere. He certainly didn't want to overlook anything obvious.

It was now four p.m. The perfect time to go canvass Joshua's former neighbors. He'd lived in the D.C. side of Chevy Chase, an upscale neighborhood filled with fancy mansions that bordered Maryland. Matt changed into his running gear and drove across town, hoping there were a lot of dog lovers there. After driving slowly past Joshua's house several times, a brick two-story colonial with a two-car garage the size of his apartment, he parked and got out.

Running shorts and a T-shirt were a good disguise since runners went pretty well unnoticed in most neighborhoods in that area of D.C. He decided to get something of a workout in even if he didn't have any luck with the neighbors. He jogged slowly up the street, and then doubled back. The trees were just starting to change color, and a few yellow leaves had drifted gently down onto the sidewalk.

Matt approached the Henley's front door warily and rang the doorbell. It chimed softly but no dog barked. The ex wasn't home and neither was the dog.

He jogged up the street hoping a neighbor would come out to walk their dog. At last a middle-aged woman with a toy black poodle strolled out of a tan brick house nearby. Matt slowed down as the dog energetically barked at him and pulled against his leash.

"Hi, doggie," Matt said, trying to sound as placating as possible.

"Charlie! Don't bark at the nice man!" Charlie's owner said. Charlie gave one last yap and then began sniffing around a shrub.

After telling her how cute her own dog looked, he asked if she knew the Henleys and their dog Rocco.

"Oh, sure. Why?"

"Rocco is missing."

The woman looked horrified. "What happened?"

"I'm not sure. But I was wondering when you saw him last."

"Maybe last week? Charlie wouldn't stop barking at him, would you?" The woman cooed at the dog and Charlie ignored her.

"So you haven't seen any dogs loose in the neighborhood?"

"Certainly not. And I would recognize Rocco, of course."

Matt thanked her for her time and continued up the block. The other neighbors with dogs all knew who Rocco was but didn't remember the last time they'd seen him. But one mused that he hadn't heard him barking for a week or so. And that was unnatural.

Finally the ex-wife, dressed in yoga pants and some kind of odd top with lots of zippers, drove up in a giant white SUV and parked in front of her garage. Maybe she'd been to the gym, but she certainly didn't look sweaty.

He walked up and quickly introduced himself. "Joshua asked me to look for Rocco."

The ex, holding her keys in front of her like a knife, went red under her layers of artfully applied make-up. "You tell that bastard I made sure he'd never see his precious dog again! I got sick of playing second fiddle to everything in his life—especially the dog. Do you know how much those things shed? He broke at least three vacuum cleaners and he never showed either of us an ounce of love."

Vindictive, but Matt knew there were two sides to every

story. "Could you please tell me if you sold him to someone local or if I need to look in Norway?"

"Oh, the dog didn't go far. In fact he went where he truly belonged." With that she turned and marched into her house. He waited for the door to slam, but it had been apparently carefully calibrated to always close softly. Not satisfying at all.

At dinner with his girlfriend Rory, he asked for advice. Her family owned Basset Hounds. "Who would buy an expensive dog like that? And how would I track them down?"

"I know the American Kennel Club keeps track of dog breeds, and people register their dogs with them."

"So if anyone bought the dog, they would register it there?"

"Maybe. It's strictly voluntary though."

The American Kennel Club was definitely next on Matt's list. Joshua said he had a chip in the dog, but that wasn't apparently a foolproof method of tracking a dog down. The dog had to be taken to the vet, and the vet had to report it.

Matt dialed the number for the AKC and insisted on talking to the big cheese. "How can I help you?" Bitsy Calhoun had a round plummy voice and sounded like she summered on Martha's Vineyard.

"I have a client whose dog is missing. Do you keep records of dog sales?"

"Not exactly. We create the paperwork to register dogs. And without the paperwork you can't sell them easily in the open marketplace or show the dogs."

"Do you police the dog breeders to make sure they're operating within the law?"

"Well, we don't really have any power to do anything to people. Just withhold paperwork."

That didn't sound like much. But he decided to ask the question that had been bugging him. "Why do you think Samoyeds are so valuable?"

"Perhaps because they are rather rare? Breeds go in and out of fashion. It's a pretty dog, but certainly isn't for everyone." Bitsy paused. "Is the dog you're looking for a Samoyed?"

"Yes. The owner claims his ex sold the dog out of spite. He wants the dog back. There's no way for you to trace the dog for him?" Matt told her a bit about Rocco.

After a few minutes he heard Bitsy sigh. "I don't have a record of the dog changing owners recently. I would only if the new owner registered the dog. That often doesn't happen until the dog is bred."

"Would you assume that someone bought the dog specifically so they could breed it and make money off its puppies?"

"Yes, definitely. Although we hope that everyone is a dog lover and wants the dog specifically for its characteristics and personality, that is sadly not always the case."

"I see." So a dog was worth seven thousand dollars because of its future potential as a stud or mother. Now it was beginning to make sense. Two litters and the dog had more than paid for itself.

"Do you know of any Samoyed breeders in the area that I should talk to? Who might know where this one went?"

Bitsy hesitated for a moment. Then she named one or two people. "They're quite reputable breeders. We do know that there are some unethical breeders who are simply in it for the money, and that's definitely not them. They want the best for the dogs."

If some unethical breeder had gotten ahold of Joshua's dog, Matt had no idea how he would get him back. Hoping for the best, Matt picked the one breeder from Bitsy's list that was actually within driving distance of D.C. Carol Warren at Rocky Top Farm. He called her and arranged to see her dogs. He decided to wait to tell her he was looking for a missing dog, since she would probably be more welcoming to a potential customer than a private eye. He wasn't opposed to a little subterfuge in order to unite a man with his beloved pet. And he invited his girlfriend Rory to go along. She worked for her family's tour business, so she knew a little bit about everything. Rory was also great at making small talk.

Rory got into the spirit of the trip, and mapped out a few restaurants and a brewpub to try in that area. They would try to hit both places, if possible. The dog breeder lived in a rural part of Maryland, north of Baltimore. The rolling hills spooled out in front of them as they drove, the tops of each touched by red and gold as the trees began to change colors. The area looked like it didn't have too many human inhabitants. Perfect for raising dogs. Especially noisy ones.

They pulled into the long isolated driveway, edged by cedar trees, and drove up a hill to a fairly modest brick ranch house. Behind the house sat a large red barn and kennels. Carol Warren came out the front door to greet them. Dressed in denim and pearls, she was a tall blonde woman who looked like she was descended from Viking raiders. She shook hands with them politely, and asked after their trip. But after that the conversation was all dog.

She gave Matt and Rory a quick tour around the spotless kennels filled with one Samoyed after another that looked, quite frankly, exactly like the one before. They were all very active, chewing, chasing their tails and barking. And barking. There was a lot of barking.

"This is Shanti. A wonderful bitch. She's due in a few weeks. I have deposits on several of her pups, but not all. The sire is Finn. He won quite a few trophies when I used to show him."

She signaled for Shanti to stay. When Shanti obeyed, she gave her a treat. She was stern with the dogs, but obviously adored them. Carol stepped back and Rory stepped in to pet her.

"She's really gorgeous. I bet her puppies are going to be adorable."

"Why pure breeds? Why not just a mutt?" Matt asked.

"You know what you're getting with a pure bred. These dogs have a long lineage and are bred to be just what people want in size, activity level and temperament."

Matt was a bit of a mutt himself, not that he'd ever minded. He guessed Carol was the type who could trace her ancestors back to the Mayflower and put a lot of stock in good breeding. Carol stopped to scratch one of the dogs on the head. "Nomadic reindeer herders selected traits in the Samoyeds to help them hunt, herd reindeer, haul sleds, etc. They're strong and independent."

"Why are they so expensive?"

"A good example of a breed can be shown and earn a lot of prize money. Plus earn a lot of prestige."

Thinking of a dog as a moneymaker contradicted the way Matt thought people should generally feel about pets. Carol obviously felt quite differently.

"Are there unethical breeders that would purchase a dog without papers?"

"Sure. And there are plenty of suckers who would buy a dog without knowing its ancestry. People take advantage of that."

"So it would be difficult to trace a lost dog? It could just vanish—even with a chip?"

"I suppose so." Carol stopped walking and looked him in the eye. "You're not really interested in getting a puppy, are you?"

Matt shook his head. "I'm looking for a dog. Rocco. He belonged to the Henleys and the wife sold him in a dirty divorce battle. Now the husband wants him back."

She looked guarded. "I know him. He was one of mine. Actually Shanti's brother." She shook her head. "The Henleys cared more about the prestige of owning a Samoyed than

Rocco himself. I should have seen that."

He wasn't surprised to find out that the Henleys had also gone to the closest breeder to D.C. to find a dog. "So you don't just sell to anyone who's interested?"

"Absolutely not. They have to pass a lot of tests. But I make mistakes."

"The Henleys were a mistake?"

"He was far more into the idea of a Samoyed than his wife. That should have been a red flag. Not taking care of a dog like that is criminal. They're not easy, but they're worth it."

"The wife mentioned that he shed quite a bit."

"That's right," Carol pivoted. "I hope you find what you're looking for. But I really can't help you. I need to get back to work."

As Matt and Rory headed back to the car, Matt's cell rang. Joshua. He was reluctant to pick up and tell him that so far he'd had no luck locating the dog. He barely got a hello in before Joshua became hysterical.

"She called and said she'd killed the dog with p-p-p-poison and buried it in the backyard!"

"Don't you think she's just saying that to hurt you?"

"She's capable of doing it! She wants more money in the divorce settlement and said she'd keep punishing me until I agreed."

Promising to give him back the dog if he agreed seemed smarter, but he wasn't imagining that either of them were thinking clearly. "I'll head back to my office and meet you there in an hour and a half," he promised. "We'll figure out a plan."

Rory was appalled when he told her what the ex had said. "What a horrible person!"

"Maybe the dog died of natural causes," Matt said as he drove back towards D.C., trying to calculate whether the

Baltimore-Washington Expressway or 95 would be quicker. Probably both were a mess.

"She's a nutcase."

Matt had to agree. But he also knew there was a chance she was lying about what happened to the dog.

Joshua was waiting outside his office pacing up and down. His hair was more disheveled than ever. "I took a pill and called my therapist, but nothing is working! I don't know what to do!"

Matt had used his travel time from Maryland to come up with a plan. He told Joshua what they were going to do and asked if he was in. It was illegal and possibly dangerous, but Joshua agreed without hesitation. If Matt wanted proof that he loved his dog he had it now.

Matt borrowed shovels from Rory's parents, changed into all black and met Joshua several blocks away from his old house after dark. Joshua wore a black Motley Cru T-shirt and black shorts. His white legs shone in the moonlight, but there was no going back now. They crept behind the ex's house and quietly entered the garden through a gate. Joshua was able to reach over and down to unlatch the gate from memory. Having the homeowner present during a break-in was useful, Matt realized, but seldom feasible.

They found a pile of fresh dirt near a bush and just to the left of a flower garden. It looked like the perfect size and place to bury a dog Rocco's size.

"Okay. Let's dig here." Joshua twitched violently in the dark next to him and stifled a sob. Matt wished there was something he could say that would assure him. But this didn't look good. Maybe the ex had finally told Joshua the truth.

The loose dirt moved easily at first. Matt got into the rhythm of push, scoop and toss after a minute, feeling the muscles in his back stretch and get warm. He could hear the murmur of traffic in the background and the quiet sound of bugs humming. But then about eight inches down they hit undisturbed clay soil. There was no way anything had been recently buried beneath it. Matt stood back panting trying to think.

Suddenly they were blinded by a bright spotlight directed at them from over the fence. "Put down those shovels and come out with your hands up!" A cop shouted through his megaphone. Matt quickly dropped his shovel and Joshua did the same. He knew it was going to take some fancy talking to get out of this mess.

Time in a jail cell that smelled like vomit and sweat, despite the loud snoring drunk and a slightly belligerent gentleman who paced around the jail cell and twitched almost as much as Joshua, gave Matt some time to think. If the dog wasn't buried in the yard, maybe the ex had lied about poisoning Rocco, too. The claim had been designed to both emotionally torture Joshua and to trap him into doing something illegal. It had succeeded at both.

One thing Matt hadn't been since taking this case was circumspect or sneaky. He'd been upfront with almost everyone and told them that he was looking for Rocco. Maybe that had been a mistake. But somewhere along the way, he suspected he'd come close enough to the truth to alarm the ex. But where?

Something Carol had said while they were at her farm had been bothering him. For the most part she had been very straight with them, but as soon as he'd mentioned Rocco she'd become evasive and uncomfortable. She'd mentioned that it was "criminal" what the Henleys had done to the dog. It was like she had witnessed something terrible that had happened to the dog recently. But how could she if she hadn't seen Rocco since he was a puppy? She had to know more than she'd let on, and he suspected she knew where Rocco was.

After Rory had posted bail for them, Matt told Joshua his

hunch. Even though he was still shaken from his adventures yesterday, Joshua insisted that he wanted to come along.

Matt drove the now familiar roads to Carol's farm and parked out of sight of the house. On foot, they skirted the driveway and looped out further around the house to get back to the kennels. Carol wasn't there. The dogs barked at them, but since they apparently barked at squirrels, flying leaves and each other, Matt didn't think they would raise much of an alarm. He methodically went down the row and studied the names. One cage was set back a bit from the others. Unlike the other healthy looking pups, he had recently been shaved. One eye looked crusty and red, and he had a wound on his leg. The dog barked fiercely at Matt. The name on the label was so faint Matt had to lean in close to read it. Rocco.

"Hey, Rocco," Matt said softly. "You're a mess." But Rocco was looking past him to Joshua.

"Rocco!" Joshua rushed forward and practically leapt inside Rocco's cage. Rocco licked his face enthusiastically and Joshua laughed with delight. Leaning in and hugging his dog, Joshua looked relaxed and happy for the first time since Matt had met him.

"Step away from the cage," Carol said behind them. "He's suffered enough."

"What have you done to him? He looks terrible," Joshua protested.

"I'm not the one who hurt him. Your wife told me about what you did to the dog and asked if I'd take him back. When I showed up to get him, he had been neglected and abused. I couldn't bear it, so I purchased him."

"I would never do anything to him," Joshua said. "He's the most wonderful dog in the world!" He turned back to the dog and fondled his ears lovingly again and received more sloppy kisses. "If I'd known she would hurt him, I would have taken Rocco away right when I left, believe me."

Carol appeared to be slowly softening as she watched the

affection between Rocco and Joshua.

"We understand that you care about him. But you can see that Joshua and Rocco love each other," Matt said. "Besides, taking dogs back isn't good for business."

Carol was first and foremost a businesswoman. Matt quickly negotiated a price that everyone was happy with. Joshua agreed to allow Rocco to come back occasionally to father a few puppies for Carol. He liked the idea of there being more little Roccos in the world, although he asked that he be able to accompany him on the stud visits. Apparently the idea of being apart from Rocco even for one night made him anxious.

On his way back to D.C. with Rocco and Joshua safe in the back seat, Matt had to admit that uniting a man with his dog had been far more satisfying than any other case he'd solved so far. He decided to take his girlfriend out to dinner to celebrate. She'd like that. Matt searched for a station on the radio and could only find country music. A singer sang about how all the riches in the world meant nothing without love. Matt couldn't have agreed more.

Not the Way It Looks
J.L. Abramo
Brooklyn, New York

Dominic Ventura was a gambler and a drunk.

Although he never raised a hand to her, he succeeded in making my mother's life miserable.

My old man did raise a hand to me—until I was old enough to warn him against it.

Dominic was a laborer. Some of his days were spent doing backbreaking work. Most of his days were spent not working at all.

I had a troubled youth—I landed in a lot of hot water. Dominic never helped me out of it and he offered no fatherly guidance to keep me from falling into it.

I don't quote my father often—He had little useful to say. But there were a few things he did say before the drinking killed him that were worth storing away.

When someone claims "it's not the way it looks," it's usually exactly the way it is, was one of them.

Brooklyn.

A stuffy, cluttered office two floors above a beauty salon on Neptune Avenue in Coney Island.

A light rap on the opaque glass pane.

"It's open."

The door swung into the room.

The visitor stood planted at the threshold.

"Nick Ventura?" he asked.

"How can I help you?"

"I need a very good private investigator."

"Come in," I said, reluctant to ask where he had heard I was very good. "Close the door, have a seat."

He walked slowly to the ancient oak table that served as my desk and offered a handshake.

I accepted.

"Jim Bishop," he said.

"Sit, Mr. Bishop," I said, releasing his hand, "May I call you Jim?"

He settled into the client chair across the table.

"I'm in danger," he began without ceremony. "There is a man out there who I believe will kill me if I say anything about what I saw."

"What did you see?"

"A murder."

"Have you talked to the police," I asked. I always ask.

"The police have no real suspects, and no solid leads. All I know is his face, and he knows mine. If I speak to the police now and he is following the investigation, he will know I came forward. Until he is positively identified and appre-hended, I'm in jeopardy. I need to learn who he is before he learns who I am—and I need help."

"What can you tell me?"

"It all happened in a matter of seconds. It was the evening before last. I was walking past the house when I heard what sounded to me like a gunshot. I moved up to the front door and I heard another shot. I tried the door, it was unlocked. I acted impulsively—I'm not a brave man. I opened the door and the shooter turned to me. We made eye contact. We both froze for a moment. He began to raise his weapon and I ran."

"And you would know the man if you saw him again."

"Yes."

"And he would know you."

"Yes. And the intent in his eyes when he turned and saw

me standing in the doorway was unmistakable. If looks could kill."

"Can you describe him?"

"I can," Bishop said. "Please, Mr. Ventura. If you can help me find this man, discover who and where he is, and do it without alerting him—then I will bring all I know to the police and pray they capture him before he gets to me."

"I don't know if I can be much help. There is not a lot to go on and, as I've learned the hard way, keeping information from the police, no matter how vague, is a recipe for grief. I need to think about it. If I decide to take the case, my fee is two hundred fifty dollars a day plus expenses. And I will need a retainer."

"Will cash do?" Bishop said, reaching into his jacket pocket.

He placed ten one hundred dollar bills on the table.

I do this job of investigation to help people in need, right wrongs, be free to bend rules occasionally, because I failed the NYPD employment background check, and sometimes it pays the utility bills.

There were more than a few debts that needed immediate attention.

"I'll need you to give me everything you can remember about the man—height, approximate weight, what he was wearing, in which hand he held the weapon, every detail of his face, hair color, eye color, distinguishing features. I'll need you to sign a standard client form."

I walked to the file cabinet. I pulled out several sheets of ruled paper, a contract form, and a fresh pen from a box of Sanford uni-ball rollers.

Bishop wrote notes. I tried to keep my eyes off the grand in cash.

He signed the contract.

"How do I reach you?" I asked.

NOT THE WAY IT LOOKS

"I'll call you," he said, rising from his seat, "and thank you."

With that he turned and left the office.

I placed the cash, the contract and the pen into the file cabinet and returned to the table. I looked at Bishop's notes.

I understood that finding the killer would be like trying to find a needle in a haystack, and that it would help a great deal if I knew which haystack.

I had the victim's name. I knew where he had been killed.

It was a start.

I needed to learn more about the victim, and learn where the police were in their investigation—learn if there were any persons of interest. The closest I had to an ally in the NYPD was Detective John Sullivan of the 70th Precinct.

John had helped me, unhappily, many times. But Sullivan was not fond of giving up information.

If I asked him what time it was, he would ask why.

The killing had taken place in Cobble Hill, covered by the detectives of the 76th Precinct. If I walked into the Seven-six, and asked about an ongoing murder investigation—the detectives would either hold me for questioning or toss me out the door.

I needed the assistance of someone who could ease suspicion—walk in, ask questions, and appear innocent of any hidden agenda.

It would also be useful if I could get Bishop's written description of the perpetrator rendered into picture form.

A sketch, even one lacking in exactness, could still be worth a thousand words.

Luckily, I knew someone who I believed might help on both scores.

* * *

Carmella Fazio was like an aunt. The connection between our families went back several generations. Carmella owned the building that housed the beauty shop and my office above. And Carmella was the proprietress of the renowned pizza parlor adjacent to the beauty shop.

Maria Leone was Carmella's niece. She was a graduate student at the John Jay College of Criminal Justice, where she had recently aced a course on sketch artistry. When she was not in class, she helped her aunt manage the restaurant. Occasionally she did a little research or field work for me—for the hands-on experience and a bit of textbook money.

I went down to the pizzeria and found Maria behind the counter.

After seeing Maria that Friday afternoon, asking her to attempt a sketch from Bishop's written description, and proposing a visit to the Seven-six the next day, I did some research on the murder—relying on newspaper accounts which offered little substance.

The victim was Richard Sherman.

Thirty-three years old, single, Caucasian, discovered by the police D.O.A. at his home following a 9-1-1 call Wednesday evening.

The investigation was ongoing.

An obituary posted in the *Daily News* informed me that Sherman was survived by his parents, brother and two sisters. The wake would be held at Cobble Hill Chapels on Court Street on Friday and Saturday, and the funeral service and burial was set for Sunday at Mount Olivet Cemetery in Maspeth, Queens.

I had a thought. Maybe the killer knew the victim. So well, in fact, that he felt obliged to show up at the funeral. I couldn't remember what movie that thought came from—so I put it on the back burner.

* * *

Maria needed to be on the upper west side of Manhattan for a class at eleven—so I drove her over to the 76ᵗʰ Precinct early Saturday morning.

Maria would claim she was working on a research paper for one of her courses and would much appreciate the opportunity to speak with one of their detectives about a current investigation. We were hoping she could subtly steer the conversation toward the case in question.

I sat in my Monte Carlo outside the police station studying Maria's drawing.

It was an excellent rendition given what Maria had to work with. The face was distinct enough to eliminate the vast majority of mankind—but not nearly distinct enough to convict a suspect. I decided I needed to show the drawing to Jim Bishop.

Maria joined me in the car a few minutes after entering the precinct.

"That was quick."

"He's in there."

"Who's in there?"

She pointed to her drawing.

"Are you sure it's him?"

"Or someone who looks exactly like him."

"It would be quite a coincidence."

"Yes."

"I could wait for him to come out."

"You should. I can walk to the subway station from here. And, Nick."

"Yes?"

"If this could be the guy," she said, "be careful."

Maria left the car.

I sat and waited.

* * *

A year can seem to pass in a moment.

Sitting alone in a car for sixty minutes without the *New York Post* sports section or an egg, bacon and cheese on hard roll can seem to last forever.

It was the Fourth of July weekend. Manhattan may have been deserted, but Brooklyn was teeming with activity. Brooklynites celebrated their national holidays close to home and mom's cooking.

The suspect finally walked out of the precinct. I followed his car out Union Street. He turned right onto 4th Avenue, heading south. I watched the vehicle enter the Prospect Expressway and followed to a house in Midwood.

I was considering my options when my cell rang.

Jim Bishop.

Checking in.

"Can you meet me at my office?" I asked.

"How about the Del Rio Diner on Kings Highway?"

"Sure. I can be there in twenty minutes."

"Twenty minutes," Bishop said.

The Del Rio was open for business twenty-four hours a day, every day. It featured a menu as thick as a Tolstoy novel. Signed and framed photos on the walls bragged of patrons from Bill Clinton to James Gandolfini to Eli Manning.

I found Bishop at a window booth, hovering over a cup of coffee.

"Is this the man you saw Wednesday night?" I asked, placing Maria's drawing in front of him as I slid into the booth.

"Yes," he said, "do you know who he is?"

"I don't—but I followed him from the 76th Precinct."

"He was at the police station?"

"For more than an hour."

"Do you think he's a suspect?"

"I don't know—and I don't know how to ask without opening myself up to a lot of questions, and my answers could involve you."

"That's still not a good idea. I won't be safe until I know my identification will put him away—and I don't think this drawing will do it. I need to positively identify him. I need to see him. And I need you with me."

I wasn't sure I was ready to go the distance with Bishop, so I hedged.

"I can't take you out there right now," I said, "give me a few hours."

"I'll call you later," Bishop said, dropping a five-dollar bill on the table for the coffee.

And he was gone.

As I left the diner, I had the feeling I was acting recklessly. Granted, I was trying to protect someone in possible danger— but I wondered if it was vanity that had me believing I was a better ally than the men in blue.

On top of that, I knew as little about Bishop as I did about his suspect—and the possibility of putting the two men in close proximity, with me in the middle, made me uneasy.

I had some thinking to do.

With a few hours to kill, I headed to my crib.

I live on a houseboat docked at Sheepshead Bay. It had taken some time to become accustomed to the constant motion of the boat—particularly at bedtime.

Eventually it had become familiar, even soothing.

The Atlantic Ocean, its bays and its inlets, have always been a major part of growing up in South Brooklyn.

We were working class kids who were a stone's throw from the seaside all summer long. We had our own island.

Growing up in Coney Island, alongside the vastness of the ocean and the mysteries that lay beyond it, always helped me appreciate my relative size in relation to the world and the universe.

It could make a kid feel small.

It could make a man battle to become big enough to contend.

I sat on the deck of the houseboat, sipping a single-malt scotch, and considered the angles. Follow through as the lone ranger, or strongly advise Jim Bishop to head straight to the police.

Maybe it was vanity, the mortal need to feel more significant. Or perhaps it was the thousand dollars sitting in the file cabinet at my office. In any case, I convinced myself it wouldn't hurt to stay in the game a little longer.

When Bishop called, I gave him my verdict.

"We need to go out there," he said.

"Is it absolutely necessary?"

"I need to see him in person, up close. When I'm sure he's the man I saw that night, we can head straight to the precinct, and I'll make a full statement. I can pick you up in front of your office in an hour."

"Take Ocean Parkway to Avenue I, take I to East Twenty-fourth, and turn left."

Bishop pulled over to the curb in front of the house. Brooklyn College was directly ahead of us.

"What now?" I asked.

Bishop began hitting his car horn repeatedly.

A light on the front porch came on.

A man walked out of the house and started moving toward the vehicle.

"Well?" I asked.

"That's him, no question."

A quick movement from Bishop caught my eye, and suddenly there was a gun in his hand. He raised his arm.

I looked from the weapon up to his face.

"It's not the way it looks," he said.

And then the lights went out.

The ammonium carbonate popped my eyes open.

I was on the ground.

A man in a white coat kneeled over me with a jar of smelling salts.

He helped me sit up.

"Sorry it took so long to get to you—we had more critical business to attend to," he said.

The EMT moved away, and a large man in a bad suit suddenly took his place.

"I'm Detective Ray Washington. You took a serious whack to the head, but you'll live," he said, taking care of the preliminaries, "and you have some explaining to do."

"What happened?"

"A man was shot less than thirty feet from where you sit and, I might add, a drawing of the man was found in your jacket pocket. We also found your PI license—your reputation precedes you."

I decide to leave that one alone.

"Is he alive?"

"He was rushed to Downstate Medical Center. The jury is still out."

"Who is he?"

"Paul Banks. He's an NYPD undercover detective."

"Was he on the Richard Sherman murder investigation?"

"Richard Sherman?" he said, helping me to my feet.

"Richard Sherman—murdered a few nights ago."

"That case was tied up this afternoon. We have the perpetrator in custody, with a full confession. The shooter's wife was suing him for divorce. Sherman was her attorney—and her lover. Detective Banks had no connection to the Sherman case."

"Are you serious?"

"I couldn't make this shit up," Washington said, "and you better start making some sense."

"I didn't shoot Banks—but I did lead the shooter straight to him."

"Follow me. I want you to start from the beginning."

We sat in Washington's unmarked motor pool car.

I gave him the story so far.

"So this client you call Bishop goes to the obituaries, pulls a name out of the hat, and sells you the Brooklyn Bridge? How smart was that?"

I had to admit it was not smart at all.

"I fucked up," I said.

"I'm inclined to believe you."

"Why would you?"

"First, I can't picture you smacking yourself in the head with a handgun. Second, I spoke to Detective John Sullivan about you. He said you were more prone to stupidity than felony."

"Sounds like something Sullivan would say."

"Detective Banks works deep undercover. Donnie Brasco shit. He is a ghost. He makes a personal appearance at a police house once, maybe twice, every three months. I didn't even know where he lived. How the hell did you find him?"

"Just my kind of luck."

"I'm still undecided about your culpability."

"So am I," I said.

"And Bishop—you have no idea how to find him?"

"None. But I could pick him out of any lineup you put in front of me when you find him. Am I under arrest?"

"I need to take you in to get a written statement," he said. And we were off to the 76th Precinct.

Washington took me into an interrogation room with a legal pad and two razor-sharp number two pencils.

I guess he didn't consider me homicidal or suicidal.

"Write it all down."

I wrote and signed a statement that included everything I cared to share with the detective.

He cut me loose with an unambiguous admonition.

"If I find you held out on me," he said, "I will personally feed your investigator's license into a shredding machine."

"Is there any word on Banks?"

"He's going to pull through."

When I left the precinct, I found Detective John Sullivan waiting outside the entrance.

"When are you going to learn, Nick?"

"Learn what?"

"That the police can be your friends—and you don't want them for enemies."

"With all due respect to you and to the Department, I'm not up for a sermon. I was played, John, and I almost got a man killed. I'm not feeling amiable."

"I can't urge you strongly enough to stand down."

"I was paid four days fees in advance. I owe the client a refund, and I would really like to settle up."

"You're making a mistake."

"I'm trying to correct a mistake. I need help. I need prints run."

"Go back in and give it to Washington."

"I'm not ready to do that."

"What's stopping me from going in myself and telling Washington you're withholding evidence?"

"I'm hoping you won't. All I want is a day."

"Do you know what you are asking?"

"I do—and I hate having to ask. If you can't help, I understand. I'll find another way. Sorry you had to come all the way down here to preach to me."

"Actually, I came because I thought you might need a ride to your car."

John Sullivan and I went back a long time. Boyhood. To say I made his job as an NYPD detective more difficult than it already was would be an understatement. Knocking heads with each other was a tradition.

John wouldn't commit to helping me—but he did agree to hear me out.

"If you have an evidence kit handy," I said when we parked on Neptune Avenue, "bring it up with you."

Up in my office, I asked him for a latex glove and a plastic evidence bag.

I lifted the pen from the filing cabinet and placed it in the bag.

"This came unused out of a box, there are only two sets of prints," I said. "One belongs to me and the other belongs to the man we're looking for."

"One condition, Nick. If we get a hit, if we identify and locate this guy, you bring it to Ray Washington"

"Deal."

"I'll call you," Sullivan said, as he moved to leave the office.

"John?"

"Yes?"

"Why didn't he shoot me when he had the chance?"

"Maybe he got to like you. Maybe he didn't want to get blood all over his car seat. Probably, he didn't consider you a threat to him. So..."

"So?"

"So hope he doesn't remember this pen and change his mind," Sullivan said, waving the evidence bag as he walked through the door.

I had failed to eat a thing all day.

I stopped into the pizzeria.

Carmella hooked me up with a veal parmigiana hero sandwich to go.

"I put a salad and a cloth napkin in the bag," Carmella said when she handed it to me.

"Why a cloth napkin?"

"It's civilized."

I picked up a cold six-pack of St. Pauli Girl on my way to the houseboat.

I took my dinner out to the deck.

I was in the cabin grabbing another beer when I heard John Sullivan call out to me.

"I'll take anything but a Coors Light."

"Drop by to watch the fireworks display?" I asked, handing him a bottle.

"I dropped by to tell you I got a hit on the prints."

"You could have phoned, saved yourself the trip."

"Sure, but then how could I stop you from doing something incredibly stupid?"

"Who is he?"

"Ted Jackson. Paroled from Riker's a week ago. Detective Banks put him away six years ago."

"I really fucked up."

"I won't argue."

"Do you know where to find him?"

"I talked to his parole officer and got an address. Now we give it to Ray Washington."

"I'm very angry, Johnny."

"We made a deal, Nicky. I don't need a debate. I need

another beer," Sullivan said, moving to the cabin.

Ted Jackson came out of nowhere.

I was seated with a bottle of beer in my hand.

He lifted his right arm and pointed a gun at my chest.

A sitting duck had a better chance.

I may have closed my eyes for a moment.

Then a bullet smashed into his shoulder, spun him around, and landed him on his back.

Sullivan was on him in a flash and had Jackson's hands cuffed behind his back in seconds.

"This should settle our argument," John said, lifting Jackson to his feet.

I rose from my chair, picked up the cloth napkin Carmella had sent with dinner, and wrapped it around my hand.

"I think the fall broke his jaw."

"What are you talking about? His jaw is fine." John said, as I moved toward them. "Nick, don't do what I think you're thinking of doing."

"It's not the way it looks," I said.

Then I swung for the bleachers and Jackson's broken jaw hit the deck.

The House on Maple Street
Janice Law
Connecticut

Harold Bain came to see me bright and early one Monday morning. That's Harold of Bain Motors, an outfit that takes up a good deal of real estate just south of town. Harold, himself, takes up a good deal of real, and psychic, estate. He's a self-made man, as he'll surely tell you, and it's probably just as well no one else has to share the credit. Harold is rich, mouthy and generous, in that order, the main object of his generosity being the Wildcats, our high school football team.

Perhaps you won't be surprised that his younger son, Harold Bain, Jr., is a high school football player? A prospect, according to his dad. A nice kid, according to his coach. A decent, but not outstanding player, according to the rest of the fans, including me. I like Friday nights down at Zabrisky Field as much as anyone, although I am definitely looking forward to Bain, Jr.'s graduation when we will no longer have to listen to Harold, Sr.'s instructions, insults, and cheers. I feel for Harold, Jr. some nights, I really do.

But if you're running a private investigation agency, you can't be too choosy. The saints and sweethearts of this world are less likely to need the services of a trained investigator than abrasive types like Harold Bain, Sr.

"Ray! How're you doing?" Harold filled the doorway. He played middle linebacker many moons ago, and he's kept the height and added weight.

"Harold!" This was a morning for exclamations, and I didn't even have Mr. Coffee gurgling yet. I took him into the office, got him a cup and considered what excuse could get me out of the latest round of business community fund raising. While Bain Motors has all the bells and whistles, Raymond Wilde Investigators is a one-man shop in our aging mill town's low rent district. Not glamorous by a long shot, but a fancy office doesn't make you any smarter even if it impresses the clientele.

"Problem, Ray."

So, a business visit. I sat down at my desk and took out a legal pad. Some people like to tap everything into their laptop. Not me. Computer data can be forever when you want it gone, and gone when it's vital. "Tell me about it," I said.

He hitched up his pant legs and leaned forward. "It's about the Wildcats," he said.

I looked up, surprised. A stealth solicitation?

"You know the Morris kid?"

"Sure." Hard to miss Laverne Morris, new to the Cats that year and a sweet QB. He was a lanky, brown-skinned kid who would probably never grow big enough for Division One, but he had a good arm and an even better eye for the game.

"He's made an impact," I said.

Harold gave a snort, like he'd grown hooves and set to paw the earth. "He belongs in Brocton," he said. "His mom lives up at the Heights. You know Brocton Heights?"

I nodded. Brocton is our bigger, tougher neighbor ten miles to the west. The town held onto its mills longer than we did, but when they went belly up, the change knocked Brocton on its ass. The Heights, particularly, had drugs, crime and unemployment, the hopeless spaghetti tangle of poverty. I see enough first hand in my present business and saw even more in my previous tenure on the Brocton force.

"See what I'm saying?" Harold asked, like I was slow on the uptake.

I shrugged. "Brocton's loss is our gain," I said.

"No, damn it! Brocton's gain is our loss. We're paying for

Laverne Morris's tuition and Brocton's saving their dime."

I saw where this was going, but thought I might head it off at the pass. "I think the Broncos are, what, one and three at the moment, while the Wildcats are four and oh?"

Harold leaned back in his chair. "It's the principle of the thing."

Beware of the principle of anything, which usually means someone's out for number one but doesn't want to admit it. That was the case with Harold, and I soon spotted his agenda. Saving a few thousand for the school board was neither here nor there. His real aim was to promote Harold, Jr. from his present position as backup quarterback.

To this end, Harold, Sr. wanted proof that Laverne Morris was not actually living with his uncle at 249 Maple Street. "It's all for football," Harold said. I supposed it was.

"He's at his mom's every weekend."

I couldn't really fault the boy on that score. "What do you want me to do?"

"Stake the place out, keep an eye on it! Find out if the Morris kid's actually living there. Early morning, late night, drive by visits! And I want to know if the guy is actually his uncle. Do that first. If he's not, bingo! Questions for the school board, right?"

"Surveillance is expensive, Harold," I said. And it's something I'm not super fond of. Working the computer, being out and about, talking to people, all okay. Sitting in my Jeep Cherokee on a cold day tightens up my bad leg.

Harold was already taking out his checkbook. I will say for Harold that he pays up front and his checks are good.

"All right," I said. "I'll establish ownership of the house, relationship to young Morris. If there's any irregularity, I'll let you know. Otherwise, I'll find out if Laverne's living there full time. Except for weekends. I think weekends with his mom you've got to allow for."

Soon as Harold left, I tidied up a few reports, made some

calls, checked the email, then went to the web. First stop, Vision Appraisal, a handy source for finding out who owns what. The owner of 249 Maple Street was listed as Johnson E. Robertson.

A little genealogical research told me that Marvina Robertson Morris of Brocton Heights had a brother, Johnson, and a chat with a pal of mine, a security guard at Brocton High, confirmed that Laverne's mother, "a hard worker, does a late shift at Walmart" had worried that her son was not getting enough guidance. "He's a nice kid but immature, too smart for his own good, if you know what I mean."

I did. I asked about his dad, and my friend shook his head. "Fallujah, I'm pretty sure. Somewhere in Anbar, anyway. One of them IEDs, I think."

I got the picture. Later that day, I called Harold and said, "Johnson E. Robertson is Laverne's uncle. Robertsons and Morrises have been around the area a long time, and Johnson's lived in town since ninety-four."

"I don't give a damn about his uncle! The kid's not living there! I'm sure he's not."

Keep your shirt on, I thought. "I'll find out," I said, although my best guess was that Laverne was spending week-days with his uncle and going back for home cooking on the weekends. Or maybe weekends was when his mom was off work and felt she could keep track of him. That was possible, too.

Maple Street is a street I know well. It's got nice, older homes that would be worth a third more if they weren't within two blocks of Main Street, formerly a row of hand-some retail businesses, now a demonstration of the perils of small business. The only survivor from the latest round of hopefuls is the tattoo parlor, and the longest standing tenant on the whole street is the liquor store.

But that made my job easier. I could park the Cherokee in the lot behind the bank and keep watch on 249 Maple Street.

No need for all day, all night, either. I figured I'd park there when football practice let out to make sure Laverne arrived. Then I'd show by seven-fifteen a.m. the next morning to see if he was on his way out the door to school. Do that for a couple of days, and, if Laverne was playing it straight, I could assure Harold, Sr. that his kid should resign himself to riding the bench or playing in the secondary.

For the next few days, I settled in around four-thirty p.m. with a cup of coffee and breaking news on my smart phone. Laverne's uncle's house was nicely located for a football player, being two blocks down and three over from the field. Unless Laverne cut through the back yards, I figured he'd walk back toward the school building, turn on Main and then onto Maple Street.

Sure enough. Five-fifteen, I see his lanky figure, accompanied by a girl in a track suit, another athlete, I guessed. They stood talking in front of 249 for a few minutes, plenty of time for me to take a photo, complete with time and date stamp, before the girl crossed to the parking lot, passed quite close to my car, and headed onto Main. Laverne went inside. That first night, I waited until dark. With no sign of the boy leaving, I had packed up my notes and started the car when I saw three figures on Maple Street. Good-sized figures. Football players? Over for a visit with their QB? Or set to go off somewhere with Laverne?

I switched off the motor and waited. They went by 249. Fine, they were no business of mine. I was ready to get home for a late supper when something kept my hand off the wheel. Ex-cops know body language; keeping an eye on rowdy adolescents, would-be vandals, addicts, and crooks of all kinds makes you sensitive to the over-the-shoulder look and furtive glance.

I snapped the boys as they passed under a streetlight before stopping at a brown house with a wide porch thickly screened by overgrown branches. I'd thought the house was empty, but one boy took out a cell phone and whatever he texted brought on the porch light. The door opened, the boys went in. Visit to a sick friend or a home-schooled buddy?

Not two minutes later, all three were back on the street and moving so fast I barely had time to snap another photo, pure habit because 253 Maple Street was not my concern. I made a note on my time sheet and went off the clock. Next morning, I arrived in the lot with a breakfast burrito and a coffee just in time to see Laverne come out the door with his school backpack. An easy morning.

That was the drill for the next couple of days. Check Laverne Morris's arrival, take a time and date stamped photo and make sure he was in for the night. Although I'd suspected after day one that the kid was a legit resident, I kept at it, racking up the photos. I like to do a thorough job, and Harold, Sr. would expect no less. I also added to my file on 253 Maple Street, a dark closed-up place with no resident adolescents that, nonetheless, had attracted half the football team, including Harold, Jr. I thought I'd like to know about that.

On Friday night, I went to the game. I'd have gone anyway because the Cats were playing a downstate team with a hot QB and a serious coach. Thanks to Laverne's arm and our stalwart line, the Cats squeaked out a win. I joined other happy fans on the field afterwards to say "Good game, Coach," and to complement everyone from the boys to the assistants, the trainer and the equipment manager. Victory makes for easy conversations.

Out on the field, it was hugs all round. The linemen, muddy and sweaty, stood arm in arm, bellowing the school song with added lyrics of their own. In between verses, they gave the mantra for the year, "Bigger, Stronger, Faster." They'd accomplished the first goal, all right. From the stands the team looked of average size. Once down on the field, I realized that some of them were massive, including Bain's boy. They had big arms, big legs, thick necks—and I sensed an attitude to go with them.

Meanwhile, the receivers and running backs, our scorers, were talking to the school reporter and to the local sports maven, who was holding his smart phone above his head to catch their accounts. Laverne was accepting congratulations beside the same athletic girl who walked home with him every evening, when a tall woman wearing a windbreaker and a red Cats' hat, came through the crowd. He put his arm around her and let himself be kissed.

"Good game, honey, but I gotta go. I clock in at eleven."

He gave the girl a hug and walked with his mom toward a beat-up Ford wagon. I guessed he was off to Brocton Heights for the weekend, and I was right. I didn't see Laverne again until he left his uncle's house at seven-fifteen Monday morning. I was ready to go back and write my report, when someone pulled up at the neighbor's house. This visitor was an adult, and like all the others, he was in and out real fast, but unlike the boys he carried a paper bag under his arm. Whatever it was, he was buying in bulk and with the sun right on his face, I got a clear photo.

Immediately I wished I hadn't, because I'd seen him on the field Friday night, patting the kids on the shoulder or slapping them five: our Wildcats' trainer. With one click of the camera, a simple surveillance job had turned into a nest of worms. I didn't need to see what was in the bag to guess what he was buying and the kids, too. I'd have bet my PI license that the Cats best season in a decade—and a huge boost to town morale—was powered by PEDs, performance enhancing drugs, most likely anabolic steroids.

I pulled out my cell phone in the hopes of getting the owner's name, but 253 Maple Street was a rental. So though my Jeep was already chilly and my leg was getting stiff, I settled down to wait, partly out of curiosity, partly to delay a decision. I hadn't been hired to scope out a funny drugs dealer, especially not one visited by Harold, Jr., who I guessed had good reasons for wanting to be "Bigger, Stronger, Faster."

On the other hand, if I was right, Harold, Jr. and his team were messing with a schedule III controlled substance that is bad stuff for boys of seventeen and eighteen. Not to mention that the dealer would definitely interest my old buddies at the state police barracks down the road.

I hadn't decided what I was going to do, so I pulled up our local school's website and tapped in Wildcat football. Sure enough, the staff was listed, including the trainer, Eustis Boyle. It wasn't hard to find Boyle's address, saved for future reference, and after more effort on the web and a few phone calls, I determined that one Matt Arsine was paying the rent at 253 Maple Street.

Right at ten a.m., out he came, pale as a mushroom, as if he and daylight were poorly acquainted. He put a large cardboard box into the trunk of his late model Honda, and when he started east on Maple Street, I cut back to Main Street and followed him onto the interstate, where the Honda's vanity plate, STRNGR, brought me an unwelcome echo of this year's "Bigger, Stronger, Faster" cheer.

He drove all the way to the shore, stopping twice at commercial gyms, allowing me to get clear photos both times, before he entered the grounds of a private college. I'd seen enough by then, and I returned to my office to complete the report on Laverne Morris's residency. By five o'clock, I had the day's work wrapped up, and I drove to the parking lot, where I was in luck. The black Honda with the STRNGR plate was already in the drive at 253 Maple Street.

I knocked on the door. No answer. Had the kids had some sort of code? I tried twice more and I was about to give up when the door opened a crack, and the pale face of Matt Arsine appeared. I got a shock when I saw him close up. He looked about fifteen; I guessed he was barely this side of twenty-one.

"I've see your S-T-R-N-G-R plate around. I'm getting to the age when I could do with a boost in the strength department. Got anything good for me?"

He moved his head to indicate I should come in. The house opened right onto the living room, now furnished with a couple of chairs and a very large flat screen TV. The shades were pulled on the windows, and even the bright afternoon sun was having a tough time making headway. There was just enough for me to see into the room beyond with its dim stacks of cartons and boxes.

"I might have something." He went into the back and shut the door. I had the feeling he had been working in there when I knocked. I scarcely had time to let my eyes adjust and to scan the room before he returned with a small bottle. "Set you back fifty dollars," he said. "But this is the good stuff."

I took out my wallet, and he handed over the drug. As soon as my hands were full, he reached behind his back and came up with a Ruger LC9 pistol. I'd let his juvenile appearance fool me.

"Interesting sales pitch," I said and stood very still.

"I've seen you around." He gestured for my wallet, and I handed it over. "Raymond Wilde Investigations?"

"Correct."

"Somebody hire you?"

"Not for you. You only came up in passing."

He was a cool one, but he was young and uncertain whether to settle the problem pronto or work out a deal. I was hoping for the latter, but before he could decide, his cell phone dinged with a text. One of his regulars, I guessed. Arsine raised a warning finger and we both froze.

A click as the door opened. My arrival must have rattled him, for he'd neglected to flip the lock. The result was a big rectangle of late day sun interrupted by a very large silhouette.

Arsine had screwed up big time, and at that realization, he took his eyes off me for an instant—I guess he underestimated me, too. I grabbed his wrist. The pistol went off, and the big flatscreen TV exploded.

Another shot and another, as I felt something sting across my back.

"Help me!" Arsine shouted as the pistol went off again.

"Keep back! Call nine-one-one!" I yelled. The last thing I wanted was some kid barreling in and getting shot.

I was both taller and heavier than Arsine, but he was younger and more agile and absolutely desperate to break free for a clean shot. We struggled back and forth until he got a foot against my damaged knee, the one that sent me off the Brocton force to the ambiguous territory mined by Raymond Wilde Investigations. I heard myself scream, then we were both bowled over, crashing to the floor as the Ruger skittered away.

The pain in my knee rocketed up my spine as I struggled to keep down lunch amidst the uproar of people arriving and Arsine's shouts. Someone said, "Oh, man!" and a girl's voice, clearly on her phone, gave the 253 Maple Street address and added "Shots fired. Someone's hurt. Send police and an ambulance. Come quick, please! Quick!"

I got my hand on a chair and managed to get myself up onto one hip. Arsine was noisy on the floor, half smothered by a very large boy, a boy I recognized. "Thanks," I told Harold, Jr.

"You all right, man?" That was the neighbor, Laverne, the ultimate reason for my presence, and from his lanky physique, one of the few players I'd bet had never sampled Arsine's dubious wares.

"Get that pistol. Bring it here so I can take out the magazine."

I had trouble focusing and my fingers seemed disconnected from the usual neural circuits, but I managed. "Give both to the troopers," I said, but he, being savvy in the ways of Brocton Heights, asked the girl, Sam, to hold them. Then he lifted me into the chair. "You shot?"

"Ricochet, maybe. Nothing serious. He kicked my bad knee." I leaned my head back against the chair, let the world go black momentarily, and thought, not for the first time, that there's no fool like a middle-aged fool.

The state police barracks are only a half mile away from Maple Street, and the troopers squealed up with sirens and flashing lights, followed shortly by an ambulance.

"The kids saved my life," I told them. "Especially Bain, here."

Harold, Jr. got up off Arsine to stand, white and shaking, with his arms around Laverne and Sam, while the troopers cuffed Arsine and hustled him out the door. The EMTs came to help me to the ambulance, where I pulled up my cell phone, found my photo reel, and hit the delete for the ones showing young Bain coming out of the dealer's house. Favoritism, I know, but I owed the kid big time.

At the hospital they looked me over and cleaned me up—I'd caught a ricocheted bullet across my upper back—and told me that the knee surgery I put off years ago was now first up on the docket. So it was two days later, with a nice new bionic knee and an assortment of aches and pains, that I had a visit from Harold Bain, Sr. Not the man I most wanted to see, but I'd discovered that morphine smooths out lots of rough edges.

"I'm out tomorrow," I said. "I'll put that report in the mail then, but I can tell you I found squat. The kid's legit."

He waved a hand dismissively, pulled up the visitor's chair and sat down. He seemed quieter and smaller somehow, as if he'd been under a big internal pressure that had fizzled away.

He didn't speak for a moment, and I said, "Your boy saved my life. He's a brave kid."

"He was on the steroids," Harold said. "They all were."

So the boy had fessed up. Good. Saved me an awkward conversation. "Mostly, not all."

He nodded his head reluctantly. "Not Laverne, no. Still skinny. A big talent. I wanted my boy to have that kind of talent. Instead, it turns out he's a goddamn hero."

"One hundred percent genuine." I said. "Football is short term. That kind of character is for the long haul."

"He and Laverne—good friends. I didn't know that. And I didn't know Harold was the leader off the field. He's the one who called the team meeting afterwards. Talked to the boys, said they had to tell the parents, tell the school. Christ!" He wiped his eyes.

'Course, the results weren't all sweetness and light. The trainer was fired, and the coach left after the season. The Wildcats finished 8-3, missing their best ever chance for a state championship. People had opinions on that, you bet, some of which came my way, and Harold, Sr. remained just as mouthy as ever in the stands.

Still, if you eliminated cranks and troublemakers, Raymond Wilde Investigations would close its doors. And sometimes I think its ambiguous territory is A-okay, for limping away after the last game at Zabrisky Field, I saw Harold, Sr. shake hands with Laverne Morris before walking out with his arm across his son's shoulders.

Finding Justice
Thomas Donahue
North Adams, Massachusetts

1.

Hoosac Mills, Massachusetts

Autumn 2004

The Mills held secrets—always did, always will. Yet simple obstacles such as fact finding never stopped Stephen Nicholson in the past. It wouldn't stop him in the present. Hoosac Mills, a staple set in the midst of Berkshire County of western Massachusetts, remained a memorable place to the part-time private investigator. Its taverns and streets and particularly its people cast an intoxicating spell that had long captivated his vision of hard work, honesty, and civic pride. He descended Route 2 in his dusted Jeep Wrangler. At the deadly hairpin turn, his radio at last caught the signal from Boston sports radio.

"*...and Dave Roberts has just stolen second base. The Red Sox have hope.*" Stephen laughed. It was the ALCS and the Sox trailed the Yankees, 3-0. Winning Game 4 could happen, he supposed. Taking it to seven games defied all probability and the notion of winning the ALCS over their arch nemesis in pinstripes was the stuff of Hollywood and fairy tales.

He parked at the Berkshire Inn parking lot; he'd catch the rest of the game from his hotel room.

The Mills defined much of Stephen Nicholson's core: first love, deaths, adventure, college years, friendship, romance, family tragedy and even recent heartbreak. Once-proud brick-and-mortar factories had long closed their doors; yet the soul of the Mills—its people—retained their pride. Stephen loved the Mills unconditionally—yet felt at times the Mills didn't love him back. Maybe that would change.

He stepped onto the hotel room balcony. Here he took in the view of his first objective: Taconic State College. The college's name was taken from the Native Americans meaning "in the trees." The institution's motto was *Fidelis-Veritas*—Loyalty-Truth.

The college's Gothic buildings, strategically positioned between non-indigenous ornamental trees and manicured sod, literally robbed the ancient Taconic Mountains of Western New England of their most precious boulders and stones, and used them to construct the very buildings gated-academics used now to revise history.

2.

"Justice Edgemont! I love her," Tamantha Parris said as she sat at the desk of her neat, economical office. "May I see your credentials?"

Stephen slid a copy of his Commonwealth of Massachusetts Private Investigator's license, plus a laminated eight-and-a-half by eleven sheet of paper across the desk. The sheet was a simplified cut-and-paste of his intent. It contained Stephen's business information, a shrunken photocopy of his private eye ID, and a quick, written paragraph explaining that Mrs. Nikki Edgemont of Jamaica Plain had hired him to locate her daughter: twenty-one year old Taconic State senior Justice Edgemont. A recent color photo in the lower left hand corner showcased Justice's blonde hair, green eyes, and exceptional looks. The photo was small—two-by-three inches. Nicholson would be walking around a college campus asking questions about an attractive twenty-one-year-old girl. He wanted to minimize innuendo of the untoward nature.

Tamantha served as the graduate student teaching assistant, or TA, in Justice's favorite course, Film Creation. Tamantha looked thirtyish. Strawberry-blonde hair, light freckles, and a curvy figure complemented her five-seven frame. Undergraduate male students frequented her office with concocted requests for help. Tamantha knew why, of course. Now she eyed Stephen. "I like your name but the initials don't work," she said.

"What did you say?"

Tamantha assessed him: mid-thirties, short cropped brown hair, Irish features and a lean yet capable build on a frame two inches shy of six feet. He wore black loafers, gray khakis and a loose-fitting, white golf shirt. She liked his physical presentation. "Your name has strength," she said. "But your initials, S and N, don't work. I like them strong, like JD or BJ or FX."

Stephen smirked. "Name and initials were out of my control."

"Understood," Tamantha said. "You carry a gun?"

"Not on school grounds."

"You are judicious," Tamantha replied. "Now to the matter at hand...I didn't know Justice was missing."

"No one really does," Stephen said. "Her mother wants her found quickly and quietly."

"What do you think happened?"

"All I know is she got off the bus and vanished. Mother's coming up tomorrow and I don't know about her father. But I hope not."

Tamantha's brow raised. "Why?"

"Guy threatened me when I showed at his apartment and started asking questions."

"What?"

"They're divorced," Stephen said. "The mother hired me but the father won't pay half. He said, verbatim, 'Ain't no screw who can't keep his own house in order gonna go looking for my daughter.'"

"He called you a *screw?*"

Stephen smiled. "Slang for correction officer. It's my full-time job in Boston. Private investigation is my side gig."

"He should want you looking for his daughter; at least I would if it were my kid."

Five years earlier Stephen had been hired to solve a cold case murder of a Hoosac Mills girl. Stephen and others—namely Detective Melanie Leary—linked the case to additional murders. They ultimately named the murderer. It came with national headlines and a morbid curiosity to Hoosac Mills. Yet, for Stephen, it came with a burden. The serial killer—coined the Olympian because he murdered every four years—was Matthew Nicholson. Stephen's older brother.

Stephen accepted Tamantha's delicate acknowledgment with a nod.

A young man with a stocky build, wearing tight denim jeans entered the office. Impressive muscle begged for space from the kid's one-size-too small polo shirt. He set down a bunch of blue essay response booklets, failing to acknowledge Stephen but ogling Tamantha without realizing he was ogling. "Anything else, Miss Parris?"

"No, Edmund," she said. Tamantha pointed to Stephen. "This is Mr. Stephen Nicholson. He's a real-life private investigator and he's looking for Justice Edgemont. She's been reported missing by her mother and he's been hired to find her."

"Nice to meet you," Stephen said, standing and extending his hand.

"Is the Olympian your brother?" asked Edmund with a dead-fish handshake.

"Edmund!" Tamantha yelled.

"Yes," Stephen said.

"He get caught yet?"

"No."

"You own a gun?" Edmund asked.

"Yes," Stephen said.

"Wicked cool," Edmund said. Then he switched gears. "Justice is a good kid. Wicked smart. Find her fast. She's in my Film Creation group and we have our first draft due on Friday."

Nothing like prioritizing your concerns, kid.

"You know her well?" Stephen asked.

"Classroom," Edmund said.

"Describe her."

Edmund hesitated, "She's about five-nine, maybe—"

"Not physically," Stephen said. "What's she like?"

Edmund's challenged mind searched for a keen response—or could that mind be vacuous? Stephen surmised the latter. "She's a good kid," he said.

"Who are her friends?"

"All the seniors."

"Boyfriend?"

Edmund rubbed his chin. "She dates a kid named Michael—he's got a weird French last name."

There were black bears on Hoosac Mountain with higher IQs than Edmund. "Thank you," Stephen said. "You've been a great help."

"Thanks!" he smiled. Edmund looked to Tamantha—for approval. She gave him a not-so-subtle gesture to leave, which he understood and promptly left the room.

Stephen had already spoken with two instructors earlier in the morning. Neither discussion revealed anything. Two remained after Film Creation.

"Tamantha, I need some time with Professor Vetrovic."

She looked at her watch. "He's unavailable; I'll schedule for tomorrow."

"Okay," he said.

Tamantha fidgeted. "Look, Mr. Nicholson—"

"Stephen."

"Thank you," she said. "I'm due in a classroom right now, but I will help with anything you need."

Stephen smiled. "You ever go to The Library?"

"Are you kidding?" she laughed. "Tonight is trivia night!"

"I'll see you there," Stephen said. "There is one thing you could do for me?"

"Name it," she said.

"The vice president promised me full cooperation. So, I asked for the student rosters of all Justice's classes. The VP went on a tangent about student rights, privacy and the school's legal department."

Tamantha paused. "Done," she said.

3.

Michael Desjardin lived in an apartment close to campus, tucked above Baran's Convenience Store. A forged-steel fire escape stairwell attached to the right side of the building provided access to the apartment. Shades were lowered. Music—specifically Jane's Addiction with lyrics attesting to what some girl Jane had to say—blared loudly.

Stephen knocked—twice. No one answered. A slightly opened window to the right of the landing caught his attention. The left half of the window positioned in front of the landing, the right set clear from the railing, fifteen feet above the ground. Hence, a window entry would be illegal, awkward, and dangerous. Stephen knocked again. No response.

He scanned the street. Nobody. He used his right hand to hoist the window; then, with a quick, athletic, movement Stephen swung his right leg over the railing and used both arms to half-jump into the apartment kitchen. He landed softly. As he rose he felt a sharp jolt of pain across his right bicep and torso. A golf club—in particular, a six-iron Spaulding—ricocheted off his body and skidded across the linoleum floor. Thankfully, the club head missed. Only the shaft connected solidly. A sloppy, poorly thrown punch landed unevenly above Stephen's right eye.

Stephen gained footing, retreated, readied his hands, then visually located his opponent. Michael Desjardin eyed the golf club only feet from Stephen.

"Don't," Stephen said. Desjardin swung a wild left hook. Stephen parry-blocked the punch with his right forearm, then swept the college senior's feet with a strong, low right leg kick. The college kid did his best *Charlie-Brown-miss-the-football* impersonation, landing flat on his back. His chest pumped up and down. Stephen kneeled over him and placed his hand onto Desjardin's shoulder. The kid weighed about a hundred fifty pounds. "I'm not a burglar," Stephen said. "I'm a private investigator, my name is Nicholson, and I'm looking for your girlfriend."

"You're looking for Justice?"

"Yes," Stephen said. "I've been hired to find her." He stood then backed away.

Desjardin rose. He turned off Jane's Addiction. "Who hired you?" he asked.

"Nikki Edgemont. Your girlfriend's been missing for three days, you're her boyfriend, so my Sherlock Holmes starter kit sent me here."

"Justice ain't missing," Desjardin said. He went to the refrigerator and pulled out two light beers; he tossed one to Stephen. "Dangerous breaking into a dude's apartment."

"Duly noted," Stephen said. "How do you know she ain't missing? She's had zero cell phone activity and no plastic transactions since getting off the bus."

Desjardin motioned toward two chestnut leather chairs. They sat across from one another. Stephen held the beer to his eye before opening it. "She came here when she got back from Jamaica Plain," Desjardin said.

"What was her disposition?" Stephen asked.

"Huh?"

"Was Justice in a good mood, bad mood, or showing emotion that was out of character?"

Desjardins shrugged. "Not really any of that," he said. "She asked me for money, and I gave it to her."

"Why'd she need money?"

"Not sure," Desjardin said. "She chilled out here for two hours then left."

"Did she say where she was going?"

"Nope," Desjardin said. "We have understandings. We don't sweat each other. She disappeared two years ago. Same deal. Mother hired a PI to find her then she showed up like nothing happened. The whole time she was at a friend's house in Southie."

"You worried?"

"Nope," Desjardin said. "You should be worried because Nikki didn't pay the last PI and she ain't gonna pay you either."

"Is that so?" Stephen said.

"Nikki knows Justice will show up," Desjardin said. "It's all about status. She just wants to tell her Moss Hill girlfriends—the ones in the short tennis skirts banging around on their old men—that she hired a private eye."

Stephen set his beer on a thick-glassed coffee table. "I need to speak with Justice's friends."

Desjardin laughed. "Good luck," he said. "They're all weird. She hangs with Lornece Atwater, Irina Dinelli...and lately some older chick named Manty."

"What's Manty's last name?" Stephen asked.

"I don't know but she's a psycho chick," Desjardin answered.

"Why's that?"

Desjardin shrugged. "Know it when I see it," he said. "These chicks all want to be in the movies and they're all obsessed with Vetrovic."

Stephen drained his beer. He scanned the apartment. The table and chairs were solid oak. A fifty-inch TV was mounted to the wall. A fully stocked bar containing top-shelf liquors sat across from the kitchen utilities. A large de-humidifier hummed nearby. Three bottles of vitamin B were in eyesight.

Stephen considered all of it.

"You sure got to me fast," he said. "When I came in it was as if you expected me."

"Say what?" Desjardin asked.

"You attacked me with a golf club like you were waiting for someone," Stephen countered.

"Thought it was a home invasion."

"Michael..."

"Yeah?"

Stephen rose and used his right hand as a make-believe wand and visually highlighted all of the luxurious amenities of a small college one-bedroom apartment. "I'll ask again: why did you come after me with a golf club?"

"I got home invaded early this morning."

"Please elaborate," Stephen said.

"Four o'clock this morning a couple dudes rolled me while I laid in bed. They wore masks—pinned me down, blindfolded me and stuck a shotgun in my mouth."

"Who?" Stephen asked.

"Don't know but my best guess is a crew outta Pittsfield that wants the college action."

This piqued Stephen's curiosity. "They say anything?"

"Nothing," Desjardin said.

"Really?"

"You don't understand," Desjardin said. "One of the dudes said, 'Say nothing.'"

"Then what?" Stephen asked.

"They left," Desjardin said.

"They rob you of money or product?"

Desjardin hesitated. "Nope."

Stephen was stumped. Could a "crew" out of Pittsfield kidnap Justice Edgemont to wrest control of a lowly college campus drug dealer like Michael Desjardin? No, that simply wasn't plausible. Maybe Justice really was stowed away with some city friend?

"Good luck, Michael," Stephen said as he walked to the door.

As Stephen descended the steps, Desjardin's parting words resonated: "I know who you are, Mr. Nicholson. You shouldn't be in the Mills."

4.

Some college kid's voice bellowed as Stephen walked away from Desjardin's apartment. "Have a good day, Professor Vetrovic!" Stephen stopped. The anonymous voice aimed toward Elder Hall—the very building where Professor Vetrovic made his name—and fame.

Stephen wasted no time. He slipped inside Elder Hall and reported directly to Tamantha Parris' office. No luck. As he turned to leave a door with stenciled lettering on the criss-cross pattern glass grabbed his attention. The name was quickly becoming familiar: Dr. Marc Vetrovic.

Stephen looked through the glass into a deep room. No movement. He knocked, twice. No response. He turned the door knob.

Click.

Acting against better judgment Stephen entered Dr. Vetrovic's office.

"Hello?"

The professor's desk and filing cabinets were at the room's

entrance. The rest of the area contained shelves lined with hundreds of movie props and paraphernalia: racks of costumes, mannequins, framed photos of Hollywood stars, movie posters, and more. A special section seemed dedicated to military and law enforcement. There were army uniforms, prop weapons, an open box of MREs, fake hand grenades, netting, Smith & Wesson and Peerless boxes, a mahogany carved wooden box fitted with prop knives, and even prop bullets. Two rows of costumes included an Evel Knievel outfit, Elvis costumes, old-style puffy Spanish or French Middle Ages dresses and blouses, and even kinky stuff reserved for adult films. A nautical section boasted portholes, rigging, sailor uniforms, flares and a flare gun.

"May I help you?"

Stephen spun. A tall, thin, fiftyish-looking man was behind him. "I'm looking for Dr. Vetrovic."

Before speaking, the man slid a hand over his blond hair and down the length of his ponytail. "I'm Dr. Vetrovic. And with whom am I speaking...?"

"Stephen Nicholson."

Stephen showed his credentials, apologized for being off-limits, then explained the purpose of his visit. "Justice loves your class," Stephen said. Vetrovic nodded. "Professor, what can you tell me about Justice?"

Vetrovic smiled and proceeded to the thermostat on the far wall, adjusting the heat.

It was a simple move on the surface, but it highlighted a tactic employed by people of power to maintain—or, in this case—establish control of a situation.

"The temperature plummets quicker in Berkshire County," Vetrovic said, a cute insult neatly aimed at Boston.

Duly noted, Professor.

Vetrovic fiddled with his tie. "Brilliant girl," he said. "I had her this past spring, I have her now, and I'll have her next semester as well."

I had her, I have her, I'll have her, Stephen thought.

Vetrovic continued. "I know little about her personal life. We at Taconic State make a concerted effort to avoid familiarizing ourselves with students away from the academic arena." The professor moved to his desk. He shuffled paperwork, yet read none of it, before looking up at the wall clock.

Why are you on edge, Professor?

"Does Justice date anyone?" Stephen asked.

Vetrovic paused. "I don't chart the dating trails of my pupils."

"Do you know any of Justice's friends?"

"I know Ms. Edgemont's classmates."

"Do you know her parents?" Stephen asked.

Vetrovic's eye twitched. "You'll have to excuse me, Mr. Nicholson, but I have an engagement. I must lock this office. Can't have more security breaches."

"Can we chat as soon as possible?" Stephen asked, handing the professor his business card.

"Of course we can," Vetrovic said, pocketing the card.

"Thank you," Stephen said, departing.

Vetrovic stood in place, frozen, for one minute. Beads of sweat had produced wet spots in his armpits and the small of his back. Vetrovic pulled his cell phone from his coat pocket. After five long rings a male voice answered. "Have you arrived in the Mills yet, my friend?" Vetrovic asked, struggleing to keep his voice light.

"Yeah, I'm here now," the man replied.

Vetrovic exhaled with relief, then said: "We may have a problem."

5.

The Library served as a one-size-fits-all tavern, catering to college kids, Millers, and sports enthusiasts. Stephen had worked there as a student and maintained a bond with Josef Kieler, the proprietor. As promised, he now sat across from the beautiful Tamantha Parris. Stephen gripped a pint of Ireland's finest stout while Tamantha worked on a Tanqueray and tonic.

The trivia maestro bellowed from the event stage. "Okay, final question: He served as the only bachelor president in U.S. history."

"Abraham Lincoln!" someone shouted, to a roar of laughter.

The speaker wore a T-shirt that was skin tight and khaki shorts that were hiked above his knees. Stephen recognized him immediately.

"Edmund doesn't hold a minor in History or Interdisciplinary Studies?"

Tamantha smiled, then belted out: "James Buchanan!"

"Right again, young lady!" the trivia maestro yelled. "That makes you tonight's winner!"

Josef Kieler walked to the table, all smiles, as always. Josef looked at Stephen, then the pint of stout. He made a gun gesture with his right thumb and index finger.

"I'm not carrying, buddy," Stephen said.

Josef showed both palms and smiled. "I never asked," he said, slipping a trivia night-winning gift certificate to Tamantha and walking away.

Stephen raised his pint; Tamantha raised her glass. "Well played, young lady," Stephen said.

"I'm twenty-nine," Tamantha answered.

"Okay, then...*señora*."

Tamantha delivered a flirtatious punch to Stephen's bicep. Pain shot up his arm—that is, the Spaulding six-iron arm. He winced. They locked eyes. "You're no longer engaged to Melanie Leary," she said.

"I'm not," he managed.

"What happened?" Tamantha asked.

The foam of his beer had settled at the high-water mark—ripe for drinking. He looked at Tamantha. An internal bomb exploded.

Melanie was the coolest and baddest and smartest detective ever in the Mills...she helped name the Olympian... she showed more heart than any fellow officer in prison...she won my heart when it had never truly been won...she made chief then quickly forgot about the correction officer on the other side of the state...she abandoned me.

"We drifted apart," he answered.

A pause.

"I see," Tamantha said, "why would she dump you?"

Stephen eyed the pint; the foam had settled. He picked it up and drained half the glass. Slowly, he placed the pint glass on the table and looked at Tamantha. "Things didn't work out," he said.

Tamantha leaned into him and touched his cheek with the back of her hand. Stephen didn't object. Tamantha possessed an indisputable academic and sexual prowess that enticed Stephen; the compassion surprised him.

"You're a beautiful woman," he said. "What's your story?"

"You're sweet," she said. "I've lived in the Mills my whole life, except for my undergrad years at UMass."

"Your family still here?" Stephen asked.

Tamantha laughed. "My family will always live here...so long as people in the Mills and surrounding towns die."

Stephen played along. "Meaning...?"

"My family has maintained Hoosac Cemetery for generations. In fact—this may sound weird—we own it," Tamantha said.

"You're kidding me," he said. "Did you ever work there?"

"Dug a grave or two," Tamantha said, winking. She jumped a seat and sat beside Stephen. With her perfume now up close and personal, Stephen had bigger things on his mind than the remaining stout. "I'm fifth-generation Hoosac Mills. My ancestor bought the land, founded the cemetery, created a trust, and we've been running it since. I'm the chair of the trust and my cousin is the foreman."

"That's creepy-on-steroids yet makes you even more sexy," Stephen said.

Did I really just say that?

Tamantha placed her drink on the table, cusped his neck and delivered a PG-13 kiss on his lips. "Thank you for saying that."

Stephen's Catholic-guilt eyes scanned the bar.

"Don't worry," Tamantha said. "Only forty people saw that kiss."

He stared into her dark eyes. "Let's roll outta here and give 'em something they won't see."

It would be a late night at the Berkshire Inn.

6.

Stephen charted a course in his Jeep that was supposed to return him to the Berkshire Inn gymnasium. But the steering wheel had a navigational mind of its own. Stephen soon found himself on a spontaneous detour that led to the Hoosac Mills City Library—the city library that is, not the college tavern.

A hulking, nineteenth-century brick and granite structure, the public library held the captured long-forgotten toils of the New England indentured servants of the robber-baron era. The hand-craftsmanship of the Roman columns, large, double-hung windows, ornate gargoyles, and wrought-iron; it was the time capsule of the forgotten artisan laborer. Ceilings hung at twenty-eight feet. Partitions scribed in specialty woods, quarter-sawn oak bookshelves chock full of antiquarian books that showed no signs of sagging after more than a century's hard duty.

At the center entrance a circular console boasted state-of-the-art computers, presided over by an elderly librarian with a classic ramrod Yankee frame and keen, gray eyes that could—at a sideways glance—spot a misshelved edition of *Little Women.*

A name tag identified her as Gertie. She studied Stephen—carefully. "Welcome back to Hoosac Mills."

"Good afternoon," he answered.

Folks of Gertie's stature had a sixth sense not preached in classroom theory; rather, it was acquired with decades of love, loss and adventure. Gertie knew that Stephen had zero interest in checking out a copy of *War and Peace.*

"May I use your Internet, ma'am?"

"You may," she said. "Unless, of course, I could assist you."

"I should be okay."

"Very well then," she said in a tone suggesting he'd blundered. She pointed to several round tables, each equipped with flat screens and keyboards. "Is it Roslindale, Hyde Park or West Roxbury?" she asked, in her silken Oxford accent.

"You're good, Ms. Gertie," Stephen said with a smile.

Stephen took a seat at one of the computers and got to work. The library was empty; clunky mechanical noises that pushed heat into the cast-iron radiators provided a soothing effect. Stephen got busy. In moments he had three separate search engines working simultaneously in three different windows. Google, Yahoo, and AltaVista—all programmed for advanced search—tracked one subject: Taconic State College Professor Marc Vetrovic.

Vetrovic didn't pass the proverbial sniff test. Stephen couldn't quantify it; it fell under the instincts umbrella. The professor had been evasive and visibly uncomfortable when speaking about Justice Edgemont. *Why was that, Professor?*

Academic achievement highlighted all search hits. Vetrovic's specialty was all things regarding film, his most decorated achievement a Cannes Film Festival Best Film award years earlier for producing and directing *Enabling Cain*. Vetrovic had also received multiple awards from the academic community.

His biography revealed little: forty-nine years old, undergrad at Emerson in Boston and earned his PhD in Film Production at the University of Southern California. Previous teaching stints included California, Michigan, and now four years at Taconic State. No information about his family.

A cup of coffee appeared near Stephen's right hand. He spun. There stood Gertie. "Compliments of the Hoosac Mills City Library," she said. Gertie pointed to a table adjacent to the wall nearest the restrooms. "There are sugar packets and creamers."

"Thank you," Stephen said. Gertie smiled. "I'm looking for a missing college girl named Justice Edgemont," he said.

Wow. Did he really blurt that?

She moved closer to Stephen and looked at the computer screen. Then she reached out, gently, and placed her right hand on his heart. The hand possessed age, wrinkles, and a light softness. The bizarre and surreal act sent chills through his spine. She removed her hand and looked at Stephen. "Your heart is pure, son," she said. "You shall find this girl because it's your destiny."

Stephen didn't speak. Gertie walked away. The emptiness of the library never felt so real, and so good. Moments later, Gertie approached again. She placed a plastic bag containing three DVDs next to Stephen. "Return these when you're done," she said. "I wish you well. And, Stephen..."

"Yes..."

"Be careful. You may know Hoosac Mills, but Hoosac Mills knows you as well."

7.

Stephen parked in the rear of the hotel lot. He considered the previous evening; sleeping with the beautiful Tamantha Parris had been a mistake. Her close association to Vetrovic could pose a legitimate problem. Simply, it had been a poor decision negotiated by the wrong body parts. A young woman remained missing and Stephen shouldn't have jeopardized the investigation.

Or was she missing? Could Desjardin be right? Maybe Justice voluntarily displaced herself.

Stephen sensed something amiss as he stepped from his Jeep. He turned and easily avoided a lumbering right-hand punch that sailed away from his head and slammed into the door jamb.

A drunken Martin Edgemont—Justice's father, snorted and charged at Nicholson. This time he threw a left-hand punch. A classic—as Stephen frequently joked—*Bonanza* haymaker. The type Hoss Cartwright would've thrown in a saloon; a punch that starts near the knotty-pine floorboards and arcs about twelve feet before landing at or near its assigned destination. Stephen glided to the right, evaded the punch and countered with a right-handed unorthodox shot that teetered somewhere between a hook and a cross. The hybrid punch landed cleanly on Edgemont's mouth. Inebriation, lack of balance, and a suspect chin were Martin Edgemont's losing trifecta. He hit the pavement but did not lose consciousness.

After several seconds, he rose. He equaled Stephen's height but weighed a sloppy two hundred pounds.

"I'm here to find your kid," Stephen said. "What the hell's wrong with you?"

"Justice is my daughter," Edgemont said. "Don't need a private eye doing a dad's job. I already warned you."

"I'm under contract with your ex-wife, not you," Stephen said.

Edgemont laughed. "I hope you got an advance."

Edgemont turned and began walking toward campus. He stopped, paused, then faced Stephen. "You don't belong in the Mills, kid. Go home."

Something bothered Stephen. He couldn't identify it. He got back into his Jeep. The sports radio guys were now talking about the Sox actually beating the Yankees.

Improbable. It could never happen.

The Jeep never moved. Then it hit him. Edgemont's word choice nudged at him.

You don't belong in the Mills, kid. Go home.

Stephen looked at the clock, then thought: *Should or shouldn't I?*

He pulled out his mobile phone and dialed. At two rings a familiar voice answered. "How are you?" Stephen said.

"Are you drunk?" Melanie Leary asked.

"No," Stephen said. "I'm actually in Hoosac Mills right now."

"What?" she said.

"Can you meet me?"

A slight hesitation followed. "Okay."

Twenty minutes later, the best looking police chief in the United States entered the Berkshire Inn lounge. About five-seven, Melanie wore one hundred thirty-eight pounds with curved perfection. Muscle. Her dark, shoulder-length hair hung below her shoulders and rested on a tight, navy-blue, cashmere turtleneck.

Melanie's face showcased Irish, and the only thing that topped its beauty were her combination of book intelligence and street smarts. She sat next to her ex-fiancé, where her beverage of choice, a light beer, awaited her.

Stephen was sipping on his second stout.

"A Taconic State senior named Justice Edgemont is missing and the mother hired me to find her."

Melanie's brow raised. "No one notified Hoosac Mills PD," she said.

"I'm notifying you now," Stephen answered.

Melanie smiled. "Any thoughts?"

Stephen apprised Melanie of his last several days. "I need some background checks," he said.

Melanie eyed him for a moment. "What're the names?"

He told her.

Melanie finished her beer, tucked away her notes, then stood.

"I'll be in touch."

"Thanks."

Melanie walked to the door, then hesitated and looked back at Stephen. "I miss your parents," she said.

Yeah, they're awesome. But how about me?

"I'll tell them you're asking for them," he said.

The lounge lights flickered. Stephen drained his stout, caught the bartender's eye to signal him for the check. When he looked back toward Melanie, she was gone. She had walked away from him.

Again.

8.

The next day Vetrovic canceled his two classes—a virtual no show. Martin Edgemont was invisible, too. A dozen more phone calls and eight interviews produced no leads. Nikki Edgemont remained in Boston. The only interesting moment occurred when Michael Desjardin drove what appeared to be a packed sedan past Stephen while he stood outside The Library.

Despite the comfortable hotel bed, Stephen couldn't sleep. He inventoried his last two days: interviews with students, professors, friends, lodging owners, business owners, looking for electronic transactions, two fights, unexpected sex, and an uncomfortable encounter with his ex-fiancée.

It all added to zero.

Maybe the refrigerator held answers? A cold sixteen-ounce became the quick solution. He popped open the beer, shut off the Sox game, and got to business. He slid Vetrovic's award-winning *Enabling Cain* into the room's DVD player. Stephen couldn't believe this short film received such high praise. The short take: a drug-addicted son steals from loved ones, leaves his fiancée, loses his job, hits rock bottom then gets clean, reinvents himself, saves another wayward soul, and returns home where he seeks and is granted forgiveness.

Good Lord.

So much for directorial originality. The film ended in unspectacular fashion. Stephen changed DVDs. A second beer steered its way into his hand.

Vetrovic's unknown short film *Jailed!* offered a bit of intrigue. Operating on a shoestring budget, Vetrovic set the plot early by detailing two young women (college-aged) being held captive in a dark, cavernous chamber. The girls were clothed in puffy white blouses and red skirts, resembling Spanish garments of past centuries. Waist chains bound the girls to the wall. The antagonist, prowling about the chamber, couldn't be seen by the viewer. Only the girls, paralyzed with fear, could be seen with frightened faces. The camera panned continuously with the antagonist, who didn't speak. The use of waist chains proved to be a wise directing decision. It permitted the girls to flail their free arms at the passing yet untouchable antagonist, who they don't seem to know. The captives screamed in 1980's Jamie Lee Curtis fashion. "Help me!" they screamed over and over.

The screen cut to a new girl, smiling, and full of energy, staring from her porch at what appeared to be her college campus. Dark skies set the tone. A car stops in front of the girl's house. Just as the driver's side door opens, Vetrovic again switched point of view. All camera angles now focus on the girl on the porch. The viewer reasonably assumes the approaching person to be a man. The girl, very attractive, smiles even wider. The point of view narrator must be a trusted person. "Hi!" she yells. "Come on in…"

Rattle, Rattle.

Stephen's mobile phone vibrated. He answered.

"Things are getting weird in the Mills."

"What you got, Melanie?"

"A couple of things," she said. "First, two more Taconic State women have been reported missing in the last hour. Names are Lornece Atwater and Irina Dinelli."

"Huh," Stephen said. "I know those names. They're—"

"Friends with Justice Edgemont," Melanie finished. "I got something else."

"Go."

"The, ah, girl…checked out clean. But guess what about your Professor Vetrovic and Justice Edgemont's father?"

Stephen sat up. "Don't leave me hanging."

"I'll paraphrase," she said. "In 1984, the University of Michigan-Flint dismissed and declined to renew the contract of Associate Professor Vetrovic."

"Why?"

"Get this," Melanie said. "Vetrovic and his TA—Mr. Martin Edgemont—were accused of unprofessional conduct by way of trying to lure three college girls into starring in a racy, low-budget film."

The Vetrovic and Martin Edgemont connection sealed all suspicions. "I wanna speak with these women," Stephen said. "What are their names and contact information?"

"You have to track them 'cause it was a long time ago," Melanie said. "The names are Iris Drake, Janet Earl—no 'e'—and Laura Anderson—spelled with an 'o.'"

Stephen recorded the names. "Okay, I'm on it tomorrow. What's your take?"

Melanie didn't hesitate. "Are you kidding? I'll be seeing Vetrovic before he takes his first attendance."

Awkward silence ensued. Then, Stephen said, "Stay in touch."

Melanie sensed something amiss. "Is everything okay?"

Stephen's thoughts raced. He assessed the better part of the last year, spent mostly without Melanie Leary. Losing her had never seemed plausible. "Actually," he said, "there's one thing, Melanie."

"Okay...?"

"When you said no 'e' in Earl, you meant no second 'e,' right?"

Melanie understood Stephen well.

"Are you getting paid for this, Nicholson?"

Stephen kept the phone close to his ear. His appreciation for the sound of her voice couldn't be measured. He missed her more than he could possibly articulate.

You abandoned me, Melanie.

"I'll see you tomorrow," he managed before disconnecting.

Jigsaw pieces of insanity tumbled in Stephen's brain. He had to concentrate. His mind produced rapid-fire questions: What is this odd relationship between Vetrovic and Martin Edgemont? Did they kidnap Justice? Why didn't Nikki Edgemont reveal this relationship? What are the odds that three girls from the same class go missing? Why doesn't Michael Desjardin care that his girlfriend is MIA and did he flee town?

What the hell is happening in the Mills?

Stephen's mind overheated; he fell back onto his bed and closed his eyes—moments later he sprang to a sitting position. He looked at the clock: eleven-eleven p.m.

Make a wish.

Vetrovic's short film neared its end. There were now three young ladies, including the young girl last shown smiling and greeting her soon-to-be-captor, all bound in chains in a dark chamber. They screamed. Arms waved, fingers clawed, but the unseen villain stayed out of reach. The chamber housed the dead—literally. Two concrete casket liners were concealed in the backdrop.

Stephen stirred. He watched the screen with detail. The villain finally emerged. A rear angle shot concealed a full view of him, but enough to show a large man dressed in vintage seaman's clothing. In his hand he carried a flare gun.

Stephen's heart rate doubled. These visuals on the screen: old puffy clothing, seamen's garb, and a flare gun—he had seen these things recently. Stephen grabbed the sheet of paper and looked at the names of the Michigan girls: Janet Earl, Iris Drake, and Laura Anderson.

Think, think, think!

Stephen snatched his pen and wrote down the names of the current missing girls: Justice Edgemont, Irina Dinelli, and Lornece Atwater. He stared at the sets of names. After a minute he made another inscription. He recorded the initials of the missing girls. Both the girls from Michigan, in 1984, and the Taconic State girls, in 2004, owned the same initials: J E I D L A.

Next he formed a circle with the letters—the same way he did when decoding anagrams in the Boston Herald. The unthinkable became reality. Stephen looked to the screen as the girls screamed even louder. The short film was the anagram, and the anagram made the film.

JAILED!

The black Jeep rolled through the Mills. Stephen called Melanie's mobile phone—which went to voicemail. He didn't mince words: "Melanie, it's Vetrovic. Get to his house now at 105 Patriot Street!"

Stephen stopped in front of Vetrovic's home. The Victorian stood tall in the hills section where the city's money and power brokers resided. Stephen knew the area well. He approached. Lights were on in all downstairs rooms. He eyed the doorbell, then simply turned the doorknob and entered. In the foyer he scanned a winding staircase and an ornate decorative interior.

Discernible male voices, namely Vetrovic and Edgemont, chatted away in the rear of the first floor.

Stephen inched ahead. Two giggles, unexpected, bounced off the walls.

Then a female voice said, "Will this get us into a real Hollywood movie?"

"My dear," Vetrovic said. "All worthy actors evolve from shallow waters."

Stephen moved closer. He looked down at his right hand. Funny—he didn't remember taking out his baby Glock semi-automatic. Martin Edgemont offered, "It'll be the easiest two grand you girls ever make."

What a sicko? Vetrovic and Edgemont were beyond repulsive—especially Edgemont.

His own daughter.

Stephen stepped into the kitchen. Five heads turned simultaneously. Stephen leveled his gun at Vetrovic's chest.

No one spoke. Stephen surveyed the girls. Two were seated and held red, plastic drink cups. The third girl stood and held a bottled water.

"What are your names?" Stephen said.

"You a cop?" bottled water girl asked.

"No, he's a—"

"Shut up," Stephen said to Vetrovic. He looked at the girls. "No, I'm looking for a girl. What're your names?"

One of the seated girls blurted, "I'm Rachel, that's Michelle and that's Patty."

"How old are you, ladies?"

"I'm nineteen," Rachel said. "My friends are eighteen."

Stephen picked up Rachel's cup and sniffed its contents. "Whew," he said. The ripe drink reeked of fruity intoxicants.

He looked at Rachel. "Are these two freaks shooting a porn film?"

The girls didn't speak. Yet Edgemont angered. "Get the hell out of here, Nicholson."

Stephen slid forward three paces. He brought his gun tight to his torso then rocked Edgemont with a left hook to the jaw. Edgemont fell to the floor. One of the girls screamed.

"They're offering us two thousand to star in a movie, but they only talked about lingerie and didn't say anything about sex," bottled water girl yelled.

Vetrovic remained calm. Edgemont rose, wobbly.

Stephen turned to the girls. "You drive here?"

Bottled water girl nodded.

"Good," Stephen said. "All of you hold up your IDs so I can read them."

"You can't—" Vetrovic began.

"Shut up!" Stephen said and again aimed the Glock at Vetrovic.

The girls obliged. Stephen ingrained a mental photograph of the three names. All lived in neighboring Pittsfield. Stephen addressed the girls. "Get out and never come back."

The girls disappeared.

"Where's Justice?" Stephen said.

Vetrovic and Edgemont stared at each other. Then, Edgemont said, "Don't know but she'll come back just like she did before."

"Where are Irina Dinelli and Lornece Atwater?"

Edgemont shot a look of confusion; body language seldom lies. This time Vetrovic answered. "We don't know where Justice or the other girls are, Nicholson. You have broken into my home and battered my colleague. These are serious criminal offenses."

"So's serving booze to minors," Stephen said. "I just left a message for the city police chief to meet me here. Speak with her if she shows. And I'm sure the school president would love your interpretation of film creation, you creep."

Vetrovic had zero leverage yet remained cocky. "Stephen Nicholson...the initials work yet your name does not."

Stephen froze. "What did you say?"

"I'm a film creator," he said. "You have good initials for my genre yet you have a phone-book name."

Stephen holstered his gun. "We ain't done," he said as he sprinted toward his Jeep. He accelerated out of the hills.

He dialed Melanie again. This time a groggy voice answered, "Can it wait, Stephen?"

"I know where the girls are!" he yelled.

9.

Vincent Price would have fit in nicely at Hoosac Mills Cemetery. Divided by a state highway, the cemetery sprawled in both directions. The east side, guarded by mature swamp maples and twisted oaks owned the dominant hill and gave the appearance of having sway over all the living creatures within their confines.

Now past midnight, the gates were locked. Stephen tucked his Jeep safely into a crevice off the road's shoulder and hidden from the moonlight. He traversed the east hill, past ancient headstones, some pre-dating the births of Emerson and Thoreau. Many of these entombed bodies had labored to build this prideful city. And while their names remained on building fronts and street corners to remind onlookers that they once lived, breathed and prepared for the future, the omnipresent Latin words *tempus fugit, momento mori* carved into the headstones throughout the cemetery, also served as a reminder:

Time flies, remember death.

Stephen reached the top. Three entry roads all led to this confluence: the receiving vault. A common fixture in New

England cemeteries, chambers were carved out of small hills and used to store bodies during cold months. Stephen neared the entrance. The large, thick-wooden door, uneven at the jamb, released a ribbon of light. He grabbed a cast-iron handle with his left hand, while the right held the Glock. Stephen battled his mind.

Don't over-analyze.

He pulled open the door and stepped inside. Several battery-operated camping lanterns lighted the cavernous chamber. To his right were three girls, gagged but fully clothed. They were bound by waist chains to the right wall of the chamber.

Just like the movie.

The girls immediately saw Stephen—and the gun. They offered muted screams. Confusion set in; then Stephen understood.

They feared him.

A voice rang out from behind a fold-up partition in the middle of the chamber. "I've been waiting for you Edmund."

Stephen recognized the voice. In the left corner of the chamber he saw a mattress.

Tamantha Parris appeared from behind the partition wearing nothing but racy, blood-red lingerie. She saw Stephen and the gun. "It's not what you think," she said. "We're re-making Professor Vetrovic's underappreciated work."

Stephen looked at the girls. He recognized Justice Edgemont but couldn't discern the difference between the presumed Irina Dinelli and Lornece Atwater. The girls now understood Stephen's role; a helper, not a villain.

Stephen stepped toward Tamantha. A few nights earlier she had shared his bed. Now she had reduced herself to a vampiress. Damn.

"Untie them," he commanded.

"But Stephen…"

He pointed the gun at her head. "Okay!" Tamantha moved toward Justice.

Stephen's eyes caught an unexpected shadow moving across the wall. The girls screamed. Sparks were now lighting up the vault with an explosion. He grabbed at his left shoulder and fell to the floor. *Was it a punch?*

Stephen rolled onto his stomach then slapped at his throbbing shoulder. It burned. He looked up. Edmund, the dopey, smitten student intern, pointed a now-empty flare gun at him.

"You okay, Manty?" he asked Tamantha.

Tamantha now held Stephen's gun. "Thank you, Edmund."

Stephen stood, wobbled, then gained his footing. He stared at Edmund.

"Don't move!" Edmund yelled. The empty flare gun no longer posed harm.

"I'll shoot," Tamantha yelled.

Stephen looked at Tamantha—making sure to lock eyes with her. "First you gotta disengage the safety."

The weapon had no safety.

Stephen put up his hands and moved. Edmund stood flat-footed—no proper balance and no sense of fighting discipline. Stephen winced with pain as he feigned a left-handed punch then delivered a crushing right-footed front kick. Edmund didn't expect this; neither did the point of his chin where Stephen's Nike sneaker connected.

Edmund fell to the floor—knocked out. Stephen turned to Tamantha.

She smiled. "No safety," she said. "Game over, private detective. You were good."

The distinct sound of a Glock 22 semi-automatic echoed. Stephen stood motionless. Blood exploded from Tamantha's right arm. Stephen's gun slid across the floor. He retrieved his weapon.

Melanie Leary stood in a perfect shooter's stance at the entrance of the receiving vault. Stephen stared. Stephen's eyes followed her every move. She secured her weapon then rolled over flabby Edmund and handcuffed him in a matter of seconds.

Melanie turned to Stephen. "Free the girls."

Their chains easily released with the standard handcuff key Stephen carried.

Tamantha slumped against the wall. Melanie approached. She leaned over so they were face-to-face, then unleashed an impressive right-handed slap. "That's for sleeping with my man," she said. Melanie handcuffed Tamantha before radioing for police and EMT response.

Stephen savored the moment. He watched everything Melanie did and listened to every word she said. He couldn't keep his eyes, ears, or mind off of her. It had taken a missing college girl for him to find Melanie. Then he looked at the pathetic Tamantha Parris. He remembered a question she had asked him at The Library. He revisited the answer—but now the truth rang clear.

Melanie was the coolest and baddest and smartest detective ever in the Mills...she helped name the Olympian... she showed more heart than any fellow officer in prison...she won my heart when it had never truly been won...she made chief and made the world proud...it was I who could not handle the relationship responsibility...it was I who stayed in Boston and said yes to the stouts and lagers when I should have been driving Route 2 west...it was I who abandoned her.

Stephen locked eyes with Melanie for the first time in months.

"I've missed you," she said.

"Forgive me," he said.

"I love you even when I hate you."

"I'll take that as a yes."

"Did you catch the end of Game 7?" Melanie asked.

"No."

"The Sox won the pennant," Melanie said. "Thought you'd like to know."

The stuff of Hollywood and fairy tales.

"Here," said the newly-freed Justice Edgemont. She approached Stephen with a bottle of spring water and poured it over his burned shoulder. Justice curiously studied the man who saved her. Then it clicked. She addressed him, not by name, but by neighborhood.

"Did you buy a triple-decker on Belgrade Avenue in Rozzie?"

"Guilty," he answered.

This was Justice Edgemont, the twenty-one year old Taconic State college student far from her native Boston. She was the kid who went missing. What she didn't know was that neither her boyfriend nor father bothered searching. Her mother Nikki remained in Boston with her tennis club friends. What Justice did know was that the man in front of her cared. She kissed Stephen on the cheek. Melanie stepped in and started guiding them out of the chamber.

As they stepped into the moonlit night, Justice looked at Melanie and then at Stephen. "You know, Nicholson, you belong in the Mills."

King's Quarter
Andrew McAleer
Portland, Maine

Margaret "Pearl" Gates was my Uncle Buddy's lost cause not mine. On my way to Pearl's that November morning, I wondered how long I'd keep telling myself this lie. In the end, not even death could save Shepherd Investigations from the Pearls of the world.

My Uncle Buddy Shepherd liked to say, "The Quarter's a stage and everybody's gotta play their part. We help our own around here." To him, this wasn't some disposable catch phrase. It represented a code to live by in our little corner of Portland, Maine known as King's Quarter. I saw little evidence anyone listened.

People said Buddy was the most loved, respected, and popular man to live and die in King's Quarter. In other words, the biggest sucker in town. I admired the hell out him, but I was no Buddy. I was twenty-seven and if I didn't get out of the Quarter before I turned thirty, I'd rot in that god-forsaken rat trap forever. I did escape once, when deployed to Afghanistan where I spent a year sniffing out IEDs as an Army combat engineer. Then I found myself back in the Quarter, investing my combat pay in Buddy's private detective business, where I eventually got my PI ticket.

Buddy ran a charity more than a business, specializing in every lost cause he could get his hands on, or every lost cause that could get its hands on him. The private eye business comes down to eat what you kill, so from now on, no more billing the bubble. And that's exactly what I planned on telling Pearl Gates over the cup of tea I knew she'd have waiting for me.

Hoofing over to Pearl's place, I zipped up my Gore-Tex field coat against the frigid November gusts sweeping off the Atlantic and rehearsed my rejection. "I'd like to help, Pearl, but I have too many commitments at the moment." Then a familiar case of the guilts raked over me as I recalled a conversation I'd had with Buddy.

"Let's help the poor old lady out, Donnie," he'd said, following this request with his loose, easy smile. "She's got no one."

I'd shrugged. "Not our problem."

He put his massive hand on my shoulder and paused his blue-green eyes on me. "We'll make it up on another case. We help our own around here."

Buddy had died a little more than a year ago. Flat broke. Nothing to show for it but his good will and a trailer up at Blue Fish Cove he called "The Quarterdeck" because it sat on the eastern most point of the Quarter overlooking the Atlantic. He was fifty-seven, took his coffee heavy on the cream and sugar, and flanked with pastries. If dinner didn't consist of steak, potatoes, and cigarettes, it wasn't worth calling dinner. He'd wash it all down with whatever tap beer happened to be on special. All hours of the night he'd be taking calls to bail out someone's kid who'd been getting jammed up by the cops. When you got snapped by five-oh in the Quarter, you didn't call a lawyer, you called Buddy. Nobody had more juice than him. On call twenty-four-seven, he became one of those classic, thirty pounds overweight, high blood pressure types who never missed a chance to say in between cigarettes, "Wha-du-I need a doctor for?"

As private detectives go, anyone here will tell you Buddy was the best, but the Quarter was all they knew, so what did they know? In the end, the only real fee Buddy collected was a pat on the back. Now it was payback time. His good will and my license would be my ticket off the block. Another five grand ought to give me a running start.

The truth: it takes only a glance in the mirror to reflect on one of his lost causes. My father, a Portuguese merchant sailor, was never in the picture. He boarded the Quarter for some quick pub, grub, and rub—and my mother served up all three. Afterward, he cast off to the four corners of the earth. Buddy took me off my mother's hands whenever he could. She hung in there until my sophomore year of high school, and then married her way off the Quarter. Buddy took me in full time and kept me in school, off the streets, off the docks at night, off the booze, off the pills and needles. Not an easy thing to do in King's Quarter. He supplemented my education by teaching me how to talk to people, how to keep my mouth shut, how to throw a right cross and, more importantly, how to avoid situations where you might need to throw a right cross.

The trouble he kept me out of landed me an opportunity to join the Army and a chance to see beyond my borders. I came back from "the 'Stan" with the usual bag of thank-you-for-showing-up-to-the-war awards, like an Army commendation medal and combat action badge. I was still Donnie Shepherd. Still five-foot-eleven, one hundred seventy-five pounds, dirty-blond hair, blue eyes, and could still coax a striped bass to swallow a hunk of mackerel. No PTSD. None I could wrap my head around anyway. And, I still had an Uncle Buddy to pass on important life tips like, "When playing the lottery, Donnie, always play the same number and always buy your ticket from Doc Burke."

"Why?" I would ask.

"'Cuz, if your number comes up, his store gets a cut. We help our own here."

Buddy liked to remind me that our roots ran deep in King's Quarter. His grandfather, Angus MacDougall, was a "two-boat" carpenter who settled in the Quarter in 1899. They got the name "two-boats" because, back in the day, they emigrated from Scotland to Nova Scotia on one boat, and then took another boat to new worlds like Portland, Boston, or New York City. Angus made it as far as Portland where he settled in this four-square mile of madness known as King's Quarter. He never left.

The way Buddy praised Angus, you'd swear Angus ran the entire eastern seaboard. On morning walks along the worn, cobblestone streets to the Down East Diner, Buddy would point to the weather-beaten shanty cottages or flat-iron buildings slapped together by nineteenth century robber barons to house and sequester their indentured servants. "Just think," he'd say, brimming with pride as he inhaled a combination of salt air and freshly-baked breads into his bloodstream, "your great-grandfather could've built this development."

Buddy had a great imagination. "Donnie, these cobblestones we're walking on would've been here during Angus's time. Bet he walked on 'em a thousand times."

Buddy's ancient claim to the Quarter by way of family folklore seemed to validate him, and he'd try to pass this family claim on to me. At Downlander's Wharf he'd sip coffee and puff on non-filtered Camels while we should've been hustling a buck. He'd squint over Snug Harbor while the early morning sun outlined his blocky profile. "I can see Angus hunched over the railing of some big ship coming down this very harbor, seeing the land of the free for the first time."

Nothing's free in King's Quarter. We call it "No Quarter" for a reason—it gives nothing. It wasn't always this way.

Commerce thrived here in previous centuries. It's hard to believe prime location once blessed King's Quarter. Before the American Revolution broke out, George III ran off what Native Americans remained and filled the bucolic island with reserve troops, securing a strategic location in the event Boston erupted. At the time, the Quarter was a small island a few hundred yards off the mainland, which meant the British

Navy could quickly blockade northern portions of the eastern seaboard and provide troops swift access to the mainland, while at the same time enjoying protection from the natural barrier of water.

The troops needed provisions and, in exchange for them, the Quarter's topsoil was stripped wagon-by-wagon load and ferried off to the mainland. There the soil was swapped out for infertile soil, which in turn was dumped into the sea, little by little extending the mainland into the Quarter. Like Boston's Back Bay, the practice of dumping infertile soil was supplemented with garbage and junk fill, ultimately consuming the shallow body of marsh water separating the once idyllic island from Portland. Now, an artery of unwanted, junk fill, covered with layers of asphalt, pumps into the Quarter.

Post Revolution, the Quarter became a convenient, lucrative port for smaller merchant vessels. Prohibition changed everything. Respectable mainlanders demanded bootleg-booze. The Quarter's once thriving merchant and fishing vessels soon fell under the control of crooked union officials, paid handsomely by crooked politicians, trafficking illegal booze for a fast buck. The working class of the Quarter didn't matter. On a voting map they were nothing but the 16th Precinct. The right people made money and that's what counted.

The Quarter got a bad reputation from the same people who underwrote its demise. You stayed away from those bootleggers, unless you wanted trouble. Yet it was okay to partake in the forbidden fruits, when it was served in respectable settings. Then the '29 crash washed over the Quarter like a tidal wave. The demand for bootleg gin dwindled. Bribe money dried up and speakeasies closed. With no payoff money left, boats got confiscated by the feds or destroyed by mainland competitors too stupid to realize the old days were caput. Overnight the Quarter became the bastard child of Portland.

The Quarter's economy never recovered. Its reputation as a "stay away" zone never changed. One did not "cross the garbage" into the 16th. It's still considered best to leave those people to themselves. From mainland society's perspective, it's the Quarter's road of garbage leaching into the mainland, not the other way around. A natural boundaries thing.

I'd never cross the garbage for good taking care of Buddy's lost causes. I'd end up like Pearl, living in a first-floor, drafty shanty spilling onto Saint's Alley, named in honor of some long-forgotten fishermen lost at sea. As I leaned into the freezing rain, I thought about what to expect from Pearl. The tea and stale biscuits would be ready and she'd start talking to me as if my showing up meant I'd fix her latest problem. I lied to myself again, muttering under my breath that her problem was her problem, not mine.

Then Buddy's ghost whispered into my ear about why we help Pearl. Back in the day, her husband Johnny got hit by a mob boss known as "Mainland" over in Portland. Shortly after the hit, Mainland disappeared. Rumors circulated that Buddy had something to do with Mainland's early retirement.

I remembered when Buddy told me about it. "Her husband Johnny was a harmless good-timer," Buddy had said. "A few bricks short, but harmless. Liked the ponies, liked the fast buck. Never understood a slow nickel's as good as a fast dime, but in his own way, not a bad family guy. Anyway, back in the day a former button man for Mainland named Chickie Meyer was supposedly getting cozy with the feds. Chickie wasn't a Q guy, so one night, after a marathon at the Dry Dock, Johnny happens to offer Chickie a ride home. Both got gunned down right before crossing the garbage. Making it a 'No Quarter' hit guaranteed the thing would get broomed. No one outside cares what happens here. Pearl got single-mommed with two boys not even in knickers. Not a dime to her name. It's a code we help her around here."

I asked, "What about her sons?"

"Needle took one and the other's doing life."

"She's got a nephew, right?" I asked.

"Junk Box. Can't do a thing but juice his veins."

"Was Johnny...?"

"What?"

"Connected to Mainland."

Buddy's lips grew tight. "Johnny had his faults, but he was clean. He got hit for no reason. We made sure he's buried here for Pearl's sake."

By "we" my uncle meant Buddy and Buddy alone. Somehow he got the cash to bury Johnny here, which is no cheap thing, since space is at a premium on the Quarter.

I tried to get Buddy to open up about Mainland's disappearance. "Any truth to that thing about you and Mainland?"

He shrugged. "Whatever happened to him he had comin'. Too many kids with needles cuzza that rat."

I sat in Pearl's kitchen, studying her face as she poured tea into a china cup decorated with shamrocks and a fancy little man riding a jaunting cart. She'd been old my whole life. Quarter women specialized in getting old. The cycle never changed. They married get-rich-quick schemers who lured them in with promises of stability through honest wages. Then, they produced sons with the same rags-to-riches DNA. In the end, they're old ladies left with little more than a tea kettle and a dimly lit shanty. If they're lucky, they'd have enough money to bury themselves. Pearl was lucky.

After pouring herself tea, Pearl flattened the backside of her thorn-proof wool skirt as she settled into a chair. A splinter of whalebone held together her white bun of hair. She was bone thin herself and, even in the poor lighting, her normally ruddy complexion now appeared jaundiced and waxy. Her kelly-green cardigan sweater hung on her shoulders the same way it might a wire hanger. I hadn't seen much of Pearl since my uncle's death and hid my shock at how much she'd aged. The Pearls of the world weren't supposed to die. They were supposed to exist forever and suffer in silence. They were supposed to be on call to counsel our own moments of grief and self-pity, and then be forgotten until needed again.

Pearl sipped tea while pointing to my cup. "I cherish that little cup. Johnny bought it for me. He promised to cart me through the lanes of Ireland someday. Oh...that would've been Heaven on earth."

I picked up the cup to take a polite look and the little delay provided her the opportunity to start in on her dilemma.

"I had a visitor, Donald. He came to see how I've been. Made some small talk while I put the kettle on. Then I made the mistake of fetching my sweater while leaving him at the table."

We both knew she was talking about her Junk Box nephew, but would never mention his name. Another code.

"When was this?"

"Yesterday."

No need to ask if she called the cops. Code again. "How much our friend take?"

"Everything."

She was talking about the burial money she'd saved her whole adult life in order to rest eternally next to her Johnny. While staring at some tea leaves floating around in my cup, I made a feeble attempt to decline taking on the case. "I'll be honest, Pearl, with Buddy gone I can't track these things down by myself without charging a fee."

Pearl removed a tissue that she'd stuffed up the right sleeve of her cardigan, and used it to dab her nose. She was busted, yet still wearing the engagement ring and wedding band given to her by the fast-buck husband who put her here.

She said, "I want you to have one third of whatever you get back."

A third of nothing is usually nothing.

"Assuming I got everything back and took a third," I said, "would that leave you with enough?"

She nodded. "Mr. O'Brien discussed costs with me and said I would have nothing to worry about after I was gone. Such a kind man."

John R. O'Brien, the Quarter's friendly neighborhood undertaker, made a handsome living selling deluxe coffins to old-school widows like Pearl. He knew how to market to the Pearls of the world. The kind who don't know how to live, but sure know how to die.

I sighed. "Mr. O'Brien's quite the man. How much our visitor walk off with, Pearl?"

She trembled. "All I had in the world. Six thousand three hundred twenty-four dollars and twelve cents."

I raised my eyebrows. "He took the twelve cents?"

She dabbed her eyes with the tissue. "Even the twelve cents. Two nickels and two pennies."

"Where'd you keep the money?"

She shifted left and pointed to an old Quaker Oats tin sitting on the kitchen counter. "In the cookie jar."

I got up and looked inside the tin. It contained a dollar and some change. "What's this?"

"I started saving again," Pearl said.

I sat down; my back slightly bowed.

Pearl broke the silence. "I don't want him in trouble with the police. He's all I have...other than you, Donald."

I gave her something between a smile and a grimace. "Yes, you got me, Pearl. Hook, line, and sinker."

I knew Pearl had had enough money to bury herself, yet didn't realize how much. Junk Box probably ran it through a needle by now, or paid off the latest leg breaker in his life, but if I collected, two grand plus meant a giant step closer to the mainland. It wouldn't take too long to track her low-life nephew down for whatever he had left. If you were from the Q, no one's tough to find since we all know each other's habits, routines and hideaways. It's the collecting part that's tough. As Buddy used to say, "Why pay when you can promise?"

I polished off my tea. "Where'd you get all that money, Pearl?"

"From when Johnny died in the accident."

I paused. "I see."

If Buddy did have anything to do with Mainland's disappearance, it'd be just like him to put together a little severance package for Pearl and say it was from Johnny.

When I stepped out of Pearl's house, freezing rain continued to pound the Quarter. I figured it would be a waste of time to check out Junk Box's digs on Arsenal Street, but wanted to check off the block anyway. I turned up my coat collar and took a few artful shortcuts to Arsenal. About ten minutes later I knocked on a loft door above a garage. No answer. I cupped my eyes with my hands, looked through the door window, and saw nothing but disarray. Utensils sticking up in cans, scattered clothes, tumbled beer cans, questionable magazines strewn across a small table in front of a battered couch, and a big screen TV. There's always enough money for reality TV and booze. I struck out on the boob tube, so figured I'd take a shot at the booze.

On my way to the Dry Dock Pub, I stepped into Burke's Pharmacy to play Buddy's daily number. I sort of inherited it from him. It was the same story whenever I saw Doc Burke. He had an unwritten rule that I have to listen to his "Sullivan Boy" story before he'll give me my ticket.

He scratched his horseshoe bald head with his left hand while working the lottery machine with his right. His light-blue pharmacist smock sported the same wear holes I remembered as a kid. He didn't need to ask my number. He moved his head and smiled. "I'll never forget that time the Sullivan kid runs in wagging a .38. I got the shakes real bad, so I empty the till for him. I'm not going down for sixty bucks and a bottle of codeine," he said, pausing, looking my way before continuing. "Must be thirty years ago." There were dozens of Sullivan kids in the Quarter, however, everyone always knew exactly who he meant. "Now meantime, Donnie, Buddy happens to be walking down the street with a piping coffee. Sullivan runs through the door right in front of him and, without missing a beat, your uncle tosses the coffee in the kid's face." He looked at me, expecting me to respond as if this was the first time I'd heard this one.

"Buddy justice," I said.

He jabbed his right index finger toward me twice. "He was top drawer. Top drawer all the way." He handed me my ticket. "Now go out and win a million, kid."

I'd settle for five grand.

Soaking wet by this point, I walked the length of Marginal Street and then took a right onto Canal, reaching the Dry Dock at about eleven-fifteen a.m. The Dry Dock sported the usual seafaring décor—battered lobster buoys, strewn fishing nets, vintage ship lanterns and shark jaws. My friend, Monica Sargent, hustled behind the bar pouring drafts and spinning up plates of comfort food for the early stampede already posted at the bar. As usual, Monica was also busy rejecting their advances firmly enough to send a message, yet polite enough to keep the tip door greased.

Other than knowing each other since kindergarten, there wasn't an intimate history between us. Whenever we looked at each other though, we didn't have to say a word to understand what each other was saying. We'd never talked about it, but we both knew each other wanted off the Quarter.

Monica was an exception to the rule that all women got old here. Her long, dark-red hair, olive skin, brown eyes that had seen everything twice, and jogger's physique tucked into tight jeans and a stretched T-shirt, seemed to pump temporary purpose into the tired men of the Quarter. Men waiting around to die, and anxious to hurry it along, one pint at a time.

As I walked the length of the bar, Monica's eyes followed me. The rank stench of a century's worth of stale beer and raw bar spillage permeated the wide-pine floors, triggering memories of Buddy. This was where he broke the news to me that my mother had crossed the garbage for good, where he bought me my first legal beer, and toasted me with shots of Maker's Mark before shipping me off to "the 'Stan" with one final reminder.

"Remember," he said, his right hand wrapped around my bicep, "no matter what happens over there, Donnie, even if you buy the farm, you got a home here."

I smiled as we clinked shot glasses. "Thanks for the pep talk, Buddy."

"Anytime. And don't be a hero, kid, just 'cuz you're a man now."

Already certain I was getting out and not coming back, I vowed that that would be the last shot I'd ever take in the Quarter. Then, after taking a few enemy shots in Afghanistan, all I could think about was how special that moment with Buddy had been. Hunkered down a million miles away, the Quarter seemed like Heaven. I dreamed about another taste. I begged for another taste of home.

When I reached the waitress station at the end of the bar, Monica held out her hand. We shook.

"Little early for you, Don."

"I'm on the wagon."

"Oh yeah...come in to give a little speech for the temperance movement?"

I smiled, then tilted my head slightly to the far corner of the establishment. "Maybe later. Came in looking for someone. Not here, so maybe I'll say hello to our friendly, neighborhood book in the corner."

She said, "That loafer makes more than book."

"I know. Can't a guy be polite around here?"

"Sure," she said, pressing a hip against the bar, "be polite and buy Mr. Book an expensive shot of single-malt."

"Looks like he's drinking Rolling Rock."

"Details, details," Monica said, pushing her hip off the bar.

In a well-practiced move, she stretched over a refrigerated compartment behind the bar and yanked out a Rolling Rock. The slinky, black, three-pocket waist apron wrapped tightly around her swinging hips managed to give the Dry Dock the only touch of burlesque it needed. In one swift move, she drew out the industrial-sized, iron bottle opener she kept squeezed into the back pocket of her sculpted jeans, snapped the cap off the bottle, and slid the opener back into its "holster." Flipping burgers, shucking oysters, bullying around kegs, and snapping bottle caps had given her restaurant hands—small burn scars, red, raw and scuffed.

She angled the bottle at me and did something with her left eye that I would argue in my dreams for the next week qualified as a wink. "Well, Don, other than single-malt, nothing says 'hello' like a long neck."

I dropped a five onto the counter and took the beer. "I'll remember that...barkeep."

With a touch of flair she scooped the five. "Thanks for saying 'hello'...sucker."

Everyone knew the man sitting in the corner as Lucky

Break—Mr. Big-Swagger-in-a-small-bar himself. Lucky's mother had a talent for cleaning up well on weekends, well enough to provide an occasional diversion for a mainland city councilor. About a decade ago, Lucky magically jumped to the head of the civil service list, landing himself a court officer's job. One day, a little more than two years into the job, he was assigned a hands-on escort of a detainee—a quick-and-dirty stroll from the holding cell to the courtroom for an arraignment. On this particular day, said detainee, hauled in on a hefty possession beef, didn't take too kindly to a hands-on escort. Said detainee attempted to head butt Lucky, so Lucky swept the detainee's left knee with his right foot. That little rebellion cost the detainee a broken nose, jaw and a handful of ribs. Afterward, Lucky said he jammed up his right knee and filed an industrial accident report and, a few doctor's notes later, said knee injury is permanent. Because the injury occurred while escorting a prisoner, Lucky was awarded full disability as a result of violence pay. Now he's known as Lucky Break because he doesn't have to do a thing other than sit back, collect and make small book. Living the dream. Like he was doing when I handed him a free long neck.

I placed the beer on the table and sat opposite him. Other than his ratty Chuck Taylor sneakers, Lucky cleaned up well himself. At thirty-something, he still held onto his dark-brown hair and a trim physique he liked to dress in a navy-blue Under Armour sweat suit, and could still breeze through the sport's page in a dim barroom corner without reading glasses. The oily redness covering his face, however, suggested the booze and greasy fare would sneak up on him long before he exhausted the good side of Medicare.

Lucky folded a newspaper up neatly and made a quick study of me before lifting the bottle closer to him and placing it smack center of a stray coaster.

"You know," he said, "I might be the only guy your uncle never bought a round for."

I shrugged. "He didn't like you for some reason."

"You?"

"I'm not my uncle."

He mock toasted me. "Okay, so you're not your uncle. Some might argue otherwise, but I have little interest in common subjects."

I shrugged. "Okay, let's chat about Sir Lucky's interest then."

He spread his hands. "Such as...?"

"You seen your friend around?"

He stared at me before dropping the chair forward. "I got lotsa friends."

"This one came into a little cash."

"Like I said, got many friends. None I talk about."

"Not asking you to," I clarified, "just wondering if you've seen him."

He polished off his beer then picked up the Rock I bought him. "Who's interested in who I see?"

I pointed to the sports pages he'd shoved to the side of the table and tried to bluff him into thinking I knew more than I did. "Curious as to how he paid off his book that's all. His big city book I mean."

Lucky started rubbing his right knee. The joke was that sometimes he forgot which knee he'd hurt and would mistakenly rub his left knee. His lips tightened and his face grew a shade redder. "I'm his book and I got jack, Shepherd."

I stood up. "Figured you'd wanna know he's cleaning slates outside the Quarter."

He swigged more beer and then extended his right leg out from under the table and started jiggling it, as if he couldn't contain his nervous energy. "Happy for him."

I remained fixed on his eyes, but could see his ratty sneaker moving faster and faster. "Funny thing, pays his aunt a visit, and presto, his big city book's paid off."

Lucky stopped rocking his foot and then started massaging his left knee. "Pearl?"

"Only aunt I know he has," I said. He was still massaging his left knee when I pointed to his right. "Taking care of your disability?" He stopped rubbing his left knee and collected himself. "See you around, Lucky," I said, walking away.

"Shepherd," he yelled.

I turned around.

He lifted his chin. "Why not go the cops?"

"Call the cops? That what we do here now, Lucky?"

"I said 'go to the cops,' not call. I hear hearsay, ya know. Junk Box got hooked last night. Old Buddy had juice with the cops."

I tightened my lips. "Buddy knew the code, pal. He never ran to the cops."

Lucky chugged more beer and once again, placed the bottle dead center of the coaster. "Yeah," he said, loudly, "but you ain't your uncle...pal."

"Enjoy your lunch, Lucky," I said, before turning around to see Monica shucking oysters.

A smile crossed her face. "You don't tip like him either, Donnie Boy."

On my way to the cop shop, I hoofed it down West Street, where I could hear the distant, rhythmic pounding of the Atlantic. My wet clothes had warmed up in the Dry Dock, but heavy gusts split by the flat irons cut into me one way, and then the next. In short order my flesh grew wet and raw. Puddles formed in depressed portions of the cobblestone streets. While dodging one, I noticed a short procession of cars alongside John R. O'Brien & Sons Funeral Home.

O'Brien's meticulous upkeep seemed out of place. As Buddy used to say, "O'Brien's is as neat as a pin." Whatever that meant. In contrast to the neighborhood's long-abandoned industrial structures, O'Brien's boasted an ornate, wrought-iron fence wrapped around a lush-green, perfectly clipped lawn, accented with beds of razor-sharp shrubs, buoyed in mounds of hemlock mulch. A brick, herringbone pattern walkway split the lawn. It led to a giant slab of granite in front of a massive burgundy-colored door, sporting panes of bull's eye glass and a spit-polished brass door handle and knocker. A slate roof trimmed with copper flashing covered the pristine, antique-white clapboards. O'Brien's reeked of the old maxim "cleanliness is next to godliness." For the right price everyone was welcome. This was the place to aspire to, for those who knew nothing beyond the Quarter's borders.

The burgundy door opened and a young man wearing a black London Fog coat stepped onto the granite slab and popped open a huge, black umbrella in anticipation of sheltering the lady of the hour. Then the owner himself, John O'Brien, draped in the same requisite black drab, stepped onto the granite. Slate-faced, gripping her elbow, he piloted old lady McDonough on her painfully slow march down the brick path to the limousine. Finally, after years of waiting patiently, this was the widow's day in the sun, and no amount of rain would cast a pall over the occasion. She would remain on display as long as she could manage.

When the walkway procession ended, O'Brien gently guided Mrs. McDonough into the back of the limo, gave her a comforting, solemn nod, and then carefully shut the door behind her. Task completed, he glanced at his wristwatch and double-timed it to the driver's side. O'Brien & Sons would likely have to make up some time to get back on schedule.

Sergeant Glenn Massey grew up on the Quarter with Buddy. I inherited the friendship. When I stepped into the 16th Precinct Police Station, stopping just inside to shake off the cold, he was working the front desk. I watched as he pulled his bifocals down to the tip of his nose with his right hand, while holding a coffee pot in his left hand. "Don't have sense enough to stay out of the rain, kid?"

I ran a hand through my hair and flicked off the wetness. "For a Downeaster like me, this doesn't even qualify as a sun shower."

A stash of distinguished wrinkles formed around Massey's eyes. "Kid, if this is any indication what a sun shower does to your fragile constitution, I'd hate to see how you'd fair in a nor'easter." He held up the coffee pot. "Cup of joe?"

I shook my head. "I'm good. Just had tea with Pearl."

He pushed his bifocals up to the bridge of his nose. "How is Pearl?"

"Not good."

Massey poured coffee into a mug with the words "time and tide wait for no one" glazed on it, and then leaned on the counter and laced his thick, blunt fingers around the mug. "Listen, kid, you didn't inherit Buddy's lost causes. Guy collected them like cut jewels."

"Keep telling myself that."

"You're a good man, Donald A. Shepherd, but try paying the bills with that. Be smart and grab a pension."

"Should've gone into the funeral business."

A toothy grin split Massey's face. "Like it or lump it, we all got stock in that one, kid. What can I do ya?"

"Heard Pearl's nephew got snapped last night?"

He nodded. "A little dance with opioids that ended in a domestic."

"He still in the jar?"

Massey shook his head. "The usual sad story. Young lady who called in the DV cash-bailed his ass outta here couple hours ago."

"Love is in the air," I said, shaking my head. "Any cash on him?"

"Didn't book him. This connected to your lost cause?"

"Like a circle hook to a striped bass."

Massey removed a hand from his mug and rubbed his lantern jaw. "That all you gonna gimme?"

I said, "Trust me, if you knew anymore, you might have to leave your little comfort station here and actually engage in real, big boy detective work out there in the harsh Maine environment."

Massey straightened out and pretended to shiver. "Goodness, can't have that so close to retirement, now can we?" He picked up his mug and walked to the end of the counter. Holding the mug with his left hand he poked the keys of his computer one at a time with his right index finger. Task completed, he read the screen before saying, "Your man had twenty-three bucks on him."

"Keep things to the penny, Sergeant?"

"We aim to please around here."

"Twelve cents?"

He pulled his bifocals back down to the tip of his nose and narrowed his eyes. "Twenty-three bucks...and twelve cents. Mean anything, kid?"

"Means he didn't blow it all."

One-third of twenty-three bucks came to about eight bucks. Things were looking brighter all the time. As long as my luck was holding out, I figured I'd head back to Arsenal Street to see if Pearl's nephew had found his way home. When I got there I could hear the TV and noticed the door wasn't fitted all the way into its frame. I looked through the window and saw Junk Box passed out on the couch, wearing nothing but a T-shirt and boxer shorts. I knocked until he stirred, which I took as an invitation to enter. I pushed open the door and stepped into such a thick haze of human stench, that I immediately grabbed fistfuls of T-shirt and propped him up so

I could take care of business and get out of there.

"Wake up," I said.

His eyes stayed closed as his head floated from side to side. The effects of the opioid du jour still coursed through his system. "Wha-what-what, man?"

"Where's the rest?" I said, pressing my knuckles against his chest.

He made a pathetic attempt to slap my hands. "Res-a-what?"

I gave another hard shake. "It's me or the cops, Junk Box. Where's the money?"

He screamed: "I don't know what you're talkin' about. Ged-off-a-me."

I looked to my right and saw a half-glass of water on a coffee table. The glass stood dead-center of a celebrity's face depicted on a magazine cover, the same way Lucky places bottles dead-center of coasters. Had he been here? Did he send me on a fool's errand to the cops? I jostled the deadhead again, thumping my knuckles harder against his puny chest.

"Where's the money you took from Pearl?"

He finally looked into my eyes. "It's mine. She's old and dyin'."

"Where's the rest, pinhead?"

Junk Box started whimpering and slapping at my hands so hard, I gave him a good shove backwards and let go. He jerked his right thumb toward his chest. "It was mine. I deserved that money. She didn't need it and now that bitch took it all."

"Who?"

"That bitch who called the cops."

I said, "The same one who bailed you out?"

"Yeah, with the hundred I gave her last night. Then we come back here and she plays all nice, until I agree to make a buy."

I shook my head. "So she figures out where you stashed

the rest of the money and helps herself."

He started rocking back and forth, his lanky arms extended between his legs. "I need that money."

"You realize that was Pearl's life savings? How much did your friend walk off with?

"Everything," he said, looking up with watery eyes. "What about me?" he whined.

"You," I yelled, getting into his face, "what about Pearl?"

Tears and confusion blotted his sweaty face. "She took everything."

"When?"

"I told you already."

"What do you mean you told me?"

He hugged his stomach. "Before, when you brought the H. I mean...I don't know. I'm confused. I thought you were here before."

I had a good idea Lucky had been the one bringing the H, but I asked anyway. "Who else was here besides the girl?"

He made fists and tightened his body and started ranting: "Oh my God what's gonna happen to me? I don't deserve this...I don't deserve this."

After Junk Box's melt down, I went looking for Lucky at the Dry Dock and a few other haunts, but he managed to evade me, so I decided to go thaw out at Buddy's trailer, the Quarterdeck.

The "Quarterdeck" was located on a little peninsula of scrubland known as Blue Fish Cove. For some reason I still called it Buddy's trailer, even though I inherited it from him, along with a small mortgage and his beach decorations consisting of jars of sea glass, driftwood, buoys, and a wooden lobster trap serving as a coffee table. A picture of Angus hung in the "living room" and under it hung one of Angus' claw hammers as if it were a museum piece. This was home. A place to lather raisin scones with wild-beach plum jam and watch the ocean through the kitchen window—and that's what I did, before carrying my scone and blueberry tea out to the enclosed porch facing the Atlantic. There, I followed the massive waves as they rose out of the sea and exploded into white foam against a natural formation of jetties locals called the "Pirate Rocks."

Local legend had us believe those Pirate Rocks splintered countless tall ships of yesteryear into kindling. As time passed, everyone agreed that some of them must've been pirate ships and, as more time passed, these pirates, being pirates, must've gone down to Davy Jones' locker with untold chests of gold waiting to be claimed by deserving locals.

A warm feeling ran through me as I recalled Buddy's response to the fool's-gold legend. He'd share it with me as we watched sunrise after sunrise turn the ocean's surface into glistening sheets of yellow foil.

"The real gold," he'd said, as we sat on the porch, "is this view of the ocean. Heaven on earth." Then he'd grown quiet and toasted the ocean with either our last beer of the night, or our first coffee of the morning. "There's gotta be more out there. When I die, Donnie, make sure tight-wad O'Brien don't get me. Scatter my ashes out there with the tides. That way I can see the world and still come back and visit. When you hear that ocean pounding, that'll be me, kid."

To my ever-lasting shame, I did as instructed. Afterward, I realized Buddy asked to be cremated because he didn't have enough money to bury himself and wanted to spare me the costs. If anyone deserved to be buried in the Quarter, it was Buddy, but the ocean had him now. As I watched seagulls drift between a slate sky and competing ocean currents, I raised my mug and toasted the salt of the earth. "Here's to the gold, Buddy, gotta be more out there now."

The wind, pounding waves, and gushes of rain sluicing off my porch helped drown out memories of the manic, self-absorbed cries from Junk Box. Pearl's life savings were with the ashes now. She had as much chance of a decent burial as the imaginary pirates clutching their imaginary booty below the Pirate Rocks. I finished my scone and tea before heading back inside. I planned to spend the remainder of the afternoon getting into a pair of dry clothes, searching for a good movie, and coming up with the right words to tell Pearl.

After a hot shower I threw on a pair of sweats and cracked open a Coke. As soon as I positioned myself on the couch, clicker in hand, my cell grumbled. It was Sergeant Massey.

"Hear the news, kid?"

"Heard nothing but the ocean talking to me for the last hour, Big Sergeant."

"A red blanket got called in about an hour ago."

"Who?"

"That little domestic thing who bailed out Junk Box today."

"Junk Box do another a dance on her?"

"Looks like a heroin-fentanyl mix."

"That'll ruin your coffee."

"Not much doesn't, kid."

Buddy had a saying, "Follow the money, Donnie. Always follow the money." That's what I did the next day. At the Dry Dock, I made a beeline for Lucky's table. I could see from the entrance he sported a new pair of sneakers. Monica stood behind the bar watching me for a moment before tracking me as far as the waitress station. The rest of the patrons likely knew they were in for a time. I stood over Lucky's table. He kept his face buried in the newspaper. He didn't bother to look up.

"Where's the rest of the money, Lucky?" I asked.

He continued to read. I swatted the paper out of his hands.

"You know I could your kick ass, Shepherd. Pick it up and I'll let it go."

I'd never squared off with Lucky before, but he was probably right about kicking my ass. I didn't care. "Not gonna happen. He and his girl called you for a buy. You delivered and took all the money. Easy marks."

"Prove it."

"She's dead, did you know that? Proof or no proof, this myth that you do nothing but make book is over."

Lucky killed his beer and, after returning the bottle to the middle of its coaster, leaned back in his chair and smiled. "What're you now, your fat loser uncle? No one gives a rat's ass."

I pointed at him. "Empty your pockets."

He shook his head. "Your man owed me nine hundred bucks."

"You'd never let him get in that deep."

"So you're my accountant now, tough guy."

From the corner of my left eye I could see Monica lift the door of the waitress station, holding something in her hands.

"Get up and I'll take an accounting of what you've got in your pockets. By the way, nice big boy sneakers, Lucky. Buy those with Pearl's money?"

Lucky's chair snapped forward, and as he shot up, he tried to sweep me with his right leg, but I was ready for it and took a step back, leaving him connected with nothing but air, his momentum spinning him left. As it did, I landed two upper-cuts to his right kidney and ribs, then worked a chokehold around his neck with my left arm, grabbed his right wrist with my right hand, and folded his arm three-quarters of the way up his back. "Nice try with the leg sweep, chump, but I'm no detox from Ten Block."

"I'm gonna kill you," he spat.

"Not today."

"You're dead."

"Empty your left pocket," I commanded.

"There's nothing there."

I tightened my chokehold. He thrust a hand into his left pocket, but when it came out, I heard the air slice and then felt a sharp pain in my left leg. Adrenalin soared through me but I refused to let go of his neck. He jabbed at my leg again and again with the switchblade, but he couldn't get a good enough angle, or momentum, to get any real meat. Every time he jabbed me, I tightened my chokehold. If necessary, I would choke the life out of him and not even care if he happened to catch a vein and I bled out in the process.

Monica suddenly ran over to us and, in one swift move, whipped the industrial bottle opener out from her back pocket and thumped it smack across the bridge of Lucky's nose. A meaty sound burst from his face. He screamed, dropped the switchblade, and buckled to his knees; face buried in the palms of his hands. Monica kicked the knife away and then punted his left ribs until he tumbled over onto his back. Balled in a fetal position, he started crying.

I held my leg. He just pricked a little muscle, so it wasn't bleeding too badly. I looked at Monica. "Thanks."

"What's this all about?"

"Nothing."

"So the usual then," she said, shaking her head. "You strong-and-silent bozos have a throw down over nothin'. I'm owed a little more, Don."

I looked straight into her eyes. I probably would've strangled Lucky to death if she hadn't intervened, so I did owe her more than unwritten codes. "It's about Pearl Gates."

"Okay...?"

"Her nephew palmed her life savings and what remained ended up with this trash."

Monica looked down at my leg. "Get out of here and get that thing looked at. I'll take care of this mess."

Monica lifted Lucky off the ground like she'd done so

335

many kegs of beer in her day and emptied his pockets. She slapped a wad of cash onto his table. Next, she practically wheelbarrowed Lucky out of the bar and tossed him onto the sidewalk.

I scooped and counted the slimy wad of tens, twenties, and fifties, all dated from the 1980s.

On my way out, Monica stopped me. "How much is left?"

"About four hundred bucks," I said, one eye on Lucky. "Better watch your back, Monica."

She reached into a pouch of her black waist-apron and pulled out her smart phone. "I filmed that sweep move he did with his right leg. Me thinks the Board of Industrial Accidents will find themselves the recipient of my film work."

I laughed. "Nothing says 'hello' like a video gone viral."

She put her left hand on my back and pushed me gently toward the street. "Go get a Band-Aid on that thing, Robin Hood."

"Roger that, Sargent," I said, saluting her.

I started to cross the street and then instinctively turned around to see Monica propped against the doorjamb, her arms folded, her eyes focused on me.

"You know," I said, "what you did in there may make you my hero."

She dead-panned me before giving up a full-blown wink.

I bit. "Can I buy you a drink, Monica?"

"Go get yourself patched up. I don't want you bleeding all over my bar."

"I thought maybe you could patch me up."

"Come to think of it," Monica said, "a real man would limp down to the ocean and just slap some salt water on his wounds."

I filled my chest with gusts of salt air. "That's what I was gonna do."

"...Then come back for a taste of Irish."

"I was gonna do that, too."

* * *

For the next couple of weeks, I visited Pearl as often as I could. She looked weaker every day, but remained in good spirits. Her nephew apologized profusely and promised to get a job, promised to pay everything back.

I shared some of Buddy's wisdom with Pearl: "Why pay when he can promise."

Pearl reached up to touch my cheek. "Seems to me I heard that one before," she said sweetly. "Anyway, thanks to you, Donald, I recovered four hundred and seven dollars. That's not chicken feed."

The last time I saw Pearl she was doubling up in a hospital room. Her shanty had already been rented to a Greenwich Village couple with their eyes set on opening up a traditional coffeehouse.

Per her instructions, I placed Pearl's special things into a box and stored them at the Quarterdeck. She'd pick them up when she got better. I brought her fancy jaunting-cart teacup into the hospital and placed it on a stand next to her bed, giving her one last vista of Heaven on earth. "I've had a tough life, but a good life," she said, her head resting sideways on a pillow. "People were good to me after we lost Johnny in the accident. He died at work you know."

I held her left hand and nodded.

They say people tell the truth on their deathbed. If Pearl wanted to believe her Johnny died as a result of sweat and toil, who was I to trouble her with the facts?

Pearl's rings disappeared after a visit from her nephew. Her teacup was spared and has now found some prominent shelf space in the Quarterdeck. King's Quarter lost Pearl the Wednesday before Thanksgiving. Her remains were carted off to a mainland morgue to be cremated sometime after the holiday.

* * *

The day after Thanksgiving came in cold, but clear blue and sunny. I swung into the Down East for a coffee and then swung over to Burke's to play Buddy's number. I was ready for Doc Burke's "Sullivan Boy" story when he yelled over the pharmacist's counter, "Let's hear it for the man of the hour! Thirty-seven hundred smackers."

A few patrons clapped and then came up patting me on the back. For what I had no idea. I looked at Doc Burke side-ways. "What're you talking about?"

He ran around the pharmacist's counter and gave me a kiss on the forehead. "Your number came up Wednesday night."

As Doc Burke hugged me, crying with joy, all I could think about was Buddy telling me, "Always play the same number. Your number's gonna come up some day, Donnie, I'm telling ya."

After a few more pats on the back, I stepped out of the pharmacy not sure where to go. With the sun on my face, salty winds at my back, and the smell of freshly-baked breads filling my lungs, I decided to swing by the Dry Dock and share the news of my winnings with Monica.

On my way, the lottery ticket—literally my ticket across the garbage—burned a hole in my pocket. With a bounce in my step, as if we'd had some secret pact all along, I fantasized about Monica escaping with me. When I reached West Street and came to sudden halt under the shadow of a flat iron, as if snagged in a web, I noticed that tight-wad O'Brien's funeral home looked neat as a pin.

Staring at the home, I thought about Pearl's life savings. I pictured her alone in a mainland morgue slated for cremation. She'd never have her day in the sun—never again be with her Johnny. No more Quarter for Pearl. I kept telling myself I wouldn't do it, but I got Quarter in my blood. I knew damn well I'd cross West Street, pass right through the wrought-iron fence, push through that burgundy door, and hand over my thirty-seven hundred in pirates' gold to the only king in King's Quarter. Before I did though, I'd walk on the same cobblestones Buddy did a thousand times before me. For whatever it's worth, I could hear the distant pounding of the Atlantic reminding me, "We bury our own here, Donald. It's a code we live by in King's Quarter."

ABOUT THE CONTRIBUTORS

J. L. Abramo was born in the seaside paradise of Brooklyn, New York on Raymond Chandler's fifty-ninth birthday. Abramo is the author of *Catching Water in a Net*, winner of the St. Martin's Press/Private Eye Writers of America prize for Best First Private Eye Novel; the subsequent Jake Diamond novels *Clutching at Straws*, *Counting to Infinity*, and *Circling the Runway*; *Chasing Charlie Chan*, a prequel to the Jake Diamond series; and the stand-alone thrillers *Gravesend* and *Brooklyn Justice*. Abramo's short fiction has appeared in the anthologies *Unloaded: Crime Writers Writing Without Guns* and *Mama Tried: Crime Fiction Inspired by Outlaw Country Music*. www.jlabramo.com/

Eric Beetner is the author of more than a dozen novels including *Rumrunners*, *The Devil Doesn't Want Me*, *Dig Two Graves*, *White Hot Pistol*, and *The Year I Died Seven Times*. He is co-author (with JB Kohl) of *One Too Many Blows to the Head*, *Borrowed Trouble* and *Over Their Heads* and co-wrote *The Backlist* and *The Short List* with author Frank Zafiro. He lives in Los Angeles where he co-hosts the Noir At The Bar reading series. For more visit www.ericbeetner.com.

Michael Bracken, two-time Derringer Award winner, is the author of several books, including the private eye novel *All White Girls* and the private eye collection *Tequila Sunrise*. He is better known as the author of more than 1,100 short stories, including private eye stories published in *Ellery Queen's Mystery Magazine*, *Fifty Shades of Grey Fedora*, *Flesh & Blood: Guilty as Sin*, *Hardboiled*, *Thrilling Detective*, and many other anthologies and periodicals. Additionally, he's edited five crime fiction anthologies, including the three-volume *Fedora* series, and has served as vice president of the

Private Eye Writers of America. He lives and writes in Texas. www.crimefictionwriter.com

Meredith Cole started her career as a screenwriter and filmmaker. She was the winner of the St. Martin's Press/ Malice Domestic competition and her first book, *Posed for Murder*, was nominated for an Agatha Award for Best First Mystery Novel. Her short stories have appeared in many anthologies, as well as *Ellery Queen Mystery Magazine.* She lives in Charlottesville, Virginia and teaches writing at the University of Virginia. meredithcoleauthor.wordpress.com

Matt Coyle's debut novel, *Yesterday's Echo,* won the Anthony Award for Best First Novel, the San Diego Book Award for Best Mystery, the Ben Franklin Award for Best New Voice in Fiction, and was named one of 2013's Best Mysteries by *Deadly Pleasures Mystery Magazine.* His second book, *Night Tremors,* was a Bookreporter.com Reviewers' Favorite Book of 2015 and is nominated for an Anthony Award, a Shamus Award, and was a Lefty Award finalist. Matt's third book, *Dark Fissures,* comes out in December, 2016. Matt is a graduate of UC Santa Barbara and lives in San Diego with his yellow Lab, Angus, where he is writing the fourth Rick Cahill crime novel. www.mattcoylebooks.com/

Thomas Donahue is the author of the well-received suspense novel, *Fraternal Bonds,* featuring Boston-based private investigator Stephen Nicholson. He served as a correction officer in Boston for more than twenty years, rising to the rank of lieutenant. He is a frequent guest speaker for various levels of aspiring writers: junior high school, high school, adult enrichment, and night college courses. Donahue's literary works have appeared in *Coast to Coast: Murder from Sea to Shining Sea,* and *Crimestalker Casebook* where he also serves as an honorary advisor. He is an active member of the

Private Eye Writers of America and served as a judge for the best original paperback 2016. Mr. Donahue is presently at work completing his second Stephen Nicholson novel and a collection of short stories. www.fraternalbonds.com

John M. Floyd's work has appeared in more than 250 different publications, including *The Strand Magazine, Alfred Hitchcock's Mystery Magazine, Ellery Queen's Mystery Magazine, Woman's World, The Saturday Evening Post,* and *The Best American Mystery Stories 2015.* A former Air Force captain and IBM systems engineer, John is also a three-time Derringer Award winner, an Edgar nominee, and the author of six collections of short fiction: *Rainbow's End, Midnight, Clockwork, Deception, Fifty Mysteries,* and *Dreamland.* www.johnmfloyd.com

Gay Toltl Kinman has nine award nominations for her writing, including three Agathas; several short stories in American and English magazines and anthologies; two collections of short stories, three children's books, Y.A. gothic novel, four adult mysteries, a novella, several short plays produced and published; articles in professional journals and newspapers; co-edited two non-fiction books; and currently writes a children's book column. Kinman has library and law degrees. www.gaykinman.com

Terrill Lee Lankford is a writer and filmmaker. He's the author of four novels: *Shooters, Angry Moon, Earthquake Weather,* and *Blonde Lightning.* He most recently worked as a writer/producer on the first two seasons of *Bosch.*

Janice Law is a retired English teacher and the author of several articles, short stories, history books and novels. Her short stories have appeared in anthologies, including *The Best American Mystery Stories, The World's Finest Mystery and*

Crime Stories, Alfred Hitchcock's Fifty Years of Crime and Suspense, Riptide, Still Waters, MWA's Vengeance, and the *New Fabulist* anthology, *Paraspheres.* Her first novel, *The Big Payoff,* which introduced her character Anna Peters, was nominated for an Edgar, and seven other Anna Peters novels followed. Other works include the contemporary novels *The Night Bus, The Lost Diaries of Iris Weed,* and *Voices from Forge,* as well as historical novels, *All the King's Ladies* and *Blood in the Water* (Wildside) a collection of short fiction. Her most recent books are a series of novels from MysteriousPress.com featuring the Anglo-Irish painter, Francis Bacon. The second volume of what became a trilogy, *The Prisoner of the Riviera,* won the 2013 Lambda award for best gay mystery. A new Francis Bacon trilogy begins in 2016 with *Nights in Berlin,* set when he was seventeen. She also has a new contemporary novel with strong mystery elements, *Homeward Dove,* came out earlier this year from Wildside Press. For a complete list of works, please see her website, www.janicelaw.com.

Andrew McAleer is the best-selling author of numerous books including the *101 Habits of Highly Successful Novelists, A Miscellany of Murder, Fatal Deeds, Double Endorsement,* and *Mystery Writing in a Nutshell,* which he co-authored with his father, Edgar winner John McAleer. He co-edited, along with Shamus Winner Paul D. Marks, *Coast to Coast: Murder from Sea to Shining Sea,* released in 2015. Past president of the Boston Authors Club, Mr. McAleer teaches at Boston College and works in public service as a senior labor relations specialist. He is a winner of the Sherlock Holmes Revere Bowl Award presented by the Speckled Band of Boston. As a sergeant in the U.S. Army, Mr. McAleer served in Afghanistan as a Combat Historian where he was awarded the Army Commendation Medal. www.coast2coastmysteries.blogspot.com

Paul D. Marks is the author of the Shamus Award-Winning noir mystery-thriller *White Heat*. *Publishers Weekly* calls *White Heat* a "taut crime yarn". His story *Howling at the Moon* (EQMM) was short-listed for both the 2015 Anthony and Macavity Awards for Best Short Story, and came in #7 in Ellery Queen's Reader's Poll Award. Midwest Review calls *Vortex*, Paul's noir novella, "...a nonstop staccato action noir." With Andrew McAleer, he also co-edits the *Coast to Coast Murder* series for Down & Out Books. His short story *Nature of the Beast* has recently come out in *Beat to a Pulp* and *Deserted Cities of the Heart* also came out in Akashic Books' *St. Louis Noir* anthology. *Ghosts of Bunker Hill* appears in *Ellery Queen Mystery Magazine*. And *Twelve Angry Days* will appear in a future issue of *Alfred Hitchcock Mystery Magazine*. Though Paul writes about other places, he considers himself an L.A. writer and lives in Los Angeles with his wife, dogs and cats. He has served on the board of the L.A. chapter of Sisters in Crime and currently serves on the board of the SoCal chapter of MWA (Mystery Writers of America). www.PaulDMarks.com

O'Neil De Noux, born in New Orleans, writes character-driven crime fiction, although he has been published in many disciplines including historical fiction, mainstream fiction, science-fiction, suspense, fantasy, horror, western, literary, children's fiction, young adult, religious, romance, humor and erotica. His fiction has garnered several awards: the Shamus Award for Best Short Story, the Derringer Award for Best Novelette and the 2011 Police Book of the Year. Recurring characters in his work include New Orleans Police Detectives Dino LaStanza (1980s), Jacques Dugas (1890s), John Raven Beau (21st Century) and as well as Private Eye Lucien Caye (1940-50s). De Noux served as Vice-President of the Private Eye Writers of America in 2013. Historical novels include *Battle Kiss*, an epic set at the Battle of New Orleans, *USS*

Relentless, a nautical saga of a US Naval officer during the Barbary War of 1803 through the War of 1812 and *Death Angels*, a novel of World War II. Other non-series novels include *Mistik* (young adult), *Bourbon Street* (crime), *Slick Time* (caper), *Mafia Aphrodite* (erotica). Collections include *New Orleans Mysteries*, *New Orleans Irresistible* and *Backwash of the Milky Way* (science fiction). His web site is www.oneildenoux.net.

Robert J. Randisi has been called by Booklist "...the last of the pulp writers." He has published in the western, mystery, private eye, horror, science fiction and men's action/adventure genres. All told, he is the author of over 650 books, 50+ short stories, one screenplay and the editor of 30 anthologies. He has also edited a Writer's Digest book, *Writing the Private Eye Novel*, and for seven years was the mystery reviewer for the *Orlando Sentinel*. In 1982 he founded the Private Eye Writers of America, and created the Shamus Award. In 1985 he co-founded *Mystery Scene Magazine* and the short-lived American Mystery Award; a couple of years later he was co-founder of the American Crime Writer's League. In 2009 he received the Life Achievement Award from the Private Eye Writers of America, on 2016 the Life Achievement award from the Western Fictioneers. Also in 2016 he was presented with the John Seigenthaler Legends Award from the Killer Nashville Conference. His most recent private eye novel, *The Honky Tonk Big Hoss Boogie*, was nominated for a Shamus Award. The second book, *The Last Song of Hammer Dylan*, will be published in 2017.
www.en.wikipedia.org/wiki/Robert_J._Randisi

Art Taylor is the author of *On the Road with Del & Louise: A Novel in Stories*. His short fiction has won two Agatha Awards, an Anthony, a Macavity, and three consecutive Derringer Awards. Stories have appeared in *Ellery Queen's*

Mystery Magazine, Barrelhouse, Needle: A Magazine of Noir, and *North American Review;* online at *Fiction Weekly, PANK, Prick of the Spindle,* and *SmokeLong Quarterly;* and in several anthologies, most notably those in the *Chesapeake Crimes* series, published in conjunction with the Chesapeake Chapter of Sisters in Crime. He teaches at George Mason University and contributes regularly to the *Washington Post,* the *Washington Independent Review of Books,* and *Mystery Scene.* www.arttaylorwriter.com

OTHER TITLES FROM DOWN AND OUT BOOKS

See www.downAndOutBooks.com for complete list

By J.L. Abramo
Catching Water in a Net
Clutching at Straws
Counting to Infinity
Gravesend
Chasing Charlie Chan
Circling the Runway
Brooklyn Justice
Coney Island Avenue (*)

By Trey R. Barker
2,000 Miles to Open Road
Road Gig: A Novella
Exit Blood
Death is Not Forever
No Harder Prison

By Richard Barre
The Innocents
Bearing Secrets
Christmas Stories
The Ghosts of Morning
Blackheart Highway
Burning Moon
Echo Bay
Lost

By Eric Beetner (editor)
Unloaded

By Eric Beetner and
JB Kohl
Over Their Heads

By Eric Beetner and
Frank Zafiro
The Backlist
The Shortlist

By G.J. Brown
Falling

By Rob Brunet
Stinking Rich

By Angel Luis Colón
No Happy Endings

By Tom Crowley
Vipers Tail
Murder in the Slaughterhouse

By Frank De Blase
Pine Box for a Pin-Up
Busted Valentines
and Other Dark Delights
A Cougar's Kiss

By Les Edgerton
The Genuine, Imitation,
Plastic Kidnapping

By Jack Getze
Big Numbers
Big Money
Big Mojo
Big Shoes

By Richard Godwin
Wrong Crowd
Buffalo and Sour Mash
Crystal on Electric Acetate (*)

By Jeffery Hess
Beachhead

(*)—Coming Soon